KU-218-822

PHOTOGRAPHY

This book is intended for the beginner with a fairly inexpensive camera as well as for the enthusiast wanting to experiment with more complex equipment or in need of a refresher on fundamental principles. For it is not the camera but the man behind it that counts, and the aim of this book is to show that technical perfection can be easily acquired.

Chapters cover the initial choosing of a camera, explanation of its parts and the different sorts of lenses, flash, films, filters, instruction about exposure, the taking of landscapes, action pictures, night photography, outdoor and indoor work, portraiture; how to develop your own film and prints; and finally how to present your prints and transparency slides in the most attractive way.

TEACH YOURSELF BOOKS

PHOTOGRAPHY

R. H. Mason, M.A., F.I.I.P., Hon. F.R.P.S.

Former editor of *Amateur Photographer*
Past President of the Institute of Incorporated Photographers
Past President of the Royal Photographic Society

TEACH YOURSELF BOOKS
Hodder and Stoughton

First printed 1974
Fourth impression 1977
Sixth impression 1979

Copyright © 1974
R.H. Mason

All rights reserved. No part of this publication may be repro-
duced or transmitted in any form or by any means, electronic or
mechanical, including photocopy, recording, or any information storage and retrieval system, without permission
in writing from the publisher

This volume published in the U.S.A.
by David McKay, Company Inc., 750
Third Avenue, New York NY 10017

ISBN 0 340 19084 1

Printed and bound in Great Britain for
Hodder and Stoughton Paperbacks, a division of Hodder
and Stoughton Ltd, Mill Road, Dunton Green, Sevenoaks,
Kent (Editorial Office: 47 Bedford Square, London WC1 3DP)
by Richard Clay (The Chaucer Press) Ltd, Bungay, Suffolk

Contents

Introduction

'Old myths die hard' and there are two widely held views on photography as a hobby which once had some validity but are not true today. One is that photography is expensive and the other is that it requires a high degree of technical knowledge.

Any hobby must involve some expense, but photography is, or need not be, any more expensive than fishing, stamp collecting, golf, archaeology or any other pursuit. It has a great advantage over many hobbies; you can spend as little as you like, as much as you like or settle for something in between.

It is possible to take good photographs with the cheapest of cameras and a minimum of expenditure on processing. Better cameras will provide more versatility and the ability perhaps to photograph a black cat in a coal cellar, but for most work it is not the camera but the man behind the camera that counts.

What technical knowledge is required? A great mystique has been built up over the last hundred years, encouraged I suspect by photographers themselves, but enormous improvements in apparatus and films have made technical failure almost impossible if reasonable precautions are taken. In fact, technical perfection is easily acquired, and this book aims to put you on the right path painlessly and without a lot of technical jargon.

Photography is unique in that it can be practised indoors and outdoors, summer and winter, day and night. When you are not taking pictures you can be making prints if you have darkroom facilities, and altogether it can provide a most absorbing and satisfying pastime which exercises your imagination and creative ability to the full.

Some people are interested only in using a camera for holiday records or family portraits, but their efforts can be improved by following some of the advice given in this book. Others are interested in photography as a complement to, or a means of recording, other interests such as natural history, motor sport or geography; they too will be able to improve their results by a basic knowledge of how photography works.

As for the enthusiast, I do not pretend that this book will satisfy all his wants because it starts from the very beginning, but a refresher on fundamental principles is always salutary and I have endeavoured to give some guidance for further study throughout the book.

Many successful professional photographers started as amateurs, and indeed are still amateurs at heart, so this book will be useful as an introduction whether you plan to use your camera just for casual snapshotting or as a tool for serious work in the future.

R.H.M.

1 Choosing a Camera

It may seem like an oversimplification to say that a camera is nothing but a box with a lens at one end and a sensitive surface at the other, together with some means of controlling the latter's exposure to the light passed by the lens. Yet that has always been, and still is, the basis of a camera. In the early days of photography before the 1840s cameras were simple, wooden, light-tight boxes having a lens and a slot or slide to take a sensitised plate. Exposures were made by removing and replacing a cap over the lens, and the camera had to be taken into the darkroom to be unloaded.

In the 1840s slide holders were introduced and other improvements such as bellows or sliding boxes, one inside the other for focusing purposes, made cameras a little easier to use. Primitive shutters to control exposure timing, together with 'stops' consisting of brass strips punched with holes of various sizes to control depth of field, arrived soon after.

Many very fine photographs were taken with these cameras and examples can be found in several museums. Nevertheless, one almost needed the strength of an ox to carry all the equipment to a desired location and, since plates had to be developed and coated on the spot, a portable darkroom was required. One of the most famous pioneers, Roger Fenton, had to convert a horse-drawn baker's van into a darkroom to take to the Crimean War in 1855; so one needed a deep pocket as well!

For sheer quality and artistry it would be hard to beat many of the pictures taken in the first thirty or forty years of photography, which goes to prove that it is the man (or woman!) behind the camera that counts. Modern cameras, even the modestly priced ones, are marvels of sophistication when compared with the early models, but the basic function is still the same. All the refinements, gadgets, aids and improvements that have been introduced make photography a great deal easier by removing many technical problems, but they do not tell you where to point the camera and how to select the subject.

Some technical knowledge is, of course, essential. Just as a painter must learn how to mix colours so the photographer must learn how to use a camera, and this means that he must also understand how it works. He must select the right camera for the purpose, and this is the first problem facing those who want to take up photography because there are a number of different types from which to choose.

Unfortunately, there is no such thing as a perfect or universal camera because the requirements for different types of photography vary and they could not be incorporated in one camera without making it so big and heavy that it would certainly not be portable. As a result there are many designs and types for special purposes, but we are only concerned here with the types in general use. They are:

Non-reflex
Single-lens-reflex
Twin-lens-reflex

There are a number of subdivisions within these categories, but before going into detail let us look briefly at the function of the various components of a camera, most of which are common to all types.

The lens

First we have the lens whose function is to project an image of the subject onto the film, and on all but the simplest cameras it is necessary to vary the distance between the lens and the film according to the distance of the subject from the camera. This distance has to be increased for near objects and reduced for distant objects. On many old cameras this was done by inserting folding light-tight bellows between the lens panel and the body of the camera. There are still a few models of quite up-to-date design that use simple bellows. However, most modern cameras, especially of the miniature type, employ some form of lens mount which goes in and out on a helical screw when the mount is rotated.

The iris diaphragm

It is also necessary under certain circumstances to control the amount of light passed by the lens, as we shall see later. In the early days this was done by inserting strips of metal with holes of different sizes pierced in them and these were known as Waterhouse stops. Today nearly all cameras are fitted with an iris diaphragm and this is usually built into the lens mount, sometimes between the component lenses. The diaphragm has a number of very thin metal leaves so arranged that they leave an aperture in the centre that can be varied in size as required— rather like the iris of the human eye.

The shutter

All modern cameras are fitted with a shutter, which controls the *time* that the sensitive film is exposed to the light passed by the lens, as distinct from the *aperture*, which controls the *amount*. There are two basic types of shutter: the 'between-lens' or 'diaphragm' shutter and the 'focal-plane' shutter. The former, as the name implies, is built into the lens mount and is something like a simpler form of iris diaphragm, except that the leaves always remain closed completely when the shutter is not actually in use. On activation they open fully to permit the passage of the light rays.

The focal-plane shutter is basically a curtain of rubberised material with a slit in it that travels from one roller to another just in front of the film itself. In its modern sophisticated form it consists of more than one curtain so that the width of the slit is variable and the speed of travel can also be regulated.

Film transport

Any camera that uses roll film or cassettes must have some means of moving the film into position for the next exposure.

On most modern cameras it takes the form of a lever, which is also coupled to the shutter mechanism in such a way that double exposure is prevented. Most shutters require 'tensioning' or 'cocking' to wind up the springs needed to operate the shutter, but some recent models operate electronically. Winding on the film also cocks the shutter, which cannot be tensioned separately. Very often the same thumb lever also winds on the film number indicator. This is important because films are too sensitive to allow red windows like those that were fitted on the back of old cameras to reveal frame numbers.

Some of the larger cameras still use the 120 size roll film which is wound from one reel to another and then removed for processing. Most cameras using this film produce either twelve negatives 6 cm × 6 cm or eight negatives 6 cm × 8·2 cm. There is also a size known as 220, which is similar to 120 but provides twenty-four negatives instead of twelve. It only fits cameras especially designed or adapted for it and will not go into all 120 size cameras. Other roll film sizes are now almost obsolete.

A vast number of modern cameras use the 35 mm cassette, and the film is drawn through the camera and then has to be wound back into the cassette before removal. Cassettes usually provide either twenty or thirty-six negatives size 24 mm × 36 mm.

A fairly recent introduction for miniature cameras is the cartridge, which is a light-proof plastic container having a reel at each end and a cut-out aperture in the centre. The camera transport winds the film from one reel to the other and the whole cartridge is then removed for processing. There are two sizes, designated 110 and 126. The former provides twelve negatives 13 mm × 17 mm and the latter twelve negatives 28 mm × 18 mm but the 126 size is losing ground to 110.

The viewfinder
Although not absolutely essential, it is obviously desirable to have some means of assessing the area of the subject that is being recorded by the camera. A simple wire frame will do this, and on many older cameras a little reflex-finder was a good

enough guide for distant subjects. Today an optical viewfinder is usually built into the camera body. It is reasonably accurate for average subjects and gives a bright picture the right way up, but it is not accurate for close-ups unless some provision is made for tilting it or allowing for parallax error, as we shall see later.

A more accurate method is found in the single-lens-reflex type of camera because this has a ground-glass screen that shows exactly what the lens is covering. On some cameras the screen is the same size as the negative and the image is the right way up but reversed left to right. On others a pentaprism is fitted above the screen so that the image can be viewed from eye level and the right way round.

All these things—lens, diaphragm, shutter, film transport and viewfinder—will be found on every camera, whatever type or price, but other facilities with varying degrees of usefulness are built into many cameras. The most popular are:

Rangefinder focusing
Exposure metering
Flash synchronisation
Automatic or semi-automatic exposure control

They are all to some extent luxuries, but they do make the technical side of photography much easier and facilitate sharp, correctly exposed negatives or transparencies. But let us consider the function of each in turn so that you can decide whether it is essential for your particular requirements.

Rangefinder focusing
All but the simplest cameras have to be focused onto the subject. Focusing is only avoided in the cheapest cameras by using a small lens and limiting the distance at which you can work to nothing less than about 10 feet. (The chapter on lenses explains this more fully.) It is therefore desirable in all but reflex-type cameras to have some means of focusing accurately.

Of course, you can measure the distance from camera to

subject and then set the lens to the corresponding footage (or metres) marked on the rotating mount. But this is not very practical, so many cameras have a built-in rangefinder based on the principle that when an object is seen from two different positions the lines of sight converge. The angle of convergence increases with the nearness of the object and decreases with distance.

Two windows are provided on the camera as far apart as the design will allow and one window is incorporated into the viewer. By rotating the lens mount, which is coupled to a rotating mirror or swinging wedge in the rangefinder, the two images that are seen in the mirror can be made to coincide. The lens is then in focus. It should be mentioned that rangefinders can be bought separately to mount on the camera via the accessory shoe, but they will not be coupled to the lens, so it will be necessary to set the lens manually to the distance figure provided by the rangefinder.

Obviously a rangefinder is not so necessary on a reflex camera that shows the image actually transmitted by the lens because focusing can be performed visually. However, on most miniature cameras the focusing screen is rather small, so a form of rangefinder is provided on the screen. A circle in the centre shows two images or a blurred image which coincide or sharpen when the lens is focused accurately. Unfortunately, these systems, known as the split-image and multiple-prism respectively, are only at their best when the lens is at a large aperture. They are also less efficient with wide-angle and telephoto or long-focus lenses. Nevertheless, they are a help, especially to people with eyesight deficiencies, some of whom find one system easier than the other. It is as well to try both before deciding on a particular make of camera and, other things being equal between two makes, this could be a deciding factor.

Exposure metering
Many of the more expensive cameras have exposure meters built into them and this can be a great convenience. On the

whole they are a reliable guide, but there are subjects of an unusual nature that call for some variation from the indicated figure. These are dealt with in the chapter on exposure, so suffice it to say that it is desirable not to follow a built-in meter blindly but to regard it as a convenient guide rather than an infallible pointer.

On some cameras the meter merely gives an indication of the exposure required and the aperture and/or shutter speeds are set by hand to correspond. On more advanced models a pointer activated by the exposure meter is visible in the viewfinder and one turns the aperture ring or shutter speed dial until another pointer coincides with it, at which point exposure will be correct for an average subject.

On so-called automatic cameras the user merely sets the shutter speed he wants to use and the meter itself opens or closes the aperture to the stop that will give accurate exposure on an average subject. With the introduction of shutters operated electronically instead of by a train of mechanical reaction, it has been possible to make cameras on which the user sets the aperture he desires and the exposure meter adjusts to the shutter speed accordingly. All of the latter are single-lens-reflex cameras and, since they measure the light coming through the lens itself, they are often called TTL (through-the-lens) to distinguish them from other SLR (single-lens-reflex) models.

However, automation has become quite common on ordinary non-reflex miniature cameras as well. They usually have a sensing cell situated on or near the lens mount so that it measures the light direct from the scene instead of from behind the lens. Such cameras are quite reliable if adjustments are made when faced with the unusual circumstances described in Chapter 6 on exposure calculation. It is most desirable when selecting a camera of this type to ensure that it has a manual override to cope with such instances. Provision is made on all cameras with integrated exposure meters to make the necessary adjustments for different film speeds.

While a built-in meter is a convenience, and it certainly makes for quick working, it is by no means essential and has certain drawbacks. If the meter should go wrong it means putting the whole camera out of action while it is being repaired, and there are certain subjects, such as colour work against the light, for which it is a distinct advantage to have a separate meter that can be turned in any direction or taken right up to the subject.

Flash synchronisation

There is hardly a camera made today that does not have provision for firing a flash at the precise moment when the shutter is open. In some of the cheap and popular snapshot cameras a bulb is inserted directly into the camera body and all the necessary batteries or firing mechanisms are built in. This may seem an ideal arrangement but, in fact, it is very bad, for two reasons.

First, nothing looks worse than flash fired from the camera position. It produces ugly, hard shadows, washed-out faces and, very often, nasty reflections from the retinas of the subject's eyes (known as 'red-eye'). Secondly, this type of camera can only use expendable flashbulbs and they preclude the use of an electronic flash, which in the long run is cheaper and more convenient.

That is why all the better cameras are fitted with sockets to take flashguns that have an incorporated mechanism or circuitry for firing the flash. The sockets are connected to the shutter mechanism in such a way that the fractional time delay in opening the shutter or for the bulb to reach the peak of its flash is taken into account and perfect synchronisation is achieved.

On focal-plane shutters it is usually necessary to keep the shutter speed down to 1/60 second or slower to allow for the time the slit in the curtain takes to traverse the negative area. Between-lens shutters can be safely operated at much faster speeds.

The independent 'guns' used for firing flashbulbs and electronic flashguns can both be fired from extension cables plugged into the camera's synchronisation socket. On the rare occasions that it is essential to use them at the camera position, they can be fitted to the accessory shoe found on most models. On some there are built-in contacts which render even the shortest cable unnecessary. These are known as 'hot-shoes'.

Automation

Camera automation has been mainly confined to exposure setting either by altering the aperture to match a pre-set shutter speed or by adjusting the speed to match a pre-set aperture. There are, however, two models with completely automatic focusing as well, but they are at present confined to a non-reflex model and an instant camera. They are not yet perfect, so we have only exposure control to consider when trying to decide on an automatic or non-automatic camera.

The former naturally cost more, so one must consider whether or not the extra convenience is worth it. Most snapshotters and non-enthusiasts would say it is because they find that they only get an exposure failure—once the bug-bear of photography—on the rare occasions that they shoot a non-average subject. On the other hand, professionals and dedicated enthusiasts are inclined to scorn them, just as most motor-racing enthusiasts deplore automatic gearboxes. Very few of the expensive and sophisticated cameras used by professionals and advanced amateurs have automation, but it is not unknown for press photographers to carry one of the compact automatics as a reserve for 'snatch' shots.

So if you plan to remain a snapshotter, buy an automatic camera, but if you are an enthusiast, or likely to become one, spend the money on a more versatile camera like a single-lens-reflex. True, there are a few single-lens-reflex cameras with automation and a manual over-ride, but these are in the very high price ranges and one pays dearly for it.

The basic types of camera

Let us now relate the foregoing to the three basic types of camera mentioned at the beginning of this chapter: non-reflex, single-lens-reflex and twin-lens-reflex.

Non-reflex cameras

This category includes any camera that does not show in the viewer the actual image thrown by the lens. It is really our basic box with a lens in the front and a film at the back, but the box has taken on many shapes. There is an enormous range of such cameras, from the Instamatic, successor to the Box Brownie, up to the high-precision Leica.

Most of these are what are known as miniature cameras, i.e. 35 mm or less. There used to be a variety of subminiature models using 16 mm film or smaller and some still exist. There are also a few known as 'half-frame' which use 35 mm cassettes but make negatives half the standard size, thus providing seventy-two shots on a thirty-six exposure roll. However, subminiatures and half-frame sizes are gradually dying out because the advantage of compactness has been largely lost through improvements in the design of the standard models.

The one exception to this is the 110 size, which has facilitated a camera that is truly pocketable and provides a sort of graphic notebook. It is very useful for the holiday snapshotter and as a 'notebook' for the serious photographer but not ideal for serious work, mainly because of its negative size limitation and the impossibility of changing lenses.

This leaves us with the 126 size and the 35 mm size. It is not too broad a generalisation to say that the former is mainly for the snapshotting public and not at all popular with enthusiasts, while 35 mm is popular in both categories.

The advantage of the 110 and 126 size is easy loading. The complete cartridge is just dropped into place, while notches on the plastic case adjust the film speed setting automatically. There is no rewinding and the whole cartridge is removed after twelve, twenty-four or twenty exposures.

The pundits' dislike of cartridge cameras is based to a large extent on the fact that the precise position of the film is determined by the cartridge itself and they say that plastic can warp. In 35 mm cameras the film is held firmly against the metal aperture by a spring-loaded pressure plate and the film cannot buckle or move. It is only fair to add that the cartridge manufacturers have hotly denied any possibility of their film buckling or leaving the precise film plane, but the fact remains that while there are many popular-priced cameras designed to take cartridges the manufacturers of the top professional and enthusiast cameras have stayed faithful to 35 mm or 120. However, this could be partly due to the fact that a focal-plane shutter cannot be fitted to a cartridge, so the facility for interchangeable lenses is excluded.

There are about eighty models that use 110 or 126 cartridges and they vary in price from about £5 to about £60, although there is one well-known make costing over £150. Some are automatic, some have built-in rangefinders for accurate focusing and all are synchronised for flash, although in most cases it is only for flash on the camera.

Non-reflex types which use 35 mm cassettes are on the whole more sophisticated and range in price from about £20 to £450. There are about sixty models on the market. A few have automatic exposure metering and most of these have a manual override. They are all synchronised for flash, using a bulb or electronic flashgun connected by a cable or fired through a hot-shoe on the camera.

There are two principal types of camera in this category: those that have a non-removable lens and those that have a screw or bayonet fitting which enables the user to change very quickly to lenses of other focal lengths, i.e. wide-angle, long-focus, telephoto or zoom. This type is always fitted with a focal-plane shutter, whereas the non-interchangeable type is usually, but not always, fitted with a between-lens shutter. Most of the automatic models are in this category.

Other facilities in this design of camera are rangefinder focusing on the more sophisticated models, delayed-action shutter releases, quick-loading spool devices and film-speed reminders. The basic principle of the camera remains the same and the difference in prices is due mostly to the quality of manufacture, especially of the lens. If a non-reflex camera is your choice it is best to decide first what price you can afford and then compare the specifications of the several models you are bound to find within a few pounds of it. In general, it is better to look for the quality and reputation of the lens in preference to the gadgets or even the looks.

Single-lens-reflex (SLR) cameras

To many enthusiasts this is the most exciting category of cameras. Most of them are designed for 35 mm cassettes, but there are a few larger models made to take 120 or 220 roll film.

There are about fifty models in the 35 mm size and prices range from about £80 to £850, with the majority in the £90 to £180 bracket. They all incorporate a hinged mirror which reflects the image up onto a focusing screen. The mirror is automatically raised at the actual moment of exposure, and this is a possible, although minor, criticism of SLR cameras because it means a momentary blackout in the viewfinder and also makes a 'clunk', which could be disturbing to a nature photographer.

On all models a pentaprism is fitted above the screen to provide eye-level viewing and in some this is removable to permit changing the type of focusing screen for special purposes. A number of the more expensive SLRs have a built-in exposure meter, which is coupled to the lens mount in such a way that adjusting the aperture brings a pointer or indicator into coincidence with a datum point or another pointer when exposure is correct. This is usually seen in the viewfinder and in some cases the measurement is based on the average of the light reaching the screen. In others it is 'centre weighted' so that it takes more notice of what is in the centre of the screen than on the outside. This avoids the underexposure that sometimes occurs when a bright sky or light background influences an out-door portrait too much.

Since the viewfinder shows the image transmitted by the lens, focusing is simplified, but most SLRs still have a rangefinder of

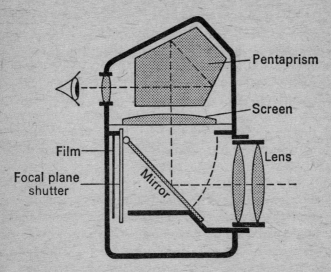

Fig. 1 Diagrammatic cross-section of a single-lens-reflex camera showing how the image formed by the lens is reflected by a mirror onto the focusing screen and then at two further angles by a pentaprism. This provides a clear image the right way up. On exposure the mirror rises automatically to permit the film to receive the image, and it also serves to mask the screen, which would otherwise let in light and fog the film.

some sort—split image, split wedge or microprism—as an additional aid. These are very useful for precision work, but many people find that in bright light they can focus quite accurately using the screen alone.

The really big plus of this type of camera is that one can change lenses, and the viewfinder will show the precise image transmitted by each lens. With the non-reflex type that has provision for interchangeable lenses it is necessary to have some means of altering the viewfinder image to match, and this can become a problem, especially with close-up work, because the lens and finder see slightly different views. There are two main methods of changing lenses. Some cameras have a bayonet ring, which allows a lens to be clipped in or taken out in a second. Others have a screw-in fitting, which takes longer but is cheaper to make and is gradually being superseded.

Another important advantage of the SLR is that there is a vast range of accessories available for the leading makes and these enable the camera to be used for nearly all types of work. For instance, close-up bellows or extension rings make macrophotography and copying easy. Microscope adaptors are available for taking pictures of microscopic specimens, while all sorts of special lenses are available for medical, architectural and press work.

The cameras of the SLR type that take 120 and 220 roll film are in some cases rather like larger versions of 35 mm cameras. The advantages of reflex operation are there, but they are necessarily heavier and in most instances more expensive.

Another type is more like a very elaborate and sophisticated version of a box camera. Apart from interchangeable lenses, this type also has interchangeable backs which hold the film and enable one to change from black and white to colour or vice versa without going through the whole roll. Although wonderful pieces of machinery, these cameras are large, heavy and very expensive, so they are favoured more by professionals, to whom the film interchangeability is a great asset.

It should be mentioned that 120 roll film, which gives twelve negatives 6 cm $\times$ 6 cm, ten negatives 6 cm $\times$ 7 cm or eight negatives 6 cm $\times$ 8·2 cm, according to the camera, is also obtainable without the paper backing. It is designated 220 size and provides twenty-four exposures 6 cm $\times$ 6 cm or twenty-one exposures 6 cm $\times$ 7 cm, but it can only be used on cameras especially designed or adapted for it. The interchangeable magazines for SLR cameras all take 120 or 220 film.

Twin-lens-reflex (TLR) cameras

This type of camera is very much like two box cameras fitted one on top of the other. The upper one is like a single-lens-reflex camera with a lens, a 45° mirror and a focusing screen, but it holds no film and the mirror is fixed. The lower half holds the film transport and the taking lens, which has a between-lens shutter. Both lenses are of similar focal length and fixed to a movable front panel so that they can be moved backwards and

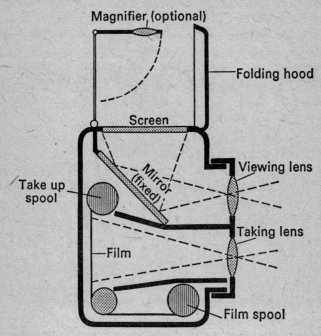

Fig. 2 Diagrammatic cross-section of a twin-lens-reflex camera in which the upper half is used only as a full-size viewer while the lower half takes the picture. The lens moves backwards and forwards for focusing, but only the lower lens has an iris diaphragm and a shutter. Most cameras of this type take 120 or 220 film, giving twelve or twenty-four negatives 6 cm square. Detachable prismatic heads are available for some TLR cameras in place of the folding hood over the screen.

forwards in tandem. Thus the top half is really a full-sized viewer that shows the image the right way up but reversed left to right.

Nearly every TLR available today takes 120 roll film or 120 and 220. The chief disadvantages of these cameras are bulk and weight. Also, it is impossible to judge depth of field or how much of the subject is in focus at a selected aperture because there is no iris diaphragm on the viewing lens. However, some people think that the brilliant viewing image at full aperture outweighs this.

Only one model of TLR camera has interchangeable lenses and these are expensive because each must have its sister viewing lens and a shutter. Nevertheless, TLR cameras in this size are popular with professionals, especially for studio work, but on the score of bulk and cost are far less popular with amateurs than the 35 mm SLR.

There are, of course, a number of cameras that do not fit any of the categories we have discussed so far. These are individual designs like Kodak and Polaroid instant cameras, stereoscopic, under-water and technical cameras.

However, the discerning reader will probably have realised by now that the nearest thing to a universal camera, although still far short of it, is the single-lens-reflex camera and its only real disadvantage when compared with others, like the non-reflex and the subminiature, is its bulk and weight. Those who intend to take photography seriously should consider it favourably and buy the best they can in that category. The versatility of the type and the uses to which it can be put will become apparent as you go further into this book.

Further reading about cameras

The Camera and its Functions, Focal Press.
35 mm, Focal Press
Camera Movements, Fountain Press.
A Short History of the Camera, Fountain Press.

Detailed test reports on all leading makes can be obtained from most camera magazines (see list on page 177).

2 The Lens

The lens is by far the most important component in any camera. The body can be built with the precision of a watch, but if the lens does not form a satisfactory image the rest of it is a waste of money. However, the enormous improvements in lens design and manufacture in the last twenty years have made it possible to take good pictures with the simplest and cheapest, provided that their limitations are understood.

The problem when an image is formed by the light rays passing through glass or any other transparent material shaped in the form of a lens is that various aberrations occur. The picture is distorted in a number of ways and often is not acceptably sharp. Overcoming these faults requires the use of very carefully treated and selected glass, plus very exact moulding or polishing. A tremendous number of mathematical calculations are required to work out the precise curvature for each component. It is reported that a famous lens designer of the 1840s, Joseph Petzval, used a whole company of military engineers to speed the calculations for a new portrait lens. Even so, it used to take anything up to two years to formulate a lens. Today, however, computers have cut it to a matter of hours or even minutes. This has naturally reduced the cost, besides increasing efficiency, and has facilitated the design of an enormous range of lenses for special purposes.

In its simplest form a lens is a circular piece of glass with curved surfaces on both sides or with one side flat and the other side curved. Glass has the property of bending, or refracting, rays of light, and the effect of the surface curvatures is to cause all rays to be refracted at different angles on entering and leaving so that they converge towards each other and meet at a point beyond.

This, of course, applies only to a lens with convex surfaces or with one flat and one convex surface—in other words, a lens that is sectionally thicker in the centre than at the edges. A lens that has concave surfaces, so that it is thicker at the edges than through the middle, causes rays of light to diverge. This means that no image is formed, but divergent lenses are nevertheless sometimes used in a compound lens having a number of components to help correct or counteract aberrations.

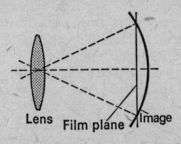

Lens Film plane Image

Fig. 3 The image formed by a single lens is curved in depth, so it is not possible to get the same degree of sharpness all over a flat film plane. If the centre rays are correctly focused, the marginal areas will be out of focus and *vice-versa*.

Nowadays most photographic lenses are made up of a number of different elements in order to overcome the aberrations existing in a single lens. The various elements are often of different shapes and curvatures, and sometimes even vary in the types of glass used.

The principal aberrations that concern us are:

Spherical aberration
Coma
Astigmatism
Curvature of the field
Barrel and pincushion distortion
Chromatic aberration

Spherical aberration

This is the inability of a lens to refract the rays falling on the marginal and central areas to the same point. Thus it is impossible to get a sharp image all over, but improvement can be obtained by 'stopping down', i.e. reducing the aperture of the iris diaphragm so that less of the marginal area is employed. Spherical aberration is present in most single lenses but not to such a degree that it is noticeable in ordinary snapshot-size prints taken with a simple camera working at about f/8 or f/11.

Coma

This is a somewhat similar defect appearing in points away from the axis. The effect is that the image of a circular subject can come out shaped rather like a spinning top. This can also be improved by stopping down. It is usually only noticeable with an extremely contrasty subject like a circular window in an interior shot.

Astigmatism

This is an inability to bring horizontal and vertical lines to focus in the same plane at the top and bottom, or sides, of the field.

Curvature of field

This is seen when rays from the outer edges of the picture do not come to a focus on the same plane as the centre rays. Both astigmatism and curvature are diminished a little by stopping down.

Barrel and pincushion distortion

This arises from a displacement in the position of image points on the outer areas of the field from their true positions so that straight lines near the edges of the picture appear curved. If the lines curve outwards it is called barrel distortion, and if they curve inwards it is called pincushion distortion. This is a common fault in a single lens but is absent or virtually unnoticeable in a corrected lens.

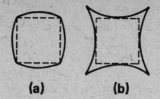

(a)   **(b)**

Fig. 4 Common aberrations in simple lenses are barrel distortion (a) and pincushion distortion (b). Straight lines such as the walls of a building that come near the edge of a picture will be curved. It can be improved by stopping down to a small aperture.

Chromatic aberration

This is a fault that results in rays of different colours coming to a focus on different planes. When the camera is correctly focused for one colour, the others are out of focus and colour-fringing results. This was a common fault with old lenses, but most

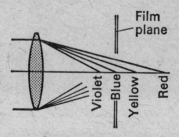

Fig. 5 Some simple lenses suffer from chromatic aberrations that cause light rays of differing colours to come to a focus at different distances from the lens. This produces softness in monochrome and colour fringes in colour work. This exaggerated diagram shows that if the lens is at the correct focus for blue rays the other rays will form circles instead of points on the film.

modern lenses, except for the very cheapest, are virtually free from chromatic aberrations.

It will be obvious from this list of possible aberrations that a single lens is not good enough for photography. Corrections must be made by using more than one lens and by selecting glass with special properties. The more thorough the correction the more complex and expensive the lens will be. Also, the wider the aperture, the more difficult it becomes to make the corrections all over, so this puts the price up as well. To some extent the *focal length* also affects the price—a wide-angle lens often being more expensive than a long-focus or telephoto lens—so let us consider this important characteristic of any lens.

Focal length

The focal length controls the linear size of the images, and it is an expression of the distance between the lens and the film plane when rays from a distant object are in focus. If it is 50 mm the lens will be described as of 50 mm focal length, and this figure will usually be engraved on the lens mount. Strictly speaking, the distance is measured from the rear nodal point of a lens, and in a compound lens this could be inside or outside the lens, but we need not worry about that here, because we are more concerned with understanding focal length than with measuring it.

Most cameras are fitted with a lens, often referred to as a standard lens, which has a focal length approximately equal to the diagonal measurement of the negative. For example, the standard lens on a 35 mm camera is usually about 50 mm (2 in) and on a 6 cm × 6 cm camera it is usually about 80 mm ($3\frac{1}{4}$ in approx.).

Anything substantially less than the standard is called a short focus or wide-angle lens and anything greater is called a long focus lens. Thus an 18 mm, 24 mm, 28 mm or 35 mm lens on a 35 mm camera is short-focus and a 85 mm, 105 mm, 135 mm or

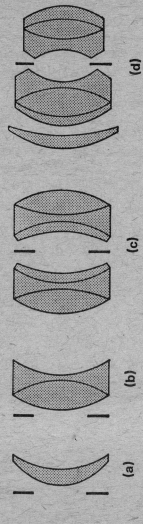

(a) (b) (c) (d)

Fig. 6 A simple meniscus lens as shown in section (a) has too many aberrations for satisfactory photography. The achromatic combination (b) is partly corrected and can be used at small apertures. The double anastigmat (c) is almost fully corrected, but its maximum usable aperture (about f/8) is very limiting. The compound lens (d) is a typical ultra-fast lens with excellent correction even at large apertures.

200 mm is long-focus. Likewise, on a 6 cm × 6 cm camera, 55 mm or less is short-focus and 105 mm, 135 mm, 180 mm, 200 mm or 300 mm is called long-focus.

The angle of view of a standard lens focused on infinity is about 55°, and the angle of view for a given size of negative gets progressively greater the shorter the focal length and can be as much as 105°. Conversely, the angle of view gets narrower as the focal length increases, and there is no limit to the focal length that can be used, except for the practical one of sheer size and length.

From this it will be seen that the ability to change lenses on a camera can be very useful. In confined spaces a short-focus lens will permit inclusion of more of the subject than a standard lens, and this is very useful in interiors and crowds. When it is not possible to get close enough to a subject to fill the negative a long-focus lens is invaluable. Sports photography and animal photography in the wild are but two of its many uses.

Telephoto lenses

To get the rays from infinity into sharp focus on the film plane the distance between the nodal point of the lens and the film plane must be equal to the focal length of the lens. On some cameras it is varied for different lenses by means of bellows or some form of extending front, but often it is produced by an extension in the lens mount.

However, with lenses of two or more times the standard focal length, the camera or the lens mount would become extremely unwieldy, so a telephoto lens provides an answer. It is a compound lens in which there is a negative back element of short-focus well separated from a positive front component. This means that the lens-to-film distance can be considerably reduced without affecting the image size. Thus a 300 mm telephoto lens may need only 150 mm between lens and film yet give the same size image as a 300 mm long-focus lens. One pays for this with a slight loss of quality, but not enough to worry about in a good-quality make.

Mirror lens

The mirror lens is another type of compromise that provides a very long focus in a relatively short mount, although is has to be rather large in diameter in order to accommodate concave and convex mirrors. It has a drawback in that it cannot be easily stopped down and it is a lens that is not really convenient for general use.

Fish-eye lens

This is an extremely wide-angle lens that has an angle of view of or near 180°. It produces extreme barrel distortion so that lines near the edge of the field are curved outward and only those through the centre of the subject appear straight. It is useful for astronomy but in other respects is something of a novelty and not suitable for general use.

Zoom lens

This is a lens of variable focal length. There are several groups of elements that can be moved by rotating the lens mount and this alters the size of the image without affecting the focus. The range of focal lengths for a 35 mm camera zoom lens is usually not more than about 100 mm, i.e. 75 mm to 175 mm or 100 mm to 200 mm, and there is sometimes a loss of quality and sharpness especially at the larger apertures. The extra weight and bulk is also a drawback, but enormous improvements have been made in recent years and the better makes perform almost as well as prime lenses.

The iris diaphragm

The iris diaphragm, which is usually fitted between the components of a lens, provides a continuously adjustable aperture that is approximately circular. In order to facilitate exposure calculation a specific range of sizes of aperture are marked on the adjusting ring.

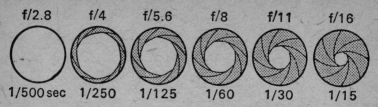

Fig. 7 The iris diaphragm built into the lens mount can be opened and closed like the iris of the human eye. Specific 'stops' are arranged at intervals so that each passes half as much light as the larger one preceding it. Shutter speeds are arranged in a progression, which also halves the exposure for each higher speed. Thus any of the combinations of speed and aperture shown in the diagram give the same effective exposure.

These are given as f numbers and they are the result of dividing the focal length of the lens by the diameter of the aperture. For example, an aperture of 10 mm diameter on a 50 mm lens would be f/5. However, a series has been standardised that runs as follows: f/1·4, f/2, f/2·8, f/4, f/5·6, f/8, f/11, f/16, f/22, and each one of these passes exactly half the amount of light of the previous one. The larger the number, the smaller the aperture, and each higher number will require double the exposure of the previous one.

Depth of field

At one time the use of small apertures, or stops as they are often called, provided a means of reducing lens aberrations. With modern lenses this is hardly necessary since the definition is generally acceptable at any aperture, although there is often a stop at which optimum performance is obtained—usually about f/5·6 or f/8 on a 50 mm lens. However, the iris diaphragm has a very much more important function in giving control over depth of field.

When a camera is focused on a plane at a specific distance there will be planes in front and behind that are acceptably

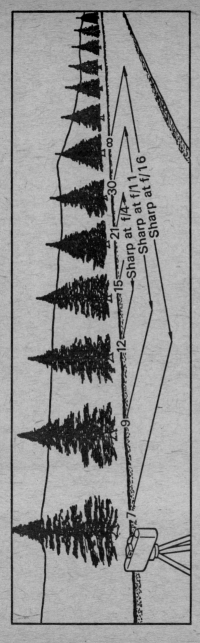

Fig. 8 The distance on which a lens is focused and the aperture in use together control the depth of field within which all objects are reasonably sharp. Here the lens is focused on 15 ft and the figures show the depth of field at three different apertures. Note that there is a greater depth beyond the focused point than in front of it.

sharp, and the distance between the nearest and furthest acceptably sharp planes is called the depth of field. This varies with:

The focal length of the lens.
The distance on which the lens is focused.
The acceptable degree of sharpness expressed as a 'circle of confusion'.
The aperture in use.

The longer the focal length of the lens in use, the smaller the depth of field when the other three factors are unchanged.

When a lens is focused on a near object the depth of field, other things being equal, will be less than when it is focused on a distant object: the variation between, say, a portrait and an object 100 feet away can be considerable.

The acceptable degree of sharpness is a variable factor, but a measurement for a 'circle of confusion' enables it to be expressed in figures and to provide a basis for comparison. It will be seen from Fig. 9 that when rays from a distant object come to a point on the film plane that object is sharp, while rays from objects nearer and further away will form circles instead of points. The largest circle that is permissible will govern the distances between which the depth of field is measured.

It is generally accepted that a circle of confusion of f/1000 (i.e. the focal length of the lens divided by 1000) is a reasonable norm, and many tables giving depth of field for different lenses at different apertures and different distances are based on it. Expressing a circle of confusion as a fraction of the focal length takes care of the fact that miniature negatives made with lenses of 50 mm or less focal length are usually enlarged much more than larger negatives made with longer focal-length lenses. It does not, however, take into account the fact that a miniature negative made with a telephoto lens will probably be enlarged just as much as one made with a standard lens, so theoretically a higher degree of sharpness should be allowed for.

The distance between the planes on either side of the film plane where the permitted circle of confusion occurs is known as the 'depth of focus'. This term is often wrongly applied to the depth of field.

Variation of the aperture gives a lot of control over depth of field. For any given distance the smaller the aperture, the greater the depth of field. Thus when it is required to throw a back-

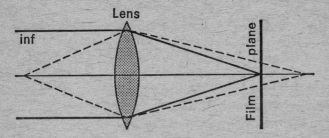

Fig. 9   Rays of light from a far distant point are nearly parallel when they enter the lens, but refraction causes them to come to a point on the film plane when the lens is correctly focused. Rays from a nearer point come to a focus behind the film, so objects at that distance appear out of focus. Conversely, if the distance between lens and film plane is increased so that the nearer objects are in focus, then those at a greater distance will appear out of focus. The circle on the film plane formed by the out-of-focus rays is known as the circle of confusion.

ground out of focus a wide aperture is employed and when it is desired to cover a great depth, as in most landscape work, a small aperture is used.

Minimal depth of field is obtained by using a long focus or a telephoto lens at full aperture on a close-up subject and maximum depth is obtained by using a short-focus lens at the smallest aperture on a distant subject. Between these extremes an infinite range of effects can be obtained and this is a useful factor in the artistic aspect of photography, as will be seen later.

It is wise to remember that for a given size of image and a given aperture all lenses show the same depth of field. However, to obtain images of the same size with lenses of different focal lengths the distances between camera and subject will vary. This has a bearing on perspective, which is fundamentally the relation in size between objects on different planes. Thus an object close to the camera will look larger in relation to a more distant object than if the camera were taken further away and a longer focus lens used to keep the main object the same size.

Perspective is purely a matter of distance, not of focal length. If an object is photographed at, say, 30 feet on two cameras, one fitted with a 50 mm lens and the other with a 135 mm lens, it will appear much larger on the 135 mm negative than on the 50 mm, but the relative sizes of the object and everything else in the picture will remain the same. In other words, both negatives could be enlarged to give identical prints.

There are many subjects where perspective must be taken into account. If we get very close to the subject in a head-and-shoulder portrait, the nose will appear much too large in relation to the ears. With a standard lens there would be a temptation to get too close in order to fill the negative, and with a wide-angle lens it would be necessary to get so close as to produce a caricature. Therefore a longer focus lens is essential in order to get far enough away to produce proportions that look natural. On the other hand, if we select a very long focus, say a 300 mm on a 35 mm camera, the ears will look too large in relation to the nose. For most portraiture a 105 mm or 135 mm focal length on a 35 mm camera gives the more natural effect.

When photographing distant scenes a very long-focus lens will appear to 'bunch-up' the planes and thus reduce the illusion of depth. This effect is frequently seen on television, where a cricket pitch is apparently reduced to a few feet in length. This is not so much because a long-focus lens is used as because the camera is so far away and the long-focus lens has been used to fill the picture with a small part of the scene.

It is useful to remember that the greater illusion of depth, other things being equal, is obtained when the camera is close to the foreground objects and a lesser impression of depth when the camera is a long way away. This, and the necessity or otherwise of filling the negative with the subject, will help you to decide what focal length of lens to employ.

Lens coating

When light strikes a glass surface a small amount is reflected back instead of passing through. In the case of a compound lens with a number of surfaces, the loss can be very considerable and internal reflections can also create a degree of fog, which has the effect of reducing contrast.

These problems can be reduced by coating the lens surfaces with an extremely thin and transparent film, usually magnesium fluoride. This is sometimes referred to as 'blooming'. Nearly all quality lenses are coated on some or all surfaces and although it gives the lens a coloured appearance, usually amber, it does not materially affect the colour transmission.

Degradation of the image by internal reflection can also be caused by allowing rays of light from outside the picture area to fall on the lens, whether it is coated or not. Such rays can cause ghost images even though they do not strike the film surface directly. This is a real danger when taking photographs 'against the light' or at an angle to the sun or other bright light source. The remedy is to use a lens hood that is long enough to shield the lens surface from such rays but not long enough to obtrude into the picture. Its use is especially desirable with modern wide-aperture lenses that have a large glass surface which is rarely very deeply recessed into the mount.

Lens converters

These are attachments that can be fitted in front or behind a lens in order to increase or decrease the focal length. When fitted behind the lens they are used to increase the focal length and are usually designated $\times 2$ or $\times 3$. Thus a 50 mm lens with a $\times 2$ converter will have an effective focal length of 100 mm. Those designed for decreasing the effective focal length are always fitted to the front of the lens.

Converters are compact and much cheaper than buying a separate long-focus or wide-angle lens, but there is inevitably some loss of quality in definition. They also decrease the effective aperture of the lens and this complicates exposure calculation. Converters for increasing the focal length are sometimes called tele-extenders.

Lens resolution

To any photographer the sharpness of the image produced by a lens is by far its most important factor. Sharpness, however, is not necessarily measured in the number of lines per millimetre that can be seen in a negative made from a test chart. Indeed, most lenses, even the cheapest, can resolve more lines than the average film emulsion.

Lines on a test chart are usually black on white, thus providing maximum contrast, whereas most photographic subjects are of considerably lower contrast. Often a photograph of a contrasty subject taken with a poor-quality lens will look sharper than a low-contrast subject taken with a good-quality lens. Also, a negative developed in an 'acutance' developer, which produces sharp contours giving a quick transition from one tone to another, will often appear much sharper to the eye.

Nearly all medium-price lenses of modern construction are adequate for normal purposes and comparatively free from aberrations, but if very big enlargements or sparkling exhibition prints are the ultimate aim it is wiser to buy the best.

Further reading about lenses

Optics, Arthur Cox, Focal Press.
Lens Guide, Leonard Gaunt, Focal Press.
200 *Filter and Lens Tips*, Fountain Press.

3 Choosing a Flashgun

Not so long ago a chapter on flash would have been at the end of a book on photography, but today it has become an almost indispensable aid that widens the scope of the camera and makes photography possible in any condition. Nearly all professional studios employ flash instead of the tungsten spotlights and floods that cluttered up the set and 'cooked' the sitter only a decade ago. You will rarely see a press photographer without flash, even in bright sunlight, and improvements in design and cost have made it available to every amateur.

There are two basic types of flash: bulbs and electronic flash. Flashbulbs are expendable—they can only be fired once and then have to be thrown away. Electronic flashguns will fire repeatedly until the tube wears out and this may mean as many as 10 000 or more flashes.

Flashbulbs

It was the introduction of foil-filled flashbulbs in 1934 that made camera synchronisation possible and today there is hardly a camera that does not have built-in provision for firing the flash during the fraction of a second that the shutter is open. The original flashbulbs were as big as electric light bulbs and not always reliable; sometimes they failed to fire and sometimes they exploded.

Continuous improvement has brought the size down to little more than a peanut and the modern bulb is both safe and reliable. In its latest form, known as a flashcube, there are four bulbs in a transparent container and each has its own tiny reflector. A variation of this, called a Magicube, does not even require an electric current to fire it.

All bulbs except the Magicube are fired by a current which is

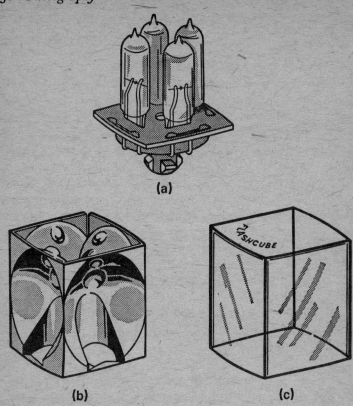

(a)

(b)   (c)

Fig. 10 An exploded diagram of a flashcube showing the four tiny blue flashbulbs. The four reflectors above slip down over them so that each bulb has its own aluminised reflector. The transparent styrene sleeve which fits over the whole is only $1\frac{1}{8}$ in $\times$ $1\frac{1}{8}$ in $\times$ $1\frac{1}{8}$ in. The Magicube is similar but has a mechanical instead of electric means of firing and can only be used on specially fitted cameras.

passed through them when the shutter is operated. In order to make sure of an adequate power supply a battery capacitor circuit is employed in most flashguns. The capacitor is charged by the battery through a resistor and when contact is made the energy is discharged direct from the capacitor instead of the battery, so a consistent 'punch' is obtained even when the battery is running down and is too weak to fire a bulb direct.

Simple 'snapshot' cameras have the capacitor built into the body, together with accommodation for a miniature battery. This means that the flash has to be used on the camera. We shall see later that this is very restrictive and useless for serious photography. Magicubes can only be used on cameras specially made for them because the firing is achieved by mechanical means. No battery is required since a trigger actuates the firing paste by friction. This means that Magicubes suffer the same 'on-camera' disadvantage as flashcubes. Nevertheless, both are an improvement on single bulbs because four flashes can be fired in fairly quick succession and they are cooler to handle after firing. Uncoated flashbulbs give a light that is too warm for daylight-type colour film, but nearly all bulbs are now coated blue in order to overcome this.

A variation of the flashcube is the 'flipflash' which is a vertical array of six miniature bulbs which fire in sequence. Some cameras, notably certain instant models, use a 'flashbar' which is similar but in a horizontal row. They can only be used in cameras designed for them.

For serious work the battery and capacitor circuit are contained in a separate flashgun unit that is connected by cable to the synchronising socket. Some are also fitted with a 'hot-shoe', which establishes a direct connection when the camera accessory shoe has built-in contacts. Flashgun units, which need not be more than about 2 in $\times$ 2 in $\times$ 1 in and only an ounce or two in weight, can be deployed at any distance from the camera with the aid of an extension cable. They are made to take ordinary capless flashbulbs or flashcubes and, in the case of the former, incorporate a reflector, sometimes of the folding fan variety.

The big disadvantage of flashbulbs is their expense. They can only be used once and the cheapest is about 10p. Allowing for the number of pictures one might have to take to get the right pose or expression, this makes portraiture an expensive pastime, so flashbulbs are losing popularity except with those who indulge in only a few sessions per year.

Electronic flashguns

Electronic flash offers a number of advantages over flashbulbs. The flash is produced by passing an electrical charge from a large capacitor or conductor through a gaseous discharge tube of glass or quartz. The capacitor can be charged from a dry battery, an accumulator or from the mains in conjunction with a rectifier, and some makes have facilities for all three methods.

The flash has a very short duration—about 1/600 second or less. This will 'arrest' most moving subjects and it has approximately the quality of daylight, so it can be used with daylight-type colour film. In the early days electronic guns were very heavy and bulky affairs, usually with the power pack separated from the case containing the tube and the reflector, but today

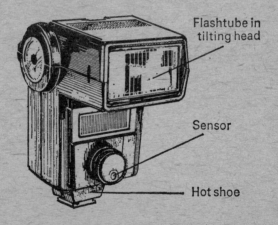

Flashtube in tilting head

Sensor

Hot shoe

Fig. 11 Electronic flashguns come in all shapes, sizes and prices. This is a popular type and it is possible to tilt it for bounce flash. No lead is necessary when the camera has 'hot-shoe' contacts. Many models like this can fire about fifty to eighty shots before the built-in NiCd battery needs recharging. Some can also be connected directly to the mains. Many recent models have automatic exposure control by means of a built-in sensor, which quenches the flash when sufficient illumination has been given.

there are many guns that are only fractionally larger than a cigarette packet and less than 8 oz in weight. True, there are professionals who still prefer the separate pack because of its extra power and the fact that it will give more flashes per charge —in some cases as many as 400. However, the smaller single units provide adequate power for most amateur purposes and give 60 to 80 flashes for each battery charge. They are not quite so powerful as the small flashbulbs, but there is not sufficient difference to take into account when weighing the pros and cons of bulbs versus electronic.

There are a number of flashguns available even in the smaller sizes, which have a built-in sensor that measures the light reflected from the foreground subject and when exposure has been sufficient the tube is quenched. All this takes place in a tiny fraction of a second and it saves calculating the exposure from the guide number described in Chapter 6. It also saves measuring the distance. On the average subject it works very well, but there are exceptions, so the guns are fitted with a switch that cuts out the sensor and allows exposure to be made with a full discharge in the ordinary way.

The disadvantage of these units when the sensor is built into the gun is that they can only be conveniently used on or near the camera, although there are a few models in the higher price class that have the sensor at the end of a cable. It can thus be placed on the camera while the flash is deployed at an angle to the subject. This also facilitates automatic exposures for bounced flash—something that is impossible with the simpler model. Some of them also have a circuitry that cuts off the flash instead of quenching it. This means that no current is wasted and more flashes per charge are obtainable.

Nearly all electronic flashguns have an angle of coverage of about 60° to 70°, which approximates to that of a standard lens. The flash has a characteristic softness, due to the use of faceted built-in reflectors or matt plastic windows over the tubes, and the pictures taken with it are generally less hard than those taken with flashbulbs.

Many of the small amateur guns use two or four penlight batteries which will give up to forty or fifty flashes. These have the advantage of convenience, and if they run down during a shooting session they can be replaced immediately. Others are fitted with a nickel-cadmium (NiCd) dry battery that can be recharged from the mains. These give sixty or more flashes on a charge, but recharging may take anything up to twenty-four hours. However, in the long run, there is a saving in cost because the battery does not have to be replaced. Electronic flashguns with nickel-cadmium batteries can also be fired by direct connection to the mains via the charging cord and plug supplied. This is a convenience at home if the battery runs out during a session.

The number of flashes obtained will obviously depend on the way the gun is used. If it is left switched on between shots current will be wasted, except in the case of large guns fitted with an automatic cut-out in the circuit.

When contemplating the purchase of a gun its use should be carefully considered. If the intention is to use it mainly for formal indoor portraiture, there is no real necessity for an automatic model and, since weight is not so important, a powerful model, possibly with separate power pack, would be an advantage. On the other hand, candid work at parties, indoors sports or theatricals calls for an easily portable model, and an automatic unit would assist quick working and in getting shots that might otherwise be missed while calculating exposure.

Flash can be useful out of doors, as we shall see later in this book, but power is not so important, so the miniature lightweight models are the obvious choice. Automatic exposure control is useless for synchro-sunlight (fill-in flash outdoors).

The strength of the light given by an electronic flashgun is sometimes expressed in *joules* or watt-seconds. This is not very reliable as a measurement of effectiveness because the watt-second figure is merely a mathematical calculation based on the storage capability of the capacitor and the voltage applied to it.

It has therefore become customary to quote a *guide number*, usually based on film of 50 ASA speed (see Chapter 4). The quoted guide number divided by the distance of the subject from the camera gives the aperture to use. For example, if the guide number quoted for the gun is 110 with 50 ASA film and the subject is 10 feet away, the aperture to use is f/11. The guide number takes into account the tube construction, reflector efficiency and any other factor peculiar to the gun. It is thus a reliable way of comparing one gun's power against another's. Most flashguns are fitted with a little rotating scale that gives the guide number for different speeds of films and indicates the aperture to use at different distances. The guide number system is also used for flashbulbs and an exposure table is usually printed on the packet.

Slave guns

A useful accessory in flashwork is known as a slave unit or slave gun. When it is desired to use more than one flashgun in synchronisation, a slave unit will obviate the necessity for cables or connections.

It is attached to and connected with one of the flashguns. Firing the other gun, which is connected directly to the camera synchronising socket, causes the slave unit to trigger the gun to which it is itself connected. This is done by means of a photocell or phototransistor which, through an amplifier, closes the contacts of a magnetic relay.

It is powered by a small dry battery and modern units are smaller than a cigarette packet. Often the slave unit is used in conjunction with a main light well away from the camera, while a second flashgun, used for filling in the shadows, is fitted on or near the camera. This is sufficient for firing the main light via the slave unit at any distance up to 20 feet or more. Any number of flashguns can be fired in this way so long as each has a slave unit, and there will be no wires or cables to trip over. Slave units can, of course, be used with either bulbs or electronic guns. Continuous light, however bright, will not affect them.

Synchronisation

On a static subject when the light level is very low it is possible to open the shutter on 'Bulb' or 'Time', fire the flash and then close the shutter. It is obvious that this cannot be done in bright light, especially with moving subjects, otherwise double images will result and so camera designers have built in a means of firing the flash at exactly the right moment. However, there is a difference in the characteristics of bulb and electronic guns that has to be taken into account. A bulb does not reach its peak until about 20 milliseconds after contact is made, but electronic flash reaches its peak almost instantaneously.

On a between-lens shutter the blades take from 2 to 3 seconds to open fully, so the contact for firing a flashbulb must be made 17 to 18 milliseconds before the shutter starts to open. To achieve this a delay mechanism is built into the shutter, and it is usually operated when the flashgun is connected to a socket marked 'M'. For electronic flash the gun must be connected to the socket marked 'X'. At this setting the flash contacts close in about 2 milliseconds, i.e. when the shutter blades are fully open. It is also possible to use the smaller-type flashbulbs on the 'X' setting at the slower speeds—up to 1/60 second. Electronic flash can be used at all speeds on 'X'.

Synchronisation with focal-plane shutters is not so easy because of the time taken by the slit to uncover the film area. A special type of flashbulb, designated 'FP', is made for the purpose and this can be used on cameras that close the contacts before the first blind begins to move. This bulb has a peak duration that is longer than the shutter travel time on most cameras and it is used via the socket marked 'F' or 'FP'.

Unfortunately, the peak duration of electronic flash is far shorter than the travel time of a focal-plane shutter, so it can

only be used at the slower speeds when the film is fully uncovered. This varies with different makes of camera but is
usually about 1/50 or 1/60 second. Anything faster will cause
only part of the negative to be exposed.

It will be seen from this that the between-lens shutter has a
big advantage over focal plane when it is necessary to use flash
in bright light conditions on fast-moving subjects. In a boxing
arena, for example, an exposure of 1/60 second might well
record a secondary image by the available light as well as the
main image illuminated by the flash. This also applies when
using flash for fill-in work in bright sunlight. The subject may
demand an exposure of 1/250 second or less, but with a focal-
plane shutter it would be impossible to synchronise electronic
flash. This could, however, be overcome by purchasing a second
gun to take an FP bulb. The guns are not expensive but the
bulbs cost a little more than the normal ones.

Further reading about Flash

The Focal Guide to Flash, Gunter Spitzing, Focal Press.
The Hobby Flash, Walther Benser, Fountain Press.
200 Flash Tips, E. Voogel/P. Keyser, Fountain Press.

4 Choosing a Film

There are three basic categories of film from which a choice has to be made before loading the camera. They are

(1) *Monochrome film*, which produces black-and-white negatives from which unlimited prints can be made by contact or enlargement. The only exception in this category is diapositive film, which can be processed to a black-and-white transparency instead of a negative. This is used mainly to copy diagrams for educational and commercial purposes and offers no advantages for normal photography.

(2) *Colour negative film*, which produces a negative in complementary colours from which unlimited colour enlargements can be produced. Black-and-white prints can also be made from colour negatives with special panchromatic printing paper.

(3) *Colour reversal film*, which produces positive transparencies in colour. These have to be viewed by transmitted light or through a projector and this could be a disadvantage, but the quality of the colour can be far superior to anything obtainable in a print which has to be viewed by reflected light. Prints, if required, have to be made by means of an intermediate colour negative and this is necessarily rather expensive. Duplicate transparencies can be made by copying, but there is some loss of quality and they are expensive.

Monochrome films

All modern black-and-white films are panchromatic, which means that they are colour sensitive and, to a large extent, translate colours into tones of equivalent strength. The only exceptions are films made for special purposes, mainly commercial or industrial, and they do not concern us here.

The characteristic that concerns us most is that of sensitivity, popularly known as speed. Some film emulsions are very much more sensitive than others and one might well ask why anybody uses the slower films rather than using the fastest for everything. The principal reason is that slower films give better resolution as a rule.

The resolving power of an emulsion is a measure of its ability to render fine detail, and this should not be confused with sharpness. A negative can look sharp and yet not show so much detail as another. Sharpness is identified by the suddenness or otherwise of the transition between dark and light tones. Thus a negative of a subject such as a checkerboard will *look* much sharper than one of a misty landscape. As a general rule, the slower the film, the better the resolution, other things being equal.

Another characteristic of a monochrome emulsion is graininess. Properly exposed and developed, the slower films do not show grain except under a considerable degree of magnification. Fast films tend to show grain even when developed in so-called fine-grain developers, but modern emulsions have been improved to a point where it only becomes obvious in quite a big enlargement. This graininess, however, is not caused by individual grains of silver halides suspended in the emulsion but by agglomerations or clumping of the grains. This tendency to clumping is greater in fast films than in slower types, although it can be controlled by keeping down the energy of the developer, as we shall see in a later chapter.

There have been a number of different methods of expressing the sensitivity of a film, but only three are in common use today. They are Gost, DIN and ASA. The Gost system is used only in the USSR and some of the satellite countries, so it need not concern us here. The DIN system (Deutsche Industrie Norm) is used in Germany and some other European countries, but in Great Britain, America and, indeed, almost everywhere else in the world the ASA system is used. This is a standard of the American Standards Association and it is uniform with the BS system (British Standards Institution) which is sometimes quoted.

Another system known as Weston, which is used on Weston exposure meters, is also based on ASA figures, but it is important not to confuse the modern Weston system with the old one that is still found on earlier models. The figures on these are about half of ASA speeds.

ASA speeds are arithmetical. In other words, a film quoted as ASA 50 is half as sensitive as one marked ASA 100 and will require twice the exposure.

Only the ASA, BSI and Weston speeds are strictly comparable because the other systems are based on different parameters, but the following table of typical film speeds in use today will serve as a guide. Scheiner speeds, an obsolete German system, are also included because there are still many cameras in existence that are marked with this system.

ASA	DIN	Gost	Scheiner
10	11	9	22°
25	15	22	26°
32	16	28	27°
50	18	45	29°
64	19	56	30°
100	21	90	32°
125	22	110	33°
200	24	180	35°
400	27	360	38°
800	30	720	41°

Monochrome films of a lower sensitivity than 100 ASA are broadly classed as 'slow', while those between 100 and 300 are called 'medium-speed' films. The range above 300 and up to

800 ASA are classified as 'fast', while anything above 800 ASA is 'ultra-fast' or 'super-speed'.

The most popular films for general use are those between 100 and 200 ASA. Although called medium speed, they are more sensitive than the very fastest were a few decades ago. They show very little grain when developed in a suitable developer and enlargements up to almost any size are possible. They give good gradation and contrast, and the speed is sufficient for ordinary use.

The fast films are usually reserved for such special purposes as press work or high-speed action subjects where it may be necessary to give short exposures in very poor light. To a press photographer, in particular, getting a picture is more important than grain. In any case, prints are rarely required larger than 10 in × 8 in and the half-tone screen used in reproduction 'kills' most of it.

Negatives of fast films tend to be rather soft, especially when developed in fine-grain developers containing a lot of restrainer, and this means printing on hard or contrasty papers which can emphasise grain. Fast films also tend to be a little oversensitive to red; this means that they do not translate colours into mono-chrome tones quite so accurately as medium-speed films, which nowadays are very good indeed. This is not important with many subjects but it is noticeable in portraiture, where flesh tones and lips tend to be rendered too light.

Monochrome films slower than 100 ASA are usually reserved for special purposes such as copying or record work where the camera is used on a tripod and the extra contrast and resolution is an advantage.

Laymen sometimes wonder why keen amateurs still use black-and-white films when colour has become so easy and so good. The principal reason is that the enthusiast can exercise so much more control. By using various filters at the taking stage he can dramatise a subject and interpret it in his own way instead of just making a record of what is in front of the camera. In the darkroom he can carry this further: select special areas for enlargement, print several negatives together, modify tones by shading, or employ one of the various allied printing processes such as tone-separation, solarisation or bromoil.

These facilities and dodges enable him to remove the picture even further from reality than a two-dimensional, monochrome picture is already. In addition, he has all the fun of doing everything himself, from taking to printing—something that is not nearly so easy in colour work.

Colour negative films

These are films that, like black-and-white, produce negatives from which positive prints can be made, but in colour. In these not only are light and shade reversed but also the colours themselves appear as complementaries. For example, blue appears as minus blue, which is yellow; green as minus green, which is magenta; and red as minus red, which is cyan.

Unfortunately, it is difficult to assess the colour quality of most colour negatives because they have an overall yellow or orange appearance due to colour 'masking'. This is incorporated to overcome the imperfections of some of the dyes that absorb some of the colours that they should transmit.

Colour negative film can be processed by commercial finishing houses through dealers or chemists and, in most cases, can also be processed by the user. It takes a little longer but can be done in the same tanks as black-and-white film. It has to be loaded in the dark, but the rest of the processing can be done in daylight or artificial light. The special kits of chemicals make it easy, but once mixed they do not keep for long, so it is only economical to process colour negatives when you have about six rolls to process, except with Photocolor II (Chapter 14).

An advantage of negative film over reversal film for transparencies is that the amateur variety can be used in a wide range of lighting without the necessity for correction filters to ensure accurate colour balance. The correction, if necessary, is done at the printing stage.

Most colour negative films are in the speed range of 50 ASA to 400 ASA.

Colour reversal films

These are films that yield positive transparencies that have to be viewed by transmitted light. In some countries they are called diapositives, and when mounted for projection they are usually called slides. The great advantage of these films over the colour negative and print process is that a very much greater range of brightness is possible. In a print it rarely exceeds about 30:1, but in a transparency the range can be as great as 5000:1. The result on projection is a brilliance that is often described as breathtaking.

The main disadvantage of reversal film is that it is a 'one-off' process. If prints are required it is necessary to make an intermediate colour negative, which is expensive and also involves some loss of quality, especially when enlarged.

Most reversal films have to be returned to the manufacturer for processing, but there are a few that can be processed at home or by a laboratory. As with colour negative films, kits of chemicals can be purchased for the purpose, but they also have a short life after mixing and are not economical unless about six films can be processed within a few days.

The reversal films that have to be sent back to the manufacturers are sold in this country inclusive of processing, and the 35 mm, 110 and 126 size films are returned in 2 in × 2 in card or plastic mounts ready for projection.

The colour balance for reversal film cannot be altered during processing and has to be balanced for a specific colour temperature during manufacture. It is therefore sold in two types, one called Daylight and the other Type A. The Daylight type is balanced for a colour temperature of about 5500 Kelvin, which is roughly equivalent to the lighting at noon by diffused sunlight. Type A is designed for use with the overrun lamps called photofloods, which burn at a colour temperature of about 3400 K.

There is also a Type B film, but this is intended for professional studios using tungsten lamps, which burn at a colour temperature of 3200 K.

An enormous range of correction filters is available and these enable extremely accurate colour rendering to be achieved under almost any lighting conditions. However, the Daylight type and the Type A are sufficient for most purposes without the use of filters. The purist or the scientist may want to make a sunset look like a midday shot because the latter shows the *basic* hues, but most people will want a sunset shot to look like a sunset and the additional warmth of the lighting will be regarded as an asset rather than a drawback.

Many people use the daylight-type film all the time because flash gives perfectly good results with it. However, it cannot be used for photoflood lighting or normal artificial lighting without using a correction filter such as a Wratten 80B. This does not give very good colour rendering, and if a lot of photoflood work is contemplated it is better to use Type A and then add a filter, such as the Wratten 85, for daylight shots. This gives better results in terms of colour balance and there is no great loss of speed caused by the filter factor because Type A film has a higher speed than the Daylight type.

It will be seen from this that it is not possible to mix lighting of different temperatures. If, for instance, Type A film is used for portraits by photoflood lighting, it is essential to ensure that windows are curtained or they will come out much too blue.

Colour reversal films are available in quite a wide range of speeds—from 25 to 400 ASA. However, the higher speeds are not achieved without some loss in quality in colour balance, colour saturation, definition and grain. Those rated at speeds of 25, 32, 50 and 100 ASA have achieved an extraordinary standard of accuracy and colour brilliance, but above 100 ASA they begin to fall off and should really be reserved for emergencies when speed is all important.

Infra-red films

There is one other category of film that interests amateurs for special purposes. This has an emulsion that is particularly sensitive to the red end of the spectrum and, in conjunction with a filter passing only infra-red rays, unusual effects are produced.

Many things, especially foliage, reflect infra-red rays very strongly and thus come out white, or nearly so, the effect often resembling moonlight. It sometimes makes scenery that includes plants, trees and fields look like a snow picture. Blue skies come out black and red or orange objects appear nearly white.

The haze that obscures the detail of a distant landscape is easily penetrated by infra-red, so it is often used for long-distance photography.

The rays from an infra-red filter come to a focus slightly behind the plane on which the equivalent visible rays meet and so it is necessary to make some adjustment to the lens focusing. Many cameras have a dot or arrow to which the lens should be rotated after focusing on the subject by visible light.

Since no exposure meter can measure invisible rays it is difficult to estimate exposure precisely. With an infra-red filter in position the film is comparatively slow—about 20 ASA—so a range of exposures should be made on either side of the exposure indicated by visible light measurement.

There is a version of infra-red for colour and this is called Ektachrome Infra-red Aero film. It reproduces most colours in totally different hues from their appearance in nature. Originally designed for the detection of camouflage from the air in wartime, it has a number of scientific applications, notably in biology, forestry and medicine.

It can only be regarded as an amusing gimmick for amateur work because the results are so unpredictable. Green often appears as magenta, blue as red, red as yellow and yellow as white. It is therefore useless for portraiture but sometimes produces attractive landscapes.

Like monochrome infra-red film, it is not possible to apply an ordinary speed rating because invisible infra-red rays cannot be measured. A deep yellow filter (Wratten No. 12) must be used because all three emulsion layers are sensitive to blue. With this filter Kodak recommends a meter setting of ASA 100 for a trial, but it is necessary to bracket exposures by several stops either way because there is very little latitude. The film can be processed by the user or by a processing laboratory using the ordinary processing solutions sold for the normal Kodak reversal films, and it must be carried out in darkness.

Infra-red films in monochrome or colour are not usually stocked by dealers and have to be especially ordered.

Further reading about films

Photography: Materials and Methods, J. Hedgecoe and M. J. Lanford, Focal Press.

5 The Use of Filters

There are two reasons for making use of filters in photography. One is to correct faults in the lighting or to compensate for deficiencies in the film's response; filters for this purpose are called correction filters. The other reason is to falsify colours or exaggerate contrasts in order to introduce extra impact or drama, and filters used in this way are called contrast filters.

Filters are made of coloured glass or gelatine and placed in front of the lens to absorb light rays from specific areas of the visible spectrum while transmitting the rest. Put another way, it means that a filter freely transmits light of its own colour but absorbs in varying degrees the rays of the other colours that make up white light. Thus a red filter will pass the light from a pillarbox and, in a monochrome print, it will come out lighter than it would do without a filter. At the same time the blue sky behind will be partly absorbed, so it will come out darker than is natural.

In normal practice there is very little need to use correction filters with modern black-and-white films. Some of the slow films are slightly oversensitive to blue, and a very pale yellow filter will correct this. Some of the very fast films are oversensitive to red, and a very pale blue filter will restore accurate tone translation. The imbalance in both cases is so small that it can be ignored, except for highly scientific work.

Contrast filters

However, filters are very useful indeed for adding contrast and altering tone values so that an object stands out from its background. In still-life work, especially for commercial purposes, a filter of the right colour can separate objects that would otherwise translate into similar tones and it can also be used to emphasise pattern or texture. For instance, the grain in a piece of wood can be made to appear much more pronounced than it does to the eye.

The filters in common use with monochrome films are yellow, yellow-green, green, orange and red. As already mentioned, each of these transmits rays of its own colour and absorbs some of the other colours, but in varying degrees. This means that in selecting a filter to darken a particular colour its effect on others must be considered. For example, consider the case of a red-brick building against a blue sky. Without a filter the sky and the building could well come out very similar in tone and the picture would look flat. A red filter would darken the sky very considerably but would probably make the building appear nearly white. An orange filter would also darken the sky and lighten the brick-work, but to a lesser extent. A yellow-green or yellow filter will have even less effect. If there is green grass in the foreground it will probably be lightened by the yellow or yellow-green filter but darkened by the orange and the red filter. The table below gives some idea of what happens, but the easiest way to decide on a filter is to memorise two rules:

(1) *To lighten* a colour use a filter of the same colour, e.g. to lighten a green lawn use a yellow-green filter; to lighten a red dress use a red filter for maximum effect or use an orange filter for a lesser degree of lightening.

(2) *To darken* a colour use a filter of the complementary colour, e.g. to darken a blue sky use a yellow filter; to darken a red pillarbox use a green filter.

Filters of every colour are available in a range of densities— the deeper the colour, the greater the effect, though naturally one has to increase the exposure accordingly because some light is being absorbed instead of transmitted. The increase required is referred to as the filter factor and is written as 2x, 3x, 4x, etc. The figure corresponds to the extra exposure necessary—for example, a 2x filter will demand twice the exposure, or one stop increase, over the exposure required without a filter.

FILTER	Darker	Unchanged	Lighter
YELLOW	Violet, Blue	Green	Yellow, Orange, Red
YELLOW-GREEN	Violet, Blue, Red	Yellow	Green
GREEN	Violet, Blue, Red, Orange	Yellow	Green
ORANGE	Violet, Blue, Green	Yellow	Orange, Red
RED	Violet, Blue, Green, Yellow	Orange	Red

It should be noted that this factor does not have to be applied with a camera that measures the exposure through the lens because it will be automatically taken into account. Automatic cameras that have the electric cell aperture close to the lens will not require adjustment if the filter used is large enough to cover the electric cell window as well as the lens. This often happens with cameras that have the cell actually in the lens mount and close to the lens.

It should also be noted that a filter, however deep, cannot give tone where no colour exists. An overcast sky that has no blue in it will not be affected, even with a red filter. Likewise, a filter is more effective in a clear atmosphere than when it is misty or hazy. This means that a very pale filter used at high altitudes or by the sea on a clear day can have an effect normally associated with a very deep one. People who habitually use, say, a 3x yellow-green filter in Great Britain often find that a 2x or 1½x gives similar results when they go on holiday in semi-tropical or tropical climes.

Another consideration is the nature of the light. Daylight is redder in the early morning and late afternoon than it is at mid-day, so a paler filter can be used to obtain the same results. If the filter used is yellow, orange or red, less exposure will be required at the extremes than at noon. Likewise, other things being equal, the filter factor for these colours is reduced when used in photo-flood or artificial lighting other than flash.

Graduated filters

A filter that is graduated from yellow on one side to clear glass on the opposite side is popularly known as a sky filter. If it is placed well in front of the lens, the blue rays from the sky will pass through the yellow part of the filter and those from the landscape will pass unhindered through the clearer half. This type of filter was especially useful in the days when films were very oversensitive to blue at the expense of other colours. Even today it can be useful because skies are usually much too bright in relation to the landscape.

No filter factor is involved, but it is important to ensure that the filter is placed well in front of the lens—at least $\frac{1}{2}$ inch in the case of a 50 mm lens. If it is mounted on the lens in the usual position for other filters, it will merely behave as if it were a pale yellow filter covering the whole lens, and a filter factor will be involved. Some graduated filters are made to fit onto the front of a lens hood, but they must be large enough to avoid any danger of cut-off and it may still be necessary to shield the filter from surface reflections when working against the light or in strong side-lighting conditions.

Blue filters

At one time nearly all films were oversensitive to blue, so yellow, yellow-green or green filters were useful for absorbing some of the blue rays. Nowadays most films are well balanced in their tone rendering and, if anything, are oversensitive at the red end of the spectrum. This applies especially to the very fast and ultra-fast emulsions, i.e. 400 ASA and upwards.

For normal subjects this red sensitivity can be ignored, but for indoor portraits by artificial light, which is warmer in colour than daylight, it sometimes results in pale lips and wan flesh tones, while blue eyes come out too dark. A pale blue filter will help to correct these faults and to make lips darker and blue eyes lighter, at the same time giving better tone and modelling in the flesh. Unfortunately, it will also emphasise freckles if they are present.

A yellow, green, orange or red filter will penetrate haze to some extent and often give a clear background when it looks quite misty to the human eye. Indeed, with an infra-red filter it is possible to photograph distant detail that is invisible to the human eye.

The artistic landscape photographer sometimes prefers to retain or even emphasise the mist or haze, and a blue filter will do this. It is even possible with a deep blue filter and a degree of underexposure to obtain pseudo-moonlight effects. A deep blue filter is also useful as a 'viewing glass' for indoor work by artificial lighting because it gives an impression of the difference in contrast between that seen by the film and that by the eye. (See Chapter 12.)

Filters for colour work

It will be obvious that the filters designed for monochrome work are not suitable for colour films because they would give an overall cast of their own colour. There are, however, a number of filters that are used to compensate for lighting that is not of the colour temperature for which the film is balanced and there are also a few filters for special purposes.

The first, and the one in general use by all photographers, is the ultra-violet (UV) filter.

This usually has a faint pink or straw colour, and its purpose is to absorb some of the ultra-violet rays and thus check the tendency for colour films to produce rather too much blue over the shadow areas in daylight shots. It also gives a slightly warmer rendering to distant landscapes, mountain pictures, seascapes and sunlit snow pictures, all of which are rich in ultra-violet.

UV filters are useful when daylight-type reversal film is used with electronic flash, which is rich in ultra-violet. It reduces the danger of flesh tones coming out too blue, especially in the shadow areas. There is no extra exposure required for the UV filters in general use, and since they have no effect on monochrome film they can be left permanently in position over the lens, where they act as a useful protection against scratches and dust.

Colour correction filters

In the chapter on films it was stated that colour reversal films are balanced for a specific colour temperature, and for amateur use there are two types: Daylight and Type A. The former is balanced for about 5500 Kelvin, which is roughly equivalent to overcast noon daylight, while the latter is balanced for photoflood lighting (about 3400 K).

Sometimes it is not possible or convenient to change films when it is desired to switch from outdoor to indoor work or *vice-versa*, so filters are available to enable the same film to be used throughout. When exposing Daylight film by photoflood lighting a blue filter will absorb the excess yellow before it reaches the film. A typical example is the Wratten 80B.

When exposing Type A film by daylight a yellow filter is required to absorb the excess blue and the Wratten 85 is commonly used. Unfortunately, the use of Daylight film with an 80B filter in photoflood lighting involves a high exposure factor —about 4x—and the results are not so satisfactory in colour rendering as those given by Type A film. The latter used in daylight with an 85 filter gives quite good results and, since Type A film is faster than the Daylight type, the filter factor is almost cancelled out. If a great deal of 'mixed' work is anticipated it is, therefore, better to use Type A film rather than Daylight.

Another type of correction filter is one used for Type A films in artificial lighting other than photoflood. A whole series of bluish filters are available for raising the effective colour temperature when the lighting is too red, as it is with tungsten lamps or under-run photofloods. A colour temperature meter is almost essential to ascertain exactly what depth of filter is required and so colour correction filters of this type are used principally for scientific or recording purposes where absolute accuracy of colour rendering is required.

This also applies to the series of brownish filters that are available to *lower* the effective colour temperature. Colour film manufacturers market filters under their own brand names and numbers; there are too many to describe here, but the Wratten Series marketed by Kodak are typical. The brown filters are known as Wratten Series 81 and the blue as Wratten Series 82. There are five filters in the former and four in the latter series.

At a colour temperature of 3200 K the changes produced by each filter are in steps of about 100 K, but at other temperatures the changes will be different. This is a weakness of the Kelvin scale of expressing colour temperatures and so the Mired scale is more often quoted.

The word Mired is derived from *Mi*cro-*Re*ciprocal *D*egrees and a Mired value is the Kelvin temperature divided into one million. Thus a mean sunlight value of 5400 K can also be quoted as having a Mired value of 185. The advantage of the Mired scale is that equal intervals on the scale correspond to equal changes in colour.

The practical advantage of this is that Mired shift values or steps can be allotted to colour filters and they will indicate the change in colour that each filter will produce. This will be the same whatever the initial colour temperature of the light. Yellow filters are given positive shift values, i.e. +9, +18, etc., and blue filters, which reduce the shift values, are designated minus, i.e. −10, −21, etc.

A correction filter called the Wratten 81C may sometimes be encountered. It is designed to enable clear flashbulbs to be used with Type A (photoflood) film. However, nearly all flashbulbs are now coated blue, so this filter is no longer necessary.

Colour compensating filters

These should not be confused with colour correction filters. Colour compensating filters—usually prefixed with CC—are employed in making colour prints from colour negatives and can also be used to effect slight modifications of colour balance when making duplicate transparencies. A full range consists of thirty-six filters—six each of yellow, magenta, cyan, red, green and blue—of varying density. Their use is outlined in Chapter 15.

Polarising filters

A polarising filter provides a means of controlling specular reflections from polished surfaces. It will reduce or even extinguish light falling on it that is polarised in any plane other than its own. By arranging the filter in a mount that permits rotation it is possible to find a position where specular reflections from shop windows, metallic surfaces or highly polished materials are considerably reduced. Complete extinction can be obtained when the polarisation plane of the filter is at right angles to the plane of polarisation of the light.

The filter has to be rotated until the desired degree of suppression is obtained. On a single-lens-reflex camera this can be seen in the viewfinder, but on a twin-lens-reflex or non-reflex type of camera the filter must be adjusted at eye-level and then transferred to the lens mount without changing the angle of rotation in relation to the subject.

The filter is a neutral grey in appearance and it can be used with colour or monochrome films. In colour work it will not alter the basic hues, but it will darken blue skies that are plane-polarised at 90° to the sun; it is often used just for this purpose. Polarising filters also absorb ultra-violet radiation and therefore tend to 'warm up' shadows and open landscapes, seascapes or mountain scenery which are normally rendered too blue.

A bonus given by a polarising filter is a greater degree of colour saturation or brightness due to the fact that all surfaces have a certain degree of specular reflection, and at least some of it will be suppressed by the filter.

An important consideration is the camera viewpoint when a polarising filter is used for suppressing unwanted reflections. To point a camera at a shop window and expect the filter to remove all reflections will only lead to disappointment. The camera will have to be moved around until a viewpoint is found where the filter has the most effect, but it is unlikely that at any point *all* reflections will be eliminated, even if it is desirable.

Polarising filters demand an increase in exposure that varies with the amount of light that is suppressed and it can only be ascertained by experiment, except when using a single-lens-reflex with built-in metering that measures the light actually coming through the lens.

Filter types

Nearly all filters are available in two forms—gelatine and dyed-in-the-mass glass.

Gelatine filters are perfectly satisfactory, economical and optically excellent. They do not affect definition in any way but, of course, they are fragile and once marked with fingerprints or scratches they are useless. They also tend to become cloudy if exposed to moisture.

Dyed-glass filters are considerably more expensive, but if they are to be used frequently they are an economy because they can be handled and cleaned. They are supplied in push-on or screw-in mounts so that lens hoods can be used in conjunction with them. It is a false economy to buy the cheapest because they are often far from optically flat and will introduce distortions or aberrations. In general, it is wise to buy the filters marketed by the camera manufacturer because he is naturally concerned to see that the lens performance is not spoilt.

Further reading about filters

Photographic Filters, L. Strackel, Fountain Press.
Kodak Range of Light Filters, Kodak Ltd.
200 Filter Tips, Fountain Press.
Focal Guide to Filters, Clyde Reynolds, Focal Press.

6 Exposure

Correct exposure presents no difficulties with modern films and apparatus, although it is an aspect of photography that seems to frighten many people. This is probably a hangover from the days when film emulsions were very insensitive or slow and the methods of exposure calculation were, to say the least, primitive.

In the early days of photography exposure had to be precise or the resulting plates were virtually unprintable through being too thin (underexposed) or too dense (overexposed). Today the films have very much more latitude and prints can be obtained from negatives made with a wide variation of exposures on the same subject. However, this can lead to carelessness; the best print will always be the one made from a *correctly* exposed negative.

Colour transparencies have far less latitude in exposure than monochrome or colour negative films because little or no adjustment can be made in processing. A transparency that is underexposed will be dense when projected and one that is overexposed will be too thin. Furthermore, the colours will not be correctly rendered and a slide show made up of transparencies of varying densities and degrees of colour saturation will be unsatisfactory.

Therefore, we should always aim at getting accurate exposure whatever type of film is used and it is wise to forget any question of latitude or, at least, not to rely on it except in emergencies. Fortunately, as we shall see, it is easy to be accurate, but it will help if we understand the four basic factors that are involved.

The first of these is the speed, or sensitivity, of the film and, as we learnt in Chapter 4, this can vary considerably and thus has to be taken into account. Fortunately, the manufacturers mark their films with a universal standard speed system such as ASA or DIN and they are remarkably consistent. The figure is always given on the film carton, cassette or cartridge.

The second factor is the strength of the light, whether it is sunlight, artificial light or flash. Obviously, the brighter the light allowed to enter the camera for a given amount of time, the greater its effect on the film—this is what makes photography possible. At one time it was also necessary to take into account the nature of the light. For example, when films were far more sensitive to blue rays than anything else, a much longer exposure had to be given for artificial light than for daylight because the proportion of red light to blue is much higher in electric, or tungsten, lighting. Nowadays this consideration is rarely necessary because all but those films made for special purposes are sensitive to all colours in the visible spectrum.

The third consideration is the amount of light that is allowed to reach the film. This is controlled by the iris diaphragm described in Chapter 2. Fortunately, the aperture formed by the iris diaphragm is also on a universal system. This means that any particular 'stop' will permit the same amount of light to pass through any lens regardless of the focal length of the lens. For example, f/8 on a 50 mm lens will pass an equivalent amount of light to f/8 on a 200 mm lens, although the diameter of the aperture on the latter will, in fact, be considerably larger.

The fourth factor is the amount of time during which the light is allowed to reach the film. This, of course, is controlled by the shutter in most cases, but for very long exposures it can just as easily be controlled by taking a cap off the lens and replacing it, or by switching the light on or off. When using flash it is very often the duration of the flash itself that is the controlling factor because it is often less than the time that the shutter is open.

Nevertheless, for most work other than flash the shutter speed is the factor to be considered in exposure calculation. Here again, a degree of standardisation has made calculation very easy. There are two basic types of shutter: between-lens and focal-plane, but both usually carry speed markings in a progression of: 1 s, 1/2 s, 1/4 s, 1/8 s, 1/15 s, 1/30 s, 1/60 s, 1/125 s, 1/500 s, 1/1000 s. Cheaper models may omit the slower speeds and the very fast 1/1000 sec.

It will be seen that each of these speeds is exactly, or almost exactly, half the one preceding it. We have already seen in Chapter 2 that each f stop on the iris diaphragm is also arranged so that the preceding one passes only half the light of the previous stop; thus by taking the aperture and the shutter speed in combination we have very precise control over the amount of light passed through the lens on to the film.

For example, in the following table all these combinations will give the same effective exposure:

f/2	f/2·8	f/4	f/5·6	f/8	f/11	f/16	f/22
1/1000 s	1/500 s	1/250 s	1/125 s	1/60 s	1/30 s	1/15 s	1/8 sec.

If we presume that any one of these combinations is correct for 100 ASA film, the correct exposures for 50 ASA film will be found by moving the top line one place to the right so that the progression starts with 1/500 at f/2, 1/250 at f/2·8 and so on. Likewise, for a film of speed 200 ASA the correct exposure for the same lighting conditions will be found by moving the top line one place to the left so that it starts with 1/1000 at f/2·8. For film of 400 ASA it would be moved two places to the left.

Thus all we have to do is find the correct shutter speed/ aperture combination for the film in use, and all the other combinations are easy to find by turning the aperture and shutter-speed scales on the camera or on the exposure meter in opposite directions.

This leaves us with only the strength of the light as an unknown factor but, nevertheless, the most important one. In the early days elaborate tables were published giving factors for different lighting conditions at different times of the day throughout the year and in different latitudes. These figures were combined with the figures for the speed of the plate, the shutter speed and the aperture, together with filter factors and other variants. The photographer of the 1850s would have welcomed this decade's electronic calculators!

Exposure meters

Today we have photo-electric exposure meters that measure the strength of the light and they are a most reliable guide if used properly. They are often built into the camera and some of these are coupled to the shutter mechanism or diaphragm. In automatic cameras they even open and close the diaphragm for you. Other meters are completely separate and the information obtained from them has to be transferred to the camera's diaphragm or shutter-speed dial, or both, by the user. There are advantages and disadvantages to both built-in and separate meters.

The big advantage of a built-in meter is convenience, and when coupled to shutter and diaphragm it makes for very quick working. The main disadvantage is that it can only measure the light falling on the camera lens. This may include lots of sky or background which is not so important as the main subject. For example, in an outdoor portrait correct exposure of the face is essential, but the influence of a bright sky might cause the face to be underexposed. It is therefore desirable to take the meter close enough to eliminate the sky and to read only the light reflected from the face. It is not always convenient or practicable to take the camera up to the subject, so a separate meter is an advantage.

There are times, as we shall see later, when it is desirable to measure the light falling on the subject rather than the light reflected from the subject. This especially applies to reversal (transparency) films and it also means that the meter should be used close to the subject and not at the camera position.

A further disadvantage of the built-in meter is that the whole camera is out of action if the meter needs repair, but fortunately this is rare—most meters are very reliable.

There are two types of photo-electric exposure meter. One

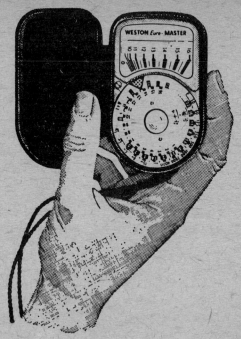

Fig. 12   A popular type of exposure meter that will measure over a wide range of lighting conditions. The cell on the back can be masked for extra bright lighting and a white opal cone can be placed over it for incident light readings.

is actuated by a selenium or silicon cell which reacts to the light by producing a tiny current that actuates a pointer or indicator. The other employs a CdS (cadmium sulphide) cell that needs a miniature mercury battery to activate it. This type is more sensitive than the selenium type, i.e. it will give a reading at much lower light levels, so it is usually the one employed in cameras. On the other hand, the selenium cell has a better all-over response which closely follows that of the human eye. Nevertheless, except for one well-known make, the selenium meter is rapidly losing favour, especially as some of the better CdS meters now have a much improved response.

Reflected light reading

Exposure readings for many subjects are taken with the meter pointed at the subject from the camera position. The pointer indicates the strength of the light and scales show the aperture/ shutter speed combinations that can be used for the particular speed of film in use. In most cameras where the meter is built in, the film speed is set and the aperture ring or the shutter speed dial can be turned until a pointer coincides with the meter's pointer. Alternatively, they can be coupled to the meter indicator, which is moved by the aperture ring or speed dial until it coincides with a mark visible in the viewfinder.

Taking readings in this way is quite satisfactory for average subjects where there is a fairly even distribution of tones and not too much contrast. The meter can only measure the overall brightness, so we sometimes have to use the meter merely as a guide and then make some commonsense adjustments.

For example, consider an open landscape on a bright sunny day. The sky will be very much brighter than the fields and foreground, so it will influence the meter to indicate an exposure that could be insufficient to get good detail in the earth. This can be overcome by tilting the meter or the camera downwards when taking the reading so that less of the sky, or even none at all, is being seen by the meter. Unfortunately, however, this cannot be done with a fully automatic camera unless it has an electronic memory facility.

We have already seen that an outdoor portrait could be very much underexposed if too much sky is allowed to influence the meter and, likewise, a portrait taken indoors or outdoors against a black or very dark background could be *overexposed* due to the lack of light. Some cameras with built-in meters allow for this by having what is known as a 'centre-weighted' reading. Working on the presumption that the centre area of a picture is usually more important than the rest, it reacts more to the rays from the centre of the subject than to the remainder. Failing this, it is necessary to make some adjustment for such subjects by opening up or closing down the aperture or speed indicated by the meter.

There is also the problem of excessive contrast. Often it is desirable to have as much detail and tone as is possible in every part of the picture, from highlight to shadow. Sometimes this will not be possible because the range of tones is greater than the film can accommodate. If the contrast cannot be reduced by using flash or reflectors, it is necessary to decide on what can be sacrificed—the detail in the highlights, the detail in the shadows or a little of both?

If it is to be the highlights, then the reading should be taken from the shadows and middle tones with the meter shielded from the highlights. If it is not possible to shield it, an average reading must be taken and the exposure increased by one or more stops, or a slower shutter speed must be used. On the other hand, if the detail in the shadows can be sacrificed, the reading should be taken from the highlights and middle tones with the meter angled to avoid the shadow areas. Again, where this is not practicable, it will be necessary to compromise by taking the meter reading as a guide and reducing the aperture by one or more stops, or by using a shorter shutter speed.

Where the decision is to lose a little of both highlight and shadow detail an average reading is probably the best, but it is far better wherever possible to reduce the contrast by employing flash or reflectors. Failing that, it is better to wait for more diffused lighting conditions—an overcast sky or a degree of haze.

Another advantage of a separate meter is that one can go very close to the subject and take one reading from the shadows and another one from the highlights. The exposure can then be adjusted to get precisely what is required—highlight detail, shadow detail or a middle-of-the-road compromise. Some of the better meters actually give some guidance on the range of tones that an average film will accommodate, but it is only a guide because film characteristics vary enormously. As a general rule, monochrome films can take in a considerably greater range than colour films.

Some monochrome films can even accommodate a range of tones of the order of about 800:1, but even this cannot cope with a really contrasty subject on a bright sunny day. Nevertheless, it is very much greater than the tone scale on an overcast day, so quite a wide variation in exposures could be given and each would still be within the capacity of the film. This is why such films are described as having a lot of latitude.

A simple way of appreciating the problem is to think of the capacity of the film to render tones from black to white in terms of a staircase with, say, twenty steps, the bottom representing black, the top being white and all the others intermediate greys in an even progression.

If the tone range of the subject is only the equivalent of five of these steps it can be placed in four positions on the stairs without going off at the top or the bottom. If, on the other hand, the range of the subject is the equivalent of twenty-five steps it will go off at the top or the bottom. If it is at the top (overexposure) detail and gradation is lost in the highlights, and if it goes off at the bottom (underexposure) detail and gradation is lost in the shadows. While the steps or tone gradation in the middle are clearly defined, the tones that are 'off' the staircase will be compressed and not so well separated. Shadows will be a solid black and highlights will be white and burnt out. Therefore it behoves the photographer to be very careful about measuring exposure for a contrasty subject.

A method adopted by some people to get a correct reading for the flesh tones on a face in an outdoor portrait is to use a light grey card or the back of the hand. This saves going right up to the subject and, as long as the light falling on the card is at approximately the same angle and is the same strength as that falling on the subject proper, it is fairly reliable. It is certainly a good compromise if there is some obstruction such as a fence between you and the subject, especially if the latter happens to be a wild animal!

Incident light reading

Sometimes there is an advantage to be gained by measuring the light falling on the subject instead of the light reflected from it.

The meter is directed from the subject position *towards* the camera and a semi-transparent white plastic diffuser, usually in the form of a cone or half a sphere, is placed over the cell window. This gives a general reading that will not fluctuate according to the tones in the subject.

Incident light reading provides correct exposure for flesh tones, so this method is especially useful for portraiture, particularly in colour. Since it concentrates on measuring the highlights, the incident light reading is much more reliable for colour-transparency work.

Exposure for flash

It is not possible to use an ordinary exposure meter for flash, but fortunately it is very easy to obtain correct exposure. There are, in fact, special meters developed for studio work, but they are too cumbersome to be practical for amateur use in addition to being comparatively expensive.

Since the duration of the illumination from a flashbulb or an electronic flashgun is generally somewhere between 1/600 and 1/1500 second, and this is usually less than the time during which the shutter is open, exposure calculation is based on the brightness and duration of the flash alone. This means that shutter speed does not have to be taken into account and the iris diaphragm aperture is the only other concern.

Every flashbulb and electronic flashgun is provided with a table of guide numbers—one for each speed of film. For example, a small bulb or flashcube may quote a guide number of 80 for 100 ASA film. This guide number is merely divided by the distance in feet to obtain the aperture to use. Thus with a subject 10 feet away the aperture to use will be $\frac{80}{10}$ = f/8. If the subject is only 5 feet away the aperture will be f/16, and if it is 20 feet away the aperture should be f/4.

On most electronic flashguns and many of the attachments for firing bulbs, a scale is provided that enables the aperture for any speed of film at any distance to be ascertained instantly and easily. Naturally the figure can be used the other way if it is desired to employ a specific aperture, say f/5·6. The guide number is 80, so the distance from the subject at which the flash must be fired is $\dfrac{80}{5·6}$ = approximately 15 feet. It must be emphasised that this distance is always that from the flash to the subject and not the camera to the subject. As you will see in a later chapter, it is rarely desirable to have the gun at the camera position. On many continental guns and tables the figures will be given in metres, which means that the guide number is much lower, but it is becoming common practice to give two sets of numbers—one for metres and one for feet—against film speeds given in both ASA and DIN.

The guide numbers are calculated for average conditions and presume that the flash is being used in a properly designed reflector. This is no problem nowadays because reflectors are always built into the gun and flashcubes even have them built into the plastic case. But if a bulb were to be fired without a reflector it would necessitate opening the diaphragm at least one stop.

The guide numbers are also based on their use indoors where there is a certain amount of reflection from walls and ceilings. If used in a large room with dark walls it will probably be necessary to open up by one stop and, if used outdoors at night, even by two stops.

Sometimes it is desirable to soften the flash by placing a diffuser of some sort, possibly one or more layers of handkerchief, over the gun (see Chapter 13). The best way to allow for the light that is lost is to point an exposure meter at a plain wall, take a reading without the diffuser and note the aperture to use at any specific film speed that is convenient. Then take another reading with the handkerchief over the cell window and note the increased aperture indicated for the same speed. It will usually be found that one layer of a linen handkerchief requires an increase of about one stop, two layers two stops and so on.

Bounced flash

Guide numbers are based on flash being directed straight onto the subject. Because this gives harsh results and very hard shadows many people 'bounce' the flash off a suitable reflector so that no direct rays reach the sitter. This reflector can be a ceiling or a wall that is light in tone and, of course, should always be white when using colour film otherwise some of the reflector's colour will be cast onto the subject.

There is no precise way of calculating exposure under these conditions, but a rough guide which usually works is to add together the distances from flash to reflector and reflector to subject. The total is then divided into the guide number and the aperture opened up one stop more to allow for absorption.

A more efficient method of employing bounced flash is to use a white umbrella on a tripod with the flashgun fixed to the tripod head so that it is facing the inside of the umbrella. Apart from the fact that this combination is easily deployed in any position relative to the subject, exposure calculation is made easy because the distance from flashgun to reflector is a constant. Once the correct exposure at any given distance has been found it can be repeated with certainty at any time. The variation between the exposure required for this and for direct flash varies with the conditions in which it is used, so it is advisable to make tests in the first place at different apertures. As a guide for starting the tests, the loss by bouncing in this way is rarely much more than one stop.

Synchro-sunlight

This is the name often given to the use of 'fill-in' flash outdoors. On a bright sunny day when the contrast is greater than the film can accommodate, flash can be used to lighten up the shadows and thus reduce the contrast to a manageable degree.

It is important that the flash is not so bright that it competes with the sun or casts its own shadows. This looks unnatural; when used properly it should be difficult to detect that flash was employed at all.

Calculation of exposure must be based first of all on the high-lights of the subject illuminated by the sun, together with the shutter speed and aperture read from the exposure meter in the ordinary way. To arrive at the flash-to-subject distance at which the flash will balance the sunlight, divide the guide number by the aperture you have already decided upon. This will light up the shadows too much—in fact, as brightly as the sun is affecting the highlights—so the distance must be substantially increased or the power of the flash reduced.

For colour work it is usually sufficient to reduce the strength of the flash by about one half with one layer of handkerchief, but with black-and-white two layers will probably provide a better picture. In monochrome we have to make use of tones instead of colours to separate one thing from another, so a little more contrast is desirable.

Another method of calculating is to give about one quarter of what would be required if the flash were being used as the main light. Since the strength of light varies inversely as the square of the distance, this merely means doubling the guide number. For example, assume that the exposure given by the meter for the sunlit side of the subject is 1/125 at f/8. The guide number for your flash is 50, but when adjusted to give only one-quarter strength it becomes 100. This means that the flash distance for giving just enough shadow fill-in with an aperture of f/8 should be $100 \div 8 = 12\frac{1}{2}$ feet. However, this may not be the right distance for the camera, so it will have to be used on an extension or suitably reduced with layers of handkerchief.

Many cameras with focal-plane shutters will not synchronise at shutter speeds faster than about 1/60 second, which means that the highlight reading must be based on shutter speeds. On very bright days this can make fill-in flash impossible because the camera has no aperture small enough to match the slow shutter speed unless a very slow film is used. Also, the shutter speed of 1/60 may not be fast enough to stop movement, so a between-lens shutter which can be synchronised at all speeds is to be preferred for this work. It should be noted that fill-in flash is the only technique that justifies having the gun on the camera or on the camera/subject axis because this is the angle where it will not cast shadows of its own.

Exposure with filters

When filters are used for black-and-white photography it is necessary when estimating exposure to allow for the fact that most of them absorb some of the light. Most filters have a multiplication factor such as $\times 2$, $\times 3$, $\times 4$, etc. marked on the mount. As a rule, these figures have a built-in safety factor and are more than necessary. They should be treated with reserve because more pictures these days are spoiled by overexposure than by underexposure. When a green or orange filter is employed to put some tone in the sky, the absorption of the blue rays can be completely cancelled out if the exposure is too long. As a general rule, it is safe to work on half the stated factor.

UV or haze filters do not require any increase of exposure either for monochrome or colour, but conversion filters that permit the use of Daylight colour film in artificial light and *vice-versa* have a multiplication factor given by the film manufacturers which should be closely observed.

Through-the-lens metering cameras automatically give the right exposure when weak filters i.e. $1\frac{1}{2} \times$ or $2 \times$ are over the lens, but with deeper filters it is wise to measure the light without the filter and then increase the exposure by the filter factor because CdS and silicon cells do not respond to all colours in the same way as the film.

Luminosity and exposure

It has already become clear that contrast must be considered when calculating exposure, and there are two factors of contrast involved. The first is the inherent contrast of the subject, which may have a reflection ratio of as much as 50:1 between a black area and a white area, even under flat or even lighting. On the other hand, a subject such as a chrysanthemum might have a ratio of less than 2:1 under the same lighting.

The second factor is lighting contrast. It is possible to increase the contrast on the chrysanthemum to something like 20:1 or more by using strong side lighting. As we have already seen, the low-contrast subject allows a lot of latitude in exposure calculation, whereas the higher contrast will need more precise calculation.

When a subject with strong inherent contrasts is also given a contrasty lighting treatment (i.e. side lighting with a minimum of shadow illumination) the overall contrast can be as high as 1000:1. This is not only more than the average film can cope with but it is also far more than any printing paper can reproduce. A good print on glossy bromide paper cannot show a range of brightness greater than about 100:1.

In a transparency the range of tones is not so limited and it may exceed 200:1 when projected. This is one of the reasons why a transparency in black-and-white or colour is capable of giving a far more convincing representation of the original subject, especially if this embraced a wide range of contrast, than can ever be obtained in a paper print.

In spite of this, however, accurate estimation of exposure is most important and, where the range of subject contrast is low, it is desirable to pitch it at the lower end of the scale. This will ensure a black-and-white negative that has all the detail but is thin enough to facilitate easy printing or it will provide a colour transparency that has good colour saturation.

Further reading about exposure

Exposure, W. F. Berg, Focal Press.
Exposure Technique, G. Gordon Bates, Fountain Press.
Exposure Manual, Dunn and Wakefield, Fountain Press.

7 Taking Landscapes

At one time most of the enthusiasts' and professionals' photographs that appeared on exhibition walls were either formal portraits or pure landscapes, and it was left to the casual snapshotter to picture life and action in a candid, natural way whenever the light was good enough.

Today the emphasis is on candour, human interest and action, both with enthusiasts and with beginners. Landscapes are still a popular subject with many, but the style and presentation has changed considerably, especially by the inclusion of figures, and they are less romantic or 'chocolate-boxy'. Nevertheless, the basic principles of approach and of composition are still valid and so worth some study.

The fact that you are reading this means that you want to improve your photographs, and no doubt you occasionally try your hand at landscapes, especially when you are on holiday or travelling to strange places. By landscapes, of course, I also mean seascapes, mountain pictures and street scenes.

There are a few simple rules that will help you to improve any of these subjects. They are:

(1) Choose side lighting or *contre-jour* lighting.
(2) Shoot early or late in the day.
(3) Select any unusual viewpoint.
(4) Use differential focusing.
(5) Add contrast with filters.
(6) Frame the main subject where possible.
(7) Avoid symmetrical effects.
(8) Choose the right format.

The angle of the light

Film manufacturers tell users to stand with the sun behind them. This is a counsel of safety from their point of view but, in fact, it is the worst possible advice. It always gives a picture if the exposure is anywhere near right, but the result is dull and flat, lacking in contrast and shadows.

It is only when the sun is to the side of the subject that we begin to get form or modelling and, in the case of a landscape, this means separation of planes. Without this separation a landscape will have little impression of depth. The more acute the angle of the light, the greater the contrast, until we reach a point where the sun is actually facing the camera—the reverse of what the film manufacturers tell you to do. This lighting, known as *contre-jour*, gives an outline of light to each separate plane and is most attractive; but it does have problems in exposure, which is why it is not recommended for snapshotters, who are the biggest buyers of film.

Incidentally, the sun does not have to be shining. Even when obscured by cloud or completely diffused by mist, the light is still directional and it is then even more important to ensure that it is to one side of the subject because the shadows will not be so obvious—and it is shadows that help to make a photograph, especially in monochrome.

The nature of the light

The advice to shoot early or late in the day is given for two reasons. First, the shadows are longer and more interesting and, secondly, the light is much warmer. In colour photography the warmth produced by early morning and late afternoon daylight is very pleasing and provides an overall patina which gives unity to the picture. All too often, a landscape taken around midday will be sharply separated into a warm green foreground and a cold blue sky so that there is little to hold these areas together. An overall warmth provides the answer.

Of course, there are times when it is quite impossible to take pictures during these hours, especially when travelling, and the only answer is to use as many as possible of the other dodges that help to turn a mundane scene into an impressive picture. Sometimes, if the weather is bad, this is easily done. Storm clouds, heavy rain with lots of reflections, snow, frost and mist all provide much more drama than an open sunny scene, so the camera should never be put away just because the sun has disappeared.

Many beautiful pictures have been made as a result of rays from the sun breaking through heavy clouds to spotlight a cottage or a field of buttercups; others have been made by pointing the camera downwards and picturing the reflections in a rain-soaked pavement—the possibilities are endless.

Choosing the viewpoint

Most landscapes are viewed from eye-level, and modern miniature cameras are used at this level. The result is that thousands of pictures are no more than a record of what the eye is used to seeing. Photographs taken from an entirely different viewpoint are much more impressive, and before making an exposure it is a rewarding exercise to kneel down, or even lie down, to see what the subject looks like from there. A very low viewpoint often makes it possible to keep the horizon low in the picture and to use the sky as an attractive but unfussy backdrop to the trees or whatever constitutes the main subject. You are thus presenting the viewer with a new and personal angle on a familiar subject.

Low viewpoints usually give an added impression of height and dignity to the subject, and this applies especially to people in the picture. On the other hand, buildings will have converging verticals, and this should be avoided unless they converge so sharply that it is obvious that this was deliberately done in order to introduce a dramatic note.

Sometimes a subject can appear more interesting when photographed from above rather than from below. This applies mostly in the mountains when it is desired to show a river winding its way through the valley or a village nestling under a massif. An advantage of shooting down on this sort of scene is that one can eliminate the horizon and the sky altogether, thus avoiding problems of contrast or colour imbalance.

Differential focusing

A good impression of depth or three dimensions is the aim of most landscape photographers and one way of obtaining it is to make use of the lens diaphragm to obtain varying degrees of sharpness on different planes.

On most open scenes exposure the light is strong, so there is a tendency to use small apertures. This, coupled with the fact that the camera is focused on infinity or at least a substantial distance, means that the depth of field is great enough for everything from foreground to horizon to be pin-sharp. For record work or picture postcards this may be desirable, but for an artistic presentation it is not.

Therefore it is better to select the plane that is the most important in your opinion and to focus on that. Then select an aperture to give you the degree of unsharpness in the foreground or the distance, or both, that looks attractive without losing identity of detail. This is easy with modern cameras and especially with single-lens-reflex models that have a pre-view button.

To summarise, it is nearly always better first to select the aperture to give the right effect and then to adjust the shutter speed to match rather than *vice-versa*. It is interesting to note that the early landscape photographers who employed differential focus usually had the foreground sharp and other planes getting progressively softer towards the far distance. It was considered undesirable to have the foreground out of focus, but today it is quite acceptable up to a point and many people concentrate on a sharp middle distance or a plane somewhere between the foreground and middle distance. This is good advice when the foreground is a 'frame' for the distant scene, for example an archway or avenue of trees, but when the foreground is the principal object, as it might be in the case of a cottage or a yacht, then that should be the point of focus. These are instances where the background can be kept well out of focus.

Contrast filters

Photographing a landscape in black and white looks deceptively simple, but often the results do not look anything like so attractive as the original scene. The colours that were clearly defined to the eye often translate into similar tones of grey, clouds are missing and the print looks flat and monotonous. Red poppies that stood out against a green background are now hardly visible and the variety of greens in the trees and bushes has dissolved into solid masses of similar tones.

The remedy for this lies in the use of filters. We have already learnt in Chapter 5 that a filter of coloured glass or gelatine placed over the lens will absorb its own colour and darken others. So if a yellow-green filter is used it will lighten most of the greens but darken the blues. Thus if there is any blue in the sky it will produce a tone dark enough to make the clouds stand out. As the trees, grass and foliage are often a mixture of yellow-greens and blue-greens, the filter will also help to separate them. In particular, it will lighten grass and this is usually an advantage.

All this is really just restoring what the eye separated by colour in the first place, so ideally we want to use stronger filters in order to exaggerate or falsify the tone values. For this reason the landscape photographer would do better to invest in a 3x or 4x filter rather than in one of the lighter ones and the enthusiast will even use an orange or red filter. The latter should be used with reserve because it can make a sunny scene look like a threatening storm, but there are occasions when it might be justified for the sake of impact.

Framing the subject

In most cases the eye is attracted to the lighter parts of a picture first, provided that the darker areas do not contain strong intrinsic subject interest. It is helpful to take advantage of this by concentrating the lighter tones in the centre of the picture space and having the darker tones towards the edges—in other words, to 'frame' the principal area and thus direct the viewer's eye to it.

Fig. 13   The eye is always attracted to the lightest part of a picture, so the right-hand diagram holds the eye in the picture much more than in the left-hand diagram. It also produces an illusion of depth.

This is very easily done in landscape pictures by shooting through an arch or doorway, through a window or the bars of a gate, or even through the legs of a horse. A very effective frame is achieved by finding a viewpoint where trees provide dark tones at the sides and overhanging branches provide some tone across the top or part of the top. With side lighting this often means that a shadow of one of the trees will provide a dark tone across the bottom of the picture space, thus completing an all round border of dark tones.

Framing like this produces a sort of peephole effect that gives luminosity to the scene beyond and it is particularly good in colour transparencies. It also helps to give a better impression of depth. It is not necessary as a rule to have the foreground critically sharp and, in fact, it is better to have it a little out-of-focus, though not so much that it is unpleasantly 'woolly' or even unrecognisable.

Fig. 14   Fig. 13 in practice. It is usually possible to find a tree, a doorway, a window or some near object to 'frame' the principal object. A small aperture may be necessary to keep both in focus, but the foreground need not be pin-sharp.

Avoiding symmetrical effects

A landscape that is symmetrical either in tones or in the arrangement of its component objects usually has a feeling of monotony. Imagine a serene and peaceful landscape with all the lines of clouds, hedges, etc. going horizontally across the picture. If the horizon line is halfway up the picture space and, worse still, goes right across without a break, the effect will be of a picture neatly halved. The horizon, with very rare exceptions, should always be well down or well up in the frame.

In terms of tone it usually takes a much larger area of light tone to balance a given area of dark tone and therefore, more often than not, it is better to keep the horizon low so that the

Fig. 15   The composition shown on the left is too symmetrical.
The right-hand sketch shows a more interesting design with
far more movement.

area of sky is greater than that of the darker landscape. This
applies both to colour and to black-and-white. The greater the
difference in tone values, the lower the horizon will need to be,
other things being equal.

However, even with a good tone balance, such a picture may
still look symmetrical or even monotonous unless an opposing
line is introduced to break the continuity of the horizontals. This
can usually be done by including a tree and choosing a viewpoint where it is well away from the centre. It is also important
to avoid including two trees or any other objects of equal size

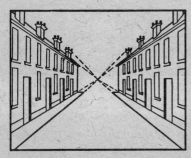

Fig. 16   Street scenes, avenues of trees or any subject having
obvious vanishing lines should preferably be photographed so that
the meeting point is well off-centre. This is simply a matter of
standing to one side or the other instead of in the centre of the
road. When one side is in shadow, make that side the smaller area.

in such a way that they appear equal in size and equally spaced out in the picture frame. It is usually possible to find a viewpoint where one tree will appear larger than the other and that one should then be nearer the centre to achieve a good balance.

Another type of picture that can so easily look very symmetrical is the one that looks down the centre of a street or an avenue of trees. When both sides are evenly illuminated and the 'vanishing point' comes right in the centre, the effect is rarely as good as it might be. A viewpoint that brings the vanishing point well down in the picture space and well to the right or left of centre is likely to look much more interesting.

To photograph a house or a bridge 'square-on' so that the main lines are horizontals and verticals is not as pleasing as to take a viewpoint to one side where form and perspective comes into play and some of the lines take a diagonal form. The former always have a static look, but diagonals have movement and therefore greater attraction.

Choosing the format

The shape of the picture can have some influence on the mood of a landscape photograph, so it is wise to give some thought to this before taking. A peaceful landscape scene made up largely of horizontals will have the mood emphasised by a horizontal format, but an upright format will tend to oppose the impression of serenity. Even more impact will be obtained by using a much longer horizontal format than the conventional picture proportions.

On the other hand, a dramatic landscape with tall trees or a stormy sky may well look much better in an upright format. Here again, the effect can be considerably increased by trimming to a narrower than conventional upright shape. This can be quite dynamic for tall trees, church towers and skyscrapers.

If you study landscapes that appeal to you it is probable that many of them will conform in a large degree to the basic guidelines of composition set out in this chapter, but there will also be the occasional picture that breaks every rule and yet has great emotional appeal. However, this is usually because of a powerful intrinsic appeal in the subject matter and further examination often shows that the composition is quite orderly. Composition, after all, is only organisation of all the elements into an ordered or logical arrangement.

Memorise and practise the eight 'rules' given at the beginning of this chapter and your landscapes, seascapes or travel pictures will undoubtedly be far more satisfying than ever before.

Further reading on landscapes

Natural Light Photography, Ansel Adams, Fountain Press.
Focal Guide to Photographing Places, D. H. Day, Focal Press.

8 Action Pictures

Modern cameras and fast films have made it feasible to photograph high-speed action and to make candid pictures of people almost anywhere. This has made it possible for camera owners to augment their interests in various sports by making photographic records.

It is not always desirable to 'freeze' the action completely and often it is preferable to show a little movement. For example, a racing car that has every detail clearly defined will look as though it had stopped and posed for the camera, but if the wheels are blurred and the spokes indistinguishable it will be obvious that the car was travelling. Therefore the selection of shutter speed is all important.

Consideration must be given to three factors:

(1) The angle of travel in relation to the camera.
(2) The distance from the camera.
(3) The speed at which the object is travelling.

It is easy to appreciate that a subject that is moving towards the camera will require far less exposure to 'stop' the movement than when the same subject at the same speed is travelling directly across the field of view, i.e. from left to right or right to left and parallel to the film plane. The relative amount of movement on the film is much greater in the latter and, while the former may need an exposure of about 1/125 second, the movement across the picture may require at least 1/500 second. Moving objects at angles in between will require corresponding adjustments to get similar results in the print. The nearer they are to a right angle with the camera, the slower the speed required, and the nearer to a parallel with the film plane, the shorter the shutter speed must be.

It would be easy to make a table of shutter speeds for different subjects if it were not for the fact that the distance from the camera also makes a big difference. The nearer the object is to the camera, the larger the image on the film and therefore the greater the movement, other things being equal. For example, an athlete 100 yards away may take 1 second to cross the field of view in your camera and he will be only about $\frac{1}{4}$ inch high on a 35 mm negative, so a shutter speed of 1/125 second could arrest most of the action. However, if he were only 5 yards away, he would be almost filling the negative and taking only about 1/125 second to cross the picture space, so a shutter speed of 1/500 or even 1/1000 second might be necessary.

Finally, the speed of the object itself must be considered. It is obvious that a car travelling at 100 miles/h is going to need a much shorter exposure than a cyclist at 30 miles/h if both are travelling at the same angle and at the same distance from the camera. Likewise, the cyclist will need a shorter exposure than a runner doing 9 miles/h, and he in turn will need a shorter one than a pedestrian at 3 miles/h.

Very often, even with the fastest films and lenses, one has to compromise. If a moving object under the prevailing light conditions is going to demand a faster shutter speed than is provided on the camera, then the angle must be changed until it becomes possible at the fastest speed available. For example, at a race track it might be impossible to stop the action of cars going past, but swinging the camera to look along the track and to picture them approaching from a distance could save the day. Without a long-focus lens this may mean smaller images on the negative, but at least it will be an acceptable picture, where otherwise only a blur would have resulted.

Experience will enable the user to judge the right shutter speed at any angle and any distance for any subject, but the table below provides some approximations that a beginner could use as a starting point for experiment. It is based on using a 2 in (50 mm) focal-length lens and will provide negatives sharp enough for a 3x or 4x enlargement. Small areas that are moving faster than the body, such as the spokes of a car or the feet and hands of an athlete, may show some blur, but this is a good thing.

			Shutter speeds		
Subject	Speed miles/h	Distance from camera ft	Moving towards camera	45° to camera	Across picture
Pedestrians	3	30	1/30	1/60	1/125
Cyclist	9	30	1/125	1/250	1/500
Horse galloping	15	30	1/250	1/500	1/1000
Train	30	100	1/125	1/250	1/500
Train	60	100	1/250	1/500	1/1000
Racing car	100	100	1/500	1/1000	1/2000

As a rough guide, the speed can be doubled at double the distance, i.e. 1/250 at 100 feet would be 1/125 at 200 feet.

Panning with the action

A technique used successfully by many sports photographers is known as panning. This involves pre-focusing on a spot, such as the middle of a race track, where it is known that the subject will appear. The camera is held with the shutter almost on the point of triggering, and as soon as the front of the object comes into the viewfinder the camera is swung smoothly in the same direction, keeping the object in the viewfinder while making the actual exposure.

This technique enables a slower shutter speed to be used, which is very useful in extreme conditions. It also blurs the background so that the object stands out well, and if there are any highlights in the background they will appear as horizontal streaks, which considerably heighten the impression of speed. With focal-plane shutters a certain amount of distortion occurs

Plate 1 A travel holiday picture which is invested with some drama because it was taken late in the afternoon when the sun was low. A yellow-green filter added tone to the sky.

Plate 2 Two ways of printing from the same negative. One with a short exposure on contrasty paper and one with a normal exposure on soft paper.

Plate 3 Two pictures showing widely different approaches but both having more atmosphere than the average snapshot. The shot of Revieulx Abbey was taken in winter just as a shaft of weak sun struck the centre of the ruins. It shows the value of 'framing' a highlight with darker tones. The aircraft shot has impact because of the sheer simplicity of its design, and this is appropriate to the subject.

Plate 4 Orange, red and infra-red filters have the power of penetrating haze. The top picture was taken without a filter and the lower one with a deep red filter.

Plate 5 This picture, taken on infra-red film with an infra-red filter, has an attractive aura because of the unreal tone values. It emphasises the value of getting away from 'picture postcard' realism.

Plate 6 Portraits of babies are easier to take outdoors because they usually act more naturally. If the sun is bright, shoot against the light. The faces of mother and child have reflected light onto each other. Note how the fussy background has been kept well out of focus.

Plate 7 Outdoor portraiture benefits from late afternoon sun, which has less contrast and gives more atmosphere. The upper picture shows the use of scenery to provide a 'frame' for the subject, but in the lower picture this was not necessary because of the dark background—a hedge well out of focus.

Plate 8 Male portraits are often better for being taken in natural environments, but it is important to avoid a lot of fussy detail and patches of highlight as seen in the bottom left example. The top left picture, taken by flash, shows the danger of pointing it at a reflecting surface. The top right picture looks rather obviously posed, but the bottom right-hand shot makes a virtue of this by getting the subject to look at the camera.

Plate 9 A holiday photograph which anyone can take. Exposure was 20 seconds at f/11 and it was made just before the sky got completely dark. This is Mont Orgeuil in Jersey, which is floodlit in different colours so that it makes a good colour shot as well.

Plate 10 The problem of reducing the contrast in church interiors can be solved by employing a long time exposure with the camera on a tripod, and firing flashes from concealed positions behind pillars, pews and rood screens. More flashes in the sanctuary than in the nave will compensate for the loss of power with distance and also light up beautiful altars like this one in Durham Cathedral.

Plate 11 Domestic pets are easy to photograph with flash, but it should never be on the camera otherwise texture rendering will be lost and the eyes will show a glare or red colour if the animal looks into the lens. This was taken with flash bounced into a white umbrella.

Plate 12 High key lighting is only suitable for a fair-haired subject and dark clothing must not be worn. Bounced flash is ideal for high-key work.

Plate 13 Daylight from a window, preferably facing north, gives superb modelling. Contrast is easily controlled by filling in the shadows with a reflector, flash or photoflood.

Plate 14 Bounced flash gives a similar softness to that produced by the daylight in the previous picture. The edges of the shadows are not defined and it is a suitable lighting for glamour subjects and babies. This was taken with one flashcube in an umbrella reflector and no fill-in was required.

Plate 15 Lighting from photoflood lamps in polished reflectors gives sharply defined shadows and is generally more suitable for low-key subjects and character portraits. It can also be used for dramatic effects, and this should be compared with the two previous pictures taken by daylight and by bounced flash.

Plate 16 Texture screens, sandwiched with the negative in the enlarger or placed in contact with the bromide paper, can provide interesting variations. They also tend to soften the image and break down detail. This was made with a Paterson canvas screen.

and wheels may come out as ovals. This is also helpful if it is not too exaggerated.

The right moment

In sports or other activities where the participants change direction it is possible to use much slower shutter speeds. A jumper leaping into the air must come down again, so there is a tiny fraction of time when he is poised to change from an upward to a downward movement. Catching this precise moment requires a little intelligent anticipation and the shutter button must be pressed in advance almost to the point of release. Fine pictures of children playing leapfrog, of ballet dancers, steeple-chasers and high jumpers have been captured in this way.

An important point to consider is the fractional time delay between seeing the action and the film being exposed. The message must be relayed from the eye to the brain and from there to the finger on the button. Add to this the time taken for the camera mechanism to open the shutter blades or release the focal-plane curtain and there is sufficient lapse of time to lose a really fast-moving shot, so the action must be anticipated, especially with single-lens-reflex cameras.

Incidentally, it is also important to avoid shooting when it may distract a player. The golfer ready to putt to win at the 18th hole will not appreciate the clunk of a shutter at the critical moment, nor will it help to get in his line of view!

People in action

In addition to picturing sports, there are innumerable occasions when it is desirable to photograph people at work or just walking along the street. Holiday and travel pictures, for example, would be dull indeed without some human interest. The same considerations of angle, distance and subject speed apply, although there is rarely enough time to consider them in detail.

It is a good rule, therefore, to use the fastest film possible and to carry the camera pre-focused on a suitable distance with the shutter set to a speed no slower than 1/250 second. The aperture should also be pre-set according to the prevailing light conditions to match that shutter speed. The camera can then be brought into action instantly. It may not always come off, but this way there is a good chance of getting something before the subject has disappeared. Press photographers who have to seize as many shots as possible, often in a few seconds, always use fast films, even on the brightest days.

Nowadays grain is so fine even on fast films that the advantage of medium-speed films is not as great as it used to be and the ability to use fast shutter speeds for this sort of work far outweighs the question of grain. In any case, the screen in a newspaper reproduction will kill the grain but, properly processed, it should be possible to get virtually grain-free enlargements from 35 mm negatives up to about 15 in × 12 in.

Composition

The composition of a sports picture or of people in action is probably less subject to 'rules' than the more conservative or static type of subject. With many sports it is desirable to set the scene by including enough background to tell the story. This could mean including the crowds in the stands at a cricket match, the scenery on a golf course or the pier behind children playing leapfrog on the beach. In such cases the principal objects are comparatively small in the picture space and the normal requirement of good balance will apply, but it is the subject rather than design that is more important in an action picture.

The main subject should preferably be somewhere off-centre and preferably light in tone against a darker background so that the eye is held in the picture. Sometimes it may be necessary to shoot from a high viewpoint to achieve this and a horizon cutting across the subjects should be avoided at all costs.

However, it is always a good idea whenever possible to get some close-up pictures as well. Here the design demands more consideration. If the action is up and down, i.e. a high jumper, a player serving at tennis or a horse clearing a hurdle, the illusion of speed and drama will be considerably emphasised if a low viewpoint is chosen. The subject then appears against the sky or a stand full of people, preferably a little out of focus.

If the subject is travelling towards the camera it is an advantage to have it at an angle rather than upright or horizontal

Fig. 17   An obvious diagonal in the composition always gives a powerful sense of movement, just as a runner leans forward when in action.

because diagonals always suggest movement. This can often be done by choosing a viewpoint near a bend where a motorcycle, cycle or runner will be leaning over. Failing this, it is sometimes possible to get the effect by tilting the camera, provided that there is no horizon or other line to give the game away.

When the subject is travelling across the picture a diagonal line is often formed naturally because a human being leans forward to run. In the case of racing cars, speedboats, etc., there is no diagonal formed, but the impression of speed can be increased by using a long horizontal format and avoiding any vertical lines in the background.

A similar consideration applies to vertical movement. One of the best pictures of a pole-jumper that has ever been published was taken from a very low viewpoint and then trimmed so that it

Fig. 18   When a picture has a number of opposing diagonals the feeling of fast movement is sometimes reduced, but a powerful impression of vitality can take its place.

filled the whole depth of a newspaper page but only two columns wide. He appeared to be 20 feet up instead of 12 feet!

Some people say that when the movement is going across the picture there should be more space left in front of the subject than behind so that there is space for the object to move into.

Others say the reverse and that if, for example, the nose of a greyhound is almost touching the edge the impression of speed will be increased. Both can be right—it depends on the subject and the other elements in the picture.

Further reading

My Way with a Camera, Victor Blackman, Focal Press.
The Leica Manual, D. O. Morgan, Fountain Press.
Camera Under Water, Horace Dobbs, Focal Press.
Focal Guide to Action Photography, Don Morley, Focal Press.

9 Outdoor Portraiture

Daylight is a great aid to natural portraiture whether the sun is shining or not because the fast shutter speeds that can be used will reduce the possibility of movement. Also, a self-conscious or timid subject will always feel easier outdoors, especially if he or she is given something to do.

It is essential to avoid formal posing, which is more suited to a studio and looks unnatural in an open-air setting, but this is one of the most common errors made by beginners. How often one sees somebody being told to 'stand still and look at me', perhaps in front of a dramatic landscape or a beautiful building! A better characterisation would result from letting the subject of his own accord look into the distance or up at some feature of the building. And how much better it would be if he were walking into the picture instead of standing as erect as a wooden soldier.

Common errors

However, strange as it may seem, more outdoor portraits are spoilt by the choice of background than by poor treatment of the subject. Unfortunately, the tiny viewfinder on most modern cameras does not show the background so clearly as the large screen on older cameras used to do. In the case of a single-lens-reflex camera the user is even less conscious of the background because he is viewing at full aperture, so the background might appear well out of focus on the screen. The fact that it will be much sharper at the smaller taking aperture is not realised. Some cameras have a 'pre-view button' that enables the exact effect at the chosen aperture to be seen before taking, and it is useful to get into the habit of employing this before making the exposure.

The most common error in backgrounds is fussiness. It takes many forms, but its effect is always to attract too much attention away from the subject proper. One of the worst examples is a brick wall, which provides a severe pattern of lines entirely out of keeping with most people, except perhaps a bricklayer. It is often used and then made worse by tilting the camera or shooting at an angle so that the horizontal lines are sloping and converging.

Red brick is also an undesirable colour for portraits outdoors. Since red is an 'advancing' colour it reduces the impression of depth and the subject will not stand out well. It also clashes with flesh colour, especially a sun-tanned face, so it is wise to avoid brickwork altogether if your primary object is to make a portrait and not just to show a figure for scale or decoration in a portrait of an important building. In such a case the subject is better shown looking at the building and therefore away from the camera.

Another very distracting background is a loose hedge or bush. The colour is probably a good choice, but highlights caused by the sky or the sun showing through tiny gaps produce a very speckly effect. Choose a hedge thick enough to exclude all light from behind it.

Confusion of interest is another error made by many people on holiday. It is always a temptation to pose the family or friends in front of Blackpool Tower or the Doges' Palace, but such backgrounds are so interesting in themselves that a viewer may well feel irritated that figures are blocking part of the view. He may be left wondering what he is supposed to look at, especially if the figure or figures are looking towards the camera. Pictures like this have some documentary value for the family album but they are not portraits.

Yet another common error in outdoor portraits which occurs through neglecting to study the background in the viewfinder is that of having a tree, a telegraph pole or something similar growing out of the top of the subject's head. Likewise, an horizon line can sometimes be seen going in one ear and out of the other, or the Great Pyramid can appear to be sitting on the subject's head like a coolie's hat.

It is obvious from all this that a golden rule for outdoor portraiture is to keep the background as simple as possible so that it does not look fussy or distract the viewer from the subject. A plain white or light-coloured wall will often serve and a thick hedge is usually very good if kept out of focus. Failing these, the sky can be used if there is some colour in it. A blue sky looks good in a colour portrait and, with the aid of filters (see Chapter 5), can provide plenty of tone for a black-and-white portrait. Remember, however, that no amount of filtering will put tone into an overcast sky that is devoid of blue, and nothing is more boring than a plain white sky in a colour or a monochrome portrait.

If none of these options is available, the only recourse is to use as large an aperture as possible so that whatever background is employed as a compromise it will be well out of focus. As a matter of fact, any background, however appropriate, should be kept at least a little out of focus. It is therefore a good idea to work with large apertures and to match the shutter speed to the one chosen rather than *vice-versa*. Large apertures will mean fast speeds, and this is an advantage because it will reduce any danger of movement as well as facilitate the use of the slower speed films.

As a general rule, it is wise to keep backgrounds fairly even all over. This means avoiding part sky and part landscape—have all of one or all of the other. By shooting downwards it is sometimes possible to get an all-over background of green grass or, by shooting upwards, an all-over background of sky. Few things are worse than the portrait taken in the back garden that has a bit of sky at the top, the line of a fence coinciding with the shoulders, and the greenhouse, some white flowers and the garden path thrown in for good measure!

Outdoor lighting

The direction of the light in outdoor portraits is just as important as it is in the studio because on it depends the modelling and form of the subject. It must be remembered that even on the most overcast day, when the sun is completely obscured and no shadows are visible, the light is still coming from the direction of the sun, so it will establish the shape of the head and the degree of texture rendering.

Film manufacturers used to say that you should always shoot with the sun behind you. But, as has been mentioned before, this was a counsel of safety and it is, in fact, the worst possible lighting. It produces very flat results because the shadows cast by various parts of the subject are unseen or at a minimum. In addition, one plane merges into the one behind and so on, thus destroying any illusion of depth.

The lighting should always be to one side of the camera to be sure of good modelling, and the ideal for outdoor portraiture is somewhere between 30° and 60°, depending on the subject. With children and women the wide angle is probably better, but for men, especially character subjects where it is desirable to emphasise ruggedness and wrinkles, 50° to 60° is better.

Lighting contrast

On a very bright and sunny day the contrast between highlight and shadow may well be greater than any film can accommodate. In other words, if exposure is short enough to retain detail and tone in the highlights, the shadows will be underexposed and devoid of detail. Alternatively, if exposure is calculated to give enough exposure to the shadows, the highlights will be overexposed and 'burnt out'.

A compromise between the two is also unsatisfactory. Both highlights and shadows will be compressed and the result will be flat. It is therefore necessary either to reduce the contrast by artificial means, to shoot in the shade or to wait for an overcast day.

When the sun is obscured by cloud the light is usually within the range of most films. Likewise, when the sun is very weak, because of early morning or evening haze, it is also manageable, although exposure must be accurately measured since there will not be much latitude.

On a bright sunny day the simplest solution is to pose your subject in the shade, because the contrast there is likely to be well within the capacity of any film—even colour, which has far less contrast capacity than the average monochrome film.

However, this is not always satisfactory. In colour the results tend to be rather cold even when a UV filter is used, although the filter will warm it a little. Also, you may want a sunny atmosphere because it is more in keeping with the mood or type of subject, so artificial means of reducing contrast by illuminating the shadows without losing the cast shadow forms is a better answer.

The simplest of these is a natural reflector. If the subject can be posed near a white wall in such a position that the light from the sun is reflected back into the shadows, a very satisfactory result can be obtained. The degree of contrast can be controlled within a wide range by varying the distance between subject and reflector. When shooting on the beach it is possible to pose a person so that the sand acts as a reflector, and, of course, snow can perform the same function in winter. Some enthusiasts always buy white cars so that they can be driven into a suitable position to act as a reflector. Many a good glamour shot has been taken with the model leaning over the bonnet or roof of a white car.

If a willing helper is available, a newspaper can be held in a position that will reflect the sunlight and it is capable of fine adjustment because the exact effect can be seen. It is always a surprise to anyone trying this for the first time to see how much light a reflector can return, but it is wise to remember that the eye is much more accommodating than film. The iris of the human eye adjusts very quickly when looking from highlight to shadow, so the subject does not appear to be nearly as contrasty as the final photograph will be. Viewing a subject through half-closed eyes helps to gain a better impression of true contrast, and some people even view the subject through deep blue glass for the same reason.

When using colour film the reflector must be white otherwise some of its colour will be reflected into the shadows, although some people think that the warmth of the reflection from sand is an advantage rather than a drawback. Lastly, it is very important to remember that the reflector is solely for reducing contrast by illuminating the shadows, so the exposure must be measured for the highlights. This means taking the meter right up to the subject highlights or using the highlight method of reading. (See Chapter 6, incident light reading.)

Synchro-sunlight

Another method of reducing contrast is to use flash for putting some light into the shadows. This technique is growing in popularity because nearly all modern cameras are synchronised for flash and electronic flashguns have made the cost per exposure almost negligible. The only drawback is that it is impossible to use fast shutter speeds with focal-plane shutters. Apart from this, it is a most satisfactory way of controlling contrast on very bright days and, with a little practice, is easy to use. (See Chapter 6 for full details of exposure calculation.)

Posing the subject

Enthusiastic photographers often have a dusty patch on the left knee of their trousers because they know that by kneeling to take a picture of a pretty girl they will be making her legs look longer; also, men will look taller and more dignified. This is not the only reason for the low viewpoint. It is part of a desire to be different or more original, so shooting from above or below normal eye-level is always a good thing. It also facilitates even tone backgrounds, as mentioned earlier in this chapter.

For more dramatic effects the subject can be posed on a wall, breakwater or ladder and this will make a good contrast to the more conventional portraits in the family album. A high viewpoint is perhaps not so desirable, except for subjects with prominent chins. Many pictures of pets and children have been spoilt because the photographer has looked down on them from a standing position. It is much better to lie on the ground, level with the subjects. By using zone-focusing (see Chapter 8) and putting a white sheet or blanket on the ground to throw light into the shadows, it is possible to get lively action pictures of young children.

Babies that are too young to sit up can be laid on a blanket on the grass and shot from above, but stand between the baby and the direction of the light otherwise there will be excessive reflection of the sky in the eyes, making them look unnaturally light.

For older children and for adults, action pictures are far more interesting and it is always advisable to give a subject something to do if he or she is not already occupied. The opportunities are too manifold to list and must depend on the photographer's imagination. But, just to illustrate the point, try getting a child to leap a breakwater while you lie on the sand and shoot up at him. A much more exciting picture will result than that obtained by posing him unwillingly against the breakwater with a command to stand still.

Another way of getting a little touch of the unusual is to take portraits at or near sunset when the light is warm and the shadows are low and long. With the subject looking into the sun or silhouetted against it there is a touch of drama and atmosphere that is lacking in the normal middle-of-the-day picture.

It is always advisable to avoid putting the subject in the centre of the picture. Try to keep him a bit to the left or right of centre and a little above or below, otherwise the effect may be too symmetrical. In a close-up portrait, when the face is almost filling the picture space, this advice applies to the eyes.

In the case of action portraits a 'directional' tendency sometimes appears. For example, if a figure is walking across the picture to the left, the viewer's eye will tend to look in that direction. Likewise, in a close-up portrait the viewer's eyes will follow the direction of the subject's gaze, presumably as a result of a natural curiosity to see what he or she is looking at. If the subject is too near the edge of the picture, the viewer's eye may be led right out of it, so there should always be plenty of background between the subject and the edge or some dark tone to 'arrest' the eye.

It is a sound rule to have people 'looking into' a picture rather than 'looking out'. This will make for a better design and a feeling of unity in the composition. Experiment with poses. Never have a subject 'square-on' and standing to attention. Women should always relax so that the body forms an 'S' curve, and there is nothing wrong with posing them with their backs to the camera but looking over the shoulder—much more interesting! Men are usually associated with action, so a pose that puts the body on a diagonal instead of a vertical is more dynamic. Diagonals, like a runner leaning forward at speed, always produce a feeling of movement and vitality.

Lastly, consider perspective. Close-up portraits taken with a standard lens at a few feet distance will show very ugly perspective, as well as an unnaturally large nose unless it is in profile. Far better to fire from 6 or 8 feet away and enlarge the result. For colour transparencies, of course, this is not so easy, and a long-focus lens is desirable, failing which the picture must be planned and composed as a three-quarter or full-length portrait.

The multiple portrait

So far we have only considered the single portrait, but often a group picture is required. The golden rule for this is never pose the subjects like a row of soldiers. Break the line by getting some to stand, some to sit and some to kneel on the ground, and also place them on different planes. Never leave gaps between the figures but arrange them to overlap so that they form a unit.

Have them carry on conversations so that they are looking at one another instead of staring into the lens and this will form an imaginary link between all the components of the group.

Even with small groups of two or three it is important to have them looking at one another and even leaning towards, or overlapping, each other. For example, a portrait of a bride and groom outside the church will be better if he stands just behind and looks down into the bride's upturned face. Thousands of full-length wedding pictures appear in the press showing bride and groom standing stiffly side by side. Much better to have them walking away from the camera, holding hands and looking back over their shoulders.

When there are more than two people in a group it is always pleasing to arrange them in a pyramid, if it is not too symmetrical. The line formed by the outlines of heads and shoulders should always be observed because it plays an important part in any group composition.

Further reading on outdoor portraiture

The Photographic Portrait, O. R. Croy, Focal Press.
Creative Portrait Photography, P. Zeemeijer, Fountain Press.
Portraiture at Home, R. H. Mason, Fountain Press.

10 Holiday and Travel Photography

Many people use their camera only at holiday times and then are disappointed because something goes wrong. Like a car that has been laid up for the winter, a camera needs some checking over after a long period of disuse.

The shutter lubrication may have got gummy, so it should be operated at every speed at least ten times. The iris diaphragm should also be opened and closed a number of times. These operations can be done without a film in the camera, but it is also advisable to expose and develop a film before going away. This is especially wise with automatic cameras because it tests the exposure meter system as well.

Make sure that the inside is completely free of dust, sand or scraps of film, and if a battery is incorporated in the camera it should be replaced. Miniature batteries are difficult to obtain in out-of-the-way places. A few thin plastic or polythene bags are useful to protect camera and film from dust and spray when not in use, but take them out at night in hot climates otherwise condensation may cause damage.

Make a note in your diary of camera and lens numbers in case of theft, and ensure that your insurance covers the camera because some policies are limited to travel in the United Kingdom. Take receipts or insurance policies to prove to the Customs, if necessary, that the camera was purchased in Great Britain and duty paid.

In some countries the electric supply is still only 100 or 110 volts, so the charger for an electric flashgun should have a voltage adjustment. Otherwise it might be safer to use flashbulbs or flashcubes. It is better to buy these before going abroad since they are cheaper here than in most foreign countries. Also, film is considerably cheaper in Great Britain than almost anywhere in the world, so take plenty with you. No country will object to a reasonable supply being imported, whatever the regulations may say.

Keep colour films in their metal containers and post them to the processors as soon as they are exposed. This will avoid any damage through humidity during storage in hot climates. Likewise, black-and-white films should be kept in metal cassettes, but they are unlikely to suffer except under extreme conditions and so can be kept until returning home. As a precaution, a little packet of silica gel can be kept in the camera bag or the hotel drawer.

A problem that exercises the minds of some enthusiasts is whether to cover the holiday in colour or black-and-white, or both. If it is decided to double everything, two cameras are necessary, because with one camera alone it will almost certainly have colour in it when black-and-white is wanted and *vice-versa*.

The ideal arrangement is to have two identical cameras, with one member of the family in charge of one camera while another member carries and uses the other. When this can be done it is an advantage to use monochrome and colour films of the same ASA speed. This will mean that only one person need carry an exposure meter and the focus, aperture and shutter speeds can be set to match on both cameras.

Planning coverage

Many slide shows or holiday albums are boring because they show an unbalanced coverage, with too much concentration on one or two events or people. It is no bad thing, and can be very rewarding, to plan the coverage of a holiday or a tour in much the same way as a film director would script a documentary. This will ensure that nothing important is missed out, although it will probably mean some ruthless rejection or weeding out afterwards.

First, list the items that will give coverage and continuity. It could read something like this: departure, arrival, venue, local architecture, the beach, family on the beach, water skiing, surrounding landscapes, excursions, flowers, animals, local characters, sunsets, cabarets, departure. It helps to study travel brochures in advance because they show the local subjects of interest and often give details of special events, such as carnivals, beauty contests, etc., that are worth photographing.

A good slide show, like a film, should have variety by including both long shots and close-ups. The general character of a scene or a building can be shown in a long shot, and it will have added interest if it is followed by a close-up of a figure in the scene or of an architectural detail. Close-ups of street nameplates, signposts, inn signs and station boards make interesting titles. In a country that has characteristic music it is also a good idea to buy a record or tape that can be used as appropriate background music for a slide show.

Remember that one landscape looks very like another unless something typical of the country is included, such as a castle in Spain, a chalet in Switzerland or a mosque in Morocco. Likewise, a seascape should have something of local interest, like a junk in Hongkong, a Thames barge off Southend or a sardine boat in Portugal.

Failing these, it is usually possible to include people—but they should be natives and not other tourists or members of the family. In most countries people do not object to being photographed, so there is no need to be shy about taking shots of people walking about or doing their normal work. In the Arab countries, where there is still some objection, it is usually found that a minority will pose in return for a small payment and tour guides can always find such people.

Some people ask 'why bother with a camera when perfectly good postcards and transparencies can be bought almost anywhere? They have been taken under ideal conditions with large format cameras.' The answer is that it is their very perfection that makes them dull. They are usually pin-sharp on every plane and taken in normal middle-of-the-day sunlight so that they are often lacking in mood or atmosphere. Nevertheless, they are worth studying because they show subjects that are important as well as landmarks that you might otherwise miss. It is fun to see how you can improve on them by changing the viewpoint, using differential focus and shooting under different lighting conditions.

Try to get plenty of local people into the shots and don't pose them like so many of the figures seen in postcards and transparencies. If you must include your friends or family, have them looking at the buildings or into the distance—anything but 'now look at the camera' expressions.

Pictures at night can convey a lot of atmosphere and fast modern films make many things feasible. Floodlighting, fireworks and market stalls lit by flares are always interesting, but support the camera where possible in order to give a long exposure. In many countries flash is not discouraged, as it is in the nightclubs and theatres of Great Britain, so carry a camera everywhere and save that sad remark so often heard 'I wish I'd brought my camera!'

Improving the quality

Everybody wants to take better pictures without becoming too involved with technicalities, and everybody can produce a set of holiday pictures that will stand out from those of their friends if a few golden rules are put into practice. They are:

(1) Shoot as many pictures as possible early in the day or late in the afternoon when the light is warm and the shadows are long and interesting.

(2) Don't wait for the sun to come out. Shoot when it is misty or when it is raining, and especially when there are dramatic cloud formations. Don't neglect reflection pictures in puddles, lakes and rivers.

(3) Take plenty of pictures facing the sun so that figures and other subjects are attractively outlined with light. These are probably the most striking and artistic pictures of all.

(4) Take pictures at night of anything that is naturally illuminated outdoors.

(5) Don't be put off by lack of light for indoor events—take a flashgun on holiday.

(6) Try to find unusual angles—low viewpoints, high viewpoints and ultra close-ups.

(7) Use filters where appropriate for black-and-white work in order to falsify tones, e.g. darker skies, for dramatic effect.

(8) Keep the composition simple in order to achieve impact. This means getting close to a foreground object, perhaps a figure, so that it dominates the picture and everything else is subordinate to it. A hundred elements all of equal interest only produce confusion. In colour it is desirable to have the dominant foreground object in a warm colour: a yellow dress is better than a blue one and will give a stronger impression of depth. Check also for opportunities to 'frame' the scene by shooting through an arch, a window or under a tree.

All these points are dealt with in greater detail in other chapters, especially Chapter 7 on landscapes, Chapter 9 on outdoor portraiture and Chapter 11 on night photography.

Exposure problems

It is all too easy to overexpose when taking a holiday abroad, especially in a tropical country, by the sea or up in the mountains. On the beach, for instance, the reflection from sand is often enough to give a false reading, even when the meter is pointed downwards to avoid taking in too much sky. There is a lot of ultra-violet in the light and this affects the film, so it is wise to close the diaphragm by one stop. The only exception would be for shooting a figure against the light, when it would generally be advisable to open up about half a stop.

An open seascape has a lot of blue in it and this is rich in ultra-violet, so give no more than half the indicated exposure, i.e. close down one stop or use the next faster shutter speed.

This also applies to mountain scenes. In both these cases an UV filter should be used to absorb some of the ultra-violet rays, and it will also help to warm up a colour shot.

Further reading

Your Holiday in Colour, Kodak booklet.
Photography in the Tropics, Agfa-Gevaert.

11 Night Photography

Photographs taken after dark have a special fascination and they are easy to take in either monochrome or colour, even with simple budget cameras.

There are two ways of taking night pictures: by time exposure or by instantaneous exposure. The former can be taken with any camera, but a tripod or some other firm support will be required and moving objects cannot be included. Instantaneous pictures usually require a large-aperture lens and the use of fast films, but the camera can be hand-held and quite a lot of action can be captured if the light level is reasonably high.

Time exposures

A firm tripod is ideal for all time-exposure work, but it is often inconvenient to carry a really rigid model, which is necessarily heavy. Lightweight tripods are useless in the slightest breeze, and even the shutter being released can cause them to vibrate. It is better, where weight is a consideration, to use a pocket camera clamp or to employ one of the miniature table-top tripods that can be set up on a wall, a pillarbox or any handy but firm support at the right height. The best of these miniature tripods fold up to make a good handle grip or stock that helps to hold the camera steady when used in the hand.

Much will depend on the weight of the camera, but a good test is to open the back with the lens focused on a light in the distance. Release the shutter and hold it open for 10 or 20 seconds and the slightest movement of the light will become obvious to the eye.

A cable release is necessary for time exposures, otherwise the camera might be left vibrating after the shutter release has been pressed. If the camera has both a T (Time) and B (Bulb) setting, the T setting should be used. This opens the shutter, which will stay open until the release is pressed again. Many cameras have only a B setting, and for these it is useful to purchase a cable release with a locking device so that it can be pressed and locked until the exposure is completed. Otherwise the release must be held throughout the exposure, which inevitably increases the risk of jarring the camera.

Under low lighting conditions and when a small aperture is employed to get a good depth of field, it may be necessary to give exposures running into many seconds or even minutes. This means that moving lights such as car headlamps can cause streaks or lines of highlight. Sometimes these can be attractive and add a feeling of movement to a street scene, but if it is desired to eliminate them it is easy enough to hold a hat or a book in front of the lens until each car is out of the picture.

When exposures run into a number of seconds, people walking across the picture are no problem because they will not be recorded unless they happen to be in a bright light area, such as the pavement in front of a lighted shop window or under a cinema canopy. In these cases they will form 'ghost' images if they are present only for part of the exposure, so it is better to wait until they have gone.

There is very much more latitude in exposure at night than in daylight and this is a real advantage for colour work, which normally requires very accurate exposure assessment. The results can be presentable over a wide range of exposures, although the colours may vary. For example, if an exposure of 1/15 second is given to a neon sign, the result may show little more than the actual tubes, but increasing the exposure to 1/2 second could well show some of the brickwork behind. Increase it still more and probably the detail in the windows, or even a glow in the sky, will appear. In all these exposures the sign will still look the same although there may be more halation around the tubes with the longer exposures, but all will be acceptable as pictures.

Most people prefer to use daylight-type colour film for night photography. The results are warmer than they would be with artificial-light film, but this, if anything is an advantage. With all colour films the exposure should be kept as short as possible because of a factor called reciprocity failure. Certain films change their characteristics when extremely long or extremely short exposures are given. This may affect the colour rendering and exposure increase is often required. This is not likely to affect most amateur work, but the film instruction leaflet should be consulted.

Unfortunately, no exposure meter is powerful enough to take readings under most night conditions, but the table below should give some guidance. It would be as well to 'bracket' exposures by taking further shots at one half and double those shown. The table is based on 50 ASA film, and exposures should

Subject	f/4	f/5·6	f/8	f/11
Big fire: well-lit outdoor stage	1/30 s	1/15 s	1/8 s	1/4 s
Boxing ring under spotlights	1/125 s	1/60 s	1/30 s	1/15 s
Well-lit shop windows: tube train interiors	1/15 s	1/8 s	1/4 s	1/2 s
Fireworks and bonfire	1/8 s	1/4 s	1/2 s	1 s
Portraits by shop-window lighting	1/4 s	1/2 s	1 s	2 s
Well-lit street scenes: Piccadilly, Times Square, etc.	1/2 s	1 s	2 s	4 s
Floodlit buildings and monuments	1–2 s	2–4 s	4–8 s	8–16 s
Floodlit buildings at a distance	4–8 s	8–16 s	16–32 s	32 s–1 min
Main railway stations	1 s	2 s	4–8 s	8–16 s
Distant scene with scattered lights	20 s	40 s	80 s	1½–3 min
Full-moon scene with snow	30 s	1 min	2 min	4 min
Full-moon landscape without snow	2 min	4 min	8 min	16 min
Stars in their courses				3 h

All the above times are for 50 ASA film

be doubled for 25 ASA and halved for 100 ASA and so on (see Chapter 6 on Exposure).

It is advisable for all night work, especially with long exposures, to use a lens hood to prevent stray light causing flare on the lens surface.

Aesthetic considerations

The beauty of a night picture is in its atmosphere and it is important not to overexpose or underprint so much that the result looks more like daylight. On the other hand, a lot of stygian black is undesirable, especially in colour transparencies, because it usually comes out as an unpleasant greenish or brown black.

As far as possible, the subject should be made to fill the picture space and too much sky should be avoided. If the picture is taken immediately after sunset when there is still a little afterglow in the sky, the result will be much more attractive, especially in pictures of floodlit buildings which may, under these conditions, also have a little detail in the shadows not reached by the floods. Sky tone is particularly important in pictures of buildings not floodlit but having a number of windows illuminated. Without some tone in the sky to outline the structure, the picture is liable to be merely a pattern of white dots.

It is also an advantage to take night photographs during or after rain. The reflections of the lights in wet pavements and roofs produce a romantic atmosphere and also help to avoid having areas lacking in detail or colour. Very often a picture may be required of a floodlit building on the other side of a river or of a ship in the docks. The water in front will show very attractive reflections if it is not too choppy and, indeed, many fine pictures have been taken solely of the reflections.

When making long time exposures it is necessary to avoid including the moon or any bright stars because they move quite a distance in the space of a minute and the moon will look elongated while the stars will appear as curved white streaks. On the other hand, amusing pattern pictures can be taken by pointing the camera at the sky and leaving it open for several hours. Likewise, some excellent lightning pictures have been obtained by placing a camera on a tripod at the window and pointed in the direction of the storm. If the shutter is left open for the duration sheet lightning will illuminate the landscape and the clouds, while forked lightning provides interesting patterns for contrast. There is obviously an element of luck in this but the results can be dramatic.

While the inclusion of the moon or other moving light source is something to treat with caution there is nothing against streetlamps or other point sources being in the picture, provided that they are not too near the camera. The halation they cause is part of the atmosphere, and sometimes the iris diaphragm will cause them to create star patterns which are also attractive.

The long time exposures that are required at night provide opportunity for multiple exposures. At a firework display, for example, the shutter can be left open long enough to allow very many fireworks to record themselves on the film, thus creating a picture full of light and colour that conveys the mood far better than a single rocket could do. Another fruitful source is the amusement fair, where such things as carousels and ferris wheels can produce unpredictable but pleasing results.

Using flash at night

With some subjects time exposures can be augmented with flash. For example, when a floodlit building or an illuminated street scene is being photographed, the exposure may still be too short to record foreground objects that are not themselves illuminated.

There are occasions when a silhouette of these objects or figures is desirable, but often a little detail is an advantage and flash is the answer. Obviously it must not be strong enough to light the foreground at the expense of the background or it would look very unnatural. A satisfactory compromise is reached in most cases by giving full exposure for the background and about one quarter for the flash. In other words, after the flash exposure is calculated by the guide number in the normal way (see Chapter 6) the aperture is closed by two stops or, if this is not convenient, the distance of the flash from the subject is doubled.

Suitable subjects for this technique are figures in front of lighted shop windows or floodlit buildings, statues in the foreground of street scenes, trees in front of houses with illuminated windows and figures in front of a bonfire. If the figures are very close to the available lighting, as they may well be in the case of the bonfire, it is most important not to overdo the flash exposure and 'kill' the fire. If the normal exposure is very long the figures must not be allowed to move very much otherwise ghost images will result, but this, of course, is no problem with statues and trees.

Instantaneous night photography

Fast films and wide-aperture lenses have made a certain amount of hand-held night photography possible. High-speed black-and-white films like Agfa Ultra, Ilford HP4 and Kodak Tri-X permit exposures of the order of 1/125 second at f/2·8 on many subjects like theatre entrances, well-lit buildings, flare-lit market stalls and big fires. Colour negative and colour transparency films are now available with a speed of 400 ASA, and they can even be used at 800 or 1200 ASA by extending development times. This inevitably incurs some loss of quality and an increase in grain.

It is therefore advisable to confine instantaneous photography to brightly lit subjects such as shop windows, the area under cinema entrance canopies, electric signs or close-ups of objects under powerful spotlights. When such pictures come off they are very rewarding because the distant scene is dark and the romantic mood of night is well portrayed. Nevertheless, it is better whenever possible to take the pictures at twilight so that there is at least a suspicion of tone or colour in the distance or in the sky.

When houses or office buildings are to be included, make sure that some of the windows are illuminated or a door is opened to reveal interior lighting. Otherwise the result could just as easily be an underexposed daylight shot or one taken by infra-red—the true night atmosphere will be lost.

If people are included, get them as close as possible to the illumination. For instance, if people are being photographed arriving at a function, wait until they are almost at the doorway and receiving the full force of light coming from it. Under canopies, shoot before they have walked so far towards the camera that most of the light is immediately above them. If they are on the far side the light will be falling on the front of them.

Apart from the fact that night photography has a greater degree of latitude in exposure than exists for daylight photography, it is also a fact that a greater degree of movement is acceptable as long as something in the picture is sharp. Add to this the great impact of a good night photograph because of its special emotional appeal and the conclusion should be obvious—always carry a camera by night as well as by day. Some exposures may not be successful, but some are almost bound to be if the advice given in this chapter is followed and they will more than compensate for a few dull frames.

12 Indoor Lighting

Photographs, especially portraits, can be taken indoors by available daylight from a window or by the normal room lighting —ceiling lights, standard lamps, etc. However, neither method is easy and one stands a better chance of successful results by the use of overrun bulbs, called photofloods, or of flash.

The main disadvantage of daylight from a window is that the contrast will usually be excessive and some fill-in light from a reflector, flash or lamp will be required. In addition, of course, photography is confined to the hours of daylight.

The chief disadvantage of using the existing house lighting is the low level of intensity, which in most cases will demand longer exposures than are practicable for live portraiture. In addition, the colour temperature is too low for colour films, even of the artificial-light type, and the results will be far too warm unless correction filters are used.

Photoflood lighting

This is an easy, economical and satisfactory form of lighting for the home photographer. It employs bulbs that plug into any lamp socket and, in fact, look like ordinary domestic bulbs, but they are 'overrun' and give a very bright light for a limited life. The popular size, known as a No. 1 photoflood, gives a light equivalent of about 275 W and is available with a bayonet or ES cap. There is a larger bulb, called a No. 2 photoflood, that gives a light output of 500 W and comes only with an ES cap.

The No. 1 is quite adequate for the average user. It will burn for about two to three hours but will last ten hours or more if two of them are used in conjunction with a series/parallel switch or a distribution board. They can then be used at half power for focusing and switched to full power only for the actual exposure.

Photoflood bulbs can be used in ordinary domestic fittings, like chandeliers or standard lamps, but this is not recommended except perhaps for party shots, where a general light of some strength is required. For portraits this does not provide enough flexibility or control over shadows and it is also inefficient because, without properly designed reflectors, much of the light is wasted.

Incidentally, it can also be dangerous to use domestic fittings because photoflood bulbs naturally get very hot and paper or fabric shades could catch fire if in close proximity. In every other respect the bulbs are quite safe and a number can be used on an ordinary domestic circuit.

The photographer who plans to do much indoor work by photoflood lighting should invest in special fittings which are economical and easily portable. These are like collapsible violin music stands but fitted with spun metal reflectors that can be angled in any direction. They can be raised or lowered from about $2\frac{1}{2}$ to 6 feet and are very light in weight.

The reflectors, which are interchangeable, are available in three forms. One is in the shape of a fairly deep bowl, often ribbed and chromed inside, and this gives a fairly hard and concentrated beam. With some makes of stand it is possible to move the bulb backwards and forwards in the reflector in order to vary the width and concentration of the beam. This is the nearest thing to the professional's spotlight and is useful as a main modelling light.

The second type is somewhat similar, but the reflector is shallower and probably has a matt finish inside. This is an all-purpose lamp and is very useful for softer modelling effects or for background lighting. The third type of reflector consists of a very shallow bowl painted matt white inside and with a baffle placed in front of the bulb so that no direct rays from it will fall on the subject. This gives the softest possible lighting and is almost shadowless, so it is used as a fill-in light to reduce contrast and to put some light into the shadows made by the main light.

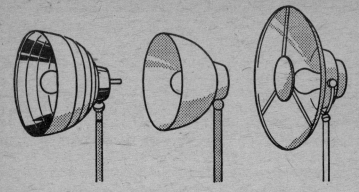

Fig. 19 Three types of reflectors for photoflood bulbs. The left-hand one is ribbed and chromium-plated internally to give a hard directional light. It can often be focused by moving the bulb backwards and forwards. The centre model is a shallower bowl, usually in spun aluminium, which gives a broader and softer beam. The right-hand drawing shows a very shallow bowl, painted matt white, and it has a mask in front of the bulb, so the lighting is very soft and almost shadowless. This one is ideal for a fill-in light. All models should be adjustable in any direction.

These reflectors are also available fitted with strong spring clips so that they can be clipped to a door, a chairback or a mantelpiece, thus avoiding the use of stands. Naturally they restrict one's freedom of placement to some extent, but one or two of these could be useful for the beginner to experiment with before investing in a number of complete stands.

It should also be mentioned that there is a certain type of photoflood bulb that is mushroom-shaped and has a built-in mirror reflector. This is useful in emergencies where proper reflectors are not available, but the type and width of the beam is fixed and so a large degree of flexibility is lost. They are also much more expensive but unlikely to give longer life.

With three stands and three different reflectors plus a series/ parallel distribution board, one is equipped to take good photographs anywhere. Their use is described in the next chapter.

Type A (artificial-light) colour films are balanced for the colour temperature of photoflood lighting, which burns at about 3400 K, so no filters are needed. Daylight-type films require a Wratten 80B filter or its equivalent.

Flashlighting

Flash has some advantages over photoflood lighting. It is more compact and portable, and does not involve trailing wires if slave units are used. Also it is cool and does not create a studio atmosphere to make a timid sitter self-conscious. On the other hand, it has one big disadvantage in that one cannot see the effect of the lighting before making an exposure, so considerable experience is required in the placing of the lamps. True, some people fit tungsten 'modelling' lamps into their flash fittings, but this defeats the main advantage of flash and is only employed in the big units used by professionals.

There are two types of flash:

(1) Flashbulbs
(2) Electronic flash

Flashbulbs and flashcubes are sealed glass envelopes containing an inflammable wire that burns with a very intense light when ignited by an electric current. The duration of the flash is extremely short—usually about 1/600 second—and the bulb cannot be re-used.

Electronic flash also gives a brilliant light of very short duration and it can be synchronised with nearly all camera shutters. The only difference is that it can be fired over and over again—up to sixty or more flashes from one charge—and the life of the tube is almost indefinite. The pros and cons of bulbs versus electronic were fully discussed in Chapter 3.

When used on the camera, bulb or electronic flash gives a very ugly effect. Faces, or whatever is the main subject, lose their form and shape, while hard, ugly shadows are cast on the background. This can be avoided by using the flash well away from the camera and connecting it to the camera synchronising socket via an extension lead. This inevitably means that some form of fill-in light will be required, otherwise the contrast will be much greater than any film can accommodate.

A reflector could be made to serve, but positioning it is very difficult because the effect cannot be seen until a print is made and slight variations in the angle and distance can make or mar the result. It is easier to use another flashgun for fill-in, and this can be placed on or near the camera because it must not cast shadows or conflict with the main light. It must also be weaker, so it should be farther away or have its power reduced by diffusing it with one or more layers of handkerchief or other white, semi-translucent material. People who use a large and powerful gun for the main light sometimes use a smaller gun for the fill-in light.

Naturally both guns must be synchronised and they can both be connected to the camera socket with a little two-way adapter; this, however, only works when both guns are of the same polarity. A more satisfactory method is to employ a 'slave' unit attached to one of the guns. It will cause the gun to fire as soon as the sensor cell receives light from the other gun. This method involves a little more capital outlay, but it is reliable and saves having trailing wires to fall over.

If a third flash is required for the background it can also be connected to the camera via an adapter if the polarity of all three guns is similar. Failing this, another slave gun can be made to fire the third flash.

Bounced flash

Much softer, and generally more pleasing, effects can be obtained by 'bouncing' the flash off a suitable reflector. If the gun is directed at a ceiling or wall at an angle that causes most of the light to be reflected onto the subject, the degree of contrast will be much lower. In a small domestic room with light walls there may even be sufficient general reflection all round to render a second light for fill-in unnecessary.

In colour photography it is important to use only white surfaces as reflectors, otherwise colour will be reflected onto the subject.

With this method of bouncing flash there is a substantial loss of light because of the extra distance it has to travel. It can be as much as four times, or two stops. A more efficient technique is to use white umbrellas as reflectors. They can be bought with universal heads that enable them to be fixed to a tripod and angled as desired. A shoe at the end of the stem takes the flashgun, which is directed towards the inside of the umbrella.

Fig. 20   White parasols or umbrellas fixed to the top of a tripod by an adjustable elbow or universal joint make ideal reflectors for bounced flash. They can be bought lined with opaque silver or gilt paint for maximum efficiency, or in white nylon for more diffused effects.

Since the distance of the gun to reflector remains constant it is easy to work out correct exposures for different distances between reflector and subject. Once this is done, accurate exposure can be achieved always and anywhere. The umbrella collects and reflects a very large percentage of the light and is not wasted by general scattering, as it is when a wall or ceiling is used. The difference between umbrella-bounced flash and direct flash can be as low as one stop.

Some people regard the effect given by bounced flash as too soft and they compromise by angling the gun so that most of the light is bounced but just a little from the edge is allowed to spill directly onto the subject.

Open flash

Flash is very useful for interior photographs that do not contain people or moving objects. The camera can be set up on a tripod and the shutter opened on 'Time'. Provided that the room is fairly dark and a small aperture is employed, the flash can then be fired repeatedly by hand in different directions. This is useful in a large room or the nave of a church which would be too deep for a single flash to penetrate. A flash fired from behind every pillar, and perhaps even two flashes behind the most distant ones, could give even illumination throughout.

Of course, the flash must never be fired towards the camera, and the gun and the user should be concealed behind the furniture or architectural features. It is also important to avoid windows, mirrors or shiny surfaces which may catch an image of the flash or cause flare.

It is impossible to calculate exposure with any precision for subjects like this, but the guide number can still be used as a rough indication for the flashes nearest to the camera. In a very large, dark interior the value of reflecting walls is lost and the exposure should be at least doubled.

From all that has been said in this chapter and in Chapter 3 it will be seen that both flash and photoflood lighting can be used for most indoor subjects, and both are available in a convenient and portable form enabling the user to turn any room into a temporary studio. In the end the choice is a personal one, but there is much to be said for starting off with photoflood lighting, especially for portraiture. Being able to see the effect and to balance the main light with the fill-in to achieve a specific degree of contrast or a particular dramatic effect is useful experience and it will help the user to a quick appreciation of the principles of lighting.

Further reading on lighting

Lighting for Photography, W. Nurnberg, Focal Press.
200 *Flash Tips*, Voogel and Keyser, Fountain Press.
Focal Guide to Lighting, P. Petzold, Focal Press.

13 Indoor Portraiture

Elaborate equipment and expensive cameras are not essential for indoor portraiture. Sophisticated apparatus provides scope for greater versatility, but good portraits can be taken in the home without it, provided that the limitations of the apparatus are understood.

A tripod or some means of supporting the camera is essential because the camera must be left in position while the lights are being deployed and the pose arranged. If close-ups are required a long-focus lens or a portrait attachment will be necessary. Taking a 35 mm camera closer to the sitter than about 6 feet will cause unpleasant perspective distortion, resulting in exaggerated noses and diminutive ears. At this distance the standard 50 mm lens will include about three quarters of the figure. When working in black-and-white the head and shoulders alone could be enlarged, but for colour transparencies selective enlargement is a costly and not very satisfactory process. A lens of 90 or 105 mm is a great asset. Two other accessories on the camera that are desirable, if not essential, are a lens hood to keep stray light off the lens and a cable release at least 12 inches long.

There are four methods of lighting the subject:

(1) Daylight from a window.
(2) Available indoor lighting. This can be ordinary electric lights or a combination of daylight and electric.
(3) Photoflood or tungsten lighting.
(4) Flash.

There are pros and cons for each method and only the user can decide which suits his purpose best.

Daylight lighting

Light from a window can be employed to produce very satisfactory portraits, but it is, of course, limited to the hours of
daylight, which in winter, when most indoor portraits are taken,
is limited in strength and duration. It is also very variable, so
exposure readings must be taken constantly and exposure cannot be standardised, as it can be with artificial lighting.

Windows that face south should be avoided. Direct sun is too
hard and it will probably make the sitter squint. The softer and
more even light from a window facing north is ideal, and it is an
advantage to mask off the lower part of the window so that the
light reaches the sitter at an angle of 30° to 40°. This is the
modelling light so much favoured by portrait painters like
Rembrandt.

In order to have room to manoeuvre, the sitter should be at
least 5 feet away from the window and placed well back so that
most of the light falls on the front of him and not behind him. It
will almost certainly be necessary to use a reflector or fill-in light
to illuminate the shadow side of the subject unless an exceptionally dramatic and contrasty effect is required.

Any large area of white will serve as a reflector—a newspaper
or a sheet, for instance. If a free-standing cine or slide screen is
available, use that because it can easily be moved about until a
position is found where it reflects the most light. For colour
portraiture the reflector must be white otherwise colour will be
cast on the subject and, of course, daylight-type colour film must
be used.

As an alternative, artificial light or flash can be used as a fill-in.
Artificial light could be used for black-and-white work, but in
colour portraits this would be mixing lights of different temperatures and the result would be most unnatural. The difficulty
with flash is that it is impossible to see the effect in advance and
it is only with a great deal of experience that the correct exposure
to obtain the desired degree of contrast can be gauged with
certainty.

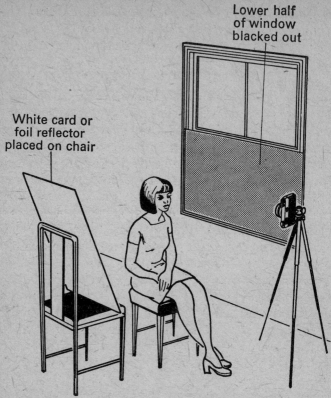

Lower half
of window
blacked out

White card or
foil reflector
placed on chair

Fig. 21 For indoor portraits, using daylight as the main light source, the window should be masked off so that the light falls on the sitter at an angle between 30° and 40°. A reflector or fill-in light will be required to illuminate the shadows and record some detail.

In any case, the flash must not be allowed to cast shadows or to conflict with the daylight, so it should be as near as possible to the camera/subject axis and should be bounced off a reflector. Umbrella flash is ideal for this, but if there is a wall behind the camera this can be used. Exposure must be based on the daylight, so a reading should be taken on that and the flash calculated to give the degree of contrast required.

For example, suppose the daylight reading indicates 1/50 at f/8 with 50 ASA film. If the guide number for the flash bulb or flashgun for this speed of film is 80, then full illumination would be obtained with the flash at $\frac{80}{8} = 10$ feet. However, the flash is reduced to about quarter strength (or two stops) when bounced, so at 10 feet the result would show a ratio of approximately 2:1, which is quite good for colour. On the other hand, if a greater contrast or more dramatic effect is required, as it might well be in monochrome work, the bulb or gun would have to be reduced in strength. In the average domestic situation it may not be practicable to extend the distance between flash and sitter, so layers of handkerchief (see Chapter 6) would be the answer. In any case, it is always a bad thing to have a flash placed behind the camera and operator because it is very easy to get in front of it and thus destroy its effect or cast a shadow over the subject.

The background can be a problem. If there is a plain wall in the right position to receive some of the daylight at the right strength, that is fine, but usually it will be necessary to light it separately unless a very dark tone is acceptable. This can also be done with flash and, in fact, it might even be possible to place the fill-in flash so that it performs both functions, but this can only be found by experiment.

Experiments made with a wig stand as a model and with careful notes made of daylight exposure and distances of flash or reflectors will provide data and experience that enable any effect to be thereafter repeated with confidence.

Available light

It is almost impossible to do serious, formal portraits in ordinary room lighting because of the fixed positions of most of the lights, and in many cases the level is so low that long exposures would be required, so the risk of movement is high. Nevertheless, there may be occasions when it is desired to 'snatch' a picture of a person at a party or function. If possible, get him or her to stand or sit below a ceiling light but a little behind so that the light falls on the face and not just on the top of the head. If the ambient light is strong enough it may provide sufficient illumination for the shadows, but there is always a danger of dark shadows under the chin and in the eye sockets. This can usually be overcome by asking the subject to hold a book or newspaper as if about to read it because it will reflect some light upwards.

If a movable desk or standard lamp is available it can also be employed for the same purpose, especially if the subject is seated, but the principles of lighting explained later in this chapter must be observed and this is not always possible with such makeshift methods. It should also be noted here that fluorescent lighting is unsuitable for colour without the use of filters, and the mixture of lighting sources such as daylight, artificial lighting and fluorescent must be avoided completely. Thus if artificial-light-type film is used, curtains must be drawn over the windows to prevent any daylight entering and any fluorescent tubes must be switched off. Note also that Type A colour film is balanced for photoflood lighting and ordinary domestic bulbs will give a rather too warm effect, so a filter such as an 82A (blue) may be necessary.

Photoflood lighting

This is a far more satisfactory method of lighting for home portraiture than either daylight or available light because the operator has complete control over modelling and contrast. In addition, it can be easily set up and used at any time, anywhere.

Using the apparatus described in the last chapter, consideration can now be given to the basic principles of lighting for portraiture. The first, and by far the most important, is the use of the main light to 'draw' the subject. This light, which is sometimes called the modelling light or the key light, is in effect the equivalent of the sun in an outdoor portrait, so it must dominate the picture. In the final result it should not be obvious that any other light source has been used at all.

It is a salutary exercise to place a simple foam-plastic wig stand or hairdresser's dummy on a table or stand about 3 feet from the floor and walk round it with a photoflood lamp in a deepish bowl reflector and with all other room lights turned off. Start by holding the lamp at camera position and the face will look very flat indeed. Walk round slowly to the left or right, keeping the light on the same level as the subject. It will gradually take on more shape and roundness until, at 90° to the camera/subject axis, the face is split into two: half lit and half in darkness.

Then do the same thing but with the lamp held much higher so that it is shining down on the head at about 45°. From the front it will look a little theatrical and at 90° there will still be a rather divided effect. However, at 45° it will be seen that the head is showing the maximum modelling and shape.

Therefore it is wise to start lighting any full-face or near full-face subject with the main light only, and at an angle of about 45° in plan and 45° up. It may be necessary in some cases to lower it slightly, even down to about 30°, or to bring it round to the front a little to avoid heavy shadows in deep eye sockets or long shadows under big noses. Many photographers use the nose shadow as a guide for the height of the mainlight and always adjust the angle so that the shadow falls at an angle across the upper lip but ends just short of the lip itself.

Naturally when the pose requires the head to be turned a little away from full face the lighting set-up will need to be adapted accordingly. It is always preferable to have the main light on the side that the subject is facing, otherwise the back of the head may be better illuminated than the more important face.

The exercise suggested will also show how the angle of the light affects texture and therefore the final effect. At 45° and beyond it is creating shadows in every nook, cranny and furrow, so it is ideal for character rendering—in other words, for men and for old ladies where it is not desired to sentimentalise them. At the lesser angles the shadows are reduced, so the effect is more

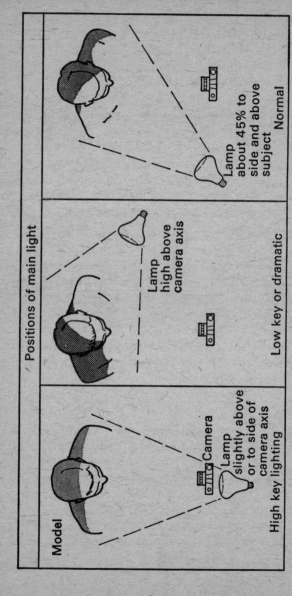

Fig. 22   The basic lighting positions described in the text. The second and third arrangements normally require a reflector or a fill-in light near the camera/subject axis.

flattering and therefore suitable for most female portraits, glamour pictures and children's portraits.

It should be emphasised here that the decision on the final contrast must be made at this point. It is no use placing the light at 45° and then trying to produce a high-key picture by adding a powerful fill-in or, conversely, putting the main light in front and then trying to get contrast by reducing the fill-in. Both results will look unnatural. The simple rule is to place the main light well up and well round for low-key, character and contrast pictures with plenty of texture, and to place it nearer the front, as well as lower, for gentler, softer or high-key portraits.

Incidentally, the positioning of the light can be done with it on half power if a series/parallel switch or circuit board is employed. It will not affect the final result and will save the sitter some discomfort, although with a little experience the correct position should be found in a second or two.

At this point the nature of the main light should also be considered. Many professionals use a spotlight that gives a concentrated beam that causes sharp-edged shadows, but for domestic purposes a deep bowl reflector is good enough and the shadows it casts are clear enough for average character portraits. In fact, it might be a little too hard for glamour subjects and a shallow bowl would be a useful addition to the outfit for high-key and low-contrast pictures.

Having established the correct angle to suit the subject and the degree of modelling required, the next consideration is the distance of the light from the sitter. The strength of the light falls off so rapidly with distance that it is dangerous to place the light too close, especially when it is at a high angle, otherwise the forehead will be much brighter than the chin. A bald-headed man will not thank you for this! Make it a rule to place the light as far away as is practicable in the space available and never less than 5 feet for a head-and-shoulder portrait. For a three-quarter or full-length picture the distance must obviously be increased accordingly. The more concentrated the type of reflector, the more likely it is to have a 'hot spot' in the centre.

When, and only when, the position for the main light has been satisfactorily settled, the secondary or fill-in light should be switched on. This light is solely for putting illumination into the shadows and is required because all films have a limited contrast range, far less than the human eye can accommodate. When the eye is transferred from highlight to shadow, the iris opens to compensate for the change, but film cannot do this. What looks reasonably well lit all over will come out far too contrasty in the negative. In other words, if the exposure is based on the highlights the shadows will be underexposed and lacking in detail, or if the exposure is long enough to record shadow detail the highlights will be overexposed, 'burnt out' and devoid of tone. In fact, the situation with a main light alone is similar to the bright sunlight discussed in Chapter 9.

It follows that the fill-in light must be, as near as possible, completely shadowless or it will conflict with the main light and cause unpleasant cross shadows. For this reason it should be kept as close to the camera/subject axis as possible and a very shallow, white-painted bowl reflector, as described in the last chapter, is ideal. Failing this, an ordinary photoflood in a bowl reflector could be bounced off a white wall or suitable flat surface.

The relative strength and distance of this light will determine the contrast of the final result. In colour photography, where the contrast range of the film is more limited than in monochrome, a ratio of about 2:1 suits the average subject. The colours themselves help to separate planes and provide modelling, whereas in black-and-white much of it is dependent on tone variation. In monochrome the contrast can be as much as 4:1 or 5:1 before it comes outside the limits that a print can show. A low-key picture where minimum detail is required in the shadows can even extend beyond this, but in general it is wise to keep the range for monochrome between 2:1 and 5:1 according to the effect required.

With the aid of an accurate exposure meter it is possible to measure both the highlight and the shadow, thus ensuring that the contrast is not too great. This should be done from a similar tone or colour for each reading, and if in doubt use a light grey card. When the meter is on the camera it will only be taking an average reading and it will not indicate the degree of contrast. As with so many things, experience teaches a lot and after a

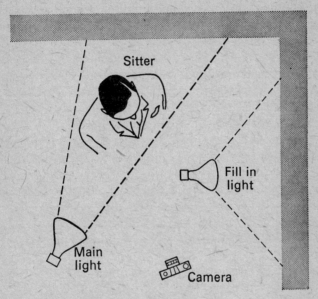

Fig. 23 When working in a confined space a corner may provide a possible background as well as a suitable reflecting surface for fill-in.

time the final effect can be judged without measuring. It helps to half close the eyes because this increases the apparent contrast and some professionals use a deep blue viewing glass for the same reason. Until enough experience has been gained several exposures should be made with the fill-in light placed at different distances and a note made of each.

When the main light and fill-in light have been satisfactorily positioned the background must be considered. It may be that the tone is satisfactory as a result of the light falling on it from the main light and fill-in light. Because of its greater distance this will come out darker than it appears to the eye, so it should also be studied through half-closed eyes.

However, it may well be found that the main light is throwing a shadow of the sitter on the background. Under no circumstances should the main light be moved further round in an attempt to move the shadow out of the picture area—once properly positioned the main light should never be moved. The answer is to move the background further back, in which case it will come out darker, or to light it separately. Of course, the sitter could be moved forward, but this would involve moving the camera, main light and fill-in, all of which have already been carefully positioned.

If the sitter is placed about 5 feet in front of the background it is easy to deploy a third light, and this makes a variety of effects

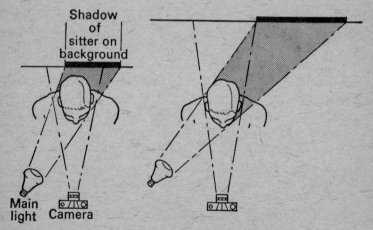

Fig. 24 Plan showing the importance of keeping the sitter far enough forward to avoid a cast shadow on the background. The nearer the light to the camera/subject axis, the greater the distance between sitter and background that will be required, unless a separate and powerful light is used to 'kill' it. But that may make the background lighter than desired.

possible. An open bulb without a reflector placed behind the subject will give a fairly even tone all over the background. Taken close to the background it will give a halo effect, with a bright centre gradually darkening towards the edges. This can be very attractive and it is quite different from a spotlight, which is more theatrical as well as much harder and therefore not so suitable for ordinary portraiture. The actual strength of tone can be varied by the use of different bulbs. If the main light is a floodlight at 5 feet, an ordinary 100 W bulb may just kill the subject's shadow on the background and leave the rest as a very dark tone. If it is not strong enough, a 150 W bulb could be employed to get a mid-key background, and changing to a photoflood will probably give a very light tone. It is hardly necessary to add that the background light should be at the same power, either half or full, for the study of contrast and tone balance as well as for the actual exposure.

The tone of the background should always suit the subject. If the lighting is contrasty and at an angle to give plenty of texture rendering, the background should be dark and preferably have some variations of tone in a minor key. On the other hand, if the subject is more delicate and a more flattering or glamorous high-key lighting scheme is employed, the background should be light in tone with subtler variations. Nothing looks worse than a dark or contrasty head and shoulders outlined against a near white background. Likewise, a high-key subject against a black or very dark background looks bad because the moods do not harmonise.

Effect lights

The only other lights that should be considered are lights used solely to add a little sparkle to a portrait by outlining the head and shoulders. These are lights used from behind or above, and they put highlights into dark hair and help the subject to stand out from the background. They are employed a tremendous amount in films and television because they ensure that the figure will be well separated, however much he moves or however much the background changes. They are not really necessary and thousands of fine portraits are taken without them, so unless one is prepared to go to all the extra trouble and expense of boom light stands they are best forgotten. Simplicity is a virtue where most portrait lighting is concerned.

Sometimes it is found that when all the lighting has been placed to give the desired effect there is a dark patch under the chin or the eyebrows that would be better with a little more light. This can often be obtained by placing a white card or an open book on the lap so that it reflects light upwards. As an alternative, try lowering the fill-in light, but if this is done watch that it does not throw a shadow on the background above the head.

This is usually necessary only in fairly low-key work because, to be in harmony, the sitter should be wearing darkish clothing which does not reflect any of the light upwards. In high-key pictures the subject's light clothing will often do the trick, but in colour beware of colour casts. For this reason bare shoulders are often better.

Lighting by flash

Exactly the same principles of positioning and balance apply for lighting by flash, but unfortunately the precise effect cannot be seen until after a print has been made. The handyman could rig up pilot lights attached to each flash unit in order to judge the modelling, but if this is done much of the advantage of flash is lost and one might just as well use photofloods.

Experience is the best teacher, but if the advice on placing given for photofloods is followed for the flashguns there is a good chance of success. There is, however, a big difference in the nature of the light. Direct flash gives a crisp, hard-edged lighting that is good for character rendering, especially in low-key, but it is not so pleasing on a glamorous or more delicate subject. It will also require a fill-in light and a separate flash for the background, both of which need precise placing. The cost per shot is high if bulbs are used, and for electronic flash the capital outlay is considerable.

Many people use flash bounced from an umbrella instead of direct because this often makes a second light unnecessary in a small, light-walled room at home. Owing to the lower level of light and the specular reflection scattered around the room, the background can be illuminated with an ordinary 100 W or 150 W domestic bulb behind the sitter.

When using colour it will make the background a little warmer than its true colour, but this is rarely a disadvantage. In fact, with a white background it is an advantage because pure white or grey is rarely satisfactory in a colour shot. Colour gels are useful, whether using flash or electric lighting, to put colours into a background, but always be careful to see that they do not spill onto the subject.

Umbrella flash gives such a diffused light that it is ideal for high-key or light-tone schemes even without a fill-in. These treatments are very suitable for the majority of feminine portraits as well as babies and young children, and the background should also be light. The final effect is almost indistinguishable from portraits taken in diffused daylight. For this reason it is perfect for colour, and daylight-type colour film should be used. In black-and-white the negative may well be a little too soft for printing on normal-grade paper, but this can be corrected by a little extra development if desired.

Quite contrasty results for low-key subjects can be obtained when required by using a single umbrella flash well to one side of the sitter and against a dark background. To obtain maximum contrast a large or dark-walled room should be used so that there is a minimum of specular reflection to light up the shadows.

Whether high-key, middle-tone or low-key lighting is required, the placing of the lamp does not need quite the same precision as for photoflood lighting. The cast shadows are so diffused that there is a great deal of latitude and this makes bounced flash an ideal light source for children and pets, who are naturally restless. They can move about within reasonable limits without any necessity for moving the main light.

Points about posing

Apart from simplicity in lighting, a good portrait generally shows a simple background, unobtrusive clothing and a natural pose. Backgrounds of patterned wallpaper or folded curtains are distracting. A white or light-coloured sheet hung from the curtain rail is ideal for formal portraiture and the interest in it should be confined to tone or colour variation. A free-standing cine or slide screen can also be used for head-and-shoulder close-ups.

The clothing should be unobtrusive. Violent patterns, polka dots and loud checks can only take the viewer's attention away from the face. Dark but fairly plain suiting is best for the male character portrait, but pure black should be avoided if possible, especially for colour pictures. Pastel colours with very subdued patterns or perfectly plain materials are better for the high-key subjects. Remember always that the face is the main object of the exercise and nothing should distract attention from it. Avoid patches of light such as a pocket handkerchief in a male portrait or a sparkling brooch in the dark hair of a female.

Posing should also have an air of simplicity, and the uncomfortable look in the eyes of a sitter who has been forced to do all sorts of contortions to satisfy a photographer's desire to be different is painful to see. Always allow the subject to get seated comfortably and have a little chat or play some music until he or she relaxes. The chair should be placed at an angle so that the sitter automatically faces away from the camera. This will ensure that the shoulders are not square-on to the lens—a position that exaggerates their width and is inclined to look gauche and inelegant. With the body at an angle and the head turned towards the camera there is a feeling of movement which is pleasing, especially when the head is tilted a little.

Most sitters, particularly women, will say that 'this side is my best side'. Often this is because there is a spot or blemish on the other, but it is not always the most photogenic. Nearly all faces are wider on one side than the other, so if the main light is directed at the wider side and the narrower side is left in shadow the final effect is of a fatter face than normal and, of course, the converse applies. If the face is already round it is rarely flattering to make it look still rounder and *vice-versa*. This is where judgment must be used.

Likewise, the desirability of suppressing less attractive features must be considered. In the case of a bald man it is better to get him to look up so that less of his pate is seen. Alternatively, the camera can be lowered to get the same effect. Double chins can be minimised by raising the camera. It is also wise to watch the nose shadow, because a large nose will look even bigger if it is allowed to cast a long shadow across the cheek.

Watch for spots of grease or perspiration, which will glisten in the lights. Keep a powder puff or handkerchief handy to make last minute corrections and ask the sitter to lick her lips to make them shine a little. Before pressing the shutter, watch for points like a jacket riding up at the back of the neck, a tie askew and wisps of hair sticking out against the background or falling over the face. Remember that retouching is practically impossible with miniature films, especially in colour.

All these points are worth watching, but the actual pose will depend on personal interpretation. 'The camera cannot lie', but the sitter can be presented in a hundred different ways to flatter, improve, eliminate or exaggerate features according to the lighting and camera viewpoint employed. A lethargic person can be made to look active by choosing a pose that has diagonals suggesting action, or another can be made to look dignified by using a low viewpoint and a tall, triangular composition.

It is a good idea to study books of good portraits and note the poses used for particular types of people. There is no better exercise than trying to copy them with appropriate subjects.

Further reading on Portraiture

Light on People, Paul Petzold, Focal Press.
Lighting for Portraiture, W. Nurnberg, Focal Press.
Portraiture at Home, R. H. Mason, Fountain Press.
Creative Portrait Photography, P. Zeemeijer, Fountain Press.

Reference book for posing
Portraits of Greatness, Yousef Karsh, Thos. Nelson & Sons.

14 Developing the Film

Black-and-white films

Anyone can develop monochrome films at home without a darkroom or elaborate equipment. It is a course much to be recommended because the individual care that can be given to the film is more reliable than the mass-machine methods employed in wholesale processing houses, especially for miniature films. In the long run it is also an economy, and there is a great deal of satisfaction to be gained from it even if the subsequent printing cannot be done at home.

The function of the developer is to turn the exposed silver salts in the emulsion into black silver and the fixing solution then removes the unexposed silver salts. Washing removes the unwanted chemicals and renders the image permanent.

The first requirement is a daylight developing tank. This can be obtained for a few pounds and the universal models will take all the standard sizes of roll film. There are also models to take one size only, and these are cheaper and use less developer. All tanks have a plastic or metal spiral into which the film is loaded and a spigot enables it to be rotated or agitated from outside. A light-tight aperture permits the developing and fixing solutions to be poured in and out.

Naturally the film has to be loaded into the tank in complete darkness. Daylight changing bags are available, but almost any cupboard or small room can be blacked out temporarily for this purpose. Loading the spiral must be done by feel, but this is surprisingly easy as long as the spiral is bone dry, and it is especially simple with several types that have a reciprocating movement.

There are also some ingenious tanks designed for 35 mm film

and 120 film that permit the entire loading to be done in daylight, but they cost about three times as much. They can be an economy if a lot of work is envisaged because only 7 oz of solution is required, against 10 to 14 oz for the other types, and they have a convenient built-in thermometer.

Much has been written about the respective qualities of different developers, but there is so little to choose between them that the wisest course is to follow the instructions given with the film. The principal manufacturers market their own developers and give precise instructions for time and temperature. Follow them and you can't go wrong. Some proprietary developers are sold in concentrated liquid form and only need diluting with water for use, after which they are thrown away. Others are in powder form, usually two separate packets, and have to be mixed with water; the solution can be used for six or seven films before being discarded.

It is advisable to filter the mixed solution before use, and in a very hard water area it might be wiser to use distilled or purified water. The makers specify the different times of development required for different temperatures between about 65°F (18°C) and 75°F (24°C), so a thermometer that reads in this range with reasonable accuracy is required. Those sold by photo dealers can be inserted in the filler aperture of the developing tank in order to keep a check on temperature during development.

The film has to be sharply agitated after the developer has been poured in so that any air bubbles on the film are dispersed. Further agitation is then required at regular intervals in order to ensure even development, but here again the instructions should be followed. Some tanks can be inverted to make doubly sure that the developer does not concentrate on any area more than another.

After development the film should be given a quick wash to remove surplus developer. Many people substitute the wash with a 'stop bath', which is a mildly acid solution that will arrest development immediately by counteracting the alkalinity of any remaining developer. This also prevents the fixing bath from being contaminated, thus preserving its life and helping to avoid any danger of stains. Stop bath, usually called 'acid-stop', can be obtained in concentrated liquid form and used over and over again, even when diluted, so its cost per film is negligible.

After the quick wash or the stop bath the film has to be 'fixed', and this can also be bought in a convenient concentrated solution. It is best to buy the acidified type rather than the plain hypo because it is cleaner working. This can be bought in two forms, ordinary and rapid. The latter is useful for the professional in a hurry but hardly worth the extra cost for the amateur.

Up to this point the tank must be kept closed, but after the hypo has been in for a minute the lid can be removed. A few minutes after the milkiness on the film has completely disappeared, the hypo should be replaced with water or the open tank placed under a running tap. Incidentally, the hypo can be bottled and re-used repeatedly until it takes more than 10 minutes or so to remove the milkiness.

The film can be washed in two ways. Either by soaking in five or six changes of water for about 5 minutes each, or in running water for about 10 minutes. In the latter case the tank should be emptied completely at intervals because hypo tends to sink to the bottom. The temperature of the stop bath and the hypo should not be more than 10°F (5°C) lower than that of the developer, and the wash water should not be more than 10°F (5°C) less than that of the hypo. Otherwise there is a danger of the gelatine shrinking and reticulating the gelatine emulsion.

In hard-water areas the film should then be given a 2-minute soak in water to which a drop or two of softener has been added. This can also be bought in very concentrated and economical form. It will prevent scum or lime deposits forming on the film, but be careful not to overdo it or streaks may result. Here again, you should follow the makers' instructions because they have really tested it out.

The film must be hung up to dry in a place free from dust. Surplus water can be removed by gently rubbing down between finger and thumb, but wash-leathers, sponges and rubber tongs should be eschewed. They are traps for minute particles of grit that cause 'tramlines' down the film while the gelatine is wet and soft.

If water softener is used the film should be dry in about 30 minutes. A clip or weight at the end will prevent rolling up or curling. It is best to cut the film into convenient lengths—about six exposures per length for 35 mm film or three for 6 cm × 6 cm negatives—and store them flat in plastic envelopes until ready for printing. Do not roll the whole film up for storage.

Colour negative film

Processing colour negative film is a little more complicated and certainly more lengthy than processing monochrome, but it is still within the capability of any amateur at home. The film manufacturers supply kits of chemicals that are very easy to mix and detailed instructions for their use are also supplied.

An efficient, and by far the most economical, developing kit is Photocolor II which can be used for all Type 2 colour negative films and also for colour prints. There are only two solutions—developer and bleach-fix—but some people like to use an acid stop bath between them instead of a rinse. The sequence of operations is:

1.	Developer (diluted 1+2)	$2\frac{3}{4}$ mins at 38°C.
2.	Stop Bath (Indicol diluted 1+30)	30 sec
3.	Bleach-fix (diluted 1+1)	3 min
4.	Wash (running water)	5 min

This shows a total processing time before hanging up to dry of $11\frac{1}{4}$ minutes, which is less than for a monochrome film. This is based on development in a drum which, once the film is loaded can be carried out in the light. Development at lower temperatures is possible but times have to be extended for both baths. If the drum and the darkroom are cold, the former must be preheated with hot water at about 34°C to 46°C. Detailed instructions are given with the kits.

A 1 litre kit will process about ten 35mm or 120 films, but if a lesser number is processed the balance can be used for making colour prints with the addition of a developer accelerator supplied with the kit.

Temperature is fairly critical and, if the instructions are not adhered to, false colour rendering can result. In monochrome a wide variation of temperatures (about 18°C to 24°C) can be tolerated if the time of development is ajdusted to correspond, but with colour negative film the tolerance for the developer is only plus or minus about ($\frac{1}{4}$°C) from the recommended time, which is usually 24°C.

It is therefore necessary to make some arrangement to keep the temperature constant for about 11 minutes. This is easily done if the room temperature is maintained at 32°C, but failing this the tank should be placed in a tray or bath of water raised to the exact temperature.

The solutions in most kits will keep for five or six weeks without deteriorating, but they will not keep more than a few days once a film has been put through them. It is obviously wise to develop as many as possible at one session, otherwise the saving in cost made possible by home processing will be nullified, except when Photocolor II is employed.

Colour reversal films

Many colour reversal films are sold at a price that includes processing and they have to be returned to a processing station specified by the manufacturer.

However, there are a few that are sold exclusive of processing because they can be processed at home in the kits marketed by the manufacturers. This is a great advantage when the results are required quickly and it is also possible to use a higher speed than that for which the film is rated. It is compensated for by a longer development time. This is useful in emergencies, but there is inevitably some loss of colour quality.

The same developing tanks can be used as for monochrome or colour negative film, but there are more processing stages.

For example, Ektachrome film processed in the Kodak E-4 kit requires the following:

1	Pre-hardener	3 min
2	Neutraliser	1 min
3	Wash	1 min
4	First developer	6 min
5	Stop bath	2 min
6	Wash	4 min
7	Colour developer	15 min
8	Stop bath	2 min
9	Wash	3 min
10	Bleach	5 min
11	Fixing bath	4 min
12	Wash	6 min
13	Stabiliser	1 min
14	Dry	

The first five steps have to be carried out with the tank sealed, but the rest can be done in normal room lighting. In some processes the film has to be exposed to white light before colour development, but E-4 uses a chemical fogging procedure for reversal. Maintenance of recommended temperatures is critical to ensure good colour balance.

All this may seem rather formidable, but in practice it soon becomes routine. Like colour negatives processes, the solutions do not keep well once they have been used, so it is uneconomical to process less than five or six films at a time. The Kodak E-4 process is gradually being superseded by the E-6 process which is compatible with the latest high speed Ektachrome reversal films.

Further reading on developing

Photoguide to Home Processing, R. E. Jacobson, Focal Press.
Developing, Printing and Enlarging, Kodak Ltd.
200 Darkroom Tips, J. Van Welzen, Fountain Press.
Darkroom Techniques, R. Spillman, Fountain Press.

15 Making Prints

We have come a long way from the days when photographers had to coat their own printing papers and then wait for a sunny day in order to expose them in contact printing frames. Today papers are very sensitive to artificial light and available in so many degrees of contrast that enlarging is feasible in any room that can be temporarily converted into a darkroom. Even colour printing is practicable for an amateur with the aid of one of the developing drums now available.

Enlarging

Miniature negatives require enlargement if the detail is to be brought out, and this demands an enlarger. There are many types available at prices ranging from £20 to £200, but they all work on the same basic principle, which is something like a camera in reverse. Light from an enclosed and light-tight lamphouse passes through the negative, and a lens placed below it projects an image onto the baseboard.

The whole unit of lamphouse, negative carrier and lens can be moved up and down the vertical supporting column in order to vary the size of the enlargement. Provision is made for focusing by means of bellows or by a helical focusing mount on the lens.

The lamphouse can be fitted with condensers or an opal diffusing glass in order to ensure even illumination all over the negative and to avoid filament images or high spots from the bulb. Condensors concentrate the light and thus require less exposure. They also add a little contrast and yield crisp images, but at the same time they tend to accentuate dust spots or scratches on the negative. Opal glass diffusers give a softer image and tend to subdue spots and scratches but are not so efficient in passing light.

Lamphouses are often fitted with a removable tray which allows colour filters to be inserted between the light and the negative in order to obtain colour correction when making

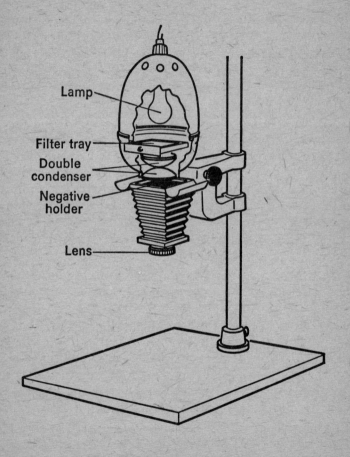

Lamp

Filter tray

Double condenser

Negative holder

Lens

Fig. 25 Cross-section of an enlarger showing the principle whereby the light is concentrated by a double condensor to provide even illumination over the whole negative.

colour prints by the subtractive method. Some models have a built-in 'colour head' containing three dichroic filters which can be 'dialled in' by outside controls in any combination. This saves a lot of time normally taken in finding and inserting the right filters, and no handling is involved. Dichroic filters are more efficient and do not fade. The lens must give coverage to the whole negative, so the focal length should not be less than the diagonal of the negative. For example, a 2 in lens is adequate for 35 mm negatives but a 3 in focal length is necessary for 6 cm × 6 cm negatives. Some camera lenses can be satisfactorily used on an enlarger, but by no means all. This is not surprising when it is realised that most camera lenses are computed to give optimum performance on subjects some distance away, whereas the enlarger demands optimum performance for an image formed only inches away. Some lenses are marked in f numbers, but most lenses made specifically for enlarging have click stops marked in a simple 2, 4, 8, 16, 32 progression, each requiring twice as much exposure as the preceding stop.

It is obvious that a good lens is the prime essential, otherwise the good definition of the camera lens will be nullified. The second important requirement is even illumination, but other facilities such as automatic focusing and built-in masking are luxuries—nice to have, but not essential.

The negative carrier can be a simple affair that holds the negative between two metal frames or it can have two sheets of thin glass to hold the negative flat. The former, the glassless carrier, is quite satisfactory for 35 mm negatives, but for larger negatives the glass carrier is better because it prevents the negative from buckling under heat. It must obviously be kept free from dust or scratches.

All enlargers have a baseboard on which the printing paper can be placed for exposure. It is more convenient, however, to employ a printing frame, which not only holds the paper flat but also provides a white border by means of adjustable masking strips. It is painted white so that the image can be focused on it.

Focusing should be done at full aperture and then the lens should be stopped down at least one stop in order to ensure even illumination and to give enough depth of field to allow for paper thickness. There are a number of inexpensive focusing magnifiers on the market and these are useful for those who find it difficult to focus precisely, especially with dense negatives.

Enlarging papers

All black-and-white printing papers, known as bromide papers, are far less sensitive to light than films are, so they can be handled in a weak amber light. Most darkroom lamps fitted with a safe-light filter take a 15 W or 25 W bulb and the paper is safe to within about 5 feet. Nevertheless, it is a good idea to make sure by placing a coin on a piece of paper under the enlarger and on the developing bench for 2 minutes or more. Then develop it for 3 minutes, and if you can distinguish a white circle the safe-light was too strong or too close.

Bromide papers are available in a series of standard sizes from $\frac{1}{2}$ plate ($6\frac{1}{2}$ in $\times$ $4\frac{3}{4}$ in) to 30 in $\times$ 24 in; probably the most popular size is 10 in $\times$ 8 in. They are also available in a large number of grades, varying from very soft to very hard. This facilitates a great deal of compensation for negatives of varying degrees of contrast. For instance, an underexposed negative or underdeveloped negative that has a very limited range of tones will require a hard or contrast paper, while an overexposed or overdeveloped negative will demand a soft paper. Most makers designate the grades by numbers. No. 0 is the softest and No. 6 the hardest, while No. 2 and No. 3 are regarded as normal and are therefore by far the most used.

Some variations in surface finish are also available, the most popular being glossy, semi-matt (or velvet matt) and matt. At one time there was a wide range of fancy surfaces such as Old Master, stipple, lustre, linen, etc., but they are falling out of fashion and even exhibition photographers use more glossy paper than anything else.

Another variation that is still available from some makers is a chlorobromide paper. It is similar to bromide but is capable of being developed to give warmer tones. It is sometimes coated onto a cream paper base, which is also going out of fashion.

For the sake of completeness, it should be mentioned that there is another type of paper known as variable contrast. Only one grade of paper is required and the degree of contrast that it records is controlled by filters placed under the enlarger lens. The British version is known as Multigrade and the American as Varigam. Both are processed in the same way as bromide papers.

Exposure

Bromide papers are much slower than films, but exposure times with normal negatives in the conventional enlarger should rarely be longer than 60 seconds at the working aperture and, in most cases, will be considerably less. Correct exposure is essential because the print must be fully developed to get good blacks and correct tone rendition. A print that is overexposed and taken out of the developer before it has reached finality will be flat and muddy, while one that is underexposed will never achieve good blacks and maximum detail, however long it is left in the developing dish.

The right exposure can be determined in a number of ways. There are several types of electronic meters available but, like exposure meters for camera work, they have to be used with judgment. The spot-reading type depends on selecting the right tone on the baseboard to measure, and the integrating type is only reliable with an average even-tone negative. Compensation must be made for subjects having a greater than normal ratio of shadow to highlight and *vice-versa*.

The most popular method is to make a test strip by placing a small piece of bromide paper, say a quarter of the final size, in a suitable place on the baseboard or printing frame and exposing it in progressive steps, such as 5 s, 10 s, 15 s, 20 s, 25 s, 30 s, by drawing a piece of opaque card across in stages.

Alternatively, you can use one of the commercially available step wedges or enlarging test negatives. These enable you to get the same result with one exposure.

After full development the test print can be examined in the fixing bath and it will be easy to see which exposure was correct. An advantage of this method is that it also gives an indication of whether or not the correct contrast grade has been chosen.

Some enlargers are fitted with an orange or red filter that can be swung into place under the lens. It is a mistake to use this for making the exposure because it is all too easy to vibrate the enlarger head and soften the print when swinging it in and out of position. The exposure should always be made by a switch that is remote from the enlarger itself—a footswitch is ideal. There are also automatic timers available. These ensure consistency and thus are useful if repeat prints are required. More elaborate models combine timer and exposure meter and, at the same time, switch the darkroom light on and off.

A great advantage of enlarging is that parts of the picture can be 'shaded'. This means that parts can be printed up or held back. For instance, if the sky in a landscape negative is very dense compared with the foreground, it can be given extra exposure by holding a suitably shaped mask cut from opaque card over the landscape portion. The card has to be held a little above the paper and kept on the move to avoid a sharp edge appearing. In portraits it is sometimes an advantage to shade a light background so that it darkens towards the edges. The keen printer keeps an assortment of different shaped masks beside him for such purposes.

However, it is obvious that such manoeuvres would be difficult to execute accurately in a space of just a few seconds and this is where the f stops or click stops on the lens can be very useful. By stopping down, the exposure time can be increased to 30 seconds or more and this is the only valid reason for using small stops on most enlarger lenses, which are generally designed to give optimum results at the larger apertures.

Contact prints in the enlarger

Many photographers like to make contact prints for filing or record purposes and this is easily done with an enlarger. If a 35 mm film is cut into strips of six negatives, it will be found that the five strips just fit neatly into a 10 in × 8 in area when placed side by side. Likewise, a 120 size film cut into four strips of three negatives each just covers 10 in × 8 in. Therefore all that is necessary is to place a piece of grade 2 or grade 3 bromide paper face up on the baseboard, lay the negatives on top emulsion downwards, and keep them flat and in place with a sheet of heavy plate glass 10 in × 8 in or larger.

Then make an exposure with the lens closed down one or two stops and develop the print. Once the correct exposure has been found it can be repeated ever afterwards if the enlarger head is always at the same height. This presumes that all the negatives are fairly constant in density, failing which a little masking during exposure may be necessary, but for filing and identification purposes optimum quality in all the pictures is not vital. If a lot of contact work is anticipated it is a convenience to use one of the inexpensive frames designed for the purpose.

Processing monochrome prints

Three dishes are required for print processing and they should be at least an inch or two bigger all round than the prints to be processed. The first dish, the developer, should also be deep enough to be able to rock it without spilling, and a minimum of 2 inches is desirable.

Print developers of a simple metol-hydroquinone formula are available as concentrates which only have to be diluted with water. Ideally, they should be kept at a temperature of about 65°F (18°C) and, since this is a comfortable room temperature, it should not be difficult. The exposed paper is slid smoothly into the developer, emulsion side up, and the dish gently rocked for a few seconds to remove air bubbles and ensure even spreading if the developer is newly mixed. It is a great temptation to watch the image come up, but this is not really necessary because the print should stay in for at least 2 minutes. Under darkroom lighting the print always looks as though it is getting too dense and there is a temptation to remove it too soon as a result.

When examined in white light after fixing, a print will be seen to be much lighter than it looked under the darkroom safelight. Therefore the test strip for determining exposure should always be examined by ordinary electric lighting or, if possible, by daylight.

After full development the print is transferred for a few seconds to an acid stop bath similar to that used in negative development. After this it is transferred to the fixing bath and the room light can be turned on. In order to avoid contamination between baths, a pair of plastic print tongs should be used to to lift the print from developer to stop bath and another pair to lift it from the stop bath to fixer. This keeps the hands dry and also enables the print to be drained of surplus liquid between each bath.

The fixing bath can be plain hypo, but acid-hypo is cleaner working and less liable to staining if the print is left in it too long. This can be bought in powder form and only needs dissolving in water. Five minutes is usually adequate for fixing if the prints are kept on the move and not allowed to cling together. A longer time, up to an hour or so, will do no harm, but longer than this may cause some bleaching.

All prints require a thorough washing or they will start fading in time. If running water is available 30 minutes is sufficient, but the prints should be kept on the move. A simple siphon can be used to adapt a bath or washbasin for the purpose and, ideally, it should drain off the water from the bottom because the salts washed out of the prints tend to sink.

Where running water is not available the prints should be soaked for 5 minutes at a time in seven or eight changes of water, and if absolute permanence is required it would be as well to employ one of the commercially available hypo eliminators.

Drying

The latest bromide papers are resin coated which means that solutions cannot easily penetrate the paper base and they will therefore dry more quickly. They should not be dried in a glazing machine because the resin melts at high temperatures, but special low temperature driers are available.

Alternatively, they can be squeegeed to remove surplus water and laid on blotting paper. Unlike ordinary bromide papers they will dry flat in about 10 minutes or so, depending on the ambient temperature. The glassy variety dries with a very high glaze.

Processing colour prints

Until recently colour printing was beyond the scope of most amateurs, but improved apparatus and material have now made it comparatively easy. The colour negative is projected through the enlarger lens just like a black-and-white negative, but the light has to be corrected with colour filters.

There are two methods: additive and subtractive. The former needs three filters in the primary colours—red, green and blue—and they can be used below the lens. It is fast becoming obsolete. In the subtractive method a set of thirteen or more colour filters are required, except when a colour head enlarger is used. These are cyan, magenta and yellow in various degrees of density, and since several may have to be used together it is better to place them in the filter drawer provided in the lamphouse of many enlargers. Gelatin filters are quite satisfactory if they are not scratched or fingermarked.

In black-and-white printing the density is controlled by the exposure, but in colour printing both density and colour are affected, so the colour of the light nearly always has to be modified by filters. This also means that there must be some form of voltage control applied to the lamp because variations in voltage can change the colour temperature of the light.

The subtractive method of colour printing is the more satisfactory and offers wider control over the final result. It would be out of place to go into detail about the selection and use of filters—there are many books on the subject—but suffice it to say that a test print has to be made without filters or with a pre-selected combination. From this, adjustments can be made if there are any colour variations or colour cast.

At one time this was very difficult and sometimes many test prints had to be made; even worse, they had to be dried before the final colour could be assessed. Today, with the aid of graded test charts containing a number of sections of different colour densities, the corrections can be made from the examination of one test print. Colour analysers make the choice of the correct filters much easier but they are expensive.

All makes of colour printing paper are naturally sensitive to light of every colour, so the handling must be carried out in complete darkness or by the very dim light of the safelight recommended by the paper manufacturer. However, the actual processing is no longer a problem because there are developing drums available which are efficient and economical.

The print is loaded into the drum in darkness after it has been exposed in the enlarger and from then on the processing is done in white light. The solutions are poured in and out through a light-tight aperture and the drum is rotated or rolled backwards and forwards to provide even working with only a few ounces of solution. In the more elaborate professional models the drum is sometimes turned by an electric motor and it is contained in a temperature-controlled water bath. Temperature is critical to within about $\frac{1}{2}°F$ ($0.25°C$) for the developer and about $3°F$ to $4°F$ ($1.5°C$ to $2°C$) for the other baths.

Temperature control is not difficult if the room is kept at the right temperature, and the bottles containing the solutions are kept in a water bath at the precise temperature required. This avoids any increase or decrease due to pouring into a cold container or drum.

Processing times vary a little between makes, but the instructions given for Photocolor II are fairly typical:

1	Developer	2 min at 38°C
2	Stop-bath	10 sec
3	Bleach-fix	1 min
4	Wash	$1\frac{1}{2}$ min

4 min 40 sec

All colour papers are resin-coated and can be dried as described for bromide papers (p.151). Extended development time will permit lower temperatures to be employed.

Colour prints from transparencies

Prints from transparencies can be made in the enlarger by the subtractive method, using reversal papers for the purpose. This naturally entails a reversal of filtration and the processing in most cases calls for a reversal exposure to white light. There are two principal processes—Kodak Ektacolor RC14 paper with Photochrome R chemistry, and Cibachrome-A. The former, which is much cheaper per print, gives very good results using four solutions at 35°C and takes $12\frac{1}{4}$ minutes, including the re-exposure necessary. Cibachrome-A has only three solutions and does not require re-exposure. It can be processed at a lower temperature (24°C) in a total time of 12 minutes. The prints are on a white polyester base instead of paper.

Monochrome prints from colour negatives

Most makes of colour negative films have a built-in orange mask which makes them difficult to assess without a lot of experience, so it can be useful to make black-and-white contact prints or enlargements before spending time on colour prints. Ordinary bromide papers can be used, but the required exposure will be very long owing to the colour of the mask and there will be some distortion of the image tones.

Special papers such as Kodak Panalure are made for the purpose and they will translate the colours into appropriate tones more accurately. As they are colour sensitive they must be exposed and developed in complete darkness or by a very, very dim safelight.

For the man with a penchant for darkroom work there is nothing more satisfying than colour printing, but makers' instructions have to be observed closely. Improvements making colour printing easier and more economical are being introduced frequently, so the keen printer should keep himself constantly up to date through the usual sources of books and magazines.

Recommended reading

Developing, Printing and Enlarging, Kodak Ltd.
Photoguide to Enlarging, Gunter Spitzing, Focal Press.
Making and Printing Colour Negatives, John Vickers, Fountain Press.
200 Darkroom Tips, J. Van Welzen, Fountain Press.
Exposure Control in Enlarging, G. Wakefield, Fountain Press.
Darkroom Techniques, R. Spillman, Fountain Press.
Focal Guide to Cibachrome, J. Coote, Focal Press.
Making Colour Prints, J. Coote, Focal Press.

16 Presentation

The impact on viewers of both prints and transparencies is greatly enhanced if they are presented properly. Even the best pictures lose a great deal if they are allowed to become dog-eared in the pocket or if transparencies are projected with specks of dust all over them.

Mounting prints

Prints, whether in colour or black-and-white, should always be mounted, even for carrying in the pocket book or handbag. Prints for preservation in an album should not only be properly mounted but also displayed in an artistic way that will add variety and interest. Page after page of photographs that are all similar in size and positioning makes an album monotonous, however good the pictures may be.

Photographs for the pocket can be mounted on card and preserved from dust and scuffing by being placed in a transparent envelope. It is also possible to have them heat-sealed in clear plastic, and experience so far would indicate that the sealing does no damage to the print.

Albums at one time had slots pierced in the pages so that prints could be dropped in or attached by the corners. They have become obsolete because one is tied to the same size of print throughout and it is impossible to trim prints or provide any variety in presentation. Adhesive corner pieces were also popular at one time and they at least gave scope for versatility in size and layout, but unfortunately they rarely stayed stuck for more than a year or two.

There are three types of modern album that overcome all these drawbacks. The first consists of leaves, or more precisely envelopes, of fairly thick clear plastic. A sheet of thin card of any desired colour can be inserted and prints mounted on either side. This enables the user to get variety by having leaves of different tints as well as black or white, and to change the pictures and the order as and when required.

The second type consists of an album with plain pages of white, grey or cream card and is often of the loose-leaf variety. One is tied to the colours provided, but there is plenty of scope for making interesting layouts and for lettering titles or captions. The loose-leaf type is usually better because it is easier to mount prints when the page is removed and it also folds out flat when being viewed.

The third type of album is one that is becoming increasingly popular. It consists of pages of fairly stout card, usually white or off-white, covered with a very thin plastic. The plastic is peeled back and prints are placed in the desired position, after which the plastic is rolled or smoothed back over the prints. It adheres to the mount between the prints because it is treated with a mild adhesive but, with care, prints can be removed if desired. The effect is very clean and modern and has the great advantage that no separate print mounting is required, but there is a disadvantage in that the mounts will not take lettering owing to the adhesive surface. This means that captions or titles must be separately typed or written on paper and mounted in place like the prints. Most of these albums are also loose-leaf.

Prints can be mounted with ordinary adhesives, but there are risks unless photo-mountants especially developed for the purpose are employed. Ordinary gums and glues sometimes have a chemical reaction with the paper or the mount which, in time, will cause staining or deterioration. In the case of water-based glues there is also a danger of uneven shrinkage or cockling, especially with large prints.

A recent introduction is a photo adhesive in an aerosol spray can. This is a quick, easy and clean method in which the back of the print is sprayed and then pressed into position. It works very well and is chemically quite safe, but it is comparatively expensive.

By far the most satisfactory method of mounting prints of any size is that known as dry-mounting. A sheet of very thin shellac tissue is attached to the back of the print with a hot iron, which can be a soldering iron. The print and tissue are then trimmed together so that they are both exactly the same size. They are then laid on the mount and a hot iron is applied over the print. This melts the tissue and a perfect bond is secured, but resin-coated papers require a special low temperature tissue.

There are special dry-mounting presses available for professional use, but an ordinary smoothing iron will make a good seal in 30 to 60 seconds. A sheet of good-quality greaseproof paper should be placed over the print to protect it from scorching; alternatively, metallic cooking foil can be used. The tissue forms an impervious layer between print and mount, thus preventing any impurities in the mount from scratching the emulsion. The shellac can be purchased in liquid form as well as tissue, but it involves an extra operation because it has to be spread on and left to dry. The saving in cost is hardly worth it.

Another advantage of dry-mounting is that it can be used on any dry and smooth surface, so prints can be mounted on wood blocks, chipboard or hardboard. The last-named is very useful for photographs that are to be framed.

Framing is very much a matter of personal taste and, in any case, should suit the surroundings in which the picture will be hung. In deciding where it is to be hung it is important to remember that colour prints are inclined to fade when exposed to sunlight for any length of time. It is possible to use an anti-fade varnish which preserves them a little longer, but it is better to hang them in the shady side of the room whenever possible.

At one time it was fashionable to mount photographs on white or cream mounting board and leave a margin of several inches all round the print; this included prints for exhibition or for framing at home. The side margins were each about one fifth of the width of the print, while the upper margin was slightly less and the lower margin slightly more. Today flush-mounted prints are the vogue and these are often on glossy paper, presumably as a result of glass going out of fashion.

For domestic showing, especially in a modern décor, prints can be mounted in very thick clear plastic—even as thick as 1 in —and this gives them an attractive and unusual 'floating' appearance. Mounted in this way they are also suitable for standing on the table. A popular type of mount for exhibition as well as for home decoration is one where the print, which is flush-mounted on hardboard, is then flush-framed at the back with wood about 1 in × 1 in. This gives the appearance of a solid block and the edges can be painted in a suitable colour or covered with a metallic tape. The effect is elegant and modern, and the picture can be easily hung flush to the wall.

For the period home, however, a normal picture frame is probably better. Curiously enough, a frame almost demands a mount around the print—something that is by no means necessary for a painting. It can be in any colour that harmonises with the print as well as the general décor, and coloured canvas is often used. For a high-key print a black or very dark mount is popular because it emphasises the luminosity of the picture, but for contrasty and deep-hued colour photographs a pastel shade is usually preferable. Try holding the print against different coloured papers or handy walls and it will be seen immediately that the colour of the mount can make a vast difference to its appearance. As with most things, simplicity, if not a virtue, is at least a safe course and in good taste.

Projecting slides

The beauty of a colour slide cannot be appreciated to the full until it is projected, but all too often the presentation is so bad that viewers get bored even when the slides are full of subject interest. Holding a slide up to the light reveals none of its detail and the colours look too cold. Battery-powered hand-viewers that magnify the picture are useful for preliminary examination or for sorting purposes and the light provided by a torch bulb gives a reasonably good colour rendering. However, one cannot conveniently share the pleasure of viewing with others by this method, so projection is the answer.

With a good projector and screen the slides are seen in a greater brilliance and range of tones than any colour print can reflect. The colours are purer and more intense, and there is often a marvellous impression of depth.

There is an enormous variety of projectors available to take 2 in × 2 in mounted slides, and they cover a wide price range

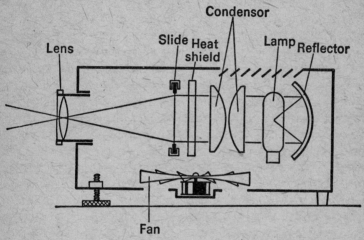

Fig. 26   Cross-section of a typical 2 in × 2 in slide projector.

according to construction and specification. This size takes 35 mm or 126 size transparencies as well as half-frame because these are all normally mounted in 2 in × 2 in card mounts when returned from the processer. Adaptors are also available to project the miniature 110 size but, of course, the picture on the screen is correspondingly smaller. If this size is used exclusively it is better to get one of the projectors especially designed for them.

There are also a few projectors made to take 6 cm × 6 cm ($2\frac{3}{4}$ in × $2\frac{3}{4}$ in) transparencies made on 120 film. There is at least one model made to take both 2 in × 2 in and $2\frac{3}{4}$ in × $2\frac{3}{4}$ in, but since two lenses or a zoom lens are required and the optical system is necessarily rather sophisticated it is in a high price bracket.

The cheapest 2 in × 2 in projectors have a comparatively low-power lamp, about 100 W or 150 W, so no cooling system is required. They will give quite a good picture up to 3 ft or 4 ft wide in a darkened room. Higher priced models have more powerful illumination, which facilitates greater magnification and some have refinements such as remote control, automatic focusing, automatic slide changing and sound synchronisation facilities. When choosing a projector the three most important considerations are the lens, the optical system and the slide-changing system.

The projector lens, like the lens on a camera, has a focal length and this controls the size of the picture on the screen at any given distance. The larger the room, or the longer the throw, the longer the focal length must be to produce a given size of picture. For example, the popular 85 mm focal length lens at a distance of 8 ft (2·2 m) from the screen gives a picture approximately 3 ft 5 in × 2 ft 3 in (1 m × 0·75 m), but at 10 ft the same lens would give a picture approximately 4 ft 2 in × 2 ft 10 in (1·25 m × 0·9 m). To obtain a picture the same size as the 85 mm lens gives at 8 ft, a lens of about 100 mm focal length will be required at 10 ft.

Most lenses have an aperture of about f/2·8 but, for obvious reasons, no iris diaphragm is fitted. There are also zoom lenses available in the higher price ranges, and these can be very convenient if the projector is used in different places that demand variations in picture size.

The table opposite shows the approximate size of image given by 35 mm transparencies with lenses of the popular focal lengths. For half-frame pictures divide the longer dimension by two, and for 110 pictures divide both dimensions by two. A separate table is given for 126 transparencies.

These sizes are rounded off to the nearest inch, but small

Image sizes for 35 mm transparencies in 2 in × 2 in projectors

Focal length	Distance from lens to screen						
	8 ft	10 ft	13 ft	16 ft	20 ft	23 ft	26 ft
50 mm	5'8" × 3'8"	7'3" × 5'	9'6" × 6'3"	12' × 8'	14'4" × 9'6"	16'8" × 11'2"	19' × 12'8"
85 mm	3'5" × 2'3"	4'2" × 2'10"	5'8" × 3'8"	7'1" × 4'8"	8'4" × 5'8"	9'8" × 6'6"	11'4" × 7'6"
100 mm	2'8" × 1'9"	3'8" × 2'6"	4'9" × 3'2"	6' × 4'	7'2" × 4'9"	8'4" × 5'7"	9'6" × 6'4"
120 mm	—	3' × 2'	4' × 2'8"	5' × 3'4"	6' × 4'	7' × 4'8"	8' × 5'4"
135 mm	—	2'10" × 1'10"	3'6" × 2'4"	4'6" × 3'8"	5'8" × 3'8"	6' × 4'	7'1" × 4'8"
150 mm	—	2'4" × 1'6"	3'2" × 2'1"	4' × 2'8"	4'8" × 3'2"	5'8" × 3'8"	6'4" × 4'2"

Image sizes for 126 transparencies in 2 in × 2 in projectors

Focal length	Distance from lens to screen				
	6 ft	8 ft	10 ft	12 ft	14 ft
50 mm	3'3" × 3'3"	4'5" × 4'5"	5'2" × 5'2"	6'7" × 6'7"	7'1" × 7'1"
85 mm	2'2" × 2'2"	2'7" × 2'7"	3'4" × 3'4"	4'1" × 4'1"	4'7" × 4'7"
100 mm	1'6" × 1'6"	2' × 2'	2'6" × 2'6"	3'1" × 3'1"	3'7" × 3'7"
120 mm	1'3" × 1'3"	1'9" × 1'9"	2'2" × 2'2"	2'7" × 2'7"	3'1" × 3'1"
135 mm	1'1" × 1'1"	1'7" × 1'7"	1'10" × 1'10"	2'4" × 2'4"	9'9" × 9'9"

variations may occur because lenses, especially the cheaper ones, are not always precisely the focal lengths marked on their mounts.

It is important to have as long a throw as the room will permit, after allowing enough room for operating the projector from behind. A short throw means that viewers will be uncomfortably close to the screen or at such an angle that the picture will appear badly distorted.

Having decided the distance available, reference to the table will show the size of picture available for each focal length. The picture must not be too big in relation to the distance or the audience will feel 'swamped' and unable to absorb the whole picture in one glance. It can also strain their necks. At 10 ft throw, a picture 4 ft wide is ample and it will still look good at 13 ft. In larger rooms and with larger audiences, correspondingly bigger pictures can be acceptable, but for home use a 4 ft picture is adequate. A popular screen with amateurs is 50 in × 50 in, but screens are also available at 3 ft, 5 ft and 6 ft square.

The optical system on a good projector consists of a bulb, sometimes with a reflector behind it and sometimes with the reflector built into the bulb, a condensor, a heat-resisting screen and the lens. Nearly all quality projectors now use low-voltage tungsten halogen lamps, which are cooler and more compact than the old gas-filled bulbs and burn with a white light that gives better colour rendering. They do not change temperature with age and they are optically more efficient because the filaments are smaller. The popular sizes are 12 V/100 W, 24 V/150 W and 24 V/250 W.

The slide is inserted between the lens and the heat filter, or where no filter is fitted between lens and condensor. The simplest form of shift carrier is of the push–pull type. It has two apertures so that, while one slide is being projected, another is being inserted in the other slot or aperture and then pushed into place when required. The previous slide comes out on the other side for removal.

This is a somewhat tedious business when there are many slides to show, so the majority of modern projectors have a carrier that holds thirty-six or fifty slides and these are pre-loaded. The carrier then moves forward automatically as each slide is shown. Another version is in a circular form and may take about eighty slides in one loading. This type permits continuous projection, which is useful for some commercial purposes. Provision is made on more advanced projectors for removing any one slide for separate examination and this overcomes an early objection to carrier projectors. Some people even use the carriers as a filing system, which saves the trouble of loading up before a show, but it is rather an expensive method of filing.

On most projectors there is provision for reversing the carriage in order to go back to a slide previously shown, and on many there is a remote control that enables the operator to control the advance or reverse from a distance. Many also have provision in the remote control for focusing by means of a button operating a small electric motor built into the projector. There are some models that have completely automatic focusing by means of a light beam which is beamed onto the transparency and reflected back to a two-part photocell. When the beam does not fall equally on each part, the motor adjusts the lens until it does.

All but the smallest and cheapest projectors have electrically driven fans that direct a current of air upwards through the slide chamber, and these are generally very quiet in operation. It is most important to ensure that the projector is clear of any obstruction so that there is a free ingress of air. Propping it up on books instead of standing it flat on its own legs may well block up the entrance with disastrous results.

Another feature found in good projectors is a masking device so that the screen is blacked out during a slide change. Without this the audience is subjected to a brightly lit screen between each slide, and this makes the slides appear less brilliant. It is also rather tiring.

Sound slide projection

The addition of sound to a slide show is becoming increasingly popular, largely due to the efficiency of modern tape-recorders, and the tape can be made to effect the slide changes. In one method the tape runs over a synchroniser attached to the tape-recorder and short strips of metal are spliced into the tape at the points where a change is required. When the metal passes over contacts connected to the remote control of the projector, the circuit is closed and the slide changes.

There is also a more sophisticated method in which the slide change signals are recorded electrically on the tape. If it is recorded on the second track of a twin-track recorder, it will be inaudible and the position of the signals can be changed at any time if required.

In recent years a number of enthusiasts have started employing two projectors so that a picture from one projector can be lapped, faded or dissolved in over the slide in the other projector as that one is faded out. The sequence can also be controlled by pulses, this time on a four-track tape, and the presentation is thus very polished and professional. However, some of its exponents prefer to do the changes by hand so that the speed of the overlaps can be varied. At least one system uses iris diaphragms in front of the lenses in order to obtain slow or fast fades and dissolves at will.

Projection screens

A good screen is essential if slides are to be seen at their best. A wall is no substitute as it is too absorbent and is, in any case, not always white or in a convenient place. Screens can be obtained for hanging from the picture rail or for permanent erection, but by far the most convenient for home use is the portable type which rolls up and has a folding stand. There is also a self-erecting type which rolls out of a box that can be stood on a table or other convenient support. Most folding or self-erecting screens have two positions: one gives the correct format for cine projection and the other is square in order to take 35 mm slides horizontally or upright.

There are three types of surface in general use: matt-white, lenticular and glass-beaded. Matt-white screens are the cheapest and are made of fairly opaque cloth. They can be viewed from a wide angle without a noticeable loss of brilliance, so they are useful in large rooms or where people have to sit at an angle to them.

Lenticular screens have minute vertical and horizontal ridges and hollows which act like a myriad of tiny lenses that have great reflective properties, so a brilliant image results. They are usually painted silver and also have a good viewing angle but, of course, they are much more expensive than matt-white screens.

Glass-beaded screens have myriads of tiny crystal glass beads impregnated in the canvas surface. They are by far the most efficient in terms of brilliance, but they are very directional and the full benefit is only seen by those sitting at no greater angle than about 20° from the centre. At a greater angle the apparent brilliance falls off rapidly, but it is still better than a matt-white screen, even at 35°. Beaded screens are therefore ideal for long, narrow rooms but not so good for domestic use if a number of people are to be seated in an average sitting-room. They have to be stored when not in use because the surface tends to turn yellow if exposed to daylight for long periods.

A cheaper version uses plastic beads instead of glass. It is naturally not so efficient but is considerably better than matt-white. At one time screens treated with silver or aluminium paint were popular, but they are not good for colour and so are now almost obsolete, except in the case of lenticular screens where colour is not affected because of the surface construction.

Mounting slides

35 mm transparencies are returned from the processors mounted ready for projection unless otherwise ordered. Kodak returns Kodachrome transparencies in 2 in × 2 in cardboard mounts that are numbered consecutively from 1 to 36 in the order in

which they were taken. The other principal manufacturers, Agfa, Perutz and Fuji, return theirs in plastic mounts, which are neater and more rigid but are not numbered. In all cases the transparency itself is exposed and therefore vulnerable to dust, damp, fingermarks and scratches.

Although transparencies can be projected in this form, they are liable to 'pop' in the projector and this can be very irritating because it demands constant refocusing. All transparencies that are of any value and are going to be retained for long periods should be mounted in glass, especially if they are going to be projected or handled frequently.

There are many ingenious proprietary brands of mounts available, most of which are in the form of two thin plastic frames with very thin glasses. The transparency is placed in position, sometimes hooked on pegs that fit the perforations, and the two halves are clipped together. This type of mount is expensive but, on the other hand, it is re-usable and the transparency can be changed as often as required. The big disadvantages of proprietary mounts are that they are neither dustproof nor air-tight.

The most satisfactory, and the cheapest, mount is the one you make yourself. All the materials can be obtained at any photodealer's shop. Thin cover glasses cut exactly to size are obtainable in packets of 50 or 100 and masks cut from thin paper or metal foil hold the transparency in the right position. The sandwich of glass, transparency and glass is then bound with a thin binding tape sold especially for the purpose. You can even buy the tape already cut and with corners mitred. An inexpensive jig makes binding easy and accurate.

One type of cover glass has a finely etched surface which reduces the risk of Newton's rings. These are concentric bands of coloured light that sometimes form between the back of the film and the glass when they are not in perfect contact. This, of course, shows up on the screen.

Properly mounted in this way the transparency will remain dust-free for life and, provided that it was perfectly dry before mounting, it will also be protected from the fungus that can form on slides stored in humid conditions.

The masks already mentioned can be purchased with apertures to take 35 mm, 126, half-frame or 110 transparencies and also with special shapes like ovals, rhomboids, circles, etc. The latter should be avoided because they interrupt the smooth flow of a slide presentation. However, some masking is often justified to improve the composition of a picture. Landscapes are sometimes improved by masking to a narrow horizontal format and many architectural pictures are better for removing some of the foreground. Likewise, tree pictures, and even portraits, are occasionally improved by masking them to a tall and narrow format. It is essential, however, that the centre line of the picture corresponds to the centre line of the slide. Nothing is worse than a picture that appears off-centre, or to one side of the screen, only to be followed by one that 'leaps' to the other side. A narrow landscape can be slightly above the horizontal centre line, but its edges must reach the edge of the screen at each side or be an equal distance from each side.

Before mounting, the transparency should be kept for a while in a warm (not hot) place, say above a radiator, for an hour or two to remove any residual damp. It and the cover glasses should be gently cleaned with an anti-static cloth or brush. Do not breathe on them or try to blow dust away—it will merely put moisture back into the emulsion. Never use any binding tape except that sold especially for the purpose. Under the influence of projector heat other tapes may dry up and come off or, worse still, ooze gum.

Every slide should be marked so that the projectionist knows which way to insert it in the gate or carrier. It is disturbing to the flow of a slide show when a picture appears upside down, on its side or reversed left to right. There are actually eight ways in which a slide can be inserted and only one is right.

The universally accepted system is to put a small white spot about a $\frac{1}{4}$ in diameter in the bottom left-hand corner when looking at the transparency the right way up and the right way round.

The projectionist, standing behind the projector, inserts the slide with this spot appearing at the top right corner, i.e. under his thumb, and the picture then appears the right way up on the screen.

Fig. 27   The way to spot a slide. With the picture the right way up and the right way round, the spot is placed in the bottom left-hand corner. The spot should come under the operators thumb when inserting the slide in the carrier or projector, i.e. with the picture upside down but the right way left to right.

Gummed spots can be bought in different colours and with consecutive numbers printed on them. They are inclined to come off if stuck on the glass, so it is better to stick them on the paper mask before the slide is mounted. It is also a good idea to put titles, name and address or any other required data on the mask rather than on the outside of the slide. Strips and spots that become detached can foul up the projector mechanism, and if slides are entered for competitions they may get lost or disqualified.

Some of the available ready-cut binding strips are black with a white strip or line arranged to appear on one side of one edge. This is an alternative to spotting, and the tape should be arranged so that the white strip appears along the bottom edge when the transparency is the right way up and the right way round. It is inserted in the projector with the white line at the top and facing away from the screen.

The total thickness of the slide should not be more than 0·125 in, but this is no problem if the materials sold for the purpose are used. It is not normally possible to bind card-mounted transparencies like Kodachromes between two cover glasses without removing the card because the 'sandwich' will be too thick for most projectors. It also leaves an undesirable air space on each side of the film.

The plastic mounts in which some makes of transparency are returned are white on one side and coloured on the other. The white side should face the rear when inserting them in the projector, but it will still be necessary to spot each slide to avoid putting it in the right way up, which will cause it to appear up-side down on the screen.

Storage of slides is important. There are many boxes and magazines available that keep the slides separated from each other, and the only essential requirement is that they are kept in a dry place. Damp and humidity is the enemy of all photographic emulsions because it encourages mould and bacteria to form in the gelatin. Slides should not be left exposed to daylight, especially sunlight, for long periods as there is a tendency for the fugitive dyes to fade.

When a show is made up it is convenient to store the slides in the correct order and the right way up in a suitable magazine or box. If a line is painted diagonally across the top edges it will be very easy to reassemble them in the correct order should they become separated or mixed up. A dab of nail varnish on each slide is good for this purpose.

Making up a show

When selecting slides to make up a show, even just for friends at home, and whether they are of holiday, travel or specialist interest, it is necessary to be absolutely ruthless and reject any

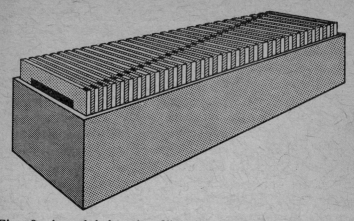

Fig. 28   A good dodge when filing slides is to paint a line across the top at a diagonal. It will then be easy to rearrange them in the right order if they get mixed up.

slides that are under- or overexposed, however important the subject matter may seem to be. Jumping from dense to thin slides is very irritating for the audience. The subject matter should be arranged in a logical or chronological sequence and there should never be more than one slide of a particular scene, however good the other shots taken at the same time may be.

As a general rule, a presentation should not exceed 100 slides, otherwise the audience will get fidgety or picture-drunk. Except for slides that require special comment or contain some important reading matter, no picture should remain on the screen for more than 20 seconds at the maximum. It is a good idea to introduce some variation by giving a picture full of detail more screen time than a close-up portrait, while a slide of a simple subject like a single flower could have even less.

Title slides give a professional touch. These can be made by lettering in black or in colour on plain white card, and adhesive letters like Letraset make this easy. The artwork is then photo-graphed and the resulting transparency can be bound in with another. For example, 'Our holiday in Greece' bound in contact with a picture of the Acropolis will set the right atmosphere from the start. Something similar can be made for the 'End' or 'Finis' slide, as well as for intermediate title slides when there is a change of subject.

A tape-recorder or record-player can be used to create an impressive atmosphere by playing appropriate music or sound-effects. Music that is typical of the country being depicted in a holiday show can be augmented at the start with the sound of an aircraft taking off. Bird pictures can be accompanied by bird calls, cars with horns blowing, etc.—the possibilities are endless. There are no problems with copyright if the music is not played in public. Most gramophone dealers now sell records of common sounds, animal noises, bird calls, trains approaching and receding, sirens wailing, thunder claps, etc., and it is easy to transfer the required parts to a continuous tape.

It is a courtesy to an audience to prepare a show in advance with the projector in position and ready focused. The carrier should be loaded into the projector with the first slide in place so that nothing is needed but to switch on. Never be diffident about showing slides and don't reluctantly drag them out when the room is already full of smoke. Have some background music playing when guests arrive, see that the room is properly blacked out, and get on with it in a meaningful and professional manner. The slides will be appreciated all the more.

Further reading

Projection Tailormade, Ernst Leitz.

Bibliography

Photographic periodicals

Weekly

Amateur Photographer. Caters for all amateur interests in still and cine photography. Published by IPC Business Press, Surrey House, 1 Throwley Way, Sutton, Surrey SM1 4QQ.

Monthly

Photography. General interest magazine with an emphasis on colour and competitions for amateurs. *Model and Allied Publications*, 13 Bridge St., Hemel Hempstead, Herts. HP1 1EE.

Photo-Technique. General interest magazine mainly appealing to the technically minded amateur. Penblade Publishers, 93 Sirdar Road, London W11 4EQ.

Practical Photography. General interest but emphasis on do-it-yourself and practical aspects. East Midlands Allied Press Ltd., Park House, Bretton Court, Bretton Centre, Peterborough PE3 8DZ.

S.L.R. Camera. General interest for amateurs but dealing almost exclusively with single-lens-reflex cameras. Haymarket Publishing Ltd., Craven House, 34 Fouberts Place, London W1.

Annual

B.J. Annual. Contains a large selection of the year's best pictures plus technical features and a section giving basic formulae. H. Greenwood & Co., 24 Wellington Street, London EC2E 7DH.

Photography Year Book. Devoted entirely to reproductions of good pictures in black and white and colour, amateur and professional. Argus Press Limited, 14 St. James Road, Watford, Herts.

Das Deutsche Lichtbild. D.S.P. Verlag Stuttgart. A representative collection of the best of European photography.

Elementary books of general interest

The All-in-One Camera Book, Walter Emmanuel, Focal Press.
Starting Photography, M. Langford, Focal Press.
The Practical Photographer, E. A. Weber, Fountain Press.

Index

There can be few contemporary novelists who, with an output as small in quantity as that of Richard Hughes, made so positive a mark and established so large a literary reputation.

Born in 1900, he was the contemporary of such literary figures as Yeats and Robert Graves, and compatriots Augustus John and Dylan Thomas. While still at Oxford, he had a play produced in London and a book of poems published.

His first novel, *A High Wind in Jamaica*, was published in 1929 to ecstatic praise and is now established as a classic novel of childhood which has 'influenced twentieth-century feeling about children as decisively as Freud'.

In 1938 Richard Hughes' second novel, *In Hazard*, was published. This had been called 'one of the best sea stories ever written'. *The Fox in the Attic*, the first volume in his planned trilogy, *The Human Predicament*, appeared in 1961, followed in 1973 by the second volume, *The Wooden Shepherdess*.

Richard Hughes also wrote short stories, children's stories, poems and plays. His achievements won him election as an Honorary Member of the American Academy which rated him among the fifty most distinguished non-American writers, painters and musicians.

Richard Hughes died in 1976 and is survived by Frances Bazley, the painter, whom he married in 1932, five children and eleven grandchildren.

Also by Richard Hughes
A High Wind in Jamaica
In Hazard
The Wooden Shepherdess
    (Vol. II of *The Human Predicament*)

Children's Stories
The Spider's Palace
Don't Blame Me

Short Stories
A Moment of Time
In the Lap of Atlas

Poems
Confessio Juvenis

Drama
The Sisters' Tragedy
A Comedy of Good and Evil
The Man Born to be Hanged
Danger

Richard Hughes

The Fox in the Attic

TRIAD PANTHER

Published in 1979 by Triad/Panther Books
Frogmore, St Albans, Herts AL2 2NF

ISBN 0 586 04883 9

Triad Paperbacks Ltd is an imprint of
Chatto, Bodley Head & Jonathan Cape Ltd and
Granada Publishing Ltd

First published in Great Britain by
Chatto and Windus Ltd 1961
Copyright © Richard Hughes 1961

Set, printed and bound in Great Britain by
Cox & Wyman Ltd, Reading
Set in Intertype Times

This book is sold subject to the condition that it
shall not, by way of trade or otherwise, be lent,
re-sold, hired out or otherwise circulated
without the publisher's prior consent in any
form of binding or cover other than that in
which it is published and without a similar
condition including this condition being imposed
on the subsequent purchaser.

NOTE

The Human Predicament is conceived as a long historical novel of my own times culminating in the Second World War. The fictitious characters in the foreground are wholly fictitious. The historical characters and events are as accurately historical as I can make them: I may have made mistakes but in no case have I deliberately falsified the record once I could worry it out.

The reader may wonder why a novel designed as a continuous whole rather than as a trilogy or quartet should appear volume by volume: the plain truth is I am such a slow writer that I have been urged not to wait.

R. H.

TO MY WIFE

and also my children
(especially Penelope)
in affectionate gratitude
for their help

Contents

BOOK ONE

Polly and Rachel

Chapter 1

Only the steady creaking of a flight of swans disturbed the
silence, labouring low overhead with outstretched necks towards the sea.

It was a warm, wet, windless afternoon with a soft feathery
feeling in the air: rain, yet so fine it could scarcely fall but
rather floated. It clung to everything it touched; the rushes
in the deep choked ditches of the sea-marsh were bowed
down with it, the small black cattle looked cobwebbed with
it, their horns were jewelled with it. Curiously stumpy too
these cattle looked, the whole herd sunk nearly to the knees
in a soft patch.

This sea-marsh stretched for miles. Seaward, a greyness
merging into sky had altogether rubbed out the line of dunes
which bounded it that way: inland, another and darker
blurred greyness was all you could see of the solid Welsh
hills. But near by loomed a solitary gate, where the path
crossed a footbridge and humped over the big dyke; and
here in a sodden tangle of brambles the scent of a fox hung,
too heavy today to rise or dissipate.

The gate clicked sharply and shed its cascade as two men
passed through. Both were heavily loaded in oilskins. The
elder and more tattered one carried two shotguns, negligently, and a brace of golden plover were tied to the bit of old
rope he wore knotted round his middle: glimpses of a
sharp-featured weather-beaten face showed from within his
bonneted sou'-wester, but mouth and even chin were hidden
in a long weeping moustache. The younger man was springy
and tall and well-built and carried over his shoulder the
body of a dead child. Her thin muddy legs dangled against
his chest, her head and arms hung down his back; and at his

heels walked a black dog – disciplined, saturated, and eager.

Suddenly the older man blew through the curtain of his moustache as if to clear it of water before speaking, but he thought better of it after a quick glance round at his companion. There was no personal grief in the young man's face but it was awestruck.

An hour later the two men had left the sea-marsh behind them: they had reached higher ground where a lofty but tangled and neglected wood traversed a steep hillside. So soft was this south-western Welsh climate, and so thick the shelter of all that towering timber round, that here a glade of very old azaleas planted in a clearing had themselves grown almost into gangling trees and dripping rhododendron-scrub had spread half across what had once been a broad gravelled carriage-drive. Deep black ruts showed where in the war years the steel tyres of heavy farm-wagons had broken through the crust of this long-derelict drive; but nowadays in places the roadway was blocked altogether with newly-fallen trunks and branches that nothing could pass.

Soon however the two men turned off by a short-cut, a steep footpath squeezed between a ferny rock the size of a cottage and a watery plantation of twenty-foot bamboos.

Beyond the bamboos their path tunnelled under a seemingly endless ancient growth of rhododendrons and they had to duck, for though the huge congested limbs of this dark thicket had once been propped on crutches to give the path full headroom many of these were now rotten and had collapsed. At the very centre of this grove the tunnel passed by a small stone temple; but here too the brute force of vegetation was at work, for the clearing had closed in, the weather-pocked marble faun lay face down in the tangle of ivy which had fallen with him, the little shrine itself now wore its cupola awry. Thus it was not till the two men had travelled the whole length of this dark and dripping tunnel and finally reached the further border of all this abandoned

12

woodland that they really came right out again at last under the open whitish sky.

Here, a flight of vast garden terraces had been cut in the hillside like giant stairs. Downwards, these terraces led to a vista of winding waterlily lakes and distant park with a far silver curl of river: upwards, they mounted to a house. The walking figures of the two men and the dog, ascending, and presently turning right-handed along the topmost of these terraces, looked surprisingly small against that house – almost like toys, for this ancient pile was far larger than you had taken it for at first. Nevertheless there was no hum from this huge house, no sign of life even: not one open window, nor a single curl of smoke from any of its hundred chimneys. The men's sodden boots on the stone paving made little sound, but there was none other.

This topmost terrace ended at a tall hexagonal Victorian orangery projecting rather incongruously from the older building, the clear lights in its Gothic cast-iron traceries deep-damasked here and there with dark panes of red and blue Bristol. In the angle this projection made with the main structure a modest half-glazed door was set in the house's ancient stone-work, and here at last the two men halted: the young man with the small body over his shoulder took charge of the guns as well and sent the furtive, feral-looking older man away. Then the young man with the burden and the wet dog went in by themselves, and the door closed with a hollow sound.

Chapter 2

Augustine was the young man's name (the dog's name I forget).

Augustine had the thick white skin which often goes with such sandy red hair as his, the snub lightly-freckled nose, the broad intelligent forehead. Normally this young face was serene; but now it was beginning to show the first effects of shock and for a full minute he stood stockstill in his dewy oilskins, staring round the familiar walls of this warm and cosy room with new and seemingly astonished eyes. Then Augustine's dilated pupils focused – fascinated, as if seeing for the first time – on his great-grandfather's gun. This stood in the place of honour in the tall glass-fronted case which was the room's chief furnishing: a beautiful double-barrelled hammer-gun damascened with silver, its blue-black barrels worn paper-thin with firing. Pinned to the wooden back of the case behind it there was an old photograph of someone short and bushy standing with this very gun over his arm; and with him two bowler-hatted keepers, equally bushy. The print was faded to a browny-yellow, but now as Augustine's abnormal gaze lit on it the faint figures seemed to him to clarify and grow – to take on for him an advisory look. At that his gaze widened to include the whole family of these beloved guns racked in that great glass gunroom case there: guns of all calibres from rook-rifles and a boy's 20-bore by Purdey to a huge 4-bore punt-gun: grouped round the veteran, they too now seemed veritable councillors.

Then his eyes shifted. In a corner of the room stood the collection of his fishing-rods. Their solid butts were set in a cracked Ming vase like arrows in a quiver; but he felt now as if their wispy twitching ends were tingling, like antennae

– *his* antennae. Above them the mounted otters'-masks on the peeling walls grinned. The tiny wisp of steam from the ever-simmering kettle on the round coke-stove seemed to be actively inviting the brown teapot that stood on the shelf above – the loaf, and the knife, and the pot of jam. In short, these guns and rods of his, and even the furniture, the kettle and the loaf had suddenly become living tentacles of 'him'. It was as if he and this long-loved gunroom were now one living continuous flesh. It was as if for the time being 'he' was no longer cooped up entirely within his own skin : he had expanded, and these four walls had become now his final envelope. Only outside these walls did the hostile, alien 'world' begin.

All this passed in a matter of seconds : then mentally Augustine shook himself, aware that his state was more than a little abnormal and reminded at the same time of that dead mite of alien world he had brought in here and carried on his shoulder still.

An old lancet window suggested this had been a domestic chapel once; all the same, not even for a moment could he put her down in *here*.

In the middle of the room a round oak table stood nowadays; but under the morning's crumbs, under the oilstains where for years guns had been cleaned on it and under the bloodstains where game had been rested on it there were still discernible faded inkstains and blurred inscriptions and knife-cuts from its earlier days in the schoolroom. As Augustine moved towards it to lay the guns down his own initials, 'A.L.P.-H.', suddenly leapt out at him from the dark wood, pricked there with his compass-points and coloured (he recalled) one drowsy morning in the schoolroom long ago — in imitation of Henry, his godlike elder cousin. For though this house had not been actually his childhood home, much of Augustine's childhood had in fact been spent here : from his earliest age his two old great-uncles used to invite him on prolonged visits, as company for Henry chiefly . . . ah, now Henry's 'H.P.-H.' had leaped out of the smudges too (ten times more elegantly tattooed than his, of course).

That little Purdey 20-bore behind the glass (momentarily it stood out from the background of its fellows as the figure in a painted portrait does) had been Henry's first gun. When Henry quite grew out of it, it had descended to teach Augustine too to shoot. That of course was before 1914: in the halcyon days before the war when the two old men were still living and *Henry* was the heir.

Augustine, still humping the little body, moved towards the telephone bracketed to the wall behind the door. This was a peculiar apparatus, evidently built to order. It had two hinged ear-pieces, installed one on each side in case one ear or the other should be deaf; and it was ancient enough to have a handle to wind. Augustine wound the handle and asked for the police, addressing the instrument in the tone-less but very articulate manner habitual to someone a solitary by his own act and choice who prefers to use his voice as seldom and as briefly as he can.

Then the machine answered him. The upshot was that the sergeant would come out this evening on his bicycle to view, but doubted he could get an ambulance to fetch it till the morning. For tonight it must just stay where it was.

When at last (in a remote and half-darkened formal place of elegance, a room he never used) Augustine did lift the morsel off his shoulder, he found that it had stiffened. This had ceased to be 'child' at all: it was total cadaver now. It had taken into its soft contours the exact mould of the shoulder over which it had been doubled and it had set like that – into a matrix of *him*. If (which God forbid) he had put it on again it would have fitted.

Augustine was absolutely alone with it in all this huge, empty house. He left it dumped there on the big dust-sheeted drawing-room sofa and hurried across the silent stone hall to wash his creeping hands.

Chapter 3

For a while, cleaning the two guns and towelling the dog took all Augustine's attention; but then he was at a loss till the sergeant should come. He craved for and gulped a spoonful of sugar but otherwise could not eat because he had become aware of his hands again : they felt large, and as if he had not washed them *enough*. Indeed he was loth to taint with them even the pages of a book.

In this dilemma he wandered from the gunroom almost without knowing it into the billiard room. This smelt of old carpeting and perished leather; it was a place he seldom went these days, but unlike most of the rest of the house it was unshuttered and now there was still enough of the failing daylight in here to see by.

Billiard rooms are never small. In childhood this one used to seem to Augustine as interminable as the vaults of heaven : it had always been a room of wonder, moreover, for what might not happen in a room where a rhinoceros – lurking in an Africa that must have been just behind the plaster – had thrust head and horn clean through the wall? (Often as a small thing he had peeped in fearfully before breakfast to find if during the night that rhinoceros in his wooden collar had inched any further through.)

This had been a man's room, which no woman except housemaids ever entered. So traditionally, it had given asylum to everything in the house no woman of taste or delicacy could stand; and Augustine himself had altered nothing. The paint was a sour chocolate brown. The chairs and settees were uniformly covered in leather. This faded purple leather covered even the top of a kind of stool made from a huge elephant's-trotter (Great-uncle William had ridden the beast in battle or shot it in the chase, Augustine could never remember which).

In a tall china-cabinet here there were some lovely pieces of porcelain – Sèvres, Wedgwood, Dresden, Worcester – and other exquisite objects too: a large conch in silver-gilt, engraved with the royal arms of the Wittelsbachs and held out invitingly by a nymph: again, a delicate tureen-like receptacle in Pacific tortoiseshell which had stood (so the printed card stated) in the cabin of Captain Cook. You wondered, perhaps, to see such beauties banished here – till you realized that this was Uncle William's unique collection of rare spittoons.

But there was even worse here than leather and brown paint and china of equivocal uses. The engravings on the walls for instance: if you looked at them closely and with not too innocent an eye you found they tended to be coarse – or even French.

Those two good old Tory bachelors, those noble Victorian figures – Great-uncle Arthur! Great-uncle William! Indeed what a powder-magazine of schoolboy naughtiness it had pleased them to sit on, in here! Hardly anything in this room was quite what it seemed at first sight. That ribbed-glass picture looked at first just an innocent rustic scene, but as you walked past you saw from the tail of your eye the billy-goat going incessantly in and out, in and out. Again, the top of that elephant-foot stool was hinged, and lifted. Absently, Augustine lifted it now: it housed a commode of course, and there was a dead spider in it; but until this very moment he had never noticed that under the spider and the dust you could just descry, printed in green under the glaze on the bottom of the china pot, the famous – the execrated face of Gladstone.

That had been typical of the fanatical way those two Tory old children felt about *Liberals*. Their treatment of Augustine's own father was a case in point. Though a Conservative himself he had married the daughter of a house traditionally Whig and for this he had never been forgiven, never asked here again. Thus Augustine's own childhood

18

visits here had always been paid either alone or with a nurse. As if the taint was one clinging to the female line, even his elder sister Mary had never once been asked here to Newton Llantony (in fairness for this deprivation, Mary had been sent alone to spend one whole summer holiday in Germany, where they had cousins. That must have been 1913: she was to have gone again, only next year the Kaiser invaded Belgium and the war came).

In addition to improper pictures, many of the lesser family portraits were hung here in this billiard room – 'lesser' in the sense that either the sitter or the painter was better forgotten: black sheep and frail ladies; and the pseudo-Lely, the Academy rejects. But as soon as Augustine's father had married a Liberal, even the lovely drawing Rossetti had done of him as an infant angel with a tabor could no longer be hung anywhere at all at Newton Llantony – not even in here! Augustine had lately found this drawing hidden away upstairs in his grandmother's bedroom drawer: whereas Henry's portrait, posthumously painted by a limited company from photographs – that vast act of worship in oil-paint hung over the fireplace in the largest drawing-room.

Henry even while he lived had been the apple of every eye. The uncles had built him his own squash-court: when he was killed at Ypres in permanent mourning for him the court was not played in any more: it became where the larger stuffed animals were housed, including a giraffe.

So much bitter fanaticism in those two old Tories: yet in practice so much actual kindness to many, including Augustine himself – the 'Liberal Woman's' child! The two things seemed hard to reconcile. Over the carved autumnal marbles of the empty fireplace there hung a huge presentation portrait of Uncle Arthur as Master, his otterhounds grouped around him; so Augustine fell to studying the face now, in the gloaming, in the hope of discovering its secret. But all it showed was that years of concentration on the animal had made the Master himself grow so like an otter

19

it was a wonder his own hounds had not rent him, Actaeon-wise. And Uncle William? The only portrait of him here was a small lady-like watercolour in full uniform painted by an artistic colour-sergeant at Hong Kong. It showed the General's eye large and liquid as a Reynolds cherub's, the rounded cheek as innocent (there can have been no Liberals in Hong Kong for Uncle William to look so much at peace).

The sky was darkening, but the mist seemed to have cleared now: through the tall uncurtained window what seemed like a single low star suddenly winked out, blurred only by the runnels on the glass.

Augustine raised the sash. That 'star' must be the lamps in distant Flemton being lit (Flemton was a little mediaeval rock-citadel eight miles away guarding the river mouth: a kind of Welsh Mont-St-Michel, or miniature Gibraltar). For a minute or two he stood watching, his solid height silhouetted against the window, what little daylight remained illumining his freckled, sensitive, sensible young face. But although his thoughts were distracted now, his features still wore the imprint of the shock he had had – like yesterday's footprints still discernible on dewy grass.

Chapter 4

Uncle Arthur the otter and Uncle William the faded general
... Augustine had been fond of both old men when he was a
child, and he warmed to their memory now – but fond of
them as objects rather than as people, for what grotesques
they were! Too old even for billiards in the end, they had
sat here day-in day-out winter and summer one each side of
a roaring fire while dust settled on the cover of the ever-
shrouded table. Uncle Arthur was stone deaf in the left ear,
hard of hearing in the right: Uncle William stone deaf in
the right ear, hard of hearing in the left (hence that peculiar
custom-built telephone). Both used enormous ear-trumpets:
Uncle William was nearly blind too, so used a powerful
monocle as well.

Suddenly it struck Augustine with force: how was it so
great a gulf divided his own from every previous generation, so that they seemed like different species?

The kind of Time called 'History' ended at the Battle of
Waterloo: after that, Time had gone into a long dark
tunnel or chrysalis called the Victorian Age. It had come
out into daylight again at the Present Day, but as something quite different: it was as impossible to imagine one-
self born a Victorian or born in 'History' as ... as born a
puma.

But wherein did the difference demonstrably lie? For the
moment he could not get beyond his starting-point that all
previous generations had been objects, whereas *his* were
people: that is, what mattered were their insides – what
they thought, what they felt. Not their outsides at all: the
natural face in the shaving-glass was not *him*, only the invisible mind and the erupting ego within it ranked as *him*.
Whereas those ... those ancient objects his uncles and their

generation were outsides only: hollow bundles of behaviourist gestures, of stylized reactions to stimuli like Pavlov's dogs. Their only 'reality' was the grotesques they looked, the grotesqueries they did.—Take Uncle William's story of old Sir Rhydderch Prydderch, a neighbour said to have torn out his staircase at the age of seventy and thereafter swarmed up a rope every night to go to bed: had such a grotesque any reality *except* as an imagined spectacle halfway up a rope?

Or take the story of that disastrous fox-hunt (it had been Uncle Arthur speaking this time, sitting on Augustine's little bed one evening and feeding him with bread-and-milk). Wolves, imported by a noble Polish exile to make his new Pembrokeshire home more homelike, were alleged to have crossed with the local foxes and brought forth monstrous hybrid young: hence, ultimately, Uncle Arthur's bedtime story of those little terrified figures in Pink clinging in trees with a pack of huge red ravening foxes howling underneath (the story had been told with relish, for the Master of Otterhounds had despised fox-hunters 'sitting dry-arse on their horses all day' almost as he had despised Liberals).

These particular grotesques were only hearsay, and perhaps even fabulous. But as well as his uncles there were plenty of other notable 'outsides' Augustine had seen among his elders with his own eyes. There was Dr Brinley, for instance: who was legendary, but living still. Dr Brinley was an aged adored fox-hunting coroner never even half sober even when on a horse. Once Augustine as a schoolboy had pulled off his cap in the High Street at Penrys Cross out of respect for the dead; but it proved to be the coroner not the corpse they were carrying into Court.

Another notable grotesque here had been the late rector: parson not person, a mere clerical keeper of pigs that used to get loose during Service. From his pulpit he could see into his rectory garden, and Sunday after Sunday what he saw there made him falter and repeat himself and then suddenly explode into a cry of *'Pigs!'* that startled strangers no end.

At that cry the rectory children (they had left the sty open deliberately of course) would rise and sidle out of their pew, bow to the altar before turning their backs on it, mince down the aisle with their muffs and prayer-books and Sunday hats . . . and the moment they were through the church door burst into loud whoops as they scampered off.

The late bishop (who had a beard like old Kruger's) came to luncheon here at Newton one day: it was 1916, and Henry was home on embarkation leave. The rector was there, but the reverend wits had now begun noticeably to fail and so Uncle Arthur asked the bishop himself to say Grace. The rector protested – etiquette was for *him* to say Grace, and he struggled to his feet. But after 'For what we are about to receive . . .' the usual form of words must have escaped him, for he stumbled on ex tempore: 'The plump chicken, the three excellent vegetables . . .' Then he sat down, seething with indignation and muttering what sounded like 'May the Lord in His mercy blast and braise us all!'

Next Sunday he announced from the pulpit a momentous discovery: Johns the Baptist and Evangelist were one and the same person! He was stuttering with excitement, but Augustine heard no more because Uncle William, startled at the news, dropped his eyeglass in his ear-trumpet and began fishing for it with a bunch of keys. Uncle Arthur in his senior corner of the family box-pew kept commenting 'Damn' young fool!' (he was unaware of the loudness of his own voice, of course) 'Oh the silly damn' fool!' then snatched the ear-trumpet from his brother's hand and dislodged the eyeglass by putting the trumpet to his lips and blowing a blast like the horn of Roland.

As the scene came back to him now Augustine burst out laughing in the echoing, comfortable room those two old men had made: which should have been Henry's: but which instead was his.

A breath of wind came through the opened window. In

the dusk something white fluttered off the marble fireplace shelf where it had been propped and Augustine struck a match to look at it. It was an engraved and emblazoned invitation-card:

The High Steward and Worshipful Court
of
FLEMTON
Request

– and then his name, and so on.

At the sight of that card his conscience pricked him; for the annual Banquet was tonight and he had not even remembered to answer. His two old uncles, of course, had attended the High Steward's Banquet yearly to the last; but wild horses could not drag Augustine to any function of that kind and surely the sooner people ceased even inviting him, the better! Bucolic banquets, flower-shows, the magistrate's bench, audit-days, hunt balls – the young squire of Newton was absolutely determined not to get 'involved'; and surely the neighbourhood ought to be only too thankful – nobody *wants* a Heavy Squire these days! In 1923 it's quite out of date. At the very least he wouldn't be missed: there are plenty of noisome little creatures who *like* doing that sort of thing. Thus he could feel his lip curl a little in derision – though quite involuntarily – as he turned himself in the dusk to contemplate once more that low fixed star which was all the lights of distant . . . of gregarious, festive Flemton.

For the moment he had clean forgotten what had just happened on the Marsh; and yet in his face that look of yesterday's footmarks had still persisted even while he laughed.

Chapter 5

Flemton, the object of Augustine's mild involuntary
derision . . .

That long line of dunes dividing the seven-mile stretch of
sea-marsh from the sea ended in a single precipitous penin-
sular outcrop of rock, and this was washed by the mouth of
a small smelly tidal river which served as creek still for a
few coasting smacks (though the trade was already dying).
The tiny, unique self-governing township of Flemton was
crowded right on top of this rock, the peeling yellow stucco
of its Regency houses bulging out over its mediaeval walls
like ice-cream from a cornet.

This was Flemton's great night – the night of the banquet
– and now the rain had stopped. Princes Street was de-
corated: Chinese lanterns hung in the pollarded limes:
signal-flags and other bunting, coloured tablecloths, tanned
sails, even gay petticoats and Sunday trousers streamed
from some of the poorer windows. The roadway milled with
happy citizenry hoping for a fight presently but not yet:
little Jimmy-the-pistol was bicycling up and down among
them letting off rockets from his handlebars, the pocket of
his jacket on fire.

Moreover the aged, famous Dr Brinley had driven himself over early from Penrys Cross along the sands in his
pony-trap. Dr Brinley knew Flemton of old: each elegant,
rotting, fungusy house and the men, women and children
who swarmed in them. He saw all these people as he tended
to see the whole world – and indeed, as the world too saw
him – with a heightening, Hogarthian eye; but he loved them
and needed them none the less. The scene tonight was meat
and drink to Dr Brinley and he paused to enjoy it.

A group of women in the middle of Princes Street had

their heads together: 'Can't think where that Dai of mine has got to,' Mrs Dai Roberts was saying.

She seemed to speak with difficulty. 'That woman has mislaid her false teeth and the ones she has borrowed are a poor fit,' thought Dr Brinley in the shadows, chuckling.

'Down on the Marsh, shooting with Mr Augustine he was very usual,' said a yellow-haired young man with a hare-lip: 'Happen they've stopped on for the evening flight.'

'My Dai'll never give the Banquet a miss, I know that!' said Mrs Roberts.

'Will Mr Augustine be attending this year, Mrs Roberts, do you know?' a woman asked her diffidently.

Mrs Roberts spat like a man and returned no other answer; but the quivering of her goitre made her look like an angry turkey and the others took their cue:

'It's a crying shame,' said someone.

'Shut away in that great house all alone – it's not natural,' said another.

'Clean mental, to my way of thinking,' said someone else. Then she lowered her voice a little: 'There's mentality in the blood, they say.'

'Mentality!' exclaimed Mrs Roberts contemptuously: 'Wickedness you mean!' Then she too lowered her voice to a sinister tone: 'Why for should he shut hisself away like that *if his life was fit to be seen*?'

A knowing and a scandalized look descended on them all:

'Flying in the face of Almighty God!'

'Enough to bring his uncles back from the grave.'

There was a brief pause. Then:

'Poor young Mr Henry . . . Pity *he* got hisself killed in that old war.'

'The little duck! I seen him guv his bath once, the little angel! Loviest little bit of meat . . .'

'Aye, it's always that way: while them as *could* be spared . . .'

'*Rotten* old Kayser!'

'Still: if most days he's out shooting with your Dai . . .'

26

' "Days"! But what about the *nights*, Mrs Pritchard? Answer me that!'

Mrs Pritchard evidently couldn't.

Dr Brinley strolled on, but now another early arrival had paused for breath after the steep ascent. This was the new bishop, whose first visit to Flemton it was. Meanwhile the talk had been continuing:

'*All alone there with no one to see – it just don't bear thinking on!*'

'*I wouldn't go near the place – not if you paid me.*'

'*Quite right, Mrs Locarno! Nor I wouldn't neither!*'

'*Not even by daylight I wouldn't!*'

The bishop sighed, closing his fine eyes. These unhappy women! So palpably striving to warm their own several loneliness and unlikeability at the fires of some common hatred . . . They were closing in like a scrum now – huddling over the little hellish warmth they had kindled, and hissing their words. But why this anathema against solitariness? 'Women who have failed to achieve companionship in their homes, in their marriages: women with loneliness thrust upon them, I suppose they're bound to be outraged by anyone who deliberately *chooses* loneliness.'

A man of orderly mind, the bishop liked to get things generalized and taped like that. Now, his generalization achieved, the tension in his dark face relaxed a little.

Meanwhile Dr Brinley had poked in his nose at the 'Wreckers' Arms' (as he always called the place). Here, and in the Assembly Room behind, preparation of the banquet was going ahead with equal enjoyment whether their rich neighbour Augustine was going to honour them with his presence or not.

All that morning, while the tide was out, farm carts from the mainland had driven down the river bank to where the track ended at a wide bight of smooth hard tidal sand. This divided the last stretch of low-water river-channel from the saltings of the Marsh; traversing the length of it, they had reached the final sickle of the dunes and the way up into Flemton. These carts had carried chickens, geese, turkeys, even whole sheep; or at least a sack of flour or a crock of butter, for the High Steward's Banquet was something of a Dutch treat and few of the guests came quite empty-handed.

But that was over, now. Now, the evening tide had welled in through the river mouth and round behind the rock, flooding the sandy bight and turning it from Flemton's only highway into a vast shallow lagoon. In the dark the shining water was dotted with little boats nodding at anchor and the slanting poles of fish-traps. Flemton was now cut off, except for an isthmus of hummocky sand leading only to the dunes. But already ducks, chickens, geese, turkeys, legs and shoulders of mutton, loins of pork, sirloins of beef, sucking-pigs – there was far more provender than the Wreckers ever could have cooked alone, and according to custom it had been farmed out among all the private ovens in the place.

Now, with all these and with huge home-cured hams boiled in cider as well, with pans of sausages, apple-pies, shuddering jellies in purple and yellow, castellated blancmanges, bedroom jugs of congealed Bird's custard, buckets of boiled potatoes, basins of cabbage – every matron of Flemton was gathered in the Wreckers' big kitchen and full of jollity. Even a happy plumber and his mate had managed to choose this day to install the new sink, and were doggishly threatening the ladies' ankles with their hissing blowlamp.

Barrels of beer were discharging into every shape of jug and ewer.

When the female kitchen company caught sight of Dr Brinley they all hilariously shrieked together. He raised an arm in acknowledgment, then slipped quietly into the deserted bar from behind.

Chapter 6

Ostensibly Flemton banquet was an occasion for men only. Only men were invited, sat down at table, delivered speeches and sang songs. But the women cooked and waited, teased and scolded the banqueters, heckled the speeches and encored the songs if they felt like it; and the women certainly enjoyed it all quite as much as the men.

To tell the truth, the men were inclined to be a bit portentous and solemn. Indeed the only really happy and carefree male in the whole Assembly Room seemed to be that fabulous Dr Brinley the Coroner – who was eighty-five, and already very drunk, and knew that everybody loved him.

They had tried to steer Dr Brinley away from sitting next to the bishop, who was new to the mitre and fifty and cold teetotal: 'That seat's Mr Augustine's, Doctor *bach*: come you along this way . . .' But the old man looked round in astonishment: 'What! Is the boy actually coming, then?'

It was no good: he read the answer in their faces and sat down without more ado.

Presently the doctor nudged the bishop with his elbow, at the same time pointing dramatically across the table at a certain Alderman Teller. Alderman Teller was trying in vain to settle his huge chins into his unaccustomed high collar.

'Do you keep fowls, my lad?' the doctor asked: 'My *Lord* I *should* say: forgive an old man, laddie, tongue's taken to slipping.'

'Yes, yes,' said the bishop: 'That is . . . no: not now, but as a boy . . .'

Leaving his outstretched arm at the point as if he had forgotten it Dr Brinley turned even more confidentially towards the bishop, breathing at him a blast of whisky and old age: 'Then you're familiar with the spectacle of a very big broody hen trying to get down to work on a clutch of eggs in a bucket that's too narrow for her?' At this the bishop turned on him a face like a politely inquiring hatchet; but the doctor seemed to think he had made his point quite clearly enough.

Opposite, Alderman Teller – hearing, but also not catching the allusion – pushed an obstinate fold of jowl into his collar with his finger, then opened his little pink mouth and rolled his eyes solemnly. 'Perfect!' shouted Dr Brinley with a whoop of laughter. 'Your health, Alderman Teller dear lad!'

As they clinked glasses the alderman's face broke into a delighted smile as sweet as a child's: 'Rhode Islands, Doctor! That's what you ought to have, same as me. But you're right, they do tend to lay away.'

However the doctor was no longer listening. He had turned in his seat and was now pointing along the table at the High Steward himself. The High Steward, bashful in his seat of honour, was giving nervous little tugs at the gold chain of office hung round his neck. 'Penalty Five Pounds for Improper Use, Tom!' the doctor cried suddenly. 'And I doubt the banquet will stop for you, at that!'

This time the bishop's lip did twitch.

'Shut up, Doc,' muttered the High Steward, amiably but just a little nettled: 'You're bottled.' Then he turned round to look at the old man with a wonder not quite free of envy: 'Why – and we haven't even drunk "The King" yet!'

That was true. The bishop began counting the twenty or more toasts on the toast-list in front of him – a toast and a song alternately: with such a start, could Dr Brinley possibly last the course? *The King* . . . *The Immortal Memory of the Founder* . . . *The Fallen in the Great War* . . . Dr Brinley was down to sing 'Clementine' immediately after *The Fallen*, he saw. And then he noticed further down it was Dr Brinley who was to propose *The Lord Bishop*! In his missionary days in Africa he had attended some curious gatherings, but this bid fair . . . indeed he began to wonder if it had been prudent to accept.

'Glad you came,' said the old man suddenly – apropos of nothing, as if reading his thoughts – and patted him on the shoulder: 'Good lad! . . . Good *Lord*' he corrected himself under his breath, and chuckled.

Meanwhile, the banquet continued. The banqueters ate fast and in almost total silence: only Dr Brinley's sallies kept ringing out in quick succession. 'A kind of licensed jester, I suppose,' the bishop ruminated. 'But really! At *his* age!'

'My Lord,' said Dr Brinley, breathing whisky and bad teeth in his face again: 'I wonder would you help an old man in his difficulties, eh?' He pushed his face even closer, and waited for an answer open-mouthed.

'If I can . . .'

'Then tell me something very naughty you did as a little nipper.'

The bishop's indrawn breath was almost a gasp – for memory had taken him quite unawares. 'A blow below the apron,' the doctor thought, reading his gasp, and chuckled: 'No, laddie – not that one,' he said aloud: 'Nothing really shaming . . . just something for a good laugh when I come to speak to your health.'

'You must give me time to think,' the bishop said evenly. That sudden ancient recollection of real wrong-doing unexpiated had shaken him, and he was too sincere a man to force a smile about it. – But was 'a good laugh' *quite* . . .?

'They'll like you all the better for it,' the old man cajoled, as if yet again reading his thoughts.

But there the matter rested, for someone was forcing his way through the crowd of women serving – the coroner was wanted on the phone. The police at Penrys Cross, it was; and they wouldn't take no for an answer, he was told. Dr Brinley sighed and left the table.

The telephone was in the stillroom, but even above the clatter of the banquet his voice could be heard everywhere: 'Eh? – No, not tomorrow: not possible, hounds meeting at

Nant Eifion . . . No, nor Wednesday neither: they're meeting at the Bridge . . . Tell ye what, I'll hold the inquest Thursday . . . Eh? You ought to be thankful, laddie: gives you longer to find out who she was . . . *Not* local: you're sure of that?'

A screech of laughter from the kitchen drowned the next few words, but everyone heard what followed: 'Mr Augustine did you say? – Then that's that! Mr Augustine will have to be summoned.'

Dr Brinley seemed quite unaware of the general hush as he made his way back to the table. He sat down, grumbling. But at his elbow, arrested in the very act of draining a whisky-bottle into his glass, stood Mrs Dai Roberts – and her triumphant eyes were now on stalks:

'*Summonsed?* What's he been caught doing, sir?'

'Who?'

'Why that Mr Augustine, of course!'

The coroner turned and looked at her judicially: 'Hasn't your Dai told you anything yet?'

'He's not come home. Missing the banquet and all, I just can't understand . . .'

So, Dai had gone to earth again! Just like him, rather than face the witness-box. Shy as a wild thing . . . ordinarily Dr Brinley sympathized with Dai's disappearances, married to that woman; but it was awkward now, just when his evidence would be badly wanted at the inquest. 'No Dai, eh?' he murmured to himself.

'Tell me, Doctor *bach*?' she wheedled. But he fixed his eye indignantly on this half-filled glass:

'Woman! Is that how you pour a drink?'

'Means opening another bottle,' she answered impatiently: 'Mr Augustine, you were just saying . . .?'

'Then fetch one and open it,' he replied implacably.

Chapter 7

Dr Brinley was happy. The room had begun to rock gently but only like – like a cradle: the motion was not unpleasant *yet*.

It was good to see old customs kept up. Flemton Banquet claimed to be as old as Flemton's Norman charter – old as the titular High Stewardship itself and the little mediaeval garrison of Flemish mercenaries out of which the place had grown (to this day no Welsh was spoken within Flemton, though all the mainland talked it). It had been well worth the long pony-drive from the Cross! Eh? It was good – *good* to be here among all these good fellows. Laddies, and lassies too: they all liked him. They liked his jokes . . . That was the point: he was among them and they all loved him so now he was on top of things . . .

He surveyed the room. It was time now to think up a new joke, else they'd forget him and start talking among themselves. A good one . . . well then a bad one, anything . . .

But his cudgelled brains went suddenly as obstinate as a cudgelled ass.

Perhaps another glass? – *A-a-a-ah!* Thank God for His good gift of whisky! Drinking . . . Yes, drinking and hunting: those were the only two times he really felt '*We*' were all one, felt he truly belonged.

Whisky . . . yes, and hunting too – in the *past*, but now you were old, now you could do no more than jog to the Meet and back . . .

This motion, now: *was* it a cradle, or was it a galloping horse titty-tup titty-tup . . . ?

'Hup! And over!' he suddenly exclaimed aloud.

The room faded and he was away: hounds in full cry, Black Bess (or was it Dandy?) between his thighs, leading the field. Hup! Black Bess it was: how beautifully she changed feet on top of the bank and then the downward plunge, the miraculous recovery and away. – *Aren't you afraid?* – Yes of course he was afraid. Broken neck, crushed ribs . . . but damn it!

That gap to the right looks a trifle easier . . . Well, perhaps, but . . . Curse her she's going for the highest place of a-a-a-all! *Hup!* – Oh, thank God!

'Gentlemen, The King!'

Dr Brinley was on his feet before any of them, and added a fervent 'God bless him!' when he had emptied his glass. – Good lad, George Five! But that boy of his (the Prince) would break his neck one of these days if they let him go on riding.

Yes, hunting was the thing . . . of *course* no doctor could practise and hunt three days a week as well! Be damned to private practice, then! They could go on their bended knees . . .

Was that the real reason, or just you were a rotten bad doctor? – Eh? – *Did you leave your practice? Or did your practice leave you?*

An angry tear rolled slowly down his nose.

A drunken doctor, a sot? – Well, they'd made him Coroner, hadn't they? That showed they respected him, didn't it? – *Maybe they'd rather trust you with the dead than the living* . . .

'Gentlemen, The Memory of the Fallen!'

A bugle sounded – shatteringly, in that enclosed space. Again the whole room rose stiffly to attention. Most had their memories (for that 1914 War had been a holocaust): all wore faces as if they had.

Briefly and gravely the bishop said his piece. As he did so he tried to keep staring at the Legion banner on the wall opposite, but his gaze was drawn down willy-nilly to a young man under it with ribands on his chest. All that young man's face except mouth and chin was hidden in a black mask which had no holes for eyes . . . and suddenly the whole room reeked overpoweringly of beer.

The Fallen . . . as Dr Brinley drank the melancholy toast his hand trembled, and his heart was torn anew at the tragedy that he himself should have been too young to serve. For what bond can equal the bond which unites for ever those who have once been heroes together, however long ago? 'I was at the Alma, I was at Inkermann . . .' Oh to have been able to say today 'I charged with the Light Brigade'! But they wouldn't have him; for alas, in 1853 he was only aged fifteen.

The Fallen . . . at one with them, perhaps, in their ever-lasting blank sleep: or conscious only at this annual moment of the raised glasses that he too was one of the forever-unforgotten. But now he must die in any case, and die alone . . .

For Dr Brinley believed he was at least doctor enough to know that in a very few months he himself would have to take to his bed. For a while the invaluable Blodwen – the fat, white, smiling Blodwen – would look after him. But only for a while. Blodwen was a wonderful nurse, so long as she thought you might recover: but not for 'the dying part'. She couldn't do with *that*. A village woman of fifty, drawn to sick beds like a moth to a candle and never yet had she seen a body dead! No, at a given stage and with nothing said Blodwen disappeared and her sister Eirwen took her place. For Eirwen was wonderful with 'the dying part', kind Eirwen had closed more eyes than any woman at the Cross. They always knew what it meant when Blodwen left them and Eirwen took her place.

Meanwhile? – Meanwhile, he drained another glass.

He felt now he was set on a pinnacle: he supposed it must be the pinnacle of his own approaching death. Anyway, from his pinnacle how remote they all suddenly began to seem, this crowd he had courted all his life! This crowd here jabbering and eating . . . hoping . . . young.

From his pinnacle (it swayed a little as in the wind, from all the whisky he had drunk) he now saw all the hearts of all the kingdoms of the world outspread, on offer – such as all his life he had coveted. But a change seemed somehow lately to have seeped into his soul from the very bottom: he found now he did not desire them any more.

Suddenly his pinnacle shot up to a towering height from which these people looked no more than minute gesticulating emmets. Moreover his pinnacle was swinging violently to and fro, now, in a full gale: he had to set his whole mind to clinging on.

He hoped the motion would not make him sea-sick.

The bishop, covertly watching him, saw that grey look, the sagging and trembling jaw: 'This man has at last begun to die,' he said to himself. But then he saw also the transparent empty eyes, and recalled looking in through other eyes like them – younger eyes, but opening on to the same unbottomed vacant pit within: 'Also he is very, *very* drunk,' he told himself understandingly.

Maybe – reckoning from the bottom up – the old doctor was indeed three parts dead already: for already there was so much nothing in him down there where once the deeper emotions had been. But at the still-living trivial brink of his mind there was something stirring even now: something which teased and foxed him, for he could not quite recognize what it was . . .

'Thursday!' that something said.

Moreover his eyes had begun to prick with tears! Was there something wrong about 'Thursday', then? '*Thursday*!' 'THURSDAY!' The word was booming insistently in his head like any bell. He took another sip of whisky to recall his wandering memory. *A-a-a-ah!* Now it had come back to him. The telephone call, the little body . . . he had to hold an inquest . . .

At that the lately too-penetrable eyes clouded over, the jaw closed, the drooping cheeks tautened to expression of a kind. He turned and gripped the bishop's arm with his bridle hand and his face was all puckered to suit his words: 'My Lord!' he gulped, 'It's a mere little maid!' The bishop turned towards him, attentive but mystified. 'A green child,' Dr Brinley went on. 'Yet here's *me* still, and *you*!'

The bishop still looked mystified; and the doctor was mildly shocked to find how little of his own pathetic words moved even himself. So he tried again – and at least his old voice now quavered dramatically enough: 'A wee maid scarce six years of age, they said. Dead! Tell me the meaning of it, you man of God!'

Then he hiccuped, burst altogether into tears and upset his glass. They all turned kindly faces on him.

'Come on, Doc,' he heard the High Steward saying: 'Give us "Clementine".'

Chapter 8

Midnight, back now at Newton Llantony . . .

As the clouds broke and the bright moon at last came out, the single point of light to which distance diminished the lamps of all roystering Flemton paled.

In the big Newton drawing-room the shutters did not quite reach to the semi-circular tops of the windows, and through these high openings the moon sent bars of light into the black gloom within. It shone on the shapeless holland bag which enclosed the great central chandelier: threw criss-cross shadows on the dust-sheets covering the furniture and covering the old mirrors on the walls. It shone on the new gilt frame of the life-size khaki portrait above the fireplace: glinted on the word 'Ypres', and the date and the name, inscribed on brass.

It glinted on the painted highlights in the dead young man's eyes.

It shone on the small shapeless dark shape in the middle of the big sofa opposite, the outstretched arms. Glinted on the little slits of eyeball between the half-open lids.

Augustine, in his white attic bedroom under the roof, woke with the moon staring straight in his eyes.

Round him the house was silent. In all its hundred rooms he knew there was no *living* being that night but him.

Downstairs a door banged without reason. His scalp pricked momentarily, and the yawn he was beginning went off at half-cock.

He who so loved to be alone felt now a sudden unmitigated longing for living human company.

His sister Mary . . .

Her child Polly, that little niece he loved . . .

For a moment, being but half-awake, he thought Polly had crept into his bed and was sleeping there, tiny and warm and humid, her feet planted firmly against his chest. But when he stirred she vanished: the bed was empty and cold.

Where would they be now, Polly and her mother? He had an idea they were away from home, there had been something in Mary's last letter . . .

Instinctively Augustine knew that this eremitical phase of his life was now over, had finally served its turn: indeed he was tempted to get out his Bentley that very minute and drive to London, drive right through the night as if he meant never to come back to Newton. '*London!*' He recalled it now: *that* was where Mary was taking Polly for a day or two, she had written; and he could be with them there by breakfast.

But he decided after all to wait till morning. He must at least be still here when the ambulance arrived, he remembered . . .

Meanwhile he lay where he was, neither awake nor asleep, in his familiar boyhood bed, cold and sweating.

Something in the room creaked.

Chapter 9

Augustine waited till the morning before starting; but the belt of rainy weather travelled eastward ahead of him across Carmarthen and Brecon. Clearing even the eastern counties of Wales about midnight, long before dawn it had arrived in London (where Polly was). There it poured heavily and steadily all day. All that wet Tuesday it felt in London as if thunder was about, though none was heard.

On the opposite side of Eaton Square from Polly's there was a certain tall house which Polly always passed slowly and with evident respect. It belonged to Lady Sylvia Davenant, but Polly called it 'Janey's house'. Seen from a window of the upstairs drawing-room of this house, the umbrellas in the street below, that Tuesday, looked like mushrooms on the run (thought Sylvia Davenant), and the tops of the cars like special sleek slugs – also very much on the run, as they cleft a passage through the mushrooms.

'A good simile,' thought Lady Sylvia, 'because mushrooms and slugs both are creatures of the rain, the very thought of them evokes wetness – but no, a bad simile because mushrooms never move at all and even slugs are . . . sluggish. But, "*run* . . ."? What does run in the rain? – Only colours I suppose,' she concluded rather wildly.

With an effort she recalled her attention to Janey at her side. For this was little Janey's 'Hour': her drawing-room hour with her aunt between tea and bedtime. Janey had flattened her nose against the pane, thus clouding it with her breath so that she could hardly see out at all.

'Darling,' said Lady Sylvia brightly, 'what do *you* think those umbrellas look like?'

'Like umbrellas,' said Janey perfunctorily. 'Auntie, why *does* it rain?'

'Darling!' said Lady Sylvia, 'You know I don't like being called "Auntie", it sounds like someone old. Why can't you just call me "Sylvia"? Don't you think that's a pretty name?'

'You *are* old,' said Janey. 'Anyway, Sylvia's a girl in the Gardens already . . . "Saliva", *I* call her.'

"*Darling!*"

Janey withdrew her face an inch or two from the misted glass, put out her tongue and licked herself a neat round peephole.

'Look!' she cried, pointing through the trees at a sudden light which appeared in a top window on the far side of the Square: 'There's Polly-wolly going to bed HOURS BEFORE ME –YAH!' she yelled: 'Polly-wolly-doodle! Pollyollywollyollydoodle-OODLE-OOOOO!"

The yell could not possibly have carried across the wide Square but it nearly split her aunt's eardrum: extraordinary it could come from so very small a body!

'Darling *please*! Not *quite* so loud! And who is this "Polly"?'

'Oh, just a person in the Gardens sometimes. . . soppy little kid.' Janey paused, glanced at the clock, considered, and added with a perceptible effort: 'I bet she wets her bed.'

Janey looked sidelong at her aunt. The 'Hour' had still twenty minutes to go, but now already Her Ladyship was crossing the room to ring for Janey's *gouvernante*. 'Goody!' thought Janey, with a chapter to finish upstairs.

Janey was an only child (and the result of a mechanical accident at that). She had been parked on her Aunt Sylvia for a couple of months interminable to both of them while her parents were getting their divorce.

Chapter 10

Janey was quite right about the light opposite. Polly was going to bed, and going to bed rather earlier than usual.

Nanny had lit the gas, although it was not really dark yet, to combat all that wet and gloom outside. Now she sat in front of an enormous blaze of coal mending her stockings (which were of black cotton with white toes and heels). The heat of the fire, and the steam rising from the round zinc bath on the middle of the carpet, made the room with its tight-shut window like a hothouse; and Polly's face was shiny with perspiration. Nanny had lit the light against the gloom but Polly *wanted* to look out: she was feeling sad, and the rain and gloom outside and all those wet hurrying people suited her mood.

Polly had a slight cold – it always happened when she came to London! This was the reason she was to have her bath in the nursery tonight instead of going down the draughty stairs to the big mahogany bathroom two floors below. Moreover, Polly had been today to the dentist. That also seemed always to happen whenever she came to London. He seldom hurt her, but he did indignities to the secret places of her mouth – shrivelling its sensitive wet membranes with a squirt of hot wind, plastering a dry cloth on to her wet tongue, poking wads of dry cotton wool into her cheek, hooking over her bottom teeth a bubbling sucking thing which plucked at the roots of her tongue . . . by the end she had felt as if her dried-up mouth had died of drought and would never be able to wet itself again. Nor could she quite breathe through her nose because of her cold . . . almost she had wished he *would* hurt, to take her mind off that horrible dryness and off the thought that any moment her nose might run and she not able to get at it.

But most of all Polly was sad because she was lonely – and that happened *only* when she came to London! She never felt lonely at home in Dorset; for at Mellton Chase there were animals to play with, but in London there were only children.

Kensington Gardens, you would have thought, were full of 'suitable' playmates for Polly. But all those children were Londoners – or virtually Londoners. Already they had formed their own packs, and nothing their nannies could say – Polly's Nanny was high in their hierarchy, so the nannies tried their best – would make them treat the little country child as one of themselves. Under orders, they would take her kindly by the hand and lead her away; but once out of sight they turned her upside down, or stood round her in a ring jeering at her ignorance of their private shibboleths.

They would call her derisively 'Little Polly-wolly-doodle', or even worse names such as 'Baby-dolly-lulu'. Any name with 'baby' in it was hard to bear, for Polly's age was just five and her struggle out of the slough of babyhood so recent a memory that the very word 'baby' seemed still to have power to drag her back into it.

Of all these groups in the Gardens, the most exclusive and the most desirable was 'Janey's Gang'. This gang had a rule: no one could join it who had not 'Knocked down a Man'. This was not impossible even for quite small children, for nothing in the rule required that he should be looking; and if you had made him fall into water you were an Officer straight away.

Janey herself was huge: she was turned seven. Janey claimed three Men to her credit, two of them in water and the third in a garden frame. She had done it so skilfully (or her curls were so golden, her blue eyes so wide) that not one of the three had suspected the push was intentional. No wonder the gang was titularly 'Janey's Gang'!

Grown-ups were ex officio Enemy to all these children, to be out-smarted on every occasion: so, their scores rose.

43

But even if Polly had been old enough and clever enough properly to understand the Rule (she was not, in fact, particularly intelligent), she could never even have made a beginning. For Polly's own grown-ups were not 'Enemy', that was the rub: they were infinitely kind, they made little pretence of not adoring Polly and it never occurred to Polly to make any pretence at all of not loving them back. Loving, indeed, was the one thing she was really good at: how then could she ever bring herself to 'knock a Man down'?

Mr Corbett, for example: the head gardener at Mellton Chase, and indeed the greatest potentate on earth: the massive sloping buttress of his front – his gold watch-chain marked the half-way line of the ascent – held him upright like a tower, and nowadays his hands never deigned to touch fork or spade except to weed Miss Polly's little garden for her; or to pick fruit, except when he saw Miss Polly coming . . .

It was unthinkable to inflict on Mr Corbett the indignity of falling!

Or even on dear Gusting (her uncle Augustine, that was). Of course he was a lesser dignitary in the world's eyes than Mr Corbett; but she loved him even more. Admired and loved him with every burning cockle of her heart!

There was magic in Gusting's very smell, his voice.

Chapter 11

'Time you got undressed, Miss Polly,' said Nanny. Slowly Polly wandered across to have her jersey peeled off.

'Skin-a-rabbit,' said Nanny, mechanically, as she always did.

'Ow!' said Polly, as she always did (for the neck of her jersey was too tight), and wandered off again nursing her damaged ears. Nanny just had time to undo the three large bone buttons on her back before she was out of reach, and as she walked away the blue serge kilt with its white cotton 'top' fell off around her feet.

The rest of her undressing Polly could do herself, given time and her whole attention. It was chiefly button work: she wore a 'liberty bodice', a White-Knight sort of under-garment to which everything nether was buttoned or otherwise attached (constricting elastic being bad for you). But tonight her fingers fumbled feebly and uselessly, fainting at the very first button; for her attention was all elsewhere.

Gusting had a game which only he played, the Jeremy Fisher Game. A little mat was a waterlily leaf and Gusting sat on it cross-legged, fishing with a long carriage-whip, while Polly swam round him on the polished floor on her stomach, being a fish . . . Polly began now to make em-bryonic swimming movements with her hands.

'Stop dawdling,' said Nanny, but without much hope. Polly made a brief effort: something else fell off her, and she stepped out of it where it lay. 'Pick it up, dear,' said Nanny, again without much hope.

'Ninjun!' said Polly indignantly (Augustine had once said her wandering manner of undressing and scattering her clothes was like a Red Indian blazing his trail, and that had hallowed it).

Minutes passed . . .

'Wake up, Miss Polly: stop dawdling,' said Nanny.

Another brief effort, and so it went on till at last Polly had on nothing but a clinging woollen vest as she stood at the window, her chin reaching just above the sill, looking out through the watery glass.

In the street far below people were still scurrying past. There seemed no end to them. That was what was wrong with London: 'If only there were fewer people in the world how much nicer it would be for we animals,' Polly told herself . . .

'We animals'! – Polly could think a rabbit's kind of thoughts much easier than a grown-up's kind, for her 'thinking' like an animal's was still more than nine parts emotion. Except for Augustine it was only with animals she could form friendships on at all equal terms; for she had no child-friends of her own age, and her love for most grown-ups was necessarily more like a dog's for a man than something between members of the same species. All the most interesting hours of the day still tended to be spent on all fours, and even in bodily size she was nearer to her father's spaniel than she was to her father. The dog weighed more than the child, as the see-saw had shown . . .

'Wake up!' said Nanny – still without much hope. 'Vest!' A final effort and the vest too lay on the floor. Nanny made stirring sounds in the bath: 'Come on,' said Nanny, 'or the water'll be half cold.'

'I'm busy!' said Polly indignantly. She had found a cake-currant on the floor and was trying to fix it in her navel, but it wouldn't stay there. 'If only I had some honey,' she thought . . . but at that moment felt herself lifted in the air, carried – her feet weakly kicking – and plumped down in the middle of the large shallow bath. Nanny's patience was exhausted.

Polly seized her celluloid frog Jeremy, and once more her thoughts were away: so far this time they were not even fully recalled when Nanny dragged off her hands and soaped her protesting ears.

'Now!' said Nanny, holding up the huge turkey towel she had been warming on the fender: 'Or I'll have to count Three!'

But Polly was loth to move.

'*One* . . .'

'*Two* . . .'

Then the nursery door opened and in walked Augustine.

Dropping into a chair, Augustine just had time to snatch the towel from Nanny to cover himself as Polly sprang squealing straight from the water into his lap – with half the bath following her, it seemed.

Well! Bursting in like that without knocking! Nanny pursed her lips, for she didn't at all approve. Nanny was a Catholic and believed it is never too young to start teaching little girls Shame. They ought to *mind* men – even uncles – seeing them in their baths, not go bouncing on to their laps without a stitch. But she knew it was as much as her place was worth to breathe a word to the child, for Mrs Wadamy was Modern, Mrs Wadamy had Views.

Meanwhile Polly, lonely no longer, was in the seventh heaven of delight. She tore open Augustine's waistcoat to nuzzle her damp head inside it against his shirt, where she could breathe nothing but his magic smell, listen to the thumping of his heart.

Reluctant at first to let his still-tainted hands themselves even touch the sacred child, he dabbed with a bunch of towel tenderly at the steaming, flower-petal skin. But with her head inside his waistcoat she grabbed his hand tyrannically to her and pressed its hard hollow palm tight over her outside cheek and temple and little curly ear, so that her lucky head should be quite entirely squeezed between *him* and *him*. But that very moment he heard Mary's voice from the stairs, calling him: he must come at once.

Augustine was wanted on the telephone: it was a trunk call.

Chapter 12

This was the dead child asserting precedence over the living one; for the untimely call was from the police at Penrys Cross. But it was only to say the inquest was put off till Friday as the coroner was indisposed.

Flemton Banquet had ended as usual – in a fight. This year the occasion had been the final torchlight procession: it had fired some of the street decorations, and Danny George declared the burning of his best trousers had been deliberate. Flemton had been happy to divide on the point, and in the fracas Dr Brinley's old pony took fright and galloped him off home in the rocking trap, splashing across the sands through the skim of ebb that still glistened there in the moonlight. He had been properly scared and shaken. Thus he had missed the Tuesday and Wednesday Meets after all, taking to his bed with a bottle instead.

The experienced Blodwen had been firm with them: Friday was the earliest the Coroner could be fit for duty.

The next day, Wednesday, Mary was taking Polly back to Dorset. The extra day just gave Augustine time to go with them and spend one night there before having to be back in Wales.

The weather had cleared, and Augustine and Polly wanted to travel together, in the Bentley; but Nanny objected. She said it was crazy in any weather to let a child with a cold travel in a thing like that; for Augustine's 3-litre Bentley was an open two-seater – very open indeed, with a small draughty windscreen and with even the handbrake outside. Mary Wadamy, on the other hand, was rather in favour. A big wind, she argued, must blow germs *away*. And it would soon be over; whereas in the stuffy family Daimler, with the luggage and Nanny and Mary's maid Fitton and Mary herself, the journey would take the best part of the day.

Trivett, their old chauffeur, was carriage-trained and had no liking for speed. But even at twenty miles an hour he drove dangerously enough for the most exacting: 'Best anyway not put all your eggs in one basket when the basket is driven by Trivett!' said Augustine grimly.

As for Polly, speech was so inadequate to express her longing that she was silently dancing it, her tongue stuck out as if in exile for its uselessness. That decided Mary: 'Being happy's the only cold-cure worth a farthing,' she said to herself, and gave her consent.

So Nanny, her face full of omens, wrapped the child into a woollen ball where only the eyes showed, and set it on the leather seat beside Augustine.

Augustine was a brilliant driver of the youthful passionate kind which wholly identifies itself with the car. Thus once his hands were on the wheel this morning he forgot Polly entirely. Yet this didn't matter to Polly. She too knew how to merge herself utterly in dear Bentley (another of her loves): the moment the engine broke into its purring, organ-like roar she uncovered her mouth and began singing treble to Bentley's bass, and for two hours Bentley and she did not for a moment stop singing, through Staines and Basingstoke, Stockbridge, Salisbury, out on the bare downs.

On the tops of those empty high downs, above the hanging woods of ancient yews clinging to their chalky sides, there was only a thin skin of rabbit-nibbled turf that was more thyme than grass and a sky full of larks. Polly had got her arms free now and waved to the larks, inviting their descant to make a trio of it.

Mellton lay in a deep river-valley folded into these bare chalk downs. In the flat bottom land as they neared the house there were noble woods of beech and sweet-chestnut, green pasture, deep lanes that Bentley almost filled, little hidden hamlets of mingled flint and brick with steep thatched roofs. Bentley and Polly sang together for them as they passed.

As Bentley rounded through the ever-open wrought-iron gates and purred his careful way on the last lap through the park, Polly was now entirely free of her cocoon and standing bolt upright against the dashboard, using both arms to conduct the whole chorus of nature. 'Home!' she was chanting on every note she could compass, 'Home! Home! Home!' And to Polly's ears everything round her intoned the answer *'Home!'*

Then at the front door of Mellton Chase Augustine switched off the engine and Polly and Bentley both fell silent together.

Augustine wiped her nose and lifted her out.

Mellton was large, nearly as large as Augustine's lonely hermitage Newton Llantony. It was all an Elizabethan house, entirely faced and mullioned with stone and with a little half-naïve classical ornament. It had originally been built as a hollow square on the four sides of a central quadrangle, like a college. In the middle of the façade there was still a great vaulted archway like a college gate: once, you could have ridden on horseback under it right into the quadrangle without dismounting, but now the arch was blocked and a modern front door had been constructed in it.

The well-known music of Augustine's Bentley could be heard afar, and the butler was standing waiting for them outside this front door when they arrived. Wantage was his name.

Wantage was a thin man, prematurely grey: his eyes stood out rather, for he had thyroid trouble.

Chapter 13

Polly greeted Mr Wantage warmly but politely (he was *Mr*
Wantage to her, by her mother's fiat). Once inside the door
she sat herself expectantly on the end of a certain long
Bokhara rug: for as usual on first getting home she wanted
to set out at once for the North Pole drawn on her sledge by
a yelping team of Mr Wantage across the frozen wastes of
ballroom parquet.

For no longer was there any open quadrangle here at
Mellton that all the business of the house had to criss-cross,
wet or fine. A Victorian Wadamy had arisen who disliked
so draughty a way of living. Fired by the example of the new
London railway-stations and of Paxton's Crystal Palace,
he had roofed the entire thing over with a dome of steel and
glass. So now in the middle of the house there was nearly an
acre of parquet dotted with eastern rugs, instead of the
former lawn and flagged paths. What now stood waiting at
the far side by the old mounting-block with its tethering-
ring, at the foot of the stone steps leading up to the State
Rooms and the Solar, was a grand piano.

The quadrangle was now called the Ballroom. Few
mansions in the country had ballrooms half its size: tradition said that on one Victorian occasion two thousand
couples had danced there, watched by the Prince and Princess of Wales. But this vast 'room' was still lit by the glazed
sky above. Its walls of weathered stone were still un-
plastered. Windows and even balconies still looked down
into it. Yet alternating with these windows and balconies
steel armoured fore-arms now projected from the walls gripping outsize electric light bulbs in their gauntleted fists; for
this had been one of the very first houses in Britain to adopt
the new lighting, with current generated by its own watermill.

Polly and Wantage may have been looking for the North Pole, but what they found at the far side of all this was Minta the under-nurse. She carried Polly off at once, and Polly went with her readily enough because Polly was always docile when she was happy and at the moment she was full of happiness – full as an egg.

As soon as Polly was gone with Minta and Augustine was washing his hands, Wantage vanished rather nervously into the dining-room. He wanted to assure himself that the cold sideboard carried everything it should for Mr Augustine's solitary luncheon. Wantage knew of old that Mr Augustine preferred not to be waited on yet objected strongly to having to ring for something which had been forgotten. If he was like this by twenty-three, Wantage often wondered, what would he be like at fifty-three? 'A holy terror and no mistake!' was Mrs Winter's forecast – unless he got married, of course.

Wantage straightened a fork that was slightly out of plumb: nothing else seemed amiss.

By rights Wantage was 'off' now, and ought to be able to put up his feet in peace. But there was still Mr Augustine's bag! Passing out through the serving-pantry he ordered a rather bucolic boot-and-knife boy, in tones of concentrated venom, to fetch the luggage out of the car and carry it up the back way.

That venomous tone of voice meant nothing: it was merely the correct way for Upper Servants to speak to Boys (indeed Wantage had rather a soft spot for Jimmy – hoped one day to make quite a proper Indoor of him). It meant no more than the tones of deferential benevolence he always used to all Gentry – who were stupid sods, most of them, in his experience. True, their word was their bond; but they acted spoilt, like babbies...

Not that *all* babbies were spoilt – not his little Miss Polly-olly she wasn't! It was her Nanny was the spoilt one – that Mrs Halloran the blooming nuisance . . . and Minta the

Under aiming to take after her: a little bitch hardly turned eighteen, I ask you! A slipper to her backside would do her a power.

Mrs Winter agreed with him about those two, but constitutionally Nursery was a self-governing province where even a Housekeeper's writ did not run.

Wantage's back was giving him gyp; but he'd got that bag to unpack before he could look to a proper sit-down. 'Off-duty' didn't mean a thing nowadays, not since the War with everywhere understaffed. Time was, he had known four footmen here at the Chase: but now – just fancy *Mellton* and the butler having to valet visiting gentlemen himself! How was he to keep his end up with Mrs Winter – her with all those girls under, and him with no one under his sole command but Jimmy?

All those girls . . . Mrs Winter, with her black silk and her keys, was hard put to it to count them all. But that's what the Gentry (the old ones: war profiteers weren't Gentry) were come down to nowadays indoors: *girls*. Why, some houses and quite good ones too nowadays they even let women clean the silver! 'Parlourmaids' . . . Mellton hadn't fallen as low as that yet, thank God.

But where was the satisfaction, rising to the top in Service and still no men under you? That was the sting. Outdoors, two keepers and a water-bailiff: an estate carpenter: six men in the Gardens still – and three (even not counting the exiled Trivett) in Stables! Only Indoors was so depleted, that's what was so unfair.

Mean! The Master ought to bear in mind what was due from a Wadamy of Mellton Chase . . .

As Wantage fitted the links into Augustine's white shirt ready for the evening he heaved a deep sigh that turned to a hiccup and left a nasty taste of heartburn in his mouth. Dead Sea Fruit! That's all his promotions had amounted to ever since he entered Service, from first to last.

Chapter 14

When at last Wantage was free to relax it was the House-keeper's Room he went to that afternoon, not his own Pantry; and he slumped into a comfortable basket chair there as near as possible to a breezy window.

Mrs Winter was sitting bolt upright before the fire on a straight-backed hard chair loose-covered in a flowered chintz. Her hands were folded in her lap. Mrs Winter never slumped – never appeared to wish to, even if her whalebone would have let her. Wantage studied her. Nowadays she looked like something poured into a mould: just brimming over the rim a little but not enough to slop. She didn't seem to possess a Shape of her own any more. It was hard to believe that once 'Mrs Winter' had been Maggie the lithe, long-legged young under-housemaid, game as any for a spot of slap-and-tickle.

That was at Stumfort Castle, when he himself was a half-grown young footman – years before they had met again at Mellton Chase. Wantage licked his lips at certain recollections. Jimminey! He'd gone a bit too far with her that one time! Might both have lost their places only they were lucky and she didn't have it after all . . .

He'd happened on her sudden, up the Tower – in the Feather-room, sitting on the floor refilling a featherbed and herself half drowned in feathers . . . with her ankles showing. Her ankles – and the sight of her Shape sunk in all that sea of soft feathers – had been too much for him. Too much for both of them, seemingly.

But *after*! Picking hundreds of downy little feathers off his livery against time before going on duty in the Front Hall, sweating he'd miss some and they'd find him out . . .

'A penny for your thoughts, Mr Wantage,' said Mrs Winter sweetly.

'Dead Sea Fruit, Maggie,' he answered hollowly.

He hadn't called her 'Maggie' for years! Mrs Winter lifted both white plump hands slightly from her lap, fitting the tips of the fingers together and contemplating them in silence. Then:

'Times have certainly changed,' she said.

Mr Wantage closed his eyes.

Suddenly he opened them again: Polly was climbing into his lap. Polly was the only person in the whole house Front Stairs as well as Back who dared wander informally into the sacred 'Room' like that. 'I've come!' she said unnecessarily, and added: 'That Jimmy's got a crown!'

'Careful, Duck,' said Mr Wantage: 'Mind my poor leg.'

'What's the matter with it?' she asked.

'Got a bone in it!' he answered dramatically. 'Minta'll be looking for you,' he went on, with quite a wicked look in his bulging eyes.

'Yes she will!' said Polly, equally delighted: 'Looking *everywhere!*'

'Hunting all over!' echoed Mr Wantage: 'You won't half cop it if she finds you here!'

But he knew , and she knew, that this was a sanctuary where even Minta'd never dare.

Mrs Winter's thoughts were browsing very gently on the visitor, Mr Augustine. For a brother and sister, how unlike in their ways he and the Mistress were! And yet, so fond. A pity to see him wilfully living so strange: no good could come of it, you can't cut loose from your Station, no one can . . . yet he had proved the soul of kindness about Nellie Gwilym's old mother – took endless pains to find her somewhere on his own property, now that the birthplace she'd hankered back to was become a waterworks. Mr Augustine

55

was better than he'd let himself be, there *were* some like that . . .

Then Mrs Winter's stomach rumbled, and she looked at the clock. But at that very moment came the expected knock and the door opened, briefly releasing into the 'Room' a distant merry burst of young west-country voices and wild laughter with even a snapshot through it of 'that Jimmy', ham-frill for crown and sceptered with toasting fork, prancing in the midst of a veritable bevy of 'all those girls'.

It was Lily, the fifteen-year-old scullery-maid, who had just come in, with her cheeks flushed and her eyes still flashing. Lily had brought their tea, of course, with hot buttered scones straight from the oven, and cherrycake.

'Like a nice slice of cake, Love?' Mrs Winter asked Polly. Even the glacé cherries in it were Mellton-grown and of her own candying. But Polly shook her head. Her cold had spoiled her appetite. Instead she begun plunging her hand in each of Mr Wantage's pockets in turn to see what she could find. Gently he began to prise open her fingers to rescue his spectacles; but she insisted on placing them on his nose.

Mrs Winter was putting on her spectacles, for the tea-tray bore her usual weekly letter from her younger sister Nellie . . . Poor Nellie! The clever one of the family – and the one Life had treated hardest. – Still, Nellie had Little Rachel to comfort her . . .

'Mrs' Winter's own title only marked professional status, like 'Dr, or Rev'; but Nellie had married, and married young. She had married a budding minister, a Welsh boy out of the mines. Clever as paint – but not strong, though, ever. Nellie was wed as soon as the young man got his first Call, to a chapel in the Rhondda Valley.

When the War came, being a minister of religion he didn't have to go – and how thankful Nellie had been! But her Portion of Trouble was coming to her just the same. 1915

– three years married, the first baby at last and born big-headed! Water, of course ... Six months later he died, the second already on the way.

Wasn't it anxiety enough for Nellie, wondering after that how the new one would turn out? Yet Gwilym (that was the father's outlandish name) must needs add to it. He took on now in a crazy fashion. He reckoned some sin of *his* had made the first one born that way: he must expiate his sin or the second would be the same.

Not to sit comfortable preaching the word in the Valleys to the ticking Chapel clock while other men died! That's how the notion took him. But the Army wouldn't have him for a chaplain: so he said he'd go for a stretcher-bearer, in the Medical Corps. It was for the unborn baby's sake he'd got to go, so he couldn't even wait for little Rachel-to-be to be born. Nellie couldn't hold him.

Nor could his angry deacons either: they were of a very pacifist turn, and counted stretchering nearly as bad as downright shooting – they'd never have him back after, not once he'd put on any kind or shape of army uniform! When he still went, they turned Nellie out of the Chapel house; for they'd have no soldier's brat born there.

Once Rachel was weaned, Nellie got a war-job teaching infant school in Gloucester.

As for Rachel – the sweetest little maid she grew and clever as a little monkey! A proper little fairy. No wonder her mother was all wrapped up in her! Her Aunt Maggie was downright fearful sometimes of the mother's doting, it was so greedy: yet even a mere aunt couldn't help marvelling at the little thing, and doting a bit likewise.

Chapter 15

Thus Mrs Winter had never quite succeeded in setting Polly
on a pedestal as the rest of the household at the Chase all
did: for she couldn't help comparing Polly with Nellie's
Little Rachel. Polly was a nice little thing, but nothing to
write home about.

Rachel was a year older than Polly, true; but anyway she
was twice as clever, twice as pretty, twice as good. A little
angel on earth. And what a Fancy! The *things* she *said*!
Nellie's letters were always full of Rachel's Sayings and
her aunt used to read them aloud to Mr Wantage: she
couldn't help it.

Polly never said wonderful Sayings like that you could
put in a book! Yet it was Polly who would grow up with
all the advantages ... This made Mrs Winter bitterly jealous
at times: but she tried to curb her jealousy. It wasn't Polly's
fault, being born with the silver spoon: there was no sense
or fairness taking it out on *her*.

When Gwilym came back from the war his deacons kept
their word: they wouldn't even see him. So he took on a tin
mission church in Gloucester, down by the docks. But then
their troubles began afresh. For now, six years after Rachel's
birth, Nellie was expecting again. She hadn't looked for it or
intended it and somehow she sort of couldn't get used to the
idea at all.

The fact was, by now Nellie had got so wrapped up in
Little Rachel she just couldn't bear the thought of having
another! She positively blamed the intruder in her womb
for pretending to any place in the heart that by rights was
wholly Rachel's.

Moreover she had a good open reason too for thinking

this child ought never to be born. Everyone knows that whatever doctors say the Consumption is hereditary, and six months ago Gwilym had started spitting blood.

Gwilym was away in a sanatorium now; so once more Nellie was left to face childbirth alone, but this time hating the baby to come and with a conviction it would be born infected – if not a downright monster like the first.

Thus it was with rather a troubled face that Mrs Winter opened the envelope and took out the carefully-written sheet of ruled paper. But the news on the whole was good. Gwilym had written to say he felt ever so much better, they'd be bound to let him home soon. Nellie herself was in good health considering, thought the birth might begin any hour now at the time of writing. No 'Sayings', for once, of Little Rachel's . . . But of course! Rachel was away visiting with her Grandma. The doctor had insisted on hospital when Nellie's time should come – ill though they could afford it; so the child had been sent off a week ago.

Mrs Winter put the letter down and began to muse. She was troubled – not by the letter but in her own mind, at herself. Why had she allowed Little Rachel to be sent to a grandmother none too anxious to have her, instead of asking Mrs Wadamy to let the child come here for a week or two? Mrs Wadamy would have been willing, no doubt of it: quite apart from her natural kindness of heart she'd have been glad of a nice little playmate for Polly. No, Mrs Winter's reluctance had come from somewhere in her own self.

'Proper Pride,' she tried to tell herself: a not wanting to be 'Beholden'. But she knew in her own heart that wasn't the real reason . . . *Mrs Winter couldn't bear the thought of seeing those two children together*, that was the fact! Miss Polly with all the world open to her: Rachel . . . Rachel, probably working in a shop by fourteen years of age and her ankles swelling with the standing.

But once she had tracked down the reason in her own mind Mrs Winter characteristically decided that it wasn't good enough – sheer selfishness! It would be lovely for Rachel here, do her all the good in the world; and it would be good for lonely little Polly too, having a real child to play with instead of just dumb animals. The children themselves wouldn't worry about their unequal futures: they'd be happy enough together, love each other kindly! At that age, Rachel the little leader no doubt and Polly the devoted little slave.

So Mrs Winter made up her mind. It wasn't too late, thank goodness, even now: Gwilym's old mother would be glad not to have the child longer than could be helped – she didn't find it too easy getting about these days, Nellie had said, yet the longer (Mrs Winter felt) the poor little new baby had a clear field, the better its chances of arousing the mother-love so strangely withheld.

She would ask Mrs Wadamy this very evening if Rachel couldn't come here after the grandmother was done with her. For a week, say, till they saw how things went. Tonight as ever was she'd write to Nellie . . .

'A penny for your thoughts, Mrs Winter,' said Mr Wantage, pretending to topple Polly off his knee.

Mrs Winter rose in silence and gave Polly so unusually loud and loving a kiss that they both looked at her wonderingly.

Chapter 16

Presently evening closed in on Mellton Chase: all over the house the sound of curtains being drawn, everywhere the lights going on – front stairs as well as back.

In spite of Trivett Mary had gone home in time to ask Jeremy Dibden (an Oxford friend of Augustine's, and a Mellton neighbour) over to dine with them. A party of three; for Parliament was sitting and Gilbert (Mary's husband) was detained in London, though probably he might be coming later.

Jeremy was tall and very thin, with narrow shoulders. 'He must have been very difficult to fit,' thought Mary (noting how well his dinner-jacket in fact did fit him): 'especially with that arm.' Polio in childhood had wilted his right arm: when he remembered he lifted it with the other hand into appropriate attitudes, but otherwise it hung from him like a loose tail of rope.

Mary's own face resembled her brother's: it was broad, intelligent, honest, sunburned to a golden russet colour that toned with her curly reddish hair, and lightly freckled. It was almost a boy's face, except for the soft and sensitive lips. Jeremy's face on the other hand had much more of a girl's traditional pink-and-white briar-rose delicacy of colouring: and yet the cast of Jeremy's features was not effeminate – it would be fairer to say they had the regular perfection of the classical Greek. In spite of his faulty body Jeremy reminded Mary a little of the Hermes of Praxiteles: his lips tended to part in that same half-smile. 'Yes, and he's aware of the likeness,' she thought; for his exquisite pale hair was allowed to curl so perfectly about his forehead it might well be carved marble.

'Somehow, though, his face isn't at all insipid because of the life in it: just very, *very* young.'

Now, dinner was ended. The white cloth had been taken away, Waterford glass gleamed on the dark mahogany by candlelight.

Undoubtedly the proper time had come to leave the two young men to their port (or rather, their old Madeira – port being out of fashion). But as Mary rose the talk had just reached the theme of the meaning of human existence. 'Don't get up and go,' said Jeremy, disappointed, 'just when we've started discussing something sensible at last.'

Mary glanced hesitantly from her brother to his friend. 'Very well,' she said slowly, sitting down again a little reluctantly (was she perhaps become lately a shade less interested than she used to be in these abstract discussions?): 'But only for a minute or two: Mrs Winter has asked to see me about something.'

'And so you've *got* to go! – That's typical,' exclaimed her brother. 'Admit I'm dead right, cutting loose from the whole thing.'

'It's known as Service,' said Jeremy to Augustine reprovingly, his light tongue flicking more meanings than one out of the single word. Then he turned to Mary: 'But tell me; there's one thing I've always wanted to know: what is it makes you continue to jeopardize your life being driven by Trivett?' Augustine snorted. 'Trivett,' declared Jeremy, 'can't even change down with the Daimler in motion: he stops dead at the foot of every rise while he struggles into bottom! Trivett – the sound of whose horn . . .' he pursued, lilting, 'makes old women climb trees. He *only* accelerates round corners and at crossroads. I believe the sole time he has ever consistently stuck to the left side of the road was that time you took the car to France.'

Augustine gave a delighted chuckle.

'Surely in Gilbert's bachelor days he used to be head

62

groom? Whatever possessed you, then, to make him chauffeur?'

The question sounded candid enough; but Mary glanced at Jeremy with a flicker of distrust, for wasn't the reason obvious? The bride had wanted to bring her hunters to Mellton and if the old duffer refused to retire voluntarily on pension what else *could* one do? For with Mary's upbringing one never entrusted a *horse* to the tender mercies of a Trivett. True, whenever he drove the car her heart was in her mouth and one day he'd surely kill them all; but similarly, one doesn't give way to fear. – But neither for that matter does one discuss one's servants with one's friends! Momentarily her eyes took on quite an angry look.

'Touché?' Jeremy murmured a little wickedly: 'Be there or be there no some method in Augustine's madness?'

Augustine snorted again. These relics of feudalism! Such relationships were so wholly false; equally ruinous to the servant and the served: he was well quit of such.

Augustine had grown up from childhood with a rooted dislike of ever giving orders. Any relationship which involved one human being constraining another repelled him. But now Jeremy executed a volte-face and attacked him on this very point: the most ominous harbinger and indeed prime cause of bloody revolution is not the man who refuses to obey orders (said Jeremy), 'it's the man like you who refuses to give them.'

'What harm do I do?' Augustine grumbled.

'You expect to be allowed to let other people alone!' blazed Jeremy indignantly. 'Can't you see it's intolerable for the ruled themselves when the ruling class abdicates? You mark my words, you tyrant too bored to tyrannize! Long ere the tumbrils roll here to Mellton *your* head will have fallen in the laps of Flemton's tricoteuses.'

Augustine snorted, and then cracked a walnut and examined its shrivelled kernel with distaste. Funny you could never tell by the shells . . .

Chapter 17

'What do you suppose would happen,' Jeremy continued, 'if there were more people like you? Mankind would be left exposed naked to the icy glare of Liberty: betrayed into the hands of Freedom, that eternal threat before which the Spirit of Man flees in an everlasting flight! Post equitem sedet atra – Libertas! Has there ever been a revolution which didn't end in *less* freedom? Because, has there ever been a revolution which wasn't essentially just one more desperate wriggle by mankind to escape from freedom?'

'A flight *from* freedom? What poppycock,' thought Augustine.

As was his wont, Jeremy was working out even the direction of his argument while he talked, leaping grasshopperlike from point to point. His voice was pontifical and assured (except just occasionally for an excited squeak), but his face all the time was childishly excited by the sheer pleasures of the verbal chase. Augustine, watching rather than really heeding the friend he so admired, smiled tolerantly. Poor old Jeremy! It was a pity he could only think with his mouth open, because he was an able chap ...

'Poor old Augustine!' Jeremy was feeling at the same time, even while he talked: 'He isn't believing a word I say! A prophet is not without honour ... ah well, never mind ... I'm really on to something this time – the flight from freedom ...' If he had read the signs of the times aright this was only too true ...

Mary began to tap the floor rhythmically with her foot. Jeremy's oratory quite drowned the impatient little noise, but she too was scarcely listening any more. Once upon a time she had thought Jeremy absolutely brilliant: she still did in a way, but somehow nowadays she seemed to be losing the power of listening when he talked. One goes on growing up (she realized suddenly) even long after one is grown-up.

Jeremy had the tiresome knack of making even sound sense appear fantastic nonsense, and moreover didn't seem himself to know which was when: yet any moment he *might* reveal some real fragment of new truth, in a sudden phrase like a flashlight going off – something the plodders wouldn't have got to in a month-of-Sundays. Tonight, though, that 'flight from freedom' idea was surely going too far. True, some people don't like pursuing freedom as fast as others but it's only a question of relative speed: surely men never turn their backs on their own freedom, it's tyrants who wrest it from them . . . Liberalism and democracy after all isn't just a fashion, it's the permanent trend, it's human nature . . . progress.

How profoundly Gilbert distrusted brilliance of this sort: Jeremy – Douglas Moss – all that Oxford kidney! 'They're hounds who can find a scent but not follow it,' he had said: 'They're babblers, they run riot . . .' Gilbert didn't really share her passion for hunting (or he could never have tolerated a Trivett in his stables) but he liked its language: he used it in the House, to tease the Tories.

Augustine seemed to prize independence and solitude above everything. But surely (thought Mary) the pattern of man's relationships with man is the one thing specifically human in humanity? And so, to the humanist, disbelieving in God, that pattern is the supremely sacred thing? You can't just contract out of . . . out of *Mankind*, as Augustine seemed to think.

Then Mary found herself wondering what it could be that Mrs Winter was so anxious to see her about. She must go in a minute – the very first time Jeremy paused for breath. Where had he got to?

'You anarchists . . .' she heard him saying to Augustine.

But (thought Mary) to do away with all government like anarchists you'd have to cut the Imperative mood right out of human grammar; for 'government' isn't just something tucked away on a high shelf labelled POLITICS – governing goes on in every human relationship, every moment of the day. One's always governing and being governed. The Imperative mood is the very warp on which that sacred pattern of humanity is woven: tamper with those strong Imperative threads and the whole web must ravel . . .

'No!' cried Augustine giving the table such a thump the glasses rang (*Heavens! How much of all this nonsense could she have been saying out loud?*) 'Your web can't ravel, because . . . Emperor's New Clothes! There IS NO web! There's no thread, even, joining man to man – nothing!'

'I see,' broke in Jeremy, delighted. 'You mean, train-bearers and train-wearers alike human society is but a procession of separate, naked men pretending? "Whom God hath put asunder, let no man . . ." '

One of the wine glasses was still singing and Mary hushed its tiny voice with her finger. 'I really must go now,' she said: 'I told Mrs Winter "Nine". If Gilbert and his friends arrive . . .'

'Don't go!' said Augustine. 'You never know with these Parliament boys: maybe they won't turn up at all!'

'But how are they getting here?' asked Jeremy. 'Is dear Trivett meeting their train at Templecombe?'

His voice was innocent but his eye unholy, and Mary was secretly smiling as she left the room. The incompatibility of Jeremy and Gilbert really was more comfortable displayed like this than hidden.

Chapter 18

Augustine closed the door he had held for his sister and sat down again.

'The voice is the voice of Gilbert!' said Jeremy sadly. 'She never used to talk like that.'

'Logically it's not many steps from Mary's "web" to horrors like the Divine Right of Kings,' said Augustine, 'once you start valuing mankind above each separate man.'

'Only one step – in History's seven-league boots,' said Jeremy. 'One glissade, rather . . . Hegel! Br-r-r! – Then Fichte! Treitschke! Von Savigny! Ugh-gh!'

Augustine forebore to ask him why he wasted his time reading such forgotten German metaphysicians – knowing that probably he didn't. They refilled their glasses.

'Politicians!' said Jeremy: 'They wholly identify their own with their country's interests.' He allowed himself a quick sardonic smile at his own quip. 'These upright Gilberts – so guiltless of favouritism they'll sacrifice a friend as readily as an enemy . . . if their career's at stake. *Poor* Mary!'

At Oxford (that intense white incandescence of young minds) everyone had been agreed that only inferior people feel an itch for power, or even consent to have it thrust upon them. 'Qualities of leadership' – as Douglas Moss once put it – 'reveal the Untermensch.' 'Ambition is the first infirmity of ignoble minds.' And so on. That might not be the kind of language Augustine used himself but it was a doctrine to which the very marrow of his bones responded. To Augustine, even honest statesmen and politicians seemed at best a kind of low-grade communal servant – like sewer-cleaners, doing a beastly job decent men are thankful not to have to do themselves. And indeed the ordinary citizen does only need to become aware of his system of government if it goes wrong and stinks . . .

And Gilbert was an M.P.! Augustine had hated his own sister marrying beneath her like this – into that despised 'Sweeper' caste. Now inevitably she herself was beginning to think 'Sweeper' thoughts.

'Poor Mary!' said Jeremy again. But then a comforting thought struck him: 'Perhaps in her case though it's only old age?' he suggested charitably: 'How old is she, by the by?'

Augustine had to admit his sister was now twenty-six and Jeremy nodded sagely. After all – as both these young men recognized – no intellect can hope to retain its keenest edge after twenty-four or -five.

'Eheu fugaces!' said twenty-two-year-old Jeremy, sighing. 'Give the decanter a gentle push, dear boy.'

Silence for a while.

Sipping her solitary coffee in the drawing-room after Mrs Winter had left her, Mary began to muse. It was time Augustine grew out of friends like Jeremy – unless Jeremy himself was capable of growing up, which she rather doubted.

Dear Augustine! That queer isolated life he chose to lead . . . Now, of course, he was going to be dragged back into society by the short hairs – inquests, newspapers and all that: was this possibly a blessing in disguise? She was sure he had great talents, if only he would apply them to something.

Mary sighed. Nature is as wasteful of promising young men as she is of fish-spawn. It's not just getting them killed in wars: mere middle age snuffs out ten times more young talent than ever wars and sudden death do. Then who was *she*, that she dared to hope her young brother whom she had so cherished and so admired was going to prove that one little fish-egg out of millions destined to survive and grow?

68

Mary set down her cup half drunk: the coffee seemed too bitter . . . *She might be going to have another baby!* It was high time, for Polly's sake. She'd know in a day or two . . .

If it was a boy it would begin all over again, the cherishing and the sisterly admiring – but this time, in little Polly.

In the dining-room the long silence was broken at last.

'Was it . . .' Jeremy began to ask a little hesitantly: 'was it . . . well, an upper-class child do you think?'

Augustine started, and suddenly paled. 'Hard to tell,' he said at last, slowly. 'N-n-no, I wouldn't say it was.'

'Good!' said Jeremy, relieved. 'That's something to be thankful for.'

The blood came back into Augustine's face with a rush: 'Jeremy!' he said, very gently, 'what a *beastly* thing to say!'

Now Jeremy blushed too – hotly, horrified at himself. 'God it was!' he blurted out honestly. Then he recovered himself a little and went on: 'But you know what I mean: not your own . . . tribe, you don't feel it quite the same. Makes it less near home, somehow.' Whereon instantly the same thought sprang into both minds: *Suppose it had been Polly?*

Augustine jumped to his feet and ground the stopper into the neck of the decanter: 'Shall we join the lady?' he said roughly, already making a beeline for the door.

Chapter 19

They found Mary in the drawing-room reading Lytton Strachey's 'Eminent Victorians' while she waited to pour their cooling coffee for them.

'But the only really eminent Victorians were Marx, Freud and Einstein!' said Jeremy. 'People poor dear Lytton has probably never heard of. And the greatest of these is Freud.'

'I suppose there can't have been such figures alive at the same time since Confucius, Buddha and Pythagoras,' said Mary, interested.

'An apt parallel,' said Jeremy: 'Society, the individual soul, mathematics...'

'Sugar,' said Mary.

'Marx is certainly the least of them,' said Augustine, stirring his cup absently, 'partly because the one most eminently Victorian...' He began to explain – with that sudden excessive rush of words to which the solitary is liable now and then – that all 'Victorian' science had been dogmatic: its aim, systems of valid answers. Now, when Einstein had lifted modern science onto the altogether higher level of systems of valid questions...

'Fair enough!' put in Jeremy: 'You can make machines to answer questions but you can't make a machine to ask them.'

'. . . Marxism is a science still fossilized at the Victorian, dogmatic level of mere answers,' Augustine continued.

'And therefore,' Jeremy nipped in, spooning the sugar out of the bottom of his cup with relish, 'rapidly degenerating into a religion! No wonder only a backward, religious people like the Russians take Marxism seriously nowadays.'

'Whereas Freud . . .' Augustine was resuming, but then stopped thunderstruck. *The great revelation which was*

Freud! He had been right, then, in the billiard room: his own generation really was a new creation, a new kind of human being, *because of Freud!* For theirs was the first generation in the whole cave-to-cathedral history of the human race completely to disbelieve in sin. Actions nowadays weren't thought of as 'right' or 'wrong' any more: they were merely judged social or anti-social, personal fulfilment or frustration . . .

'But that lands us with two dichotomies instead of one,' said Jeremy, 'and sometimes they clash . . .'

Soon they were at it again, hammer and tongs. But on one thing Augustine and Jeremy were agreed: theirs was a generation relieved of the necessity even of active envangelistic atheism because the whole 'God' idea had now subsided below the level of belief or disbelief. 'God' and 'Sin' had ceased to be problems because Freudian analysis had explained how such notions arise historically: i.e. that they are merely a primitive psychological blemish which, once explained, mankind can outgrow . . .

'Conscience is an *operable* cancer . . .'

In the age of illimitable human progress and fulfilment now dawning the very words 'God' and 'guilt' must atrophy and ultimately drop off the language. People would still be born with a propensity for being what used to be called 'good'; but even goodness would become innocent once its name was forgotten.

Meanwhile Mary busied herself with her quilting: a simple, pleasant little coverlet for Polly's bed. Suddenly she frowned. Suppose that child she had invited (Mrs Winter's little niece) turned out to be religious? Wasn't her father some sort of dissenting minister? She ought to have thought of that before accepting her as a fit companion for Polly.

Children talk so! – Of course children *should* talk freely about sex, and about excreta and so on; but there are still words and ideas that tender childish ears like Polly's ought to be shielded from, at least till they are old enough to resist or succumb of their own free will: such words as 'God' and 'Jesus'. In Mary's own case and Augustine's those words had been knotted in their very navel-strings...

Wantage must be made to go to bed but she must remind him to leave the whisky out in case Gilbert and his friends were very late. Some sandwiches too: railway food was practically uneatable. And Gilbert had said these guests might be important. There was a movement on foot for reuniting the Liberal party, with much coming and going in the inner councils. Gilbert wasn't perhaps quite 'in' those councils yet, but he was a rising young man with his foot in the door at any rate: he could be a Go-between even if he wasn't yet quite a Gone-between.

Gilbert hoped to be bringing someone important down to Mellton that night – Mond, perhaps, or Simon, or Samuel. If a significant step towards Liberal reunion was taken at a Mellton houseparty it would be a feather in Gilbert's cap worth wearing...

Gilbert had told her the Little Man (Lloyd George) seemed ready enough to be reconciled: it was Asquith who was being rather wary and uncordial. 'He acts as if he has something on his chest!' So L.G. – surprised at it, apparently – had confided to someone who had confided it to Gilbert. Said L.G., 'The old boy is different to me, he just doesn't know when to forget.'

In private life (she continued musing) it would be looked on as rather despicable if an Asquith did 'forget' – if he ever spoke to a Lloyd George again, the nasty little goat. But now, even his own friends were blaming him. For in public life you aren't free to act on your inclinations or even your principles: in order to acquire power you have to forfeit free-will, which seems rather paradoxical.

And how much more so must it be in a dictatorship! A man like Lenin must have about as much choice and freedom of action as the topmost acrobat in a human pyramid...

Mary opened her ears for a moment: but the boys' discussion had reached the late-evening stage of merely going round and round. 'It's eleven o'clock,' said Mary: 'I think I'm going to bed, but don't you . . .' Whereon Jeremy sprang to his feet, full of apologies for outstaying his welcome.

Augustine saw Jeremy to the front door and helped him light his bicycle lamp. For Jeremy's father was a country parson and far from well-off (Jeremy might even have to go into the Civil Service).

'Well I *have* enjoyed myself!" Jeremy exclaimed, with an enthusiasm bordering almost on surprise: 'I don't know *when!*' He flung his leg over the saddle and pedalled off one-handed down the drive.

Augustine set off for bed. He was just crossing the ball-room when he heard that distant, desolate scream.

Chapter 20

For Polly was having a nightmare – Polly, the child so cushioned on love!

Often, when Polly was just dropping asleep, the air would suddenly be full of hands. Not threatening hands: just hands. Hands coming out of the floor, reaching down from the ceiling, coming out of the air – small as she was, there was hardly room to wriggle between them. That wasn't exactly frightening; but tonight she was having a proper nightmare – the worst she had ever had.

It began in Mr Wantage's serving pantry, where Mrs Winter was sitting in Sunday bonnet and cape. But this wasn't quite Mrs Winter . . . actually, it was more a lion dressed in Mrs Winter's clothes and it said to Polly in quite a pleasant voice: 'We're going to have you for our supper.'

Shrinking back, she now saw many of the other grown-ups who best loved her ranged stiffly round the wall, surrounding her. All were principally turned to beasts of prey, even if they didn't entirely look it.

That was the moment she caught sight of Gusting, standing idly by the baize swing-door which led to the kitchen passage . . .

This surely was entirely Gusting, for *he* could *never* turn! She dashed to him for protection.

But even as she flung herself into his arms she saw what a big mistake she had made: for this was in fact a huge gorilla in disguise, stretching its arms across the door of escape and smiling down cruelly at her with exactly Gusting's face.

A trap, baited with Gusting's convincing image! At this moment of panic and betrayal she began to wake. She still saw him there, but now realized with a flood of relief she was dreaming – this monster wasn't real. So she hit him in the stomach with her fist and cried triumphantly: 'I'm not afraid of you! I know you're only a dream!' Then she opened her mouth to scream herself entirely awake, only . . . only to find she was not as near waking as she had thought, and the scream wouldn't come. She had only 'woken' from one level of sleep to the level next above – and now she was slipping back . . . the figure was growing solid again.

'Oho, so I'm only a dream, am I?' he said sardonically, and his dreadful hands began to close on her murderously . . . Gusting's hard hands which she always so much loved.

In this extreme of terror her strangled voice just came back: she managed at last to scream, and woke herself in floods of tears – with the Gusting-Gorilla still shadowy against the billowing darkness of her room (where no night-light was kept burning, for modern atheist children have no need to fear the dark).

When Augustine on his way to bed heard that scream he raced up the stairs three at a time, but Nanny had reached the night-nursery before him and was already rocking the sobbing, nightgowned little figure in her arms.

Polly was quieter already; but now at the sight of Gusting really standing in her bedroom doorway she began to scream again so wildly and in a voice so strangled with fear it was more a hysterical coughing than a proper scream, and she was arching her spine backwards like a baby in a fit.

Nanny signed to him so imperiously to be gone that he obeyed her; but only with feelings of violent jealousy and distrust. 'That woman ought to be sacked!' he muttered loudly (half hoping she would hear), as he retreated down the nursery passage. For of course it was all her fault – she must have been frightening the child . . . goblins . . . tales of black men coming down the chimbley if you aren't good . . . What on earth was the use of Mary trying to bring the child up free of complexes in the new way while confiding her to an uneducated woman like Nanny? 'You can never trust that class!' Augustine added bitterly.

—There is no hell of course but surely there ought to be one for such a woman, who could deliberately teach a child to be afraid! Augustine's anger with that horrible woman gnawed so he would have liked to have it out with Mary there and then: but alas, she had gone to bed.

He knew there'd be a fight, for Mary seemed almost hypnotized by Nanny Halloran: which was surprising, seeing how often and how deeply they disagreed . . .

There's no need nowadays for any child even to know what Fear is – nor Guilt! Not since the great revelation which was Freud . . .

Half-way down the long drive, Jeremy on his way home was dazzled by the lights of an approaching car. He jumped off and dragged his machine right into the bushes.

But it wasn't Trivett driving at all. This was a big limousine with brass and mahogany upperworks like a yacht, and lit up inside: the hire-car from the Mellton Arms, which the Wadamys sometimes bespoke on these occasions.

It seemed full to bursting with young men with sleekly brushed hair and black overcoats, and they were all turned inwards – like bees just beginning to swarm on a new queen – towards the central figure wrapped in a tartan rug in the middle of the back seat: the elongated figure and well-known hawklike face of Sir John Simon.

Chapter 21

Wantage had been shocked at the idea he should go to bed before the Master got home, and was there to attend to his needs. But Mary was already asleep when Gilbert and his guests arrived, and it must have been an hour or two later that she woke abruptly. Something was worrying her – what someone had said earlier about religion subsiding 'below the level of belief or disbelief'. Surely that wasn't quite right? 'Below the level of argument' he ought to have said. We have learned to distinguish these days between concepts which are verifiable and those by nature unverifiable – and which therefore can't be argued about: so really we now need two words for 'belief' and two for 'truth', since we don't mean the same things by 'belief' and 'truth' in both cases.

After all, even Aquinas spoke of faith as an act involving the will: that distinguishes it entirely from verifiable truth – which is the only real truth, of course, she hastened to assure herself.

Through the dressing-room door Mary could hear Gilbert snoring: so he had arrived all right. She hoped they would pull off Liberal Reunion this time ... it was bound to come sooner or later, of course – it takes more than a rift of personalities to dissipate so mighty a force as Liberalism. In fact, Gilbert had said this Asquith v. Lloyd George split was just a repetition of the Rosebery-Harcourt split at the turn of the century; and that had been prelude to the solidest victory the Liberals had ever achieved, the general election of 1906.

Mary could still remember being driven to the village, that sunny January polling-day, in the governess-cart with little Augustine: everyone wore coloured rosettes and even the politest gentry children put out their tongues at children of a different colour.

At this rate (she forecast) the Liberals should be back in power by 1930 or so; and by that time Gilbert...

Having tidied in her mind these two incongruous loose ends, Mary sighed and went to sleep again.

But now she dreamed – the first time for many years – of her German cousin, Otto von Kessen.

It was in 1913 – ten years ago – that Mary had gone on her visit to Schloss Lorienburg. Walther, the eldest von Kessen brother and owner of Lorienburg, was already married then of course – he had at least two sweet children, ten-year-old tow-haired Franz and the wide-eyed little Mitzi. But Otto was 'married to his regiment', they said. Handsome in uniform as some Ouida hero, in white flannels Otto played tennis with the beauty and vigour of a leaping white tiger ... Mary had been sixteen at Lorienburg, that last summer before the war, and the magnificent Otto thirty. Mary had fallen blindly, hopelessly in love; and had developed a boil on her unhappy chin.

Augustine that night was a long time getting to sleep at all, for the moment he was alone his mind reverted uncontrollably and quite fruitlessly from the living to the dead child. He was still racked with pity, and he thought of the coming inquest with foreboding.

Pictured on the darkness he kept seeing again the deep black pool, the sixpenny boat floating just out of reach, then the whitish something in the water . . . He had had no choice, when they found she was quite dead, but to carry her home; for on the Marsh a duck shot at dusk, if the dog failed, was no more than a scatter of feathers by the time daylight came. Thus when Augustine fell asleep at last he dreamed horribly of those hungry rats that the whole Marsh teemed with.

Mrs Winter also stayed awake late, but deliberately. She was sitting up in bed, wearing the little bed-jacket Mrs Wadamy had given her last Christmas over a white linen nightgown with a high frilled collar, and writing a letter – by candlelight, for there was no electricity in the servants' rooms.

Mrs Winter's 'shape' looked natural now, comfortably buxom: her whalebone stays were neatly rolled on a chair. But her greying hair looked unusually skimpy; for it owed its daytime bulk to certain brown pads, and these now lay on the dressing-table. Her cheeks too looked sunken, for her pearly teeth also were on the dressing-table. They stood in a tumbler of water between two photographs in velvet frames: one was her late father, the other showed Nellie holding the baby Rachel.

'Dear Nellie,' she wrote, 'I spoke to Madam about you and Gwilym and darling Rachel and she was kindness itself. She said at once ...' Mrs Winter wrote slowly, weighing every word. For now she had made up her mind she had come to want more than anything else in the world that Nellie should consent.

It would be lovely having Rachel here. Pausing, she tried to picture dear little Rachel now as she must be that very moment, asleep in bed somewhere. But that was difficult, for she had never visited the parts where Gwilym's mother was living these days.

Augustine was woken at six in the morning by the jackdaws arguing in his wide bedroom chimney. He lay awake listening to them, for he was interested in birds' minds and would have liked to be able to make out what all the palaver was about. Jackdaws are notoriously social birds, and it sounded very much as if they were holding some sort of court of justice: certainly someone was getting generally pecked ...

'Getting generally pecked'! – Yes (he thought), that's about all Social Co-operation ever seems to amount to in practice. Then surely it's high time we humans gave up behaving like *birds*?

But just then the door clicked. It was Polly, and she climbed quickly onto his bed in expectation of a story.

At eight that same chilly morning, when the postman arrived, Mrs Winter had already licked and stamped her letter for him to take. But he had a telegram for her, from Gloucester: it was a boy, and mother and child were both doing well.

Nellie's pains had begun the previous evening and the doctor had carried her off to hospital in his car himself. The birth was quite normal: it was the baby's safety *after* birth the doctor had been anxious about in the mother's unnatural mood; but in fact Nellie gave her breast quite readily when they brought the infant to her, because in her drowsy state she believed it was somehow Baby Rachel come again.

Mrs Winter added a few words on the back of the envelope, then re-addressed her letter to the hospital; for the sooner now it was fixed about Rachel coming here the better.

Another telegram to the sanatorium told Gwilym, even this little buff envelope bringing an unmistakably 'outside' smell into the faint odour of illness which tainted everything round him there. The news excited him wildly and brought on a fearful fit of coughing.

A *son*! Then his name should be called Sylvanus . . .

How pleased little Rachel would be! How he longed to be watching her face the first time they let her hold her baby brother! Surely the doctors must let him go home now (indeed they probably soon would – but because they needed his bed for some less hopeless case).

Little Rachel . . . how long would it be before she got the news, he wondered? Wales must be a nice change for her after Gloucester Docks but the place was terribly cut-off. For his mother's new home had been a lonely sluice-keeper's cottage once – in the piping days of farming, when the sluices were still kept on Llantony Marsh.

None of these people knew yet that Rachel lay under an official rubber sheet in the mortuary at Penrys Cross.

Gwilym's old mother lived alone, and on Tuesday had somehow walked alone the whole nine miles to the Cross to report the child missing. She knew already that whatever his letters said her son was dying; she knew that Nellie was about to be brought to bed at any hour: they showed her the body on the slab and she collapsed. She recovered, but for the time being had lost the power of speech.

Thus Augustine had already left for the inquest at Penrys Cross by the time the news reached Mellton.

Chapter 22

The cold had come early to the Continent that Autumn: in the next few days it crossed over, driving Dorset's late mellow muggy autumn away before it.

Mary's mind at Mellton these days was full of the tragedy: she was cudgelling her brains how best Nellie behind the barrier that was Mrs Winter could be helped; but now the cold had come and her brains refused to respond. Dorset never got quite so cold as central Europe of course; but at Mellton she had not those gigantic porcelain stoves she had once laughed at in Schloss Lorienburg, nor the double windows, nor even central heating: houses in Britain were nowadays no warmer than before the war – yet, as if they had been, women had ceased wearing wool next to the skin, ankle-length drawers and long thick petticoats. Thus in a large and draughty place like Mellton Mary always found it difficult in winter to think: her blood kept being called away to do battle in her extremities, leaving her brain on terribly short commons. Thus Mary in winter had to do most of her thinking in her bath, where her brain responded to the hot water like a tortoise in the sun: she saved up most of the day's knottier problems for the bath she took each evening before dressing for dinner: and it was in her evening bath that Mary now had her brainwave about the Hermitage as somewhere for Nellie with her baby and her diseased husband to live.

That morning Mrs Winter had told her the doctors were going to send Gwilym home. There had been a pleading look in Mary's eye as she offered to help, for she was deeply moved and longed to be allowed to. Nellie must be desperately hard-up: naturally there was no question of Gwilym working 'yet' (that 'yet' which deceived no one except Gwilym himself!): with a husband to nurse and a new baby Nellie couldn't go out to work, even if she could find work now there were millions unemployed...

But Mrs Winter had shaken her head. Not *money*: in a life-time of domestic service she herself had saved nearly three hundred pounds, and that should at least last out Gwilym's brief time: it was her own privilege to support her sister, not an outsider's. Yet Mrs Winter felt quite sorry for her mistress, for Mrs Wadamy looked so sad at being shut out.

Moreover there was one kind of help they could surely properly accept. If Gwilym was 'to get well' they had to find somewhere to live right out in the country: somewhere high up and windswept, such as the chalk downs...

Mary's face had lightened at the 'chalk downs': she would speak to the Master about it at once. But when she did so, Gilbert had astonished her by being 'difficult': he had practically ticked her off for even suggesting he might let these people have a cottage! In the end she hadn't dared confess to him she had virtually promised Mrs Winter.

Now, while Mary lay long in the hot water thinking about the Hermitage as a solution, Gilbert was already tying his evening tie and also thinking. His brisk game of squash with the doctor's son ought to have left him enjoying unalloyed that virtuous feeling which is the chief reward of exercise when you are sedentary and thirty; but thoughts of the morning's argument with Mary were troubling him.

A most pathetic case ... yes, but a question of Principle was involved. Yet he doubted if Mary even in the end had hoisted in fully how right he had been to refuse – and the doubt pained him, for he loved Mary. The point was that these people were strangers. His first duty was to his *own* people, he had tried to show Mary; and cottages were scarce: at the moment even his own new carpenter was having to live in lodgings till a cottage fell vacant for him.

But Mary had seemed unimpressed (her picture of the dying Gwilym refusing to be ousted from her mind). The bachelor carpenter was quite comfortable at the Tucketts', she had urged: couldn't he wait?

Couldn't Mary see it would be morally wrong to give strangers a Mellton cottage over Mellton heads? If you don't draw the line somewhere (Gilbert argued), you soon cease being able to do your duty by your own people, the people to whom it is *owed*. One's duty to mankind at large isn't in that same way a personal, man-to-man relationship: it's a collective duty, and one's services to Liberalism rather are its proper discharge – not random little drop-in-a-bucket acts of kindness. Surely no one supposed he ought to rush off to Turkey personally to rescue a massacred Armenian or two? But he'd certainly make time to address that Armenian Atrocities Protest Meeting next month; and similarly his correct Liberal response to these strangers' plight was to campaign for improved National Insurance, more Houses for the Poor: not try to take these particular poor under his own personal wing . . .

As Gilbert stood there tying his tie the lean face which looked back at him from the glass ought to have been re-assuring: with its firm jaw and permanently indignant grey eyes it was so palpably the face of a Man of Principle. But was Mary truly a Woman of Principle? That was the trouble. Alas, Mary yielded all too easily to irrational instinct! There were times lately you almost sensed a distaste in her for all a-priori reasoning, however clearly it was put . . .

Gilbert loved Mary; but was he perhaps a little afraid of her always in any ethical context?

Gilbert was silent and distrait at dinner that night – not on Nellie's account however, or because of the Poor: no, it was something of vital importance. For as he left his dressing-room he had been called to the telephone and what he had heard was disturbing. The speaker knew someone very close to L. G. (with him now, on his American tour).

It had been noised widely abroad that lately the Little Man seemed bent on concocting his own little economic ideas unaided, and from what this chap said might not be quite sound even about Free Trade any more! Then the cat was among the Liberal pigeons indeed.

In short, Liberalism just then had problems on its plate more immediate than slaughtered Armenians and the Poor ... imprimis, there was the split in the party itself to heal – or to exploit; and Gilbert was involved in all that up to the neck.

Thus at dinner Gilbert hardly understood Mary at first when she mentioned the Hermitage: his mind flew first to St Petersburg, then to his wine-cellar.

'No – up on the downs! In the chase. As somewhere for Mrs Winter's sister.'

That place – for her to *live* in? – Lumme ... but after all, why not? Certainly no one else would want it.

This lonely Hermitage was a little romantic folly in eighteenth-century gothic: an architect's freak, built of the biggest and knobbiest flints they could find and designed to look like a toothy fragment of ruined abbey (the largest window was a lancet, the rest more like arrow-slits). But it had been built for a *habitable* hermitage: indeed a professional hermit had originally been persuaded by a good salary to live there, groaning and beating his breast dutifully when visitors were brought to inspect him. Once hermits went out of fashion however it had mostly stood empty: it was too remote, as well as too uncomfortable ... the well even was a hundred feet deep, which is a long way to wind a bucket up.

Aesthetically in Gilbert's opinion so arrant a sham deserved dynamite. However, it still stood; and at least you could be sure the woman wouldn't roost there long! Moreover his consent would stop Mary ...

'Stop Mary' doing what? – 'Nagging him' was the dire meaning he expunged before it could even form in his mind. (Jeremy had once remarked unkindly that Gilbert didn't

85

know how to be insincere: 'He believes every word he says – as soon as he has *said* it!' Thus Gilbert had to be most careful what thoughts he allowed into the reality of words even in the privacy of his own head.)

'By all means – an inspiration, my dear!' he answered. 'But now, if you'll excuse me . . .'

He had much to think over. Whether or not this was true about L. G. and Free Trade the Tories would soon get wind of the rumour – and what then?

Mary had never been inside that hermitage: only seen it in the distance. But the site though remote seemed so exactly what was wanted; and actually it was only about four miles from the house, an easy bicycle-ride for Mrs Winter on her afternoons off. She was so elated she told Mrs Winter about it that same evening.

Mrs Winter was very pleased. She too had never seen the place; but how lovely to have her Nellie at last so near, and be able to share her grief!

Chapter 23

Discovery that the dead child had been Mrs Winter's famous little niece was not the only shock the inquest had had in store for Augustine. Apparently the deceased had *not* died of drowning, the police-surgeon said in evidence as soon as the proceedings opened: he had found hardly any water in the lungs and the skull was cracked.

He went on to testify he had found no medical signs whatever pointing to violence: the child's skull was abnormally thin: perhaps her head had hit something as she tumbled in, reaching after her toy boat – even a floating branch could have done it. But this ghoulish sawbones had already had an effect on the court that nothing he said later could alter or undo.

Moreover as it turned out Augustine had found himself sole witness to the finding of the body: his companion Dai Roberts was still untraced.

In the front row of the public seats sat Mrs Dai Roberts with her Flemton coven: as he told his story their glittering eyes never for a moment left his face. But the jury seemed unwilling to look at him at all: so long as he was in the box they averted their eyes to the well of the court where the public sat, and their faces were wooden and uneasy.

The police for their part said they also had found nothing on the spot either that suggested foul play – nothing at all. But when the police-witness protested perhaps over-much how satisfied they were, Mrs Roberts under the eyes of the jury took out her purse and looked inside it. The sergeant at the door reddened with anger; but there was nothing he could do. Then a juryman asked for Augustine to be recalled, and put a suspicious question to him, in a suspicious voice: 'Why ever did you move it, mun?'

Throughout the still court the questing breathing of those Flemton women could be *heard* . . .

A scatter of torn frock and a bloody bone half-gnawed . . . Augustine's mind's-eye flash of the reason he'd had to bring the body away at once was so beastly he just stood there in the box tongue-tied and at last Dr Brinley the coroner himself had blurted it out: 'Rats, laddie!' he said to the juryman reprovingly. The juryman of course misunderstood Dr Brinley's meaning and flushed with mortification; but the old man never noticed.

Meanwhile a fly had settled on Dr Brinley's bald head and polished its dirty legs while the aged voice under it continued: 'A very natural, decent thing to do!' But on this the juryman set his jaw and looked more obstinate still.

Dr Brinley was troubled. The whole neighbourhood had got it in for that boy . . . but *why*? Notoriously wrongheaded, certainly . . . tactless . . . a bit of a recluse . . . With that inadequate eggshell of a skull the wonder was the child had lived so long! The very first fall from her pony . . . but she wouldn't have had a pony, of course . . . Why, too – Dai had been with the boy when he found her! – Damn Dai for his eternal Law-shy elusiveness: his presence today could have made all the difference . . .

But at that point Dr Brinley was distracted by the appearance of something lying on the desk before him. It was a hand; and a very old hand – the loose skin was blotched with brown under the white hairs, and wrinkled: the joints were knobbly, the ribbed nails horny and misshapen. The withered object was so redolent of old age it was seconds before he realized that this aged hand was his own. – *Now*, when he had never felt younger or better, when even those pains a week ago he had thought mortal were quite gone! But if all over he looked like *that*, all these idiots here must regard him as . . . how dare they, puking puppies the whole sort of them!

Thrusting the offending hand out of sight he glared at his middle-aged jury as if he would like to slipper the lot; and they wriggled resentfully . . . the old fool!

When the evidence was all taken the coroner strongly suggested a verdict of accidental death; but the verdict the jury obstinately returned was an 'open' one.

The Flemton women looked gleeful: Dr Brinley looked worried.

Meanwhile the police had found the Bentley in the street outside with its windscreen smashed, and belatedly had set a guard on it. After adjourning his court Dr Brinley took one look at the damaged Bentley and then surprised Augustine by asking him for a lift home in it. He ignored someone else's offer and insisted he wouldn't mind the draught from the broken windscreen; but in fact his old eyes watered painfully the whole way back to his house.

The pavements in the High Street as they passed were unnaturally deserted – but not the windows.

At Newton that night two of those unshuttered billiard-room windows got smashed and late flowers in the garden were deliberately fouled. But of that Augustine knew nothing, for straight after dropping Dr Brinley he had started for the north. He was embarked on what was presently to prove a none-too-satisfactory visit to Douglas Moss – the former Oxford luminary and leading philosophic wit. This was their first meeting since both went down. But Douglas was a native (surprisingly) of Leeds and already, alas, beginning to revert to native ways: he was out all day at the 'Works', leaving Augustine to his own devices – and then Augustine couldn't get that inquest out of his mind, his thoughts kept returning to it. The Mosses' home was a vast and almost bookless mansion in grimy crimson brick, built on the outskirts of the city. The old people made him as welcome as they could, but still the inquest continued to rankle. That accusing question: Why had he moved the body? That juryman's suspicious voice, asking him *'Why ever did you move it, mun?'*

The whole thing was indeed an intractable cud to chew . . .

What was that phrase Jeremy had once used? – 'Flemton's tricoteuses.'

Chapter 24

Waking next morning Mary did wonder a moment if she had been rash, telling Mrs Winter without having even seen the place: but it was all settled now, so she put the thought from her. After breakfast, though, she would ride that way ... there might be repairs needed. There might even be no sink!

It was a golden mid-October morning when Mary started out: sun above, and in the hollows mist. There was a smell of frost in the air but none properly in the ground yet, and the oaks in the park still held their yellow leaves.

Polly was out exercising her pony there, under a groom's surveillance: a tiny, narrow piebald pony off the Prescelly hills Augustine had given her like a miniature Arab, and perfectly schooled. Polly had a remarkable natural seat for so young a child, and the beauty of their effortless performance together under the trees that autumn morning plucked at Mary's heart. Should she take Polly with her for company, then? But no, it might be too far (or was the real reason a fear Polly might not like the Hermitage?) – Anyway, Mary rode on alone, collecting her mare to take the low wall from the park into the stubble (no wire was allowed anywhere on Mellton land, however much the farmers grumbled).

The soil in the valley was still soggy with autumn water though today the tufts were frosted; but on the high downs where lay the chase (a misnomer nowadays, with its ten-mile circuit of high wall) the going was crisp and solid, and the air was sharp.

As she entered the chase at last by the crumbling castel-lated gateway even the green unrutted track she had fol-lowed came to an end, and Mary realized fully for the first time how ungetatable this hermitage was. Once more she felt a twinge of anxiety; but again drove it from her, for Mrs Winter would be bitterly disappointed by adverse reporting *now*.

Moreover as Mary neared the Hermitage all practical thoughts were banished by the beauty of its setting. This chase, this tract of land preserved unchanged by man for a thousand years or more, was a piece of Ancient Britain itself. In the middle distance red-deer grazed warily: this was where they had always grazed since the dawn of time, for this turf under the wide sky had never known the plough – not since ploughs were invented. These thickets had never known the axe, these huge hollow yews and holly and random natural timber all tangled in old-man's beard and bryony.

This was the very Britain King Arthur knew! In this setting, even the romantic fragment of the Hermitage looked almost true. In this setting, Mistress Mary Wadamy felt quite mediaeval herself . . . she hitched her palfrey to a thornbush and let herself in.

The kitchen was smaller even than most town kitchens. It was darker and gloomier too because of that ruby-tinted lancet which provided the only light. Mary's heart sank . . . still, it would probably just take a table for two . . . the stained-glass in the lancet could be replaced with clear (and perhaps even made to open): white walls would work wonders, and in any case whitewash is far healthier than wallpaper when there are germs about.

The reason the kitchen was so cramped was that two-thirds of the space in the Hermitage was occupied by the grandiose beginnings of an ascent of corkscrew stone stairs. This stairway had been concocted so wide and ornate as proof of the fabulous dignity and wealth of this abbey-which-never-had-been: seen from outside, the stairs extended several feet even above the façade of the building, then the corkscrew broke off dramatically against the open sky (effectively masking from sight the kitchen chimney but perhaps rather spoiling its draught).

Off these stairs, just before they emerged through a trap into the open, a low door led into the hermitage's only room other than the kitchen: an attic bedroom, contrived in the small space available under the sloping, hidden roof. It had no window – but surely a skylight is adequate ventilation for quite so tiny a room? The slightly-slanting floor was triangular, and so were the only two walls (on the third side the roof itself sloped to floor-level). Presumably, though, it was here the hermit had set his truckle-bed . . . and indeed there *would* just be room here for a single bed for the mother if she didn't sit up too suddenly, and even for the child's cot too.

As for the invalid, Mary had made up her mind before starting out: an opensided wooden shed out-of-doors should be built for him such as she had seen in Swiss sanatoria. She was thankful there was no possible room for Gwilym here in the house: it saved argument. In times past, when the warm sweet breath of cows was thought sovereign for consumption, folk would have contrived him a little dark loft in some crowded cowhouse close over the cows and there they'd have been shut up all winter, he and his raging tubercles and the milking-cows together. A more scientific age now realized the danger to the *cows*; so they prescribed chalk downs, and the warm sweet breath of a loving wife and child . . . Mary had little patience with doctors who sent infectious cases home to their families like this: they seemed too much like farmers doing a grim seeding for next year's crops.

As her eyes got more used to the half-dark in the kitchen she saw now there was moss growing on some of the beams. The place could certainly do with a good drying out, and Gilbert *must* provide a sink (there was no piped water or drainage, but a sink can be served with buckets). Workmen must be sent up at once, so that the woman could move in and have it ready for her husband when he arrived.

As her eyes grew still more used to the ruby-tinted gloom she saw that the open grate was nearly solid with wet ashes. The chimney-throat was plugged with a wet sack: Mary poked it with her crop and it collapsed, discharging a barrow-load of sodden soot and jackdaw nests. Under this weight the front of the grate fell out too.

As Mary rode home she wondered how best to describe the place to Mrs Winter. It was indeed a fairy-tale little place; but its charms were not altogether too easy to put into simple words.

However, when Mary got home she found a new problem awaiting her to consider in her bath that night. A letter from Augustine in Leeds: he told her he thought of travelling in China for a bit.

Chapter 25

Even before the inquest Augustine had known the Hermit-of-Newton phase of his life was ended. His obsession that every man *is* an island remained, but his craving for physical solitude had been transitory and was now gone. It had been succeeded by a similar compulsive craving to 'see the world'.

Because of the war, Augustine had come to manhood without ever setting foot even on the further shores of the Channel. Even Calais would have been strange to him. But his temperament was not one ever to do things by halves, and hence his letter to Mary that he thought of going to China. He had 'once met a chap who had actually set out to *walk* to China and had got as far as Teheran when the war broke out and stopped him. Perhaps . . .'

Mary's answer suggested : 'Fine, but first why not go to Germany?' She could write to Lorienburg . . . And now Douglas had commented : 'After all, why not? – if you don't mind remoteness; for Germany of course is so much *remoter* than China.'

The friends were alone together, after dinner, in the huge but darkling and unventilated pillared pannelled 'lounge'. Tonight Douglas seemed a little more like his old self : business forgotten for once, he lay on his back in a deep armchair with his long legs higher than his head and his suède-shod feet tinkling the bric-à-brac beside them on the top shelf of the chiffonier, while he purported to be composing a love-letter in modern Greek. Augustine looked at him hopefully. There was sound truth in what he had said : Germany was indeed singularly 'remote', in the sense that Germany was somewhere utterly *different*.

On Augustine's wartime mind of course had once been deeply impressed the concept of Germans as quintessential

95

'they' – as Evil Absolute, the very soil of Germany being poisoned. Since then, victory had somehow set all one's wartime 'we-they' axes in a flat spin. However, that hadn't made Germany 'ordinary' soil again: the evil magic emanating from it had not been disspelled, it had become good magic. Today it was rather one's own country and one's own wartime allies that tended to look black in young English eyes like Augustine's, while Darkest Germany was bathed in a mysterious, a holy light ...

'The new Germany? Hm ... I see what you mean ...'

'Yes-s-s-s!' Douglas almost whistled, with all his old Oxford sibilance: 'The *new* Germany!'

Except for those hissing sounds his voice was always quiet, and he had learned to make this sort of speech without the least betraying tinge of irony in his tone as he continued: 'For it is indeed utterly new, isn't it? The Kaiser being gone, the power of the Prussian Army forever broken, out of the shattering of that hard and horny chrysalis has emerged the *new* German s-s-soul ... a tender and shimmering angel, helpless among the cynical guilty victors and yet with so much to teach them! Yes-s-s – well worth a visit! A *Weimar* Germany – all Werfels, Thomas Manns, Einsteins, Ernst Tollers – all nesting swallows, democracy and peace!'

'Shut up!' said Augustine, stirring uneasily. 'All the same, I think I'll go.'

'Do, dear boy, do ...' said Douglas absently, appearing to bury himself again in his Demotic. But in fact he was silently wondering what accounted for these fantastic notions about Germany 'everybody' now held. It could hardly be *just* that little bit of eloquence from Keynes ... nor even *just* the blessed word 'Weimar' brightening Ebert's aura with a few rays from Goethe's and Schiller's ... then too there had been the shock of victory, coming just when the pendulum had reached the other furthest teetering-point of the absurd ... 'Perhaps any picture so garishly coloured as our wartime one of Germany must inevitably reverse its colours if stared-at till suddenly the eye tires.'

Moreover the concrete British imagination tends always to project its fictive Utopias on to some map – and it was still at Germany that the atlas lay open.

—But in any case, this dear naïve was better among new scenes for a bit, after that beastly business ... though not quite so far off as China!

Chapter 26

This was the post-war generation – Augustine and Douglas and the like. Unconsciously, and from below, those four war years would condition their thinking and feelings all their lives through.

Five years had passed since the war's ending, and already it was difficult for an Augustine consciously to remember that so short a while ago unnatural death had been a public institution; that there had indeed been a time when the tiny thud of such a falling farthing sparrow as Little Rachel would have gone quite unheard in all the general bereavement (except by the ears of God). Even the impression of the Armistice was growing dim. It had come like waking with a jolt out of a bad dream, that sudden victorious ending of the 'Great War' in 1918: one moment in the grip of nameless incubi, the next – sweating, but awake and incredulously safe between the crumpled sheets. 'Everyone suddenly burst out singing' – so wrote Sassoon at Armistice-time: 'O, but everyone was a bird, and the song was wordless, and the singing will never be done!' But now, even that brief singing aftermath seemed to be forgotten too: at least, by the young. It had quickly subsided, together with the bad dream it ended, below the threshold of recollection – as dreams do.

But buried beneath that threshold the war years persisted in these young men indestructible – as dreams do. Thus it is imperative for us to draw for our own eyes some sort of picture, however partial – some parable of the impact of this war upon them, and of the reasons.

That impact had been from the first on British minds something unique in history; for in 1914 Britain had known

98

no major war for ninety-nine years – a unique condition; and most folk in Britain had come to believe in their bones such wars were something Western man had quite outgrown. Thus its coming again in 1914 had been over the head of a bottommost belief it couldn't. So people's reactions tended to be 'as if' they were now at war rather than 'that' they were at war: almost more appropriate to make-believe than to belief.

Yet there is reason to talk as we have done of their state rather on the analogy of 'dream' than of 'make-believe': for this was no voluntary make-believe, they were soon to discover – this was the true dreaming: compulsory, compulsive, like Polly's nightmare. If their state, then, was dreamlike, was this war 'dream' at least in part a projection of some deep emotional upheaval such as compulsive Freudian dreams like Polly's are born of – an upheaval by which familiar things and people were all *changed*, just as in dreams? An upheaval from the very roots of being, like earth's queasy belly abruptly gurgling up hot lava onto the green grass?

That could be, if modern man had been trying to ignore (as perhaps he had been) what seems to be one of the abiding terms of the human predicament.

Primitive man is conscious that the true boundary of his self is no tight little stockade round one lonely perceiving 'I', detached wholly from its setting: he knows there is always some overspill of self into penumbral regions – the perceiver's *footing* in the perceived. He accepts as naturally as the birds and beasts do his union with a part of his environment, and scarcely distinguishes that from his central 'I' at all. But he knows also his self is not infinitely extensible either: on the contrary, his very identity with one part of his environment opposes him to the rest of it, the very friendliness of 'this' implies a balancing measure of hostility in – and towards – 'all that'. Yet the whole tale of *civilized* man's long and toilsome progress from the taboos of Eden to the psychiatrist's clinic could be read as a tale of his efforts, in the name of emergent Reason, to confine his concept of self wholly within Descartes' incontestable cogitating 'I'; or alternatively, recoiling rebuffed off that adamantine pinpoint, to extend 'self' outwards infinitely – to pretend to awareness of every one as universal 'we', leaving no 'they' anywhere at all.

Selfhood is *not* wholly curtailed within the 'I': every modern language still witnesses the perpetuity of that primitive truth. For what else but affirmations of two forms of that limited overspill of '*I*'-ness are the two words 'we' and 'my' (the most potent words we have: the most ancient meanings)? These are in the full sense 'personal' pronouns for they bring others right inside our own 'person'. Moreover the very meaning of 'we' predicates a 'they' in our vocabulary, 'meum' an 'alienum'.

That primitive truth about selfhood we battle against at our peril. For the absolute solipsist – the self contained wholly within the ring-fence of his own minimal innermost 'I' and for whom 'we' and 'my' are words quite without meaning – the asylum doors gape. It is the we–they and meum–alienum divisions which draw the sane man's true ultimate boundary on either side of which lie quantities of opposite sign, regions of opposite emotional charge: an electric fence (as it were) of enormous potential. Yet emergent Reason had attempted to deny absolutely the validity of any such line at all! It denied it by posing the unanswerable question: Where, in the objective world, can such a line ever reasonably be drawn? But surely it is that question itself which is invalid. By definition the whole system of 'self' lies within the observer: at the most, its shadow falls across the objective observed. Personality is a *felt* concept: the only truth ever relevant about selfhood must be emotional, not intellectual truth. We must answer then that objectively the we–they dividing line 'reasonably' lies . . . wherever in a given context the opposing emotional charges for the moment place it: wherever it brings into balance the feelings of owning and disowning, the feelings of loving and hating, trusting and fearing . . . 'right' and 'wrong'. For normally (at least up to now) each of these feelings seems to predicate its opposite, and any stimulus to the one seems to stimulate the other in unregenerate man. In short, it is as if it were *the locus of this emotional balance* that circumscribes and describes the whole self, almost as the balance of opposite electrical forces describes the atom.

Perhaps in the neighbourhood of death or under the shadow of heaven man, in a dissolution as potent as the splitting atom his analogue, *can* experience love only . . . or, in the shadow of madness and hell, conceivably hate only. But normal man seems not to be able to, normally, unaided; and even the all-loving Christ still kept one counterbalancing 'they' outside for utter hatred and spurning: *Sin*.

In terms of our picture of the 'self', then – of this our parable of a system contained within the observer, its shadow (only) shifting like the shadow of a cloud across the landscape–'objectively' old we–they dichotomies will appear to be continually replaced by new. On the scale of history, old oppositions such as Christian and Paynim will in time give way to Papist and Protestant: these in turn to distinctions of colour and race, local habitation, social class, opposite political systems: but whatever the changing content of the opposing categories, the love–hate balances of kinship and alienation inherent in man would, unaffected, continue.

But suppose that in the name of emergent Reason the very we–they line itself within us had been deliberately so blurred and denied that the huge countervailing charges it once carried were themselves dissipated or suppressed? The normal penumbra of the self would then become a no-man's-land: the whole self-conscious being is rendered unstable – it has lost its 'footing': the perceiver is left without emotional adhesion anywhere to the perceived, like a sea-anemone which has let go its rock.

Then surely, in this entropy of the whole self, the depleted voltages *must* cry out for a re-charge and dichotomies new! In comparison with that psychic need material security will suddenly seem valueless. Reasonable motive-constructs such as 'Economic Man' and the like will be revealed as constructs, their motivation being quite overthrown or adapted as conduits for much deeper springs. In such a state the solipsist-malgré-lui may well turn to mad remedies, to pathological dreaming; for his struggles to regain his 'footing' would indeed be an upheaval from being's very roots ... gurgling up hot lava suddenly on to the green grass.

Chapter 27

Especially in modern England had it been held to be the measure of man's civilization, how much they strove to kick against these particular pricks. Elsewhere, nationalism or the class-struggle were in the comforting ascendant; but here, Liberal 'Reason' had done its utmost to keep both emotionally weak. Thus here there had been *no* adequate replacement for the once-unbridgeable hereditary castes and trades which had now so long been melting: now, too, that derided nigger-line at Calais was growing shamefast, weakening: so was the old damnation-line between Christian and heathen; and even (since Darwin) the once-absolute division between man and beast.

Moreover in the last century the once-dominant Liberal mystique of laissez-faire had called on man to renounce even his natural tendency to love his neighbour – the workless starving craftsmen, stunted women sweating in the mills, naked child-Jezebels dying in the mines and the sore chimney-boys. Ignoring what an unnatural and dangerous exercise this is for ordinary men (this trying not to love even mildly even such neighbours as those), the earliest English 'Liberals' had loudly denounced that strong implanted urge: not only as a Tory obstacle to economic progress, but worse – as a blasphemy against their rational doctrine of total *separation of persons*, a trespass on the inalienable right of the helpless to be helped by no one but himself.

Now, coming full circle, you were called on to love all mankind at large, coupled for good measure with all created nature! The Humanist 'we' of infinite extension. Yes, but *how*? For 'Sin' nowadays evoked nothing stronger than a mild distaste – the lifted eyebrow, not the lifted rod; and they had found no substitute for Sin.

In 1914, then, there was something of an emotional void in England: and into it war-patriotism poured like Noah's Flood. For the invasion of Belgium seemed once again to present an issue in the almost-forgotten terms of *right* and *wrong* – always incomparably the most powerful motive of human conduct that history has to show. Thus the day Belgium was invaded every caged Ego in England could at last burst its false Cartesian bonds and go mafficking off into its long-abandoned penumbral regions towards boundaries new-drawn.

The effect was immediate. The boy Jeremy, lying on his sickbed paralysed throughout that hot 1914 summer, had seen with the clear and detached eye of the child who has nearly died just such an extraordinary change overtake his elders when 'war' was declared – so he told Augustine afterwards, wondering: he had *seen* his father that gentle clergyman suddenly lift up his nose and begin baying for blood as naturally as any foxhound.

The dim world had come out for them all in clear contrasting colours again, like a landscape after rain: everything, taking sides at last, looked nobler or more villainous. And thus in simple minds and minds not-so-simple too had quickly been conjured all that whole new potent 'we–they' dream-phantasmagoria typical of 1914 (thought Jeremy): *Martyred Belgium . . . our brave little Servia, with the big benignant Russian Bear lumbering to his rescue;* and against them, *Decrepit, tyrannical Austria,* with chiefest 'they' of all *GERMANY, Belgium's Ravisher,* who now unmasked features of wickedest quintessential THEY!

Their 'we' too had been re-born; for the two-ended compass needle, ceasing to dither, cannot point to the north without faithfully pointing to the south as well. If war (and lesser crime too, for that matter) pointed to hate alone, would man find the difficulty he palpably does find in renouncing them both – war, and crime? Surely love, rather, is the lode: it is the love two-ended war points to which will always suck us into it if deprived of enough

104

natural loving to do in the ways of peace. Certainly the enthralment over Britons in 1914 of this their war-dream was not hate but that it enabled Britons to love Britons again. Officers found themselves now able to love the Regiment, soldiers their officers: the non-combatant loved both – every uniform designated a Hero and a gallant grave among the nodding poppies of Flanders was to be their guerdon, so

> *So sing with joyful breath:*
> *For why, you are going to death . . .*

The public dream was now in full pelt: moreover as the dream deepened everything grew even more symbolical. *Grey hordes of 'THEY' raven on the lovely virginal flesh of La Belle France:* the Russian Bear turned into a Steamroller, but was thrown back on his haunches in an agonizing halt: indeed, now *tridented Britannia herself stands with her back to the wall;* but

> *Loudly over the distant seas*
> *The Empire's call rang across the breeze:*
> *'Children of mine! Your liberties*
> *Are threatened now by might!'*

Then Britain's bronzed sons overseas lay down the sheep-shears and the reaping-hook, hastening at the Mother's call, and

> *Tramp, tramp, tramp, the boys are coming . . .*

After the war, in a 'waking' state, it was just such potent love-fantasies as these which came most particularly to be derided: the most implausible materialist motives were invented to account for the Empire's whole-hearted entry into the war (as for Britain's too). Yet surely all this had been true dreaming! Why need there have been anything faked, anything despicable, anything wrong or ridiculous about these love-fantasies? Surely for the most part they were noble and quite true – come through the Gate of Horn.

After the war, war-emotion was assumed ex hypothesi to be all hatred because men then *wished* to believe war-making something easy to slough off; and hatred is akin to suffering . . . so what sane man ever positively wishes to hate?

They deliberately forgot the love war stimulates too.

The public dream was now in full pelt: but not yet the public nightmare it was presently to become.

A private nightmare too can begin nobly, pleasurably. Silver ponies skimming summer meadows . . . a soaring on wings among restless star-fronted towers, over alabaster domes mirrored in shining lakes . . . but then suddenly the dream changes phase, the wings shrink to a tight winding-sheet and the dreamer plummets, the topless towers turn to dizzy unbanistered stairways climbing to nowhere up nothing.

Then the translucent lakes become the rocking oceans paved with accusing faces: then come the staring idiot monkeys and the hollow derisive parakeets, the stone coffin at the heart of the pyramid, the 'cancerous kisses of croco-diles', the slimy things and the Nilotic mud . . .

The *Flanders* mud, the slime of putrefying bodies. The accusing sunken eyesockets trodden in the trench floor. The gargled pink froth, and an all-pervading smell.

Chapter 28

There had never been so much death in any earlier war: nothing comparable.

In the one battle of Passchendaele alone the British lost nearly half a million men. But mostly it was war hardly separable into battles – a killing going on all the time: without apparent military object, although in fact a deliberate military policy called 'attrition'. For while so many men on both sides were still alive between the Alps and the Narrow Seas the generals on both sides had no room for manœuvre; and in manœuvre alone (they both thought) lay any hope of a decision.

But so prolific had civilized western man become it proved no easy task, this killing enough in the enemy ranks and your own to make room to move. Even after some four years, when some fourteen million men all told had been killed or maimed or broken in nerve, it had scarcely been achieved. Always there seemed to be new boys in every country growing to manhood to fill the gaps; whereon the gaps had to be made all over again.

Boys of Augustine's age had been children when the war began and as children do they accepted the world into which they had been born, knowing no other: it was normal because it was normal. After a while they could hardly remember back before it began; and it hardly entered their comprehension that one day the war could end.

Merely they knew they were unlikely to live much beyond the age of nineteen; and they accepted this as the natural order of things, just as mankind in general accepts the unlikelihood of living much beyond eighty or so. It was one of those natural differences between boys and girls: girls such as Mary would live out their lives, but not their brothers. So, generation after generation of boys grew big, won their colours, and a few terms later were . . . mere names, read aloud in chapel once. As list succeeded list the time of other littler boys for the slaughterhouse was drawing nearer; but they scarcely gave it a thought as they in turn grew into big boys, won their football colours.

After all, it is only grown men ever who think of school as a microcosm, a preparation for adult life : to most boys at any time school *is* life, is itself the cosmos : a rope in the air you will climb, higher and higher, and – then, quite vanish into somewhere incomprehensible anyhow. Thus in general they seemed quite indifferent. Yet sometimes the death of someone very close – a brother, or a father perhaps – would bring home to them momentarily that being killed *is* radically different from that mere normal disappearing into the grown-up shadow-world : is being no more even a shadow on the earth.

When Augustine's cousin Henry was killed – the heir to Newton Llantony – the change in Augustine's 'prospects' had still meant nothing to him at all; for his real prospects were still unchanged : to tread the universal path that Henry had just trodden. But Henry's death did make a deep impression on him of this other kind, a sudden blinding intimation of mortality.

Augustine at this time had been seventeen, a sergeant in the school Officers' Training Corps. That afternoon with his mother's opened letter in his pocket he was taking a squad of little boys in bayonet-practice. Scowling as savagely as he could he jerked out the staccato commands 'In! – Out! – On guard!' while the little boys struggled with their heavy rifles and bayonets to jab the swinging sacks of straw called 'Germans', piping as they did so the officially-taught obscenities supposed to arouse blood-lust in them.

Suddenly the moment of self-revelation came to Augustine, more vividly than he had ever felt it since the first time in childhood – the realization that within his 'we' and distinct from it there was too one irreplaceable 'I'. But this time there came with it the awful corollary: it is the 'I' which *dies* . . . '*I* shall die . . .' and at the same moment he felt the tender flesh of his belly and the very guts within shrinking back as from a stabbing bayonet-point.

For a moment his face went grey with fear.

Just then a pretty four-foot choirboy shrilled: 'Knock his b . . . s out of the back of his bloody neck!' – The child took a flying punt-kick at the swinging sack and landed on his behind in the mud, the rifle clattering from his hand.

Some bigger boys laughed. But Augustine angrily reproved their frivolity and the solemn bayonet-practice went on.

Augustine had left school and was on the last lap of all – at a training camp for young officers – when the guns stopped.

The war had ended. He was eighteen. The shock was stupendous.

No one had warned him he might after all find himself with his life to live out: with sixty years still to spend, perhaps, instead of the bare six months he thought was all he had in his pocket. Peace was a condition unknown to him and scarcely imaginable. The whole real-seeming world in which he had grown to manhood had melted round him. It was not till Oxford he had even begun to build a new world – he, and his whole generation – from the foundations up.

Perhaps then the key to much that seems strange about that generation is just this: their nightmare had been so vivid! They might think they had now forgotten it, but the harmless originals of many of its worst metamorphoses were still charged for them with a nameless horror . . . Just as Polly that night, when after waking she saw Augustine's harmless real figure standing in her bedroom doorway, had screamed at it so. Just as next morning, her dream ostensibly forgotten, she had yet lain away from him on the mattress's extreme edge – as companionable as a three-foot plank of wood.

Oxford is always luminous; but at first in those post-war days Oxford had been an older and more hysterical society than in normal times. Colonels and even a brigadier or two twisted commoners' gowns round grizzled necks: young ex-captains were countless. But between the Augustines who had never seen the trenches and these, the remnant who for years had killed yet somehow had not been killed back, an invisible gulf was fixed. Friendship could never quite bridge it. Secretly and regretfully and even enviously the men yet felt something lacking in these unblooded boys, like being eunuchs; and the boys, deeply respecting and pitying them, agreed. But the older men understood each other and cherished each other charitably. *They* knew they sweated sometimes for no reason, and the sweat smelt of fear. Their tears came easily, making the boys ashamed: they had moments of violence. They tended to find knowledge difficult to memorize.

That was in the first twelve months or so, before they hardened over; and in two years most of them were gone. The young ex-captains and the uncrowned kings like Lawrence departed, their places were taken by freshmen younger than Augustine still – the Jeremies, milk-fresh from school. But one belief had been shared absolutely on both sides of the gulf, and in England continued for a long time to be held by those who came thereafter: it was built into the very structure of Augustine's new world: *never till the end of Time could there be another war.*

Life in the years so unexpectedly to come might hold many hazards for this and for succeeding generations; but that hazard could be discounted.

Any government which ever again anywhere even talked of war would next minute be winkled out of Whitehall or the Wilhelmstrasse or wherever by its own unanimous citizens and hanged like stoats.

BOOK TWO

The White Crow

Chapter 1

In his little office in Lorienburg, the castle Mary had visited in her girlhood before the war, sat the magnificent Otto von Kessen she had so lately dreamed of. He was rubbing his chin, which felt pleasingly rough to the touch after the papers he had been fingering all afternoon.

'Thursday November the Eighth' said the calendar on the wall. The cold had come early to Bavaria this autumn, with ten degrees of frost outside. But this office was in the thickness of the castle's most ancient part: it was a tiny twilight room with a sealed double window, and it was like an oven. There were beads of sweat on Baron Otto's forehead, and the hot air over the huge blue porcelain stove quivered visibly: it kept a loose strip of wallpaper on the wall in constant agitation like a pennon.

This monumental stove was too big: with its stack of wood it more than half filled the room and the space left only just housed the safe and the little kneehole desk Otto was sitting at. On the desk stood a huge ancient typewriter of British make, built like an ironclad and with two complete banks of keys (being pre-shiftlock), and that incubus also took up far too much space: the files and ledgers piled high beside it leaned, like Pisa. In such a cubbyhole there was no possible place to put the big wire wastepaper basket other than under the desk, yet that left a man nowhere to stretch his artificial leg in comfort and now the socket was chafing: a nerve in the mutilated hip had begun to throb neuralgically against the metal of the heavy revolver in Otto's pocket.

Otto tried hard to concentrate on the sheets of accounts in front of him (he acted as factotum for his half-brother Walther these crippled days). These were the last and craziest weeks of the Great Inflation when a retired colonel's

113

whole year's pension wouldn't cobble him one pair of shoes: Walther's cheques however vast were still honoured, but only because he was able to keep his bank account nowadays in terms of the corn he grew and a cheque drawn for trillions of marks would be debited as so many bushels according to the price that actual hour. This galloping calculus of the currency, this hourly acceleration in the rise of all prices and the fall of all real values, made endless difficulties for Otto; and now the shooting pains in the leg which wasn't there were getting worse ...

'November the Eighth' said the calendar: almost five years to the day since the old world ended.

The sound of wind ... the bitter Munich wind which had swept down the wide spaces of the Ludwigstrasse that scudding winter day nearly five years ago, alternating with moments of unearthly calm: whipping the muffling rags of the uncertain crowd, wildly flapping the revolutionary red banners on the public buildings and then leaving them pendulous and despondent.

The sound of marching feet ... it was in one of the lulls of the wind that Otto had first heard that dead thudding sound, and a sudden stirring and a murmur had passed through the crowd for this could be none of Eisner's 'Red Guard' rabble, only trained Imperial troops marched with such absolute precision. But to Otto's professional ear, keen as a musician's, from the first there was something wrong in the sound of that marching. A hollowness and a deadness. No spring in the step – it sounded ... wrong: like the knocking of an engine, which is also a precise and regular sound yet presages a breakdown.

Then, through the front ranks of the crowd, a blur of field-grey and steel helmets as the first men began to pass. Many were without packs: some even without rifles: their uniforms were still caked with French mud. Someone in the crowd tried to cheer – for this was their menfolk's homecoming, home from the war, home to be demobilized; but

114

the solitary cheer ended in a fit of coughing and nobody took it up.

The men marched in close formation, in small parties that were token platoons, detachment after detachment, with wide spaces between, so that the dead sound of marching came in waves, rising and falling regularly, like sea-waves on shingle – only varied by the sullen rumbling of a baggage-wagon like boulders rolling.

A small child, pushed forward a little in front of the crowd, stood motionless, a bunch of wilting flowers held out in front of her in a chubby fist; but no soldier accepted it, no one even looked at her, not one smiled: they did not even seem to see the crowd. They marched like machines dreaming.

Even the officers – the first these five chaotic weeks to appear on the Munich streets in uniform – wore that empty basilisk look, marching with men they hardly seemed to see; but at this sight of *officers* there rose from the onlookers here and there a faint and almost disembodied growl . . . someone behind Otto on his new crutches jostled him aside and pressed right forward out of the crowd, right past the child too: a big elderly woman with a massive bosom and a huge protruding stomach, upright as a ramrod from carrying all that weight in front: a flaunting hag with a lupus-ridden face and hanging dewlaps, wisps of grey hair under a railwayman's peaked cap. Deliberately she spat on the ground just where a young major was about to tread. But he seemed to see nothing, not even that. For a moment it looked as if she was going to attack him; but then, as if appalled, she didn't.

If there was any expression at all on any of these wooden military faces it was a potential hatred: a hatred that had found no real object yet to fasten on, but only because nothing in the somersaulted world around seemed real.

God! That German soldiers should ever have to look like that, marching through a German crowd!

Why had God chosen to do this thing to His German Army – the very salt of His else-unsavoury earth?

115

Otto bundled his papers into the safe and locked it, for that obsessive dead sound of marching made work impossible: then hoisted himself to his feet, facing the window.

Chapter 2

In England the ending of the war had come like waking from a bad dream: in defeated Germany, as the signal for deeper levels of nightmare. The symbols and the occasion had changed but in Germany it was still that same kind of comprehensive dreaming. The ex-soldier, expelled from the crumbled Gemeinschaft of army life, had stepped out into a void. The old order had shattered: even money was rapidly ebbing away from between men, leaving them desperately incommunicado like men rendered voiceless by an intervening vacuum: millions, still heaped on top of each other in human cities yet forced to live separate, each like some solitary predatory beast.

Now in 1923 prices were already a billion times the pre-war figure and still rocketing. These were the days spoken of by Haggai the prophet, when 'he that earneth wages, earneth wages to put it into a bag with holes': by Monday a workman's whole last-week's wages might not pay his tramfare back to work. The smallest sum in any foreign currency was hoarded for it would buy almost anything; but nobody held German money five minutes. Even beer was an investment for presently you got more for the empty bottle than you had paid for it full.

The salaried and rentier classes were becoming submerged below the proletariat. Wages could rise (even if always too little and too late); but interest and pensions and the like, and even salaries, were fixed. Retired senior officials swept the streets. The government official still in office had to learn to temper his integrity to his necessities: had he tried to stay strictly honest a little too long, he would have died.

When the solid ground drops utterly away from under a man's feet like that he is left in a state of free fall: he is in

117

a bottomless pit – a hell. Moreover this was a hell where all were not equitably falling equally together. Some fell slower than others: even peasants could resort to barter (you went marketing with your poultry, not your purse); and many rich men had found means of hardly falling at all. There they were still, those Walther von Kessens and the like, tramping about solidly up there like Dantes in full view of all the anguished others who were falling. People who could buy things for marks and sell them for pounds or dollars even rose.

A hell where justice was not being done, and seen not being done.

Consumption has always to be paid for. Their war had been very conspicuous consumption but in Germany there had been virtually no war-taxation to pay for it on the nail. Thus there was nothing really mysterious about this present exhaustion into outer space of every last penn'orth of new value as fast as it was created: this was a kind of natural, belated capital-cum-income levy – though levied now not equitably by any human government but blindly, by Dis himself. Of this rationale however the sufferers had no inkling. They could not understand their suffering, and inexplicable suffering turns to hatred. But hatred cannot remain objectless: such hatred precipitates its own THEY, its own someone-to-be-hated. In a hell devoid of real ministering devils the damned invent them rather than accept that their only tormentors are themselves and soon these suffering people saw everywhere such 'devils', consciously tormenting them: Jews, Communists, Capitalists, Catholics, Cabbalists – even their own elected government, the 'November Criminals'. Millions of horsepower of hatred had been generated, more hatred than the real situation could consume: inevitably it conjured its own Enemy out of thin air.

On the heels of that hatred came also the inevitable reacting love. All those egos violently dislodged from their old penumbral settings were now groping desperately in the face of that dark enveloping phantasmal THEY to establish a new 'footing', new tenable penumbral frontiers of the Self: inevitably they secreted millions of horsepower of love that the actual situation also couldn't consume, and therefore precipitating its own fictive WE – its myths of Soil and Race, its Heroes, its kaleidoscope of Brotherhoods each grappling its own members with hoops of steel.

Its Freikorps, its communist cells: its Kampfbund, with all its component organisms: its Nazi movement.

After the official cease-fire in 1918 fighting still went on for a time in the lost Baltic provinces that the Armistice had raped. These freelance wars were a more amateur and even obscener carnage for they were all ill-armed and merciless Kilkenny-cats all-against-all, where fanatical bands of Germans in a state of bestial heroism fought with Latvians, Lithuanians, Poles, Bolsheviks, British – even Germans of the wrong kidney. It was one way of staving off this generation's Nemesis of 'Peace'.

Otto's young nephew, Franz (the 'ten-year-old tow-haired Franz' of Mary's pre-war memories), had a best schoolfriend called Wolff; and in 1918 Wolff had enlisted in those wars when not quite sixteen.

There Wolff had vanished; but these were wars fought without benefit of war-office and no published casualty lists. Even now no one could say for certain that Wolff had been killed.

Wolff's younger brother Lothar (for one) would never believe it. Before the débacle this Lothar had been sent to the same fashionable cadet-school as Wolff and Franz (their father the gaunt old Geheimrat Scheidemann was a retired colonial governor, an ex-colleague in Africa of Goering père). But come the inflation the Scheidemanns had not the same solid resources as the von Kessens, nor foreign investments like the Goerings. The old widower was too arthritic now to work: he let lodgings in his big flat near

119

the 'English Garden' in Munich, but there was not much left nowadays under any of those lofty ornate ceilings of his except hard-lying lodgers, several to a room.

Eighteen-year-old Lothar who was supposed to be studying law thought himself lucky to have landed a part-time desk-clerk job at the Bayrischer-Hof hotel in Munich where most of the clerks and waiters were sons of just such middle-class families as his, and were nowadays virtually their families' sole support. At the Bayrischer-Hof, too, some at least of Lothar's meals were provided. But no one could expect so good a job all to himself, and Lothar shared his turn-about with a fellow student. On his off-days he lived chiefly on memories of his hotel meals, dining in retrospect. One night when he was supperless like this he dreamed he had been sacked, and woke screaming: other times he dreamed of his brother Wolff – the wild one who had vanished – and woke in tears.

This morning at the hotel Lothar had had a windfall: a young Englishman who had spent the night there asked him to change an English ten-shilling note.

Lothar had changed it out of his own pocket: no one would be such a fool as to put good English money in the till. He buckled it safely inside his shirt. He had changed it into marks for Augustine quite fairly at the rate current that morning; but even by midday it was worth ten times as much.

Chapter 3

So Augustine with his pocket full of marks caught the main-line train for Kammstadt where he had to change, and soon after his departure Lothar came off duty.

Habitually Lothar spent most of his time off duty at a certain gymnasium near the Southern Station. The neighbourhood was a bit medical, but convenient for the Teresienwiese Sportsground with its running-tracks. He went there for physical training and to meet his friends as in Sparta of old; for the company he met here was indeed a noble sodality, the very flower of German youth; and Lothar was proud and humble to be accepted as one of them.

He found here that decent, modest, manly kind of idealism as necessary to youth everywhere as desert watersprings. 'True', thought Lothar, 'we are come here to exercise only our brute bodies; but in fact how innocently do Body and Spirit walk hand in hand! How much more often the Eye of Horus' – their private name for that rare hawklike eye that pierces to the spiritual behind every material veil – 'is found in the faces of simple athletes than of philosophers or priests!' Lothar himself was intelligent enough but had found it only a hindrance in this company; and he had the more need for friends now that his brother the noble Wolff was gone.

So Lothar with Augustine's half-Bradbury still safe inside his shirt betook himself to his gymnasium; and at the first whiff of all the delicious manliness within its echoing portals he snorted like a horse. The abiding smell of men's gymnasiums is a cold composite one, compounded of the sweet strawberry-smell of fresh male sweat, the reek of thumped leather and the dust trampled into the grain of the floor and confirmed there by the soapy mops of cleaners;

but to eighteen-year-old Lothar this tang meant everything that the wind on the heath meant to Petulengro and he snorted at it now like a horse let out to spring grass.

Today Lothar began with a few loosening-exercises, starting with neck and shoulders, then the fingers, and ending with ankles and insteps. After that he hung from the wall-bars, raising and lowering his legs to strengthen the abdomen; for that muscular wall is of the greatest importance, since not only does it control the body's hinge on which everything else depends but it also protects the solar plexus with its sacred emotions.

At the far end of this bare hall filled with the echoes of young men's staccato voices the wall was painted a light green with a broad off-white band at the height of a tennis-net, for solo practice. Lothar was fond of tennis, but alas in May 1919 when von Epp was 'cleansing' Munich someone had stood Reds against it so now the brickwork (particularly in and close to that white band) was too badly bullet-pocked for a tennis-ball ever again to return off it true. Thus if the arms and shoulders of some quill-driver like Lothar needed building up he had really nothing more interesting to turn to than dumb-bells and Indian clubs. Today moreover when he came down off the wall Lothar found the vaulting-horse crowded and also the parallel bars; so he went straight to the mat of the small pug-nosed world war sergeant who taught them all ju-jutsu.

Ju-jutsu (or Judo), being the art of using unbearable pain for the conquest of brute force, has an irresistible attraction for young imaginations, boys' almost as much as girls'. Lothar was obsessed by it these days. Since it is the technique of unarmed self-defence the instructor taught you how to take your enemy unawares and break arm or leg before he can even begin his treacherous assault on you: how to fling spinning out of a window a man big enough to be your father, and so on. Lothar was slightly, almost girlishly built but he had a quite exceptional natural quickness of movement, and lately at political meetings or the like

he had sometimes had occasion to use that natural quickness and these acquired skills outside and in earnest. At
grips with some older and angrier and stronger but help-
lessly-fumbling human body he had then been astonished to
find how deeply his aesthetic emotions could be stirred by
his own impeccable performance. The aesthetic satisfaction
of that culminating moment could be almost epileptically
intense: Lothar was not uncultured, but surely no poem nor
even music had ever offered him one tenth part of this.

O happy, happy youths – hungry and happy!
'Isn't life wonderful!' thought Lothar, towelling his lean
body in the changing-room that afternoon: 'What a dis-
pensation of Providence that *we*, the German Remnant,
should have found each other in this predestined way and
grappled ourselves so tight with our comradely love!' For
with the secret enemies of Germany ever ceaselessly at work
tension these last few weeks was everywhere mounting:
surely any minute now the storm must break . . .

But then suddenly Lothar remembered that this was a
Thursday, and at that his heart leapt. At week-ends most
of this same sodality went out from Munich, drawn by the
silence and the purity of the ancient German forests, to sing
ancient German songs together as they marched down the
rides between the echoing tree-trunks: to meet in secret
deer-haunted glades to perfect their formation-drill: to
practise in that pine-sweet air such quasi-military pastimes
as 'the naming of parts'.

Such times as Captain Goering himself was coming the
whole band of brothers wore death's-heads in their caps,
and carried arms.

Chapter 4

Schloss Lorienburg was built on a precipitous tree-clad mound in a bend of the stripling Danube. Under the small window of Otto's office, in its deep embrasure, there was a nearly sheer drop of a hundred and fifty feet or so into tree-tops, so that everything nearby was hidden from where he stood. All he could ever see from here was the far distance dimmed and diminished by its remoteness – today, a horizonless pattern of small dark patches that were forest a little darker than the canopy of cloud, and small patches a little lighter and yellower than the cloud that were rolling withered winter fields under a thin scumble of rime: the high Bavarian plateau, stretching away into purple immensities under a purplish slate sky.

Otto could not see the river for it was almost directly beneath him. He could not see the village, crowded between the river and the hill's foot. He could not even see the valley, but he could hear – though faintly, through the two thicknesses of glass – the melancholy mooing of the little daily train as it wound its way down the branch line from Kammstadt; and that recalled him. The unknown English cousin was arriving on that train – cause of all his unease.

Bavarian Otto had served in Bavarian Crown-Prince Rupprecht's Sixth Army during the war, being posted to the 16th Reserve Regiment of Foot. It was at Bapaume he had lost his leg, to an English mortar-shell. Nearly all the time it had been the English he was fighting – Ypres, Neuve-Chapelle, the Somme. So what was it going to feel like, meeting an Englishman again for the first time since the Western Front?

Relatives of course are in a special category: indubitable bonds transcending frontiers connect them. Not that this was a close kinship, it was merely the kind that old ladies like to keep alive by a lifetime of letter-writing. In fact, these Penry-Herberts were really the Arcos' relatives rather than their own. It was some niece of someone in the Arco tribe who had married a Penry-Herbert, generations ago: but the Kessens and the Arcos were themselves related many times over, so it came to the same thing in the end – and even the remotest relationships ought to count.

Moreover, this was the younger brother of that little English Backfisch – he had forgotten her name, but she came to stay at Lorienburg the summer before the War, and rode in the bullock-race.

Somebody had told him, too, this boy was quite a promising young shot. His grandfather of course had been the world famous shot – even in his eighties still one of the finest in Europe: Otto's own father had felt it a great honour when invited to Newton Llantony for the snipe . . . or would that have been this boy's *great*-grandfather? It was getting difficult to remember how quickly the generations pass. Indeed what Otto found hardest of all to envisage as he faced the wintry prospect beyond the window was that the little brother that girl had so prattled about in 1913 was now a grown man – the master of Newton Llantony – and yet had been too young to serve in the War.

Beneath his clipped correctness of manner Otto was a devout Catholic with tinges of mysticism.

Most Imperial German officers those days were avowed Christians. Perhaps they found in the code of their Officers' Corps the closest earthly simulacrum possible (in their eyes) to the selfless ethics of the Sermon on the Mount, and in 'Germany' an identical name under which to worship God. Be that as it may, Man, among all God's vertebrate creatures is in fact the *only* species which wages war – man alone, in whom alone His image is reflected – and how could that awful monopoly mean nothing? War, surely, is a pale human emblem of that Absolute of Force; and human power, a portion of *His* attribute incarnate in us *His* earthly mirror-images: fighting, *His* refiner's furnace to brighten the gold and burn away the material dross.

Otto's present deep conviction that all this is the true teaching about war had come to him more slowly, perhaps, than to many; for he had seen the 'dross' burn (some of it) with so very lurid a light. But in the end it had come even to him ineluctably, for it seemed to derive honestly from his own experience of himself and those around him in four years of war. For instance, at Bapaume when his leg was shattered three willing volunteers in turn had carried him from the front line, succeeding each other instantly, as each was shot: a thing no man could easily forget, or ignore.

Because of his pride in his calling Otto was personally humble but he was not one whose convictions once formed were easily shaken or complicated. He had not argued all this out with himself step by step but had reached much the same frame of mind as if he had: he believed that for every man war is the essential means of Grace.

Whatever a cripple could do, working secretly, towards the rebuilding of the proscribed German Army, Otto was doing. But hostilities were suspended now, Germany so shattered and the civil crowd so rotten that it might be many years before war could be resumed; and suddenly he was moved by a deep pity for this young English cousin such as he felt for his own German nephew Franz. He must needs pity that whole generation everywhere whose loss it was that the last war had ended just too soon: for the next might come too late.

Presently one-legged Otto left his office and made his way with difficulty (the stone treads being sloping and uneven) down the stairs. Reaching the courtyard, he caught sight of his brother Walther who was crossing it towards the Great Gate. In spite of Walther's abnormal size and massive strength he walked lightly and springily like a cat; it was all on the ball of the foot, his was a hunter's gait rather than a soldier's . . .

It was typical of Walther's courtesy (Otto thought with affection) to feel he must go to the station himself to meet even so young a guest.

Chapter 5

Meanwhile in the crowded one-class branch-line train from
Kammstadt Augustine was agog with interest. These peaceful fenceless fields! These forests, that looked cared-for as
chrysanthemums – so utterly unlike wild natural English
woods! These pretty pastel-coloured villages with pantile
roofs, onion-top churches . . . all this, rolling past the half-
frosted windows – all this was *Germany*! Moreover these
friendly people in the compartment with him . . . they looked
almost ordinary humans but were they not in fact all 'Germans' – even the quite small children?

The old peasant opposite Augustine had the kind of belly
which made him sit with knees wide apart, and he was
smoking a decorative hooked pipe which smelled like fusty
hay. His face was brimming over with curiosity : earlier he
had tried to talk to Augustine but Augustine's Swiss-taught
school German could alas make little of this slurry dialect
even with the words tapped out for him on his knee. The old
man's wife, too, had a kindly wrinkled face with intensely
wild humorous eyes . . .

How happily Augustine could spend the rest of his days
among such simple, friendly people! He had no feeling *here*
of being in enemy country. But for want of a better vehicle
he could only project his love on a broad and beaming
smile.

The little train, raised high on trestles above a stretch of
frozen flood, hooted a warning to itself as it neared a bend.
With a warm forefinger Augustine melted himself a further
peep-hole in the window-ice.

From under the voluminous black skirts of the old
peasant-woman opposite there came the faint, drugged
crooning of a half-suffocated hen. A moment later the

128

woman's whole nether person began to heave with unseen poultry. She leaned forward and slapped at her skirts violently to reduce them to silence and stillness, but at that the vocal hen only woke up completely and answered the more indignantly; and then others began to join in. She glanced anxiously towards the Inspector – but luckily his back was turned . . .

What *lovely* people! Augustine began to laugh out loud, whereon the old woman's eyes flashed back at him with pleasure and merriment.

Last night Augustine's express from the frontier had reached Munich after dark: that was how it happened that his first night on German soil had been spent at the old Bayrischer-Hof hotel. Since then it has been rebuilt, but Augustine had found it a majestic yet rather worn and despondent hostelry those days. As he had stood signing himself in that evening it had struck him that all the clerks and waiters there seemed *distraits* – as if they had something rather more important on their minds than running hotels. This surprised and rather charmed him: he sympathized with them, for – coming of a class which practically never used hotels – Augustine disliked and despised them *all*. No wonder the characteristic stale hotel-foyer smells here seemed to irk their clean young noses: these diluted, doctored alcohols, the coffee-sodden cigar-ends: the almost incessant rich eating which must go on somewhere just upwind of this foyer where he stood so that even its portières smelt permanently of food; and the nearer, transient smells of brand-new pigskin suit-cases and dead fur, of rich Jews, of indigestion and peppermint, of perfumes unsuccessfully overlaid on careless womanhood.

Later on it had greatly surprised this novice traveller, too, to find on his machine-carved bed a huge eiderdown in a white cotton cover but *no* ordinary top-sheet or blanket to tuck round him. And it had surprised him yet further to find, half-hidden by the washstand, such mysterious scribbles on the bedroom wall . . . for there, among mere lists of names, he *thought* he had made out this:

> *A.D. 1919 February 27*
> *With six others, innocent*
> *hostages . . .*
>> (then something
>> undecipherable, and then:)
> *ADELIE! FAREWELL! ! !*

Authentic dungeon-scribbles – in a hotel bedroom? – But then Augustine had taken more particular notice of the date. '1919'? *Since* the war? '1919'? – Why, that was surely the Golden Age when the young poet Ernst Toller and his friends had ruled Munich! The thing was impossible.

The message was scrawled in a difficult Gothic hand . . . he must have read it wrong – or else it was a hoax.

In the morning Augustine had perforce to pay his bill with English money. He had only tendered a ten-shilling note but the German change he was given appeared to be noughted in billions! What a joke! That pleasant-looking, dark-eyed young desk-clerk with the speed and dexterity almost of a conjurer had whipped *billions* loose out of his pocket, flipping them like postage-stamps . . . 'Lothar Scheidemann' the desk-card named him; and the name as well as the face somehow fixed itself in Augustine's memory.

Augustine would have liked to talk to him, for he looked certainly educated; but on a second glance decided – N-n-no: perhaps rather too formal and detached a chap for any such casual approach.

Now, in the train, Augustine took out his new German money to count those incredible noughts yet once more. It was quite true: today he was indeed a billionaire! It made his head swim a little. But then through his peep-hole in the frosted window he sighted a familiar flight of mallard: these at least were in normal non-astronomical numbers even in Germany, and his brow cleared. Involuntarily he crooked his trigger-finger, and smiled . . .

'*Lothar Scheidemann, Lothar Scheid* . . .' the train wheels repeated; and Augustine's smile faded. For there had been something in the eyes of that attractive young clerk he couldn't quite get out of his mind. Then suddenly the train passed off its trestles on to solid earth again with a changed sound.

Chapter 6

At Lorienburg station the engine of Augustine's train halted on the very brink of the swift unfrozen Danube and stood there hissing. Augustine climbed happily down and followed the other pasengers across the tracks.

On the low station 'platform' – so low it hardly deserved the name of one – a tall truculent young Jew was chaffing with a group of farmers, gesticulating with the duck he held by its fettered feet. These farmers, like the ones on the train, all seemed to wear a kind of civilian uniform: thick grey cloth trimmed with green, and huge fur collars. One was affectionately nursing a hairy piglet in his arms: another, a murmuring accordion.

But now a burly, almost gigantic figure was making a beeline for Augustine. His little corded and feathered 'Tyrolean' hat bobbed high above the crowd. He wore the same kind of uniform the peasants wore but newer and better cut: strong as it looked – that acreage of heavy close-woven cloth – the muscles of his massive shoulders seemed almost bursting it. He walked with the gait of someone who likes to be out-of-doors walking all of every day . . .

Behind him followed a small dark man with a monkey face, some sort of servant who seized Augustine's luggage. So this must be Cousin Walther – the Freiherr von Kessen come in person to meet his guest!

It must be . . . and yet it surprised Augustine to find his host wearing such obviously *German* clothes. Somehow he hadn't thought of the Kessens as being Germans, the way those peasants were. Surely gentlemen were much the same everywhere: a sort of little international nation, based more or less on the English model. However, he soon found that the Baron talked excellent informal upper-class English, except that his slang was ten years out of date.

Walther shook Augustine warmly by the hand, then captured his arm and whisked him through the tidy village, enquiring the while after English relations most of whom neither of them had ever met and at the same time answering jovially the soft, respectful greetings on every hand: *'Grüss Gott, Herr Baron . . .'*

'Grüss Gott, Zusammen!'

''ss Gott z'sammen!' It sounded almost like 'Scotch salmon!' the abbreviated way this Bavarian baron said it, Augustine thought – and smiled. How spick-and-span everything was here, he noticed. The butcher's window did not look very well stocked by English standards, but it was orderly as a shrine: in comparison, what slatterns the English were!

Augustine wished his boisterous cousin would give him time to look about him at all these wonders – he was almost having to trot. Indeed it was a mystery how the man managed to keep his own footing so securely on this icy ground, for rounding a sudden corner in the village by a chemist's Augustine himself skidded altogether and cannoned into an old Jew peddling laces, so that both of them nearly fell. Just then, too, descending the side-street and missing the pair of them by a hair's-breadth, something shot by like an arrow. This was a youth on skis. The skis – to their detriment – rattled and sparked, almost uncontrollable on the iron-clad surface (for there was no proper snow at all), and it was only by a miracle of sheer balance that the skier managed to swerve just clear of an ox-cart in the middle of the cross-roads. Then he shot away down a steep bye-road towards the frozen water-meadows.

Walther was just beginning to explain 'Ahah! The eldest of my young devils, Fr . . .' when something else followed, but this time something more like a low ricochetting cannon-ball than like an arrow. It was a small toboggan with two little girls on it rounded out to packages with extra clothing,

133

the two pairs of pigtails standing straight out behind them with the acceleration of their transit. They too just managed to skid past the slow-moving ox-cart. But they failed to make the counter-swerve: the toboggan hit a pile of gravel ice-bound into concrete and somersaulted.

The two children rose into the air and landed on their heads. The wonder was they weren't clean stunned, or even killed. But no – for they got up; though slowly, dazed. They were obviously quite a lot hurt and Augustine's tender heart went out to them. The knees of both were wavering under them. Then one began lifting her fist uncertainly towards her eyes . . . but at that Walther in a brutal voice shouted something mocking, and instantly both stiffened.

They hadn't seen their father was there watching them till then; but now they didn't even stop to rub their bruises. They managed to right their toboggan – giddily, though without quite toppling over again – and dragged it away (though still moving as if half-drunk) after their brother and out of sight.

'Little milk-sops: they make me ashamed,' said Walther; but he sounded quite proud and pleased, as if expecting to be contradicted.

Augustine said nothing: he was too deeply shocked. He had omitted to take stock of his cousin's face when they first met and now needed all his eyes for the going; but from that voice, that behaviour, that massive bulk, he assumed now it must be very like an ogre's, or some gigantic stony troll's.

Chapter 7

That icy sunk lane leading up from the village, the lane the
skis and the toboggan had just traversed, was very steep;
but Walther took it still at the same breathless speed. Augustine began to suspect his cousin (who must have been more
than twice his age) of trying to walk him off his legs; but
Augustine had got his second wind now and could hold his
own.

Ultimately the castle on its mound was approached from
the high ground behind it along a raised causeway lined
with linden-trees, ending in a wooden bridge. Just where
you reached this bridge there stood on one side of the way
a little closed summer beerhouse shanty – rather decrepit,
and with a deserted skittle-alley full of dead leaves. But on
the other side stood a life-size crucifix, skilfully carved and
realistically painted; and this crucifix looked as if it was
brand new – its newness astonished Augustine more than
anything else he had seen here yet.

The heavy ironbound gates in the massive gatehouse stood
open. Times were quieter now and they were only closed at
sunset, Walther explained: all the same, some of the iron
sheathing on them also looked brand new and this was surely
almost as odd an anachronism as the new crucifix. In the
porter's cubbyhole a lynx-eyed old woman sat permanently
knitting. She rose and curtsied to them, but her dropped
hands did not even cease their knitting while she curtsied.

The first court of the castle they now entered had long
byres built against its high crenellated walls and from the
nearest of them there came a gentle lowing, the slow clank
of headchains. The cobbled yard itself was as clean as a
drawing-room floor, the dung stacked tidily in masonry
tanks that steamed in the frosty air: 'Still, what a queer

approach to one's front door!' thought Augustine. He was used of course to lawns and wide carriage-sweeps leading to gentlemen's houses: to rhododendrons and begonia-beds, with the facts of country life tucked well out of sight.

In the second court there did seem to be some attempt at a garden but now all the beds were covered with spruce-boughs against the frost ... but surely it could never get much sun in here even in summer, for nowhere was the court surrounded by less than fifty-foot lowering walls ...

'*Herunter!*' Walther suddenly bellowed against Augustine's ear: 'The little imps of Satan! – Rudi! Heinz!'

Augustine looked up. High overhead against the sky, almost like tight-rope performers there on the narrow un-protected cat-walk of the battlemented wall which formed the castle enceinte, two six-year-old boys were riding little green bicycles. At their father's shout they wobbled wildly, and Augustine gasped; but somehow they dismounted safely. Walther called out again in rapid German and they scuttled into a turret doorway.

Then Walther turned to Augustine: 'That is something forbidden. They shall be punished.' The bull-like voice sounded calm; but the iron hand which still gripped Augustine's upper arm was actually trembling; and the face ... surprisingly, Walther proved to have just an ordinary, anxious, *human* parent's face – not at all a stony troll's. The features were small and fine and by no means commanding. The brows beetled a bit but the brown eyes under them peeped down at Augustine almost timidly: 'Don't you agree? I mean, would not even an English father also forbid?' When Augustine nonplussed said nothing he added rapidly: 'Not that *I*'m a fusspot – but if their mother knew ...'

The main house itself now towered in front of them. There were four storeys of stuccoed stone and then four more of steep pantiled roof with rows of dormers in it all boarded up. On the topmost roofridge was fixed a wagon-wheel, sup-

136

porting a tattered old stork's nest. Augustine took this all in at a glance, for today he was still absorbing everything with the unnaturally observant eye of a first arrival somewhere totally strange: not till tomorrow would he even begin to notice less.

Now Walther opened a wicket in an imposing, church-size door (remarking lugubriously: '*Twins!* It is fated that they will die together!') and Augustine found himself ushered into a darkling, stone-vaulted space. This seemed to be a kind of above-ground cellarage or crypt, for it had no windows and immensely stout squat pillars upheld the weight of the castle overhead. Between these in the half-dark were parked a Victoria and a wagonette, together with two horse-sleighs and various other vehicles. Right at the back there was a pre-war vintage Benz – as cobwebby as a bin of port, and evidently long out of use.

Again, what a curious front-entrance for a gentleman's house! But it was indeed from here, apparently, that the main staircase led.

This narrow, twisting stairway too proved to be merely massive and defensible between its whitewashed stone walls: the stairs themselves were treaded with solid tree-trunks roughly squared with the adze.

At the first floor a heavy, wormy door opened straight off these stairs. It offered none of the flattering perspectives for entrances and exits social architects use – yet how magnificent the hall that hulking door opened into! Augustine caught his breath, for the sight was so unexpected. Not only was this hall quite vast in size: its length stretched nearly the whole width of the house; its proportions seemed to August-ine quite perfect – a most civilized room!

The floor was flagged with squares of some pale yellowish stone so shiny they reflected the chalky blues and faded crimsons of the primitive unvarnished portraits hung on the white walls – reflected even the dove-grey that the many doors opening off it were painted, and their delicate fillets picked out in gold leaf. Some of these stone floor-tiles were cracked and loose, clinking under them as they walked . . .

'Adèle!' roared Walther so that the painted rafters echoed: 'Here is our guest and cousin!'

Walther flung open the double doors at the far end of the hall, and stood aside in the outrush of hot air for Augustine to pass. A rather faded lady in her forties rose from an escritoire. She had very bright blue eyes, an aquiline nose, and a slightly pursed mouth which only just knew how to smile; but in general her pale sandy face seemed to Augustine of a rather unmemorable kind. She thrust her hand firmly into Augustine's, English fashion; for she guessed he would be embarrassed if he thought he ought to kiss it.

Once the greetings were over, and the introductions (for there was a girl there too, and some middle-aged brother of Cousin Walther's who seemed to be lame), Augustine began looking about him again. It seemed to him sadly incongruous with the room's simple hexagonal shape and the delicate Adamsy traceries of its high coved ceiling that the place should be quite so crowded with furniture and knicknackery.

The walls were thick with pictures: amateur water-colours, mostly, and photographs. Most of these photographs were inclined to be old and faded; but there was one big enlargement in a bright gilt frame surmounted by a big gilt crown and this frame looked new, while the photograph itself looked also pretty recent – at any rate post-war. It showed an outdoor group centred on a rather dishevelled old gentleman in baggy trousers, with a grey beard and steel spectacles . . . *certainly* not the Kaiser, even in retirement; and yet the frame looked unequivocally regal . . . the background was some mammoth forest picnic: there were some forty or fifty children in their Sunday best – but also a bit dishevelled, the thing must have ended in a most un-regal romp!

In a firm but old man's hand it was signed: 'Ludwig'. But of course – 'Ludwig of Bavaria'! Thinking of 'Germany' one tended to forget that Bavaria had remained a sovereign state-within-a-state, with her own king (down to

138

the revolution five years ago), and her own government and even army. Moreover Augustine remembered hearing that this peaceable-looking old gentleman had carried to his recent grave a Prussian bullet in his body: a bullet from the war of '66, before there was any 'Germany' – a war when Prussia and Bavaria had been two sovereign countries fighting on opposite sides. To an Englishman, used to long perspectives and slow changes, this was indeed History telescoped: as if King George V had been wounded at Bannockburn.

'Germany': that formidable empire which had lately so shaken the whole world – its entire lifetime then had lasted less than a normal man's, a bare forty-eight years from its cradle to its present grave! Even the still adolescent U.S.A. was *three* times 'Germany's' age. Everything here confused one's sense of time! There was something Victorian about Augustine's hostess, Cousin Adèle, with her lace and her chatelaine; but equally something of an earlier, sterner century too ...

There was something at least pre-war even about the young girl standing behind her. That cold and serious white face, with its very large grey thoughtful eyes. The carefully-brushed straight fair hair reaching nearly to her waist, tied back in a bunch with a big black bow behind her neck. The long straight skirt with its shiny black belt, the white blouse with its high starched collar ...

But he mustn't stare! Augustine lowered his gaze deliberately; and behold, curled on the sofa in an attitude of sleep but with his bright eyes wide open, lay a fox.

Chapter 8

They dined that night off wild-boar steak, grilled (it tasted more like young beef than any kind of pork), with a cream sauce and cranberry jam. There was spaghetti, and a smoky-flavoured cheese. They drank a tawny Tyrolean wine that was light on the palate but powerful in action. Augustine found it all delicious: there wasn't much 'starving Germany' here, he thought.

Franz (the young skier) had shot the boar, he learned, marauding in their forests – though Heaven knows where it had come from, for they were supposed to be extinct here-abouts. Baron Franz – Lothar's former schoolfellow, Mary's 'ten-year-old, tow-haired little Franz' – was now a lad of twenty. He was very fair, and smaller than his father but with all his father's energy of movement. His manner towards Augustine was perhaps a little over-formal and polite as coming from one young man to another, but in repose his face wore permanently a slightly contemptuous expression. This the father's face totally lacked and it made Augustine's hackles rise a little in the face of somebody quite so young, quite so inexperienced in the world as this Franz – his own junior by three years at least.

The only other male person present was that rather dim ex-officer with a game leg, Walther's brother. He swallowed his food quickly, then shook hands all round murmuring something about 'work to do' and vanished. Augustine ticketed him 'Cheltenham' and thought no more about him; thus he missed the quick glance of intelligence that uncle and nephew exchanged, Franz's almost imperceptible shrug and shake of the head.

At dinner the conversation was almost entirely a mono-logue by Walther. The mother and that eldest daughter (the

140

younger children were in bed, presumably) hardly spoke at all. Augustine had failed to catch the girl's name on introduction and no one had addressed her by it since, so he didn't know what name to think of her by; but he found himself peeping at her more and more. It never entered his head to think her 'beautiful' but her face had a serenity which promised interesting depths. Her eyes hardly roamed at all: he never saw her glance even once *his* way; but already he surmised she might be going to prove rather more sympathique than that cocky brother, once she opened out a little.

She looked always as if she were just going to speak: her curving upper-lip was always slightly lifted and indeed once he saw her lips actually begin to move; but it proved to be only a silent conversation, with herself or perhaps some absent friend. In fact, she 'wasn't there': she seemed to have shut her ears entirely to what was going on around her. Perhaps she had heard them all before too often, these stories her father was interminably telling?

Walther had begun his harangue with the soup, asking Augustine how many seats the Socialists held in the new British parliament elected last winter. From stopping his ears inadequately when at Mellton Augustine had a vague idea the Socialists had temporarily outstripped the Liberals who had suckled them, but that was the most he knew. He tried to convey without downright rudeness that he neither knew nor cared; such things were none of his business.

Walther looked incredulous. 'Ah!' he said earnestly: 'Their leader, that Macdonald: he's a gaol-bird, isn't he? How can you trust him? England ought to take warning by what happened *here*!'

And so the tale began.

Five years ago, on the night of November 7th, 1918 – almost the actual eve of the war's ending – Walther and some fellow-members of the Bavarian parliament had met in the blacked-out Park Hotel. Bavaria had reluctantly to make certain constitutional changes (such as instituting the

141

formal responsibility of the royal ministry to parliament) as a gesture to the American, Wilson: so these legislators had met to discuss the next day's necessary measures. Most of the Centre Party deputies were there, except those away with the army or stricken by 'flu.

Another problem they had discussed was the coming demobilization. But everything was already taped, it seemed: the plans were ready and the men would go straight into jobs, so his friend Heinrich von Aretin assured the company. Industry would need all the labour it could get, in the switch to peace-production. But then someone (said Walther) casually mentioned a socialist mass-meeting happening out on the Teresienwiese Sportsground that very hour . . . Eisner, the demagogue from Berlin, was addressing them . . . and Gansdorfer, the blind farmer . . . 'Hetzpropaganda'. But it seemed that too was taped: the police were confident, and Auer (one of the Socialists' own leaders) was assuring everybody there'd be no sort of rumpus. Indeed only Aretin had seemed even faintly anxious: 'How little even *we* knew then of the unscrupulous Socialist mentality!' said Walther pointedly. 'You are aware what happened, of course?'

'What?' asked Augustine, half polite, half curious. To Augustine, who elected to ignore public events anyway, the events of 1918 already seemed centuries ago – lost in the mists of time; but even now Walther could hardly pronounce *Eisner*'s name in a normal voice – the rabble-rousing animal Eisner, from Berlin, with his straggling beard and floppy black hat like a seedy professor of pianoforte . . . marching into the city that night with lorry-loads of all the hooligans of Munich at his heels! It was red revolution, of course . . .

'They tore off my uniform in the Odeonsplatz,' said Walther. 'I was lucky to get home safely in borrowed mufti, I can tell you! And the dear old King chased from his bed: Bavaria is to be a republic, forsooth, after a thousand years of Wittelsbach rule! And Ei . . . that Kurt Ei . . . Ei . . . *Eisner*, with a gang of Galician Jews like himself for his cabinet – lunatics, lamp-lighters, gaol-birds, Judases . . .'

Having reached this surprising (but in fact literally truthful) peroration Walther had to pause for the moment for breath and for his blood to cool; and Franz at once slipped into the breach, speaking suavely and rapidly, hoping to head him off: 'The careful demobilization-plans – torn up, of course. No one any more did what he was told. Even years afterwards . . . Papa, do you remember how we found a gang of deserters *still* living in the forest years afterwards, when we were out with the Bristows? You were shooting particularly well that day,' he added cunningly.

As the conversation seemed now to be taking a turn towards sport Augustine pricked up his ears. But it all sounded very un-English. Indeed he soon jumped to the conclusion that here in Germany people shot wild-boar, roe-deer, foxes and wandering cats indiscriminately, from platforms built high among the trees like an Indian tiger-shoot.

Augustine in turn tried to describe the hides which at home he used to dig in the half-frozen tidelands: water-logged mudholes where he was happy to crouch for hours waiting for the honking of the wild geese in the dawning half-light.

Chapter 9

But the dinner-table talk of gentlemen ought to be on serious subjects, not sport! Walther was itching to get back to politics. The bolshevik danger was after all world-wide and Augustine's indifference truly alarming.

A few polite enquiries about Augustine's journey soon gave Walther his cue, for he learned that Augustine had spent last night at the Bayrischer-Hof. 'I hope,' said Walther, 'they made you more comfortable than they made me, the last time *I* was a guest there?' An almost audible sigh and a shifting in their chairs went round the table. Franz's diversion had failed! Papa was off again. 'That of course was February 1919 – the time when Toni had just shot the animal Eisner; whereupon the Red Guards . . .'

'You ought to meet our joint eminent kinsman, Count Toni Arco-Valley,' Franz told Augustine, desperately. 'He's been in prison of course for the last four years or more, but I'm sure Papa could get you a pass . . .'

'The Red Guards arrested me,' Walther swept on, frowning at Franz. 'They dragged me – your Bayrischer-Hof Hotel was their headquarters in those days, four years and nine months ago, and I was locked up there with the others: six of us, innocent hostages. They told us we should all be slaughtered at Eisner's funeral – a human sacrifice on their hero's pyre!'

'*Prison,* did you say?' Augustine asked Franz: 'The chap who actually shot Thingummy only *prison*? How didn't he get killed?'

'Toni *was* killed,' Walther said coldly, resenting the interruptions more and more: 'Or so they thought: five bullets instantly in his neck and mouth, kicked half across the street . . . but to return to myself in the Bayrischer-Hof . . .'

But Cousin Adèle was clearing her throat rather like a clock that is going to strike, and now she spoke for the first time: 'Toni counted the bullets as they hit him,' she said, speaking English slowly and distinctly but without expression, her eyes on Augustine: 'They were using his own revolver, and he tried to remember how many shots were left in it.'

'In the Bayrischer-Hof . . .'

'One bullet knocked over a wisdom-tooth,' Adèle persisted. 'His throat was full of blood. He was choking, and they were kicking; but he dared not move because if they knew he was not yet dead they would have torn him in pieces and suddenly he very much wanted to live.' She was crumbling a piece of bread nervously as she went on: 'They dragged him into the courtyard of the Ministerium and there left him as dead; but not before he heard someone say that Eisner was dead first, and he rejoiced. After a time a bandage was put round his neck but presently again someone tore it off.'

'Then the police picked him up,' said Walther resignedly, 'and Sauerbruch, the great throat-surgeon . . . but that *Toni* of all people should have done it! A boy of twenty nobody had ever looked at twice!'

Instantly memories of his own twentyishness at Oxford flashed across Augustine's mind and he recalled touchy old Asquith's visit to the Union. *Shooting* politicians! In England it was inconceivable. 'Was it a conspiracy?' he asked: 'Was he detailed for the job?'

'No conspiracy – just Toni,' said Adèle, her brow puckered.

'There were people he told,' said Walther, 'but they never dreamt of taking him seriously.'

'Such as, he told the maid in his flat to run a specially hot bath because he was going to kill Eisner that morning,' said Adèle. 'Then, as he waited in the street for Eisner to pass,

145

a friend stopped and asked him to dinner. "Sorry!" says Toni, "I shall be engaged – I'm going to shoot Eisner." His friend looked only a little startled.'

'Eisner left the ministry on his way to parliament and passed Toni quite slowly, with a crowd following him,' said Walther. 'I understand that Toni carried a map to hide his revolver.'

'Eisner's staff were close all round that awful man!' said Adèle. Then her voice went suddenly gruff: 'Toni kept saying to himself "I must be brave, I must not shoot any innocent man – only Eisner!" Then at two metres' range he shot him; and a second later comes the beginning of to be shot himself.'

To end the long ensuing pause Augustine asked Walther how he had escaped 'being slaughtered on Eisner's pyre'. He was told the police had somehow got hold of the hostages and transferred them to Stadelheim Gaol: 'There we had quite a welcome – "*Prosit, Servus!*" And lanky Poehner – later he was Chief Commissioner of Police for Munich, but then he was the prison governor at Stadelheim and he did his best for us, every privilege. As well as myself there was General Fasbender, Fritz Pappenheim, Lehmann the publisher, Buttman, Bissing and both the Aretins – all the élite of Munich! We had *most* interesting talks. It was far worse for our poor wives, without news except rumours that we'd been shot already.' The look of love and reverence with which he now glanced at Adèle astonished Augustine on so middle-aged a face: 'Ah, she was the heroine then! – My Adelie, my Sunshine!'

At that the expression on Adèle's faded sandy features scarcely altered but a faint flush mounted half way up her neck. Even Walther had never known the lengths she went to, that awful time, less than five years ago. The twins had been babies then, scarcely weaned . . . and all – for what?

But already Walther had begun to laugh: 'Ha! Heini Aretin – that was very funny! Somehow his wife got news of his danger sent to Haidenburg – smuggled a note to the

146

village priest in a prayerbook. Whereon the Haidenburg innkeeper comes to Munich, barges his way with his big shoulders into the so-called "Central Council", bangs his fist on the minister's desk and says he can't have his brewer shot or where's he to get his beer? – Heini owns the Allersbach brewery, you know. After that they decided to let us go. They saw that anyhow Poehner would never let them kill us.'

Chapter 10

Walther was drinking the Tyrolean wine copiously (it came from his last bin, broached in Augustine's honour) and his neck had begun to sweat.

Augustine's own head was getting a little dizzy. All this – it was straight from the horse's mouth indubitably, but it sounded so unreal! The sort of thing which happened to people in 'history', not people today, not *real* people. Anyway it was surely over now . . . well – if only those crazy vindictive Frenchmen in the Ruhr . . .

Meanwhile Walther rambled on with great seriousness and much emphasis. Eisner had seized power in November 1918: but his 'Red Guards' (Walther related) were sailors from the Kiel mutiny, Russian ex-prisoners and such-like riff-raff: their maraudings hardly endeared Eisner to the peasants, and he had little following outside Munich itself and industrial towns like Augsburg. Thus, after a few months of office, in the January Bavarian elections he had only won three seats! But he intended to cling to power. For as long as he could he prevented the new parliament from meeting; and then, for its opening session, prepared a second *coup-d'état*: he packed the public gallery with his armed communists. He was on his way to that very session when he was killed.

Proceedings began – but where was Eisner? Then the news of his death reached the Chamber. Instantly a fusillade from the gunmen planted in the gallery: two members killed outright, Auer wounded, the blind Gansdorfer escaping down a drainpipe.

The Munich mob went mad. Walther's own arrest . . . the Red Reign of Terror: March, April . . .

Then May Day 1919 at last, the blessed Day of Liberation! At long last General von Epp's valiant forces from outside advanced on Munich to free it from Bolshevism. At that point Walther turned a beaming gaze on his son: 'Our brave young Franz here . . .' But Franz at once put on so glittering a frown that his father looked nonplussed, and began to mumble: 'Von Epp enters the city . . . the dear white-and-blue flag again! Bavaria a republic still, alas – but decent people in control: von Kahr, Premier . . .'

Just then Augustine's brain having long stopped listening gave an unexpected and uncomfortable lurch. He pushed his wine glass resolutely from him: this wine was too potent, the people across the table were beginning to slide past like a procession starting off. So he chose that passing girl opposite for an experiment: fixed his eyes resolutely on her and with a big effort willed her to a halt.

That crystal and yet unfathomable face of hers was like a still pool . . . Augustine found himself acutely wishing his eyes could pierce its baffling surface, could discern the silent thoughts that must all this while be gliding to and fro in the lucid maiden mind beneath, like little fish . . . but no, not the flick of a tail could he descry tonight, not a freckled flank, not a fin!

Girls' minds . . . Of course, when they *know* you're watching they'll deliberately send all the little tiddlers in them dimpling to the surface, start fretted rings of ripples which meet and cross and render everything opaque! But in unsuspecting tranquillity like this they're transparent . . . or so at least they should be.

Girls' clear minds . . . in tranquillity like this how lovely they often are to watch! First, a whitish motion, deep in the bottom-darkness: an irised shadow on the shining gravel . . . then suddenly, poised beautiful and unwitting in the lens-clear medium, that whole dappled finny back of some big thought – as blue as lead . . .

But *this* girl's mind? Here surely it must be that the thoughts swum altogether too deep: lurking in the darkness of some unnatural shadow, perhaps, hiding in some deep pit.

While Walther's mind? *Hoo-hoo!* Just old dry bones shaken endlessly under one's nose in a worn-out basket that cried 'Look! Look!'

Augustine just managed not to hiccup – but indubitably he was now more than a little drunk.

Augustine was startled by a sudden silence. Walther's voice had tailed off and stopped. Walther was looking from face to face. That young Englishman with so much to learn – conceited flushed young fool! Obviously his attention had wandered. But then Walther looked at his own wife as well, his two children: their attitudes also were politely attentive and their faces blank.

Walther *so much* loved them! He had learned at his own painful costs how the world wagged – and *Gott in Himmel* wasn't it the very world they too would have to live in? Yet whenever he tried to tell them they shut themselves in their shells like this and stopped their ears. Their *own dear papa* had suffered these perils and done these deeds – not some stranger . . . Ah, if only he had been born a poet with winged words hooded on his wrist ready for the slipping! But Walther had been born instead proud heir to the long line of Knights of Lorienburg – so damn all snivelling low-born poets!

Walther took a deep breath and tried again: 'The Red rabble that faced von Epp that spring, four-and-a-half years ago – just imagine! It appointed for itself a self-styled *poet* in command, the Jewish scribbler Toller.'

'*Toller* . . .' In all Walther's rigmarole that name had come to Augustine as the first tinkle of the Germany of his suppositions, the 'real' Germany he had come to see: the Germany of Toller, Georg Kaiser, Thomas Mann, Werfel, Einstein, the world-famous architect Mendelssohn. Here at last, perhaps, was the moment for knowledgeable comment: '*Ernst* Toller?' said the rather fuddled Augustine helpfully: 'Surely one of the greatest German dramatists of all time! – A feather,' he added acutely, 'in Munich's crown.'

There was a stilly pause. Franz's gasp was audible, while Walther looked vastly startled – as if Augustine had suddenly used improper language in mixed company. 'Indeed? I have not had the privilege of reading the young scoundrel's works,' he said presently with cold distaste.

Augustine had not read them either: he was only repeating Oxford tattle, where it was known that Romain Rolland had praised them, and Bjorn Bjornsen.

Augustine hadn't of course had any intention of giving offence. But now Adèle rose. The girl rose too: she passed quickly round the table, trailing her finger negligently along the edge: then she held and kissed her father's frowning forehead and vanished from the room behind her mother.

On that, Augustine found himself actually wondering for one brief moment what impression *he* might be making on *them*. – Lord, he supposed he had better watch his step . . . he must make things right with Walther, straight away.

Suddenly though he realized that Walther also was bidding him good night.

Chapter 11

Augustine's bedroom was a large low one opening off the stairs, with white walls and dark furniture. It was heated by an iron stove standing out in the middle and the wood was crackling so merrily when he went to bed that a foot or more of the long iron flue-pipe glowed red-hot. Augustine wrestled in vain with a window in the hope of letting out some of all this heat. He was not used to a heated bedroom and it made him somehow afraid to go to sleep. Thus he lay awhile in his bed awake, watching the flue-pipe glowing in the dark.

As the wine receded his mind began to race, rather like an engine with a slipping clutch; but presently its chaotic involuntary plungings began to take shape as a new poem:

> *Oft have I stood as at a river's brim*
> *In girls' clear minds to watch the fishes swim:*
> *Rise bubbling to their eyes, or dive into places*
> *Deep, yet visible still through crystal faces . . .*

He was rather pleased with that beginning, at first – its detached attitude was so adult. But then he grew disgruntled with its idiom. Why didn't his few poems, when they came, arrive spontaneously in modern idiom – the idiom of Eliot, or the Sitwells? They never did . . . 'Oft . . .' *This* idiom was positively Victorian. *Victorian* idiom . . .? 'Idiom Makyth Man,' Douglas Moss had once said; and the recollection gave him now a most uneasy feeling.

In the night-silence he could hear someone in the far distance somewhere playing a piano. It was too powerful for a girl's playing, these swelling thunderous chords were a very Niagara of *lacrimae rerum*. It must be Cousin Walther, not in bed yet – or else unable to sleep.

Augustine began to wonder about people like Walther. Were they actually the way they *talked* – unreal creatures, truly belonging to that queer fictive state of collective being they seemed to think was 'Life' but which he thought of as 'History'? Or were they what they looked – real people, at bottom just as human and separate as Englishmen are? Was Walther the freak he seemed? Were all the others here – indeed, all Germans – like him? Perhaps he'd be nearer the answer when he got to know the girl better . . . or even Cousin Adèle. For Women (he told himself sagely and now very sleepily) are surely, surely always the same, the whole world over,

> In every time . . .
> In every clime . . .
> Every time . . .
> Clime . . .
> *Climb* . . .

Augustine found himself climbing a long, long rope to get to his bedroom. He was at Mellton and very reasonably he had had the staircase taken out – Gilbert was on it – and put on the lawn. It was somewhere out there on the lawn now, with Gilbert still mounting it.

Presently a queer, high-pitched howling mingled itself with these dreams. It was shriller and more yappy than a dog's and almost too heartless to sound sorrowful. It came first from the big hall : then presently something passed his half-open door and the howling began again, above.

Squatting in her thick dressing-gown high in the middle of her hard huge bed of dark carved wood, by the shaded bedside light of a focused reading-candle, the girl (this was Mary's 'wide-eyed little Mitzi', of course, and she was now seventeen) sat writing a letter. Her face looked very different now in spectacles – much livelier than at dinner : kinder,

153

and cleverer too, and her head was cocked on one side with one cheek almost on the page, like an infant child's . . .

She wrote to Tascha every night, in her big straggly writing that she couldn't read herself. If she missed even one night Tascha thought she had stopped loving her and sent Mitzi a keepsake damp with reproachful tears (Princess Natascha was a Russian girl of her own age with a deep contralto voice who lived in Munich).

Mitzi paused and laid the letter on the quilt beside her. Then she hunched up her bare bony knees inside her nightgown against her bare soft chest and hugged them extravagantly, considering: what should she say this time?

Papa at dinner had been awful again, but that wasn't news . . .

Usually the words came with a run, even when nothing had happened. Nothing much ever did happen, at Lorienburg . . . but today there had surely been a real event – the arrival of this young Englishman in a house where visitors were rare.

It was difficult to guess what he was really like, inside his outside; hard to know if he would turn out to be nice *inside* or not. Hard enough to imagine what the mere feeling of being any Englishman must be like, that unknown breed, without distinguishing between them. As for his 'outside' . . . he talked German haltingly and with a rather unpleasing accent (rather like that Swiss tutor who once looked after Franz). But when he talked his own English his voice was quite different: she hadn't thought of 'English' – that dour schoolroom task – as capable of ever sounding like that! An honest, feeling voice: one you could trust not to laugh. His clothes had an extraordinary smell: a wistful smell, rather like wood-smoke – no, peat . . . his shoes were curiously silent: they must have rubber soles.

The sudden howling in the hall just outside her door sent momentarily a goose-shiver down her spine. She jumped out of bed and went to investigate. As soon as she opened her door the howling stopped abruptly. She whistled, softly;

154

but the little fox didn't come to her, instead she heard his almost soundless stealthy padding towards the stairs. For a moment she stood, listening: he went up, not down.

The night was turning colder still.

After she was back in bed and settled again wholly within the warmed spot in it she faintly heard the howling resumed; but now, high in one of the desolate uninhabited storeys overhead where nobody ever went.

The obvious thing was to write to Tascha about *him* – the unknown English cousin 'Augustin'. His coming was important. But it was almost a heard voice within her that kept warning her: *'No, Mitzi: better not!'*

When Otto left the table he went to his office and for some hours worked on the papers he had abandoned earlier. Then he looked at his watch: it was time to put through his call to Munich.

It had begun to snow. Outside the pane a succession of flakes like white moths fluttered through the beam of light.

But when he asked for his number they told him there were 'no lines to Munich'. So he asked for his call to be kept in hand; but they told him no calls for Munich were being accepted tonight. – Were the lines down? – They didn't know, but they could accept no calls. – But this is to the Minister himself, Herr Doktor . . . There was a pause, and then another voice answered, coldly, that regrettably that made no difference – *no* calls were being accepted.

Kahr's orders, presumably; or General Lossow's? Or perhaps actually Colonel Seisser's (he was now police chief). What were they up to, then, those Munich triumvirs? Otto hung up the receiver, and his brow was wrinkled. The snow was falling faster but clearly this wasn't a question of faulty lines: something was happening in Munich tonight!

As he creaked along the dark passages on his way to his room he wondered what it was, this time; there were so many things it might be. The situation was so tense it could only break, not bend; but there were half-a-dozen places the fracture could occur. – Still, no use worrying. He put his keys under the pillow, then oiled his revolver and put it in a drawer. Then he undressed, unstrapped his leg and laid it on a chest, and hopped to his bed.

But once in bed the pain began again : extraordinary how difficult it is to lie comfortably in bed with only one leg!

'*No calls to Munich accepted* . . .' On second thoughts he got out of bed again, hopped to the drawer, fetched his revolver and put it under the pillow with his keys.

When Otto heard the howling he wondered what ailed Reineke; for surely the mating season was three months off as yet?

Indeed there was only one person in the whole household seriously perturbed by that faint, high-pitched howling when it sounded from the desolate upper regions.

This was Franz. As soon as he was sure where the sound now came from he slipped a dark coat over his pyjamas, blew out his light and quietly opened his door. The hall outside was pitch-black. He listened : no one else was stirring. As he stealthily felt his way up the stairs in the dark his bare feet were even more noiseless than reynard's own had been.

Here, in the curving walls of the stair-pit, the howling echoed eerily. On the first half-landing he passed Augustine's room – the last room inhabited. The door must be ajar; for he could hear Augustine muttering in his sleep. So, as he passed it on his way up, Franz felt for the English cousin's door and quietly closed it; for least of all did Franz want *him* rendered inquisitive about those floors above.

Chapter 12

In Munich tension had risen all that day – to fever-level. Everyone knew that von Kahr (who had lately been appointed a dictator in the old Roman, caretaker sense) was holding a meeting that evening at which fatal decisions were expected. Kahr wanted Prince Rupprecht on the throne of his fathers: an independent Bavaria, perhaps. The meeting was private but all the bigwigs in Bavaria had been invited and several from outside.

The situation was indeed so tense it could only break, not bend: no wonder those young clerks and waiters at the Bayrischer-Hof had seemed to Augustine that morning to have something more important on their minds than running hotels! At the gymnasium too all nerves had been on edge today: even the pug-nosed instructor was so distrait he nearly broke Lothar's pliant back in a new lock he was teaching him.

Lothar himself was not consciously aware of nervousness or foreboding, but he was moved by a sudden overweening upsurge of the love he felt for all these his friends and for that incomparable brotherhood to which they all belonged. Presently a gust of it almost swept him off his feet as he stooped in the changing-room tying his shoes.

On that the lace broke, and while he knotted it his mind's eye contemplated this signal image: *Germania*, a nymph chained white and naked to the cruel Rock of Versailles. Her soft skin was ravened and slobbered by the sated yet still gluttonous Entente Powers; but it was being even more cruelly mauled and torn (he saw) by the talons of her hungry secret enemies – the Bolsheviks, the Berlin government, the Jews . . . the hooded Vatican and her Bavarian separatist brood. But just then in the nick of time Lothar's boyhood hero and present commander the brave young Hermann Goering (that nonpareil among Birdmen!) swooped down in shining armour to save her – with *Lothar* at his side.

Before that picture Lothar's heart quite brimmed over with love; and while the mood was still on him he slipped his precious ten-shilling note almost surreptitiously into the Party chest.

In the throng behind Lothar as he did this his comrade the massive (though rather muscle-bound) Fritz nudged young Willi, and pointed: 'Watch out!' he whispered hoarsely: 'The artful little bourgeois scab – what's *he* trying to pull?'

Fritz's indignant croak was meant to be confidential, but it had come out louder than intended. At once his suspicious eyes blinked and he glanced round anxiously over his huge, humped shoulder: for Fritz was working-class (his father being a skilled burglar), and he feared that most of these bourgeois wet rags here already looked on him as no better than a Red. Who knows? That perishing little twister young Scheidemann! With his foreign Valuta he might have wormed his way in with the Top Ones here *already* . . . in which case poor clumsy Fritz had put his foot in it proper. – Look! Even Willi the pariah was edging away from Fritz now . . . or was it Lothar Scheidemann Willi was giving the cold shoulder to? – Which? – God's Mother, *which*?

(Willi was edging away from both, probably; for with a 'Roman' nose like Willi's for sole birth-certificate it was surely only prudent for a young Trooper to tread a bit delicately.)

But this evening there was to be not much time for prudent little manoeuvres like these. For while Lothar was still dreaming about Germania and Willi was still debating in his mind who to stand next to at roll-call it was announced that the troop had special orders tonight. They were to cross the western sector of the city in twos and threes by different routes and to rendezvous at the Drei Katzen – an obscure but spacious beerhouse just off the Nymphenburger Strasse past the Löwenbräu. There the 'Hundred' they were enrolled in would mobilize, with certain other 'Hundreds', and be told what to do.

Nothing more was said to them now than just that: no word about Kahr's meeting at the Bürgerbräu beyond the river, on which all day all surmise had centred: yet there was something electric in the air, and everyone knew that at last this was no routine assignment. At once all prudent little manoeuvres were forgotten quite, for at once all the jealousies and suspicions which inspired them had vanished like smoke. You could almost hear the click as those 'hoops of steel' settled into place, binding all these ardent young men together into one body like well-coopered barrel-staves.

As dark fell they had set out: in twos and threes, as ordered. Larger numbers might attract attention: to go alone would be imprudent, for it was at any time none too safe after dark in certain streets near here for these known Galahads alone – even partly armed, as they were tonight. The Reds had been driven underground – the treacherous beasts . . .

Thus the uncouth but sterling Fritz lingered in the doorway for his friend Lothar (who had a quick hand and a cool head in a scrimmage, as Fritz well remembered), and the two linked arms; whereon they both of them felt almost frightened at the intensity of the comradeship each other's touch engendered.

Arm-in-arm like that they had moved off, keeping well to the middle of the roadway, well clear of doors and alleyways. Each had one hand on the bludgeon in his pocket, each with his weather eye searched the shadows his side. They were confident even without having to look round that the trusty Willi was following a pace or two behind and guarding their rear.

But there were no Reds on the streets this bitter evening: only other young men like themselves moving purposefully

159

in twos and threes; and heavy covered lorries, which roared along the streets in increasing numbers and skidded round the icy corners with crashing gears.

Crossing the Stiglmaierplatz, however, our Lothar and Fritz and Willi had several reminders that (Reds apart) theirs was by no means the only 'patriotic' private army in Munich those days. There were other – and potentially hostile – loving 'German Brotherhoods'. The Löwenbräu-keller they saw was full to the gills with men of the Reichskriegsflagge, with steins in their hands and their danders up, roaring their heads off . . . well, these (as Willi, who had an insatiable curiosity about such things, pointed out to them) were Captain Roehm's own men now, since the show-down – and Roehm seemed to be a grand chap, it was he indeed who had put our own leaders on the map! So, on Willi's instructions the three young musketeers hailed Roehm's men in passing. But in that uneasy alliance under old Ludendorff's titular presidency called the 'Kampfbund' these two were almost the only component parts which could fully trust each other. Those 'Oberland' men outside the Arzbergerkeller –Weber's crowd . . .? Well (said Willi) these . . . and perhaps Rossbach's henchmen too . . . these might be trustworthy up to a point, but there were others – the 'Vikings' for example – who were an altogether different kettle-of-fish. The 'Vikings' resembled Captain Goering's gymnasium brotherhood only in their love for their country and hatred of its government and of public order: they were too Catholic and monarchist by half to stomach the blas-phemies of a Ludendorff or a Rosenberg. These would be Kahr's men and Prince Rupprecht's if brass-rags were ever irrevocably parted with those two.

These 'Vikings' were Commander Ehrhardt's chickens. Ehrhardt, of course, was already famous: a veteran of the guerilla fighting that raged for two whole years after the 1918 'armistice' in the lost Baltic provinces, it had been he too who had led the Naval Division in the Kapp Putsch on Berlin. And Rossbach as well was famous: he also was one of those young veteran outlaws of the Baltic shambles who had gone to ground in Bavaria when cowardly Berlin disowned their private wars. Lone warrior-patriots of the lost lands in the East, such as prove lodestones to angry young men any time, anywhere! What a godsend, then, it had been to an unknown unglamorous little H.Q. bell-hop with his own splinter-party to build when at last he had been able to counter the attractions of such heroes as these with the prestige of *his* young Captain Goering! For Hermann (the old African governor's handsome son) had been the ace of Richthofen's famous wartime 'Flying Circus', and now had all the panache on him of his *Pour le Merite* (Germany's V.C.).

By the time they had reached the Drei Katzen and reported, that too was filling up: older men, mostly – ex-soldiers; but all their *own* men however, except for a small and rather secluded, unwanted knot of 'Vikings' (who seemed all eyes and ears).

Two hours later they were still at the Drei Katzen, waiting – with steins in *their* hands now and their danders up, roaring their heads off – when a car drew up outside with a squeal of brakes. Hermann Esser was in it (Esser the young journalist and scandal-buster). He looked wild-eyed and feverish tonight. They crowded round him: Esser had come straight from the Bürgerbräu and he gave them the news: thirty-five minutes ago precisely the balloon had gone up! They cheered till the building shook. Then Esser gave them their orders: to march in parade order right through the heart of the city to the Bürgerbräu. It was 'action' at last!

As Lothar's company with banners flying and drums beating swung down the Brienner Strasse by lamplight – with *guns* in their hands now and their danders up, roaring their heads off – people poured everywhere out of the side-streets: men, women and children marched with them and behind them and in front of them and all round them, cheering wildly for the 'Revolution' – though just whose revolution most of them scarcely knew. Was this the Catholics' monarchist and separatist one, or . . . whatever the Kampfbund themselves were after? – Cross or Hakenkreuz? – Either meant mud-in-the-eye for Berlin: thus both were almost equally attractive to Bavarians after fifty years of Prussia calling the tune.

So they traversed the Königsplatz in style, with one proud little boy just in front of the marching column doing handsprings, handsprings – handsprings all the way.

It was a cold night all night in Munich – that exciting night of Thursday November the eighth – but still no snow there; and bitter and windy was the 'Kahr-Freitag' morning which followed.

Chapter 13

At Lorienburg, when Augustine had gone to bed last night the room had been too hot; but by morning his bedclothes had slipped off, the stove was dead and the room down to freezing-point. There was ice in the jug on his wash-stand.

Here at Lorienburg moreover there had been quite a heavy fall of snow in the night. This morning the sky was still as slaty-grey as before, but with all that whiteness outside indoors it was appreciably lighter than yesterday. As Augustine on his way to breakfast entered the hall he found the few touches of colour in it picked out by the snowlight: the blue tablecloth on the little round table, a green chair, the gold scroll-work on the big black settle. The ancestral paintings looked brighter than yesterday, and the pale cafe-au-lait stone floor-tiles glistened as if they were wet.

Then came a brief flicker of shadow over everything as a cloud of snow slipped silently off the steep roof: not in one heavy lump as when it melts, but more like a slowly falling cloud of smoke. Augustine turned, and through the window saw it drifting away like smoke on the almost imperceptible breeze. Someone (he noticed) had left a bottle of beer on the sill overnight: it had frozen solid and then burst, so that the beer still stood there – an erect bottle-shape of cloudy amber ice among the shattered glass!

As he turned again from the window Augustine caught sight of two little girls. They were half hidden in the embrasure of a door; but he recognized them as the tobogganers by the bumps on their foreheads, glistening like the floor-tiles. He smiled at them; but they didn't smile back: they were too intently watching something, with shocked expressions.

It was only by following their eyes that he caught sight

of the twins also, Rudi and Heinz. Those perilous trick-cyclists were crouched now under a tall Gothic breadchest, withdrawn as far as possible from sight; but they couldn't quite hide that they were wearing heavy brass-studded dog-collars and were chained by them to the legs of the chest with long dog-chains. Ashamed – not at all of yesterday's crime but acutely of today's punishment – they glared out at Augustine with unruly and unfriendly eyes.

With her back to him, and squatting on her heels so that the long fair tail of hair hanging down her back was actually touching the ground, that older sister who had so interested him last night was dipping hunks of bread in a bowl of coffee and feeding them. Intent on scowling at Augustine one of the boys got a crumb in his windpipe and choked, coffee and other liquids pouring from nose and eyes. In a paroxysm of embarrassment Augustine tip-toed past with averted head, hoping against hope the girl would not look round and see him.

At breakfast there was an atmosphere of suppressed excitement mounting. It bewildered Augustine, who knew nothing of the night's mysteries.

At six that morning Otto had got up and again tried to telephone to Munich; but still 'no lines'. He had then rung the railway-junction at Kammstadt and learned that during the night no trains had arrived from Munich and no news either. What could have happened? Services elsewhere, they told him, were normal. This narrowed the field somewhat; for if Berlin had marched on defiant Munich – or Munich on Berlin, for that matter ... or if Kahr and Lossow had loosed the *Freikorps* mobilized on the Thuringian border against Bavaria's leftist neighbours ...

No: this must be something confined –for the moment – to Munich itself. And since Kahr was in control in Munich, surely something Kahr himself had started: that could only be one thing, the thing everybody expected Kahr to start.

Walther thought so too, when he heard the meagre facts:

it *could* only mean . . . and now Walther was finding the suspense unbearable, waiting for the expected news in front of his untouched coffee dumb.

Franz also looked pre-occupied; but withdrawn, as if his anxiety was his own and something neither his father nor even his uncle shared (nor he theirs). Yet it was Franz alone who remembered to ask Augustine politely how he had slept (had the little fox woke him? No?), and to pay him the other small attentions of a host. Franz was heavy-eyed, as if he himself had not slept at all, his expression more contemptuous than ever.

'Heavens!' thought the simpleton Augustine, looking from face to face: 'What hangovers they've all got!'

It was at that moment Mitzi entered the breakfast room, followed by her two little sisters. She too seemed curiously inattentive; for she would have collided with a displaced chair if Franz, polite as ever, had not whisked it out of her way.

'Dreaming again!' thought Augustine.

At breakfast Augustine found himself noticing how strangely Mitzi spread her fingers – like antennae, like feelers – when stretching out her hand for something small such as a spoon, or a roll off the dish. Sometimes it would be the little finger which touched it first, whereon the others would instantly follow. But even at twenty-three he was still at an age when, as in childhood, there are things which can be deemed too *bad* to be true. Thus this bad truth was bound to be slow in forcing an entry into so young and happy a head as his – the truth that already, at seventeen, those big grey eyes of Mitzi's were almost completely blind.

'Listen!' said Otto.

Churchbells – no doubt of it! Faint but wild, the churchbells in the village below had begun ringing. Hard upon the sound came Walther's foreman forester, his dark hair powdered with fine snow off the trees, panting and jubilant with the news he carried. It was the expected news of course

165

(the first news always is). Solemnly Walther filled glasses and passed them round. 'Gentlemen!' said Walther (everyone had already risen to his feet): 'I give you – The King!'

'*Rupprecht und Bayern! Hoch!*' There was a tinkle of broken glass.

'What fun!' thought Augustine, and drained his glass to King Rupert with the rest and smashed it: 'What nonsense – but what *fun*!'

Neither Augustine nor anyone else noticed that Franz smashed his glass with the drink in it untouched.

Chapter 14

The first wave of rumours which spread nearly everywhere across the Bavarian countryside that Friday morning spoke, quite simply, of a Wittelsbach restoration. No one quite knew whence the news came or exactly what had happened: only that there had been 'a great upheaval' last night in Munich and now Prince Rupprecht the Field-Marshal was to be king of Bavaria (his father, the ex-king Ludwig III with his Prussian bullet in him, had died two years ago).

No one was surprised. Kahr was back at the helm these days with special powers, and everyone knew Kahr was an open royalist who was manoeuvring to declare the Bavarian monarchy restored at the first ripe moment. Presumably his recent deliberate defiances of the federal authorities in Berlin were no more than moves in that separatist game. Lately moreover there had been no lack of know-alls to whisper, knowledgeably, that now it was only a matter of days. Last Sunday at the big Totengedenktag march-past in Munich it was Rupprecht who had taken the salute, not Kahr and not the Minister-president! Everyone had commented on that.

So now it was only the expected which had happened. Mostly, people were jubilant. Churchbells rang and villages were beflagged. In the past people had tended to laugh a little unkindly at the late ex-king's concertina-trousers and his passionate interest in dairies; but in Bavaria fanatical republicans had always been few. Even since the republic villages still used to be beflagged and churchbells rung, children dressed in their holiday best and fire-brigades paraded, for ex-king Ludwig's 'private' visits. When Ludwig died two years ago Munich gave him a state funeral. It turned into the warmest demonstration of public affection you'd have found anywhere in all that 'thousand years of Wittelsbach rule'.

Thus today there were only a few who wore long faces: but those were the very few who allowed themselves to wonder *What next?* For surely this must make the present open breach with Berlin final, must make wastepaper of the Weimar constitution? An independent Bavarian kingdom, then . . . but where do we go from there? Other German states had their would-be separatists too; as well as royalist Bavaria there was red Saxony; there were rebellious reds in Hamburg; and at Aachen there were those despicable paid stooges of the French who even talked of an 'independent' Rhineland.

But Walther von Kessen was not among these long-faced, long-sighted ones as in bubbling spirits he saw to the hoisting of flags, ordered the firing of feux-de-joie, plotted processions and ox-roastings, planned thanksgiving Masses with the village priest, even bruited a memorial obelisk on the Schwartzberg. Moreover Augustine had caught the infection and was bubbling too: possibly the drinking of toasts (no heel-taps) in plum-brandy at breakfast contributed to his care-free attitude of 'Ruritania, here we come . . .' Presently he waved his glass and asked 'M'Lord Baron' for a boon: surely so happy an occasion should be celebrated by granting a pardon to all poor prisoners in the castle, chained in durance vile?

For several seconds Walther gazed at him pop-eyed, as if Augustine had gone stark mad: for Walther's mind had been far away, and in any case he was somewhat unused to fooling. But at last the light dawned – and then, Walther was delighted. How very charming of Augustine! What an appropriate sentiment and how wittily expressed! Walther indeed was quite astonished: for the first time he felt for his young English cousin something that was almost affection, and clapped him on the shoulder till the dust flew. Then he commanded that the boys' dog-collars should of course be undone ('That was your meaning, wasn't it? I have divined rightly?') and sent the two little sisters happily scurrying to see to it.

For the fact was that Walther was only too glad of this excuse for an amnesty. It was forced upon him that in this exemplary punishment he had let his sense of fitness run away with him: the boys were taking it harder than he had expected. There was nothing naturally cruel in Walther – only a belief that in punishing children one ought to be imaginative as well as stern: that the modern parent doesn't go on just unintelligently beating his children for ever.

Thereafter Walther had to go about his feudal festive occasions with Otto: so the three young people, feeling excited and pent-in, went down to the courtyard, Franz and his sister arm-in-arm, out into the keen cold air. The courtyard was deep in snow. The ramparts on its surrounding walls where yesterday the boys had bicycled were now covered in a slope of untrodden snow, the crenellated twiddles of the parapet smoothed out by snow. A snow-hush was on all the world this morning, in which the distant sounds of loyal merriment – the churchbells and the sleigh-bells and the gunshots and some far singing – floated unaccompanied: the only near sound was the tiny (indeed infinitesimal) shriek of the snow you trod.

They passed through the Great Gate. Below them, white snow blanketed the treetops and the village roofs, the church-tower rocking under its bells; and all the forests and fields beyond were also a dead white under the dun sky. In all that whiteness the tints of the painted crucifix outside the castle gate took on a special brilliance: the crimson gouts of blood that trickled from the snow-covered crown of thorns and down the tired face: the glistening pinks and ivories of the emaciated naked body with its wisp of loin-cloth: the blood and blue-white snow round the big iron spike driven through the twisted, crossed, riven feet. Under the cross but quite unconscious of it stood a group of small mites who just toiled up there from the village with their toboggans: red caps and yellow curls, shell-pink faces in-

169

toxicated with the snow, they stood out against the background colourlessness as rich as butterflies, they and the Christ together.

Here Franz halted the trio and they stood in contemplation. 'Grüss Gott,' the children whispered.

Augustine peered inquisitively down through the treetops towards the half-hidden village celebrating beneath. But Franz and Mitzi, their arms still linked, stood with their two smooth yellow heads close against the crucified knees. Franz's face was working with emotion. Instinctively Mitzi at his side turned towards him and with her free hand felt for and stroked his shoulder. As if that released something he began speaking: his face was averted from Augustine but his voice intended for him . . . this English Augustin even though English was young and so *must* understand him!

'Papa,' said Franz (and each word was charged with its peculiar tension), 'is a monarchist: we are not, of course.' He paused. 'You see, Papa is a Bavarian, but I am a German.' With a careful but unconscious finger he was pushing the snow off the spike through Christ's feet. One after another the children on their toboggans and bobsleighs dived head-foremost into the trees below, leaving the three alone. 'Papa lives in the Past! *We* live in the future, I and Mitzi.'

'. . . And Uncle Otto,' Mitzi added quietly.

'Uncle Otto too? Yes, and no . . . not without reservation . . .'

At that, Mitzi drew a sudden, startled breath.

As they passed in through the great gate and saw the house again Augustine glanced up at the roof, for from the tail of his eye he seemed to have caught a flicker of movement there. That *open* dormer on the fifth floor: yesterday surely it had been boarded up like all the rest?

170

Chapter 15

'All the same,' Franz was saying as the trio re-entered the garden court, 'to me, this morning's news is good news . . . so I *think* . . . for now things will begin to move.' Just then the twins appeared in a doorway, watching them. Augustine stooped to make a snowball, but these little fellows looked so solemn they might take it for a deadly affront. 'Kahr – Rupprecht – they are themselves of no importance,' Franz was explaining. 'Gustav von Kahr is merely the Finger of Fate: "Fate's *Little* Finger," if I may be permitted the trope. Supposing it possible to harness too-great forces to too-small ends, today he has released in Germany disruptive powers he will not be able to control. And certainly no one in Berlin will be able to control them now Walther Rathenau is dead. – That was why the great Rathenau *had* to die,' he added in a curious husky parenthesis, his eyes suddenly large and gloating and horribly human.

'But if things do get quite out of control . . . what is it you're hoping to see happen?' asked Augustine, idly amused.

'Chaos,' said Franz, simply and sombrely. 'Germany must be re-born and it is only from the darkness of the hot womb of chaos that such re-birth is possible . . . the *blood-red* darkness of the hot womb, etc,' he corrected himself, sounding for the moment very young – a child who had only imperfectly learned his lesson.

'Golly!' murmured Augustine under his breath. This queer German cousin was proving a rather more entertaining character than he had suspected.

But just then Augustine's attention was distracted from Franz, for Mitzi stumbled over something in the snow. Franz was still holding her by the arm but had ceased to pay much heed to her, so that now she almost fell. 'Whoa there, hold up!' cried Augustine blithely, and slipped from his place to take her other arm.

Usually Augustine rather avoided touching people, if he could: girls, especially. So that now he had deliberately taken a girl's arm it was somewhat a strange experience to him. True, it seemed quite devoid of any electrical discharges; but it was embarrassing all the same. Thus at first he found himself gripping the limp, sleeved thing much too hard. Then he would have liked to let go of it again but found he didn't know how, gracefully, and so had to keep hold of it willy-nilly. All the while he was acutely anxious lest Mitzi should take him for one of the pawing kind.

Whereon in a curiously emphatic – indeed almost tragic, and yet unhurried voice, Mitzi ignoring him began to talk to her brother about their uncle. Perhaps (she admitted) Franz had been right in his 'reservations'; for one had to admit that Uncle Otto did *not*, in his every endeavour, show signs that he sought absolute chaos and ensued it. Indeed, the work he was doing for the Army ...

'I'm afraid that is in fact so,' said Franz, frowning. 'Our uncle has not, I regret, so clearly understood the philosophical pre-necessity of chaos before creation as we have, you and I and ... and certain others.' Now that his brain was active and his emotions engaged, Franz's habitual conceited and contemptuous expression had given place to something a good deal simpler and nobler: 'Hence arises our uncle's mistake – to be working too soon for the re-birth of the German *Army,* when he ought to be working first rather for the re-birth of the German *Soul.* He sets too much store by cadres and hidden arsenals and secret drilling: too little by the ghostly things. He forgets that unless a nation has a living soul to dwell in the Army as its body, even an Army is nothing! In present-day Germany an "Army" would be a mere soulless zombie ...'

'Hear-hear!' Augustine interrupted: 'Naturally! This

time the soul of the *new* Germany has to take unto itself a civilian "body" of course – and that can't be an easy pill for soldiers like old Otto to swallow.'

'The soul of Germany take a *civilian* body?' Franz looked startled, and there was a prolonged pause while he turned this strange idea over in his mind: 'So! That is interesting . . . you carry me further than I had yet travelled. You think then that our classical Reichswehr, with its encumbering moralistic traditions, will prove too strait an outlet for so mighty an upsurge of spirit? So, that the re-born Soul of Germany will need to build for itself some new "body" altogether – some "body" *wholly* German, wholly barbaric and of the people? Is that your thought?'

Now it was Augustine's turn to look startled. In some way they had got at cross-purposes but just how? And where?

But before he could gather himself to answer Franz had begun again: 'The ghostly things: those must indeed not be lost sight of. Do you know what General Count Haesler said even thirty years ago? – No? I will tell you. It was in an address to the Army: *"It is necessary that our German civilization shall build its temple upon a mountain of corpses, upon an ocean of tears, upon the death-cries of men without number . . ."* – Prophetic words, profoundly metaphysical and anti-materialist: an imperative to the whole German race! But how to be fulfilled, please, Augustin, excepting through the Army?'

So Franz continued, yet even while he was speaking his words were growing faint in Augustine's ears – fading, as at a departure, into silence. For suddenly and when least expected the magic moment had come. That soft, living arm in the thick insulating sleeve – Mitzi's arm, which his fingers had almost forgotten that they held – had warmed . . . had thrilled. Now it seemed to be rapidly dissolving between his tingling fingers into a flowing essence: an essence moreover that felt to him as if it hummed (for it was indeed more a feeling than a sound, this humming) like a telegraph-wire

173

on a still evening. Then all at once his own trembling hand which did the holding began too to dissolve away in this 'Essence', like a sandcastle in a rising tide. Now there was direct access – a direct union between the two of them through which great pulses of Mitzi's soul seemed to be pumped up his arm, thence gushing into his empty chest, his head, his singing ears.

Augustine turned himself and stared down into Mitzi's face, wild-eyed. What must she be thinking about this extraordinary thing which was happening between them? For it was surely happening to her arm and his hand alike – it was happening to them both, to the very separateness of their being. Her enormous soul was pouring every moment more deafeningly in and out through the steaming gates of his, while the whole world clanged about them. Yet Mitzi's expression was cool and calm and unfathomable as ever: her incredibly beautiful face perhaps even stiller . . .

'Beautiful'? – Why, this young face out of the whole world was the sole incarnate meaning of that dumb word 'beauty'! In the whole world's history, the first true licence for its use! Her inscrutable face under his gaze was so still it hardly seemed to breathe. Her wide grey eyes neither met his nor avoided them – seemed to ignore them, rather.

'Her wide . . .' It was then at last that the truth about those purblind eyes struck home to him! Struck him moreover with a stab of panic – for pity as well as fear can attain the mad intensity of panic.

Evidently Franz was expecting an answer. Augustine had quite ceased hearing him talking yet now heard him stop talking, sensed his expectancy. So Augustine hurriedly searched his ears for any unnoticed words which might be lingering there, like searching sea-caves for old echoes. 'Well: surely lately we've had enough of all that in all conscience!' he said at last, half at random.

'Enough of all what?' asked Franz, puzzled.

'Of . . . well, corpses and tears and what's-it.'

'How "enough", when Germany is not yet victorious?' Franz countered, now even more puzzled still by this queer English cousin.

Chapter 16

Already by mid-morning more detailed rumours about what
had happened last night in Munich were reaching Lorienburg. But once these stories began to contain even a scrap of
truth they began to sound quite incredible. For now the
name of General Ludendorff came into them – and what
part had he in Rupprecht?

The legendary Ludendorff! For the last half of the late
war he had been supreme arbiter of a German realm that
stretched from the North Sea to the Persian Gulf. On the
collapse in 1918 prudently he had withdrawn to Sweden for
a while (leaving it to Hindenburg to get the defeated armies
home unaided): but he had reappeared lately, and had
immured himself in a villa near Munich at Ludwigshöhe,
where he practised ancient pagan rites (it used to be
rumoured) and kept pretty queer company: succouring con-
spirators, baiting the Jesuits from time to time, and abusing
the Bavaria he lived in. Yet now Rumour was saying that
today the great *Feldherr* had come out of his retirement like
an Achilles from his tent: that he had thrown in his lot with
Rupprecht: that the Bavarian restoration had grown to a
'National' revolution.

Rupprecht (said Rumour) was to be not only Bavarian
king but German Kaiser, and Ludendorff and Rupprecht
were to march on Berlin shoulder to shoulder! Otto and
Walther looked at each other completely disbelieving, for
how could two such sworn enemies ever join forces? Was it
conceivable for His Most Catholic Majesty to begin his
reign by countenancing in any way the discredited Ludendorff – a professed anti-Christian, an unblushing Prussian, a
parvenu moreover whose forbears were hardly any of them
even noble? It was inconceivable that Rupprecht would

accept an Imperial crown at Ludendorff's hands. Yet Ludendorff's name persisted, even when the stories grew more circumstantial. Other lesser names too began to be added: Colonel Kriebel (Ludendorff's Kampfbund leader) and Major Roehm of von Epp's staff, and even some egregious pocket-demagogue of Roehm's who (it appeared) also tagged in somehow with the Kampfbund: all these were in some way involved. There seemed no doubt that Ludendorff was indeed playing a big part: rather, it was the part played in all this by Rupprecht which seemed as time went on to grow more and yet more nebulous. Indeed, was Rupprecht even in Munich? And where was the Cardinal?

At last someone declared that since last Sunday's 'Unknown Soldier' parade Prince Rupprecht had positively never left his castle in Berchtesgarden. Had he been made even King of Bavaria at all, then? Once that was doubted, someone else was positive that the restoration wasn't even scheduled to be triggered for three whole days yet.

These counter-rumours too flew fast. Down in the village, whoever it was had been pealing the bells got tired of it and stopped. Up in the castle, Walther put what was left of his plum-brandy back in the cupboard and locked it. There seemed to be reasonable doubt whether anything had happened, or even was going to happen. At least, anything fit to celebrate: Walther had no desire at all to celebrate *Ludendorff's* pranks. He'd save his liquor for Monday . . . if Rupprecht really was to be made king on Monday (the 'emperor' idea he had dismissed wholly from the start).

All this passed quite unheeded by Augustine: his mind was too full of Mitzi. For Augustine had fallen in love, of course. As a well-made kid glove will be so exactly filled with hand that one can't even insert a bus-ticket between them, so the membrane of Augustine's mind was now exactly shaped and stretched to hold Mitzi's peerless image and nothing more: it felt stretched to bursting by it and couldn't conceivably find a hair's-breadth room for anything else.

Augustine navigated now whenever he crossed a room. I mean, like the yachtsman working along the coast who takes some point on his beam to steer by instead of looking straight ahead – some bold headland, or rock-girt lighthouse – and fills his mind with that cynosure: keeps taking new bearings on it, and reckoning his changing distance from it. This was very much the way Augustine now shaped his course across any room that had Mitzi in it. Even when his back was turned to her the very skin under his clothes seemed aware of the direction Mitzi lay: just as the body through its clothes can feel the direction of the sun's rays falling on it.

Augustine was now twenty-three: but had he ever been in love like this before? Certainly not . . . at least, not since his kindergarten days.

Chapter 17

Presumably the whole party had luncheon presently, but Augustine was too deeply besotted to be conscious of such things any more. Afterwards however came something that he had to take cognizance of: Mitzi vanished, and reappeared dressed all in furs. Franz too appeared, looking handsome and mediaeval in a long sleeveless belted sheepskin jerkin (he liked his arms free for driving, he said). Then Walther insisted on lending Augustine his own fur coat, a magnificent sable of dashing but antique cut – and much too large for Augustine, which caused great hilarity. Finally Adèle produced a sealskin cap for him, and as she fitted it to his head with her own hands her face suddenly went young again: fleetingly it was almost as if Mitzi herself peeped out of it.

Apparently it had been arranged a long time ahead that this afternoon Augustine was to be shown to some neighbours. These were the Steuckels, who lived very comfortably in a large villa at Röttningen ten miles away. Originally it had been planned for the whole Lorienburg family to descend on Röttningen in force, but in view of the dubious political situation surely Dr Steuckel would understand . . .

—Anyway, now it was to be just the three young people alone.

The Steuckels (Augustine was informed) were not nobility; but they were distinguished intellectuals (a class, Walther explained carefully, which *he* considered deserving of every respect). Dr Steuckel owned an old-established Munich publishing firm of high repute, which – like the even more famous Hanfstaengl outfit – specialized in Fine Art; and he controlled an exhibition-gallery and picture-business as well (pounds and dollars!) in a very good

179

position on the Promenadestrasse. That was *Ulrich* Steuckel of Röttningen, of course – 'Dr Ulrich': his brother Dr Reinhold (the eminent Munich jurist) had once been like Walther himself a Centrist member of the Landtag but now (also like Walther) by his own wish kept out of party politics. He still knew everybody, though.

Dr Reinhold was particularly able . . . here Walther digressed to describe one of the previous season's meetings of 'Gäa' (a serious and distinguished circle whose proceedings began with an authoritative lecture on some worth-while subject and continued with brilliant informal discussions over veal sausage and free beer). Walther himself had been present on that occasion but had hardly dared to speak, whereas Reinhold Steuckel had covered himself with glory by totally confounding the lecturer over some technicality of monetary theory – the lecturer being no less a person than Dr Schacht himself, the great Dr Hjalmar Schacht. 'People are saying,' Walther now digressed, 'that Schacht will shortly be called on to direct the financial affairs of the nation . . .'

But at that point Mitzi started off down the stairs, whereon Augustine (to whom in any case the name of Schacht meant nothing) instantly closed his ears against Walther and followed her hot-foot.

When they reached the courtyard Augustine realized the reason for all these furs and this wrapping-up. They were to travel perched high on a light one-horse sleigh, sitting abreast there the three of them as open to the weather as three birds on a branch.

Augustine's heart leapt; but Franz chose to sit in the middle between them, alas, since he was driving.

As soon as the little monkey-faced man let go of the horse's head and the sleigh moved off – even while still at a walk – Augustine was assailed by a curious giddy, swimming feeling; for the sleigh began slipping about, like a car in an uncontrolled skid. Instinctively Augustine's motoring foot felt gingerly for a brake, his motoring hands clutched for a steering wheel. The sleigh was yawing about behind the horse like a raft on tow. But horse-sleighs, Augustine soon found, don't mind yawing and skidding: they are not intended to behave like staid vehicles on wheels: they don't even need to stick to the road. As soon as they were free of the perils of the causeway Franz left the road altogether. He turned aside into the fields at a canter, his sleigh sliding and pitching on its squeaking runners in the rushing clear cold air, taking his own beeline across this open unfenced country like a hunt.

Once Augustine was able to persuade his muscles to relax, and to acquiesce in this helpless-feeling motion as a baby's would do, he found his mind also relaxing (in sympathy) into a state that was almost infantile. He felt an overwhelming desire to sing: not any proper song with a regular tune, but just to warble aloud in Mitzi's honour much as a bird sings when it is in love – much as Polly had 'sung' that day they had driven down to Mellton. Moreover, when he had slammed his ears tight shut in Walther's face just now Walther's last meaningless syllables had got caught inside: '*Schacht! Schacht! Doktor . . . Hjalmar . . . Schacht,*' Augustine began to carol. Then he stopped, to comment in his ordinary speaking voice: ' "Hjalmar"! What an in*eff*ably ridiculous name! I bet he parts his hair in the middle – eh, Franz?'

But Franz paid no attention: his mind was all elsewhere, was in the past . . . von Epp's crusade of four years ago to turn the Reds out of Munich . . .

Papa last night had wanted to make a great fuss over coupling Franz's name with it all as if it wasn't a matter of course that Franz had volunteered! Hadn't he been already a trained cadet by then, and turned sixteen? – No younger than his friend Wolff; and by then the dedicated Wolff had already been away fighting in the Latvian marshes for the past six months. There had been plenty of others from

181

Franz's cadet-school too with von Epp. Even Wolff's little brother Lothar – ex-Governor Scheidemann's other boy – had wanted to join, and they'd have taken the lad if Lothar hadn't looked so obviously only a child . . . Lothar's voice hadn't broken even.

Why then had Franz minded it so last night when Papa blurted . . . after all, it was not true any more to say that . . . that whatever-it-was had happened to 'him': it had happened to a boy: the very sixteen-year-old boy as it chanced that *he* used to be – but he wasn't that boy now.

Toller . . . last night those two had both spoken Toller's name (the Reds' young commander); and that had touched something on the quick.

There had been that day when the Reds counter-attacked unexpectedly and for a few hours Franz had found himself Toller's prisoner . . . The loathsome taste of imminent death bitter on his lips whenever he licked them (and he had kept on licking them as he stood there with tied hands expecting it): was that the sensitive spot?

If not, *what else?*

After their Spring campaign – the gun-booms and the bomb-bangs, the excitement and the fright – May Day 1919 had been the final day of triumph for the White forces, the day of victory and glory. There had been a cock-a-hoop triumphal march into Munich under arms, down the broad but battered and littered Ludwigstrasse, across the Odeons-platz – goose-stepping between the Residenz and the stately Feldherrnhalle and down the narrow canyon of the Resi-denzstrasse, past the Max-Josefs Platz to the gothickated Marienplatz beyond. There had been a Te Deum and an open-air Mass: the Red Flag had been hauled down and the 'dear white-and-blue flag' of old Bavaria had been hoisted over the city again.

That surely was the end: after May Day, volunteers such as the schoolboy Franz had hoped to go straight home. But there had been work still to do, it seemed: Munich had not only to be freed it had to be cleansed ...

That 'cleansing' ... suddenly Franz's hands on the reins trembled and the galloping horse threw up its head and snorted: for suddenly twenty-year-old Franz was sixteen and living that boyhood *whatever-it-was* over again.

Chapter 18

The triumphal May Day was over: Munich entirely in 'white hands' but seething still ...

Mechanically Franz's hands still guided the sleigh with his sister and Augustine in it, but he was scarcely conscious of it for in his reverie he was transported backward in time to an enormous hostile Munich tenement-building on the far side of the river Isar right beyond the Bürgerbräukeller: it was the grey small hours of the morning, and Franz was quite alone there, and lost.

This young cadet had never been in such a place as this before: he had scarcely in his life before even seen the urban poor. But now he was left alone here, alone in this dark would-be-clean but old and rotting and hence stinking wet warren of endless decaying dark corridors and broken stairs and stuffed-up windows: surrounded in the darkness by innumerable woken waspish voices repeating '*Toller!*' in different tones – and rude things about him (little Franz) and fierce blood-curdling threats.

Franz had been sent here with a patrol which was searching for Toller; for this was the sort of place Toller might be expected to take refuge in. Most of the other Red leaders had been caught and shot by now or clubbed to death; but Toller had hidden himself, the dirty Jew! The patrol had brought Franz along because he alone had ever seen Toller face-to-face.

That of course was the day Franz had been Toller's prisoner: the day the Reds had surprise-attacked in front and then armed women from the local munitions-works had suddenly taken the Whites in the rear as well, and while most of the Whites had managed to escape to Pfaffenhofen Franz had stuck loyally close to his commandant, until ...

Hey, presto! The canny White commandant himself had escaped from the little town solo on a railway-engine and Franz and the few who had remained with him were taken.

At last they had been brought before the bloodthirsty Toller: a slim, small-bodied young student-ogre with big brown dramatic eyes and wavy black hair. They thought that now they would surely be shot. But instead Toller had said something sentimental and a huge navvy had untied the blond, childlike Franz and given him his own hunk of sausage: whereon Franz had burst into tears under Toller's very eyes and Toller had turned all his prisoners scot-free loose – the dirty Jew!

So now, in the grey dawn that as yet had scarcely penetrated indoors, they were searching this place for Toller the fugitive; and Franz was there to identify him, if he were found.

'Open! *Open!*' The doors seldom opened quickly enough, and again and again the sergeant had to kick down these doors. Doors entering on rooms with sagging, gravid ceilings and with lamps hastily lit. Entering on dark rooms filled to the peeling walls with beds. Collapsing rooms, filled with threadbare beds laden with whole bony families – whole families which night after night had bred on them those innumerable bone-thin children now smelling, in the darkness, of urine and of hate.

All the same, they had not found Toller; and presently for some reason Franz had been left alone like this in the darkness to guard the stairs while the rest of the patrol moved on elsewhere . . .

Just at that point in his recollections Franz turned the horse's head towards the forest. All at once the sleigh plunged in among the trees down a broad ride, and Augustine in his snow-bound loving ecstasy gave loud utterance to a hunting-cry. At that happy, wholly animal sound a tremor passed across Franz's quailing, hunted face: for now in the paling darkness countless shadowy figures in their

185

ghostlike nightclothes were hustling him and again hustling him, and the tide of them had begun to carry him away – in a twinkling that woman had snatched at his rifle and underfoot the child had writhed and bitten him and his falling gun had gone off lethally right among them, the women and the children – a deafening bang, and then the howling . . .

Augustine failed to notice that tremor, for he was leaning right forward so as to be able to see past good old Franz and steal a glance at Mitzi – Aha! At the happy, noble, British animal sound he had just emitted her parted, frost-pink lips had smiled.

Augustine leant back again in his place, content.

Mitzi had smiled . . . but surely the smile lingered on her lips rather overlong? Indeed in the end it seemed frozen to a mere physical configuration, no pleasure nor humour remaining in it.

Once Mitzi's childhood cataracts had been removed the only vision she ever had when without spectacles to give things some semblance of shape (those spectacles which might never be worn in public) was a sort of marbled mingling of light and shade. But this morning she had woken plagued with dark discs floating across things – discs which even the spectacles could not dispel; and now these swimming discs, or globules, had begun to coalesce in a queerly solid black cloud, curtaining totally one part of the field. Now too that black cloud had begun to emit minute but brilliant blue flashes along its advancing edge . . . for it *was* advancing, every now and then the cloud jerked forward a little further and blocked out a little more of the field (moreover, in such an absolute way!).

Six months ago without even this much warning one eye had wholly collapsed, ceased to be a sense-organ at all. 'The retina had detached,' they said. But that was the eye which had always been the weaker, quite apart from those cata-

racts in both of them; and the doctors were so full of comforting assurances about the remaining, stronger eye! Until
now she had completely believed them; but was after all the
same thing now happening to her 'good' eye too? In a
matter of hours or minutes – hastened perhaps by the jolting
of the sleigh – might she find herself for ever afterwards
stone blind?

That was the sudden premonition which had made Mitzi
so suddenly abandon that smile of hers and leave it lying
derelict on her lips, discarded and forgotten while she
prayed:

Mary, Mother ... Oh Mary, Mother ... Heart of Jesus ...

So the sleigh glided on with them, and slid – all three
swaying together, these three separate identities bundled up
in one bundle: a trio, pressed flank to flank in such close
physical communion as almost to seem physically one
person. On and on through the whiteness and the blackness
of the endless snow-burdened forest.

In the ears of all three of them similarly the silvery music
of their sleigh's sweet bells echoed off the endless equidistant
serried boles.

Chapter 19

It surprised Franz when at last they arrived at Röttningen
to find Dr Reinhold there. The eminent jurist was a busy
man and seldom came to his brother's house; but now Franz
heard his unmistakable throbbing voice as soon as they
entered the hall.

It seemed to come through the open library door where
Dr Ulrich had just appeared to greet them: '*Two* shots!'
the exciting voice thrilled in tones rich with pathos: 'Straight
through the ceiling! *Phut-phut!* Surely a remarkable way of
catching the chairman's eye at a meeting . . . and indeed he
caught *every* eye, balancing there erect on a little beer-table
– all those grandees in full fig, and him in a dirty mackintosh
with his black tails showing under its skirts – like a waiter
on the way home. In one hand a big turnip-watch, and a
smoking pistol in the other . . .'

A subdued buzz of appreciation was audible from the
library. In the meanwhile Franz had been trying to murmur
his parents' excuses, but Dr Ulrich seemed in a towering
hurry and wouldn't stop to listen to them – he would
scarcely let the Lorienburg party get their furs off before
he shepherded them in front of him into the already crowded
library and pushed them into chairs. 'S-s-s-sh!' he admonished them excitedly: 'Reinhold was there, he saw
everything! He left Munich before dawn and has just got
here by way of Augsburg. They're all in it – Ludendorff,
Kahr, Lossow, Seisser, Poehner . . .'

'You muddle everything, Uli! It's all that Hitler!' said
Reinhold plaintively, 'I keep telling you!'

'. . . and Otto Hitler too,' Dr Ulrich added hurriedly: 'One
of Ludendorff's lot,' he explained.

'*Adolf* . . .' his brother corrected him. 'But not "*and* Adolf

Hitler *too*"*!* As I'm trying to explain – only you will keep running in and out – little second-fiddle Hitler entirely stole the show! Ludendorff, today? Kahr?' he continued with ironical disdain, and snapped his fingers: '*Pfui!* – For months those two have both been stringing this Hitler along, each trying to use that empty brain and hypnotic tongue for his own ends: now Hitler has turned the tables!'

'It must all have been richly comic,' someone remarked comfortably.

'But on the contrary!' Dr Reinhold was palpably shocked. 'How can I have conveyed to you any such idea? – No, it was deeply impressive! – *Macabre*, if you like: a mis-en-scène by Hieronymus Bosch: but in no way comic!'

Once more everybody settled down to listen. 'The hall was packed – by exclusive invitation only, for a pronouncement of Great Importance. Everybody who was anybody was there including our entire Bavarian cabinet – and Hitler too of course, he'd somehow been invited . . .'

'*When was this, and where?*' Franz whispered to Ulrich, aside.

'*Last night. Munich.*'

'*But WHERE?*'

'*S-s-s-sh! The Bürgerbräukeller: Kahr had engaged their biggest hall.*'

'We all knew what we'd been summoned for, of course – more or less. It would be monarchy, or secession – or perhaps both . . . federation with Austria, even. But Kahr seemed in no hurry to come to brass-tacks. He droned on and *on*. That tiny square head of his – for anthropometrically he's a veritable text-book Alpine, that old boy, and his little head sank lower and lower on the expanse of his chest till I truly thought it would end up in his lap! Nothing about him looked alive except those two little brown eyes of his: from time to time they'd leave his notes and take just one peep at us – like mice from the mouths of their holes! *Eight-fifteen – eight-twenty – on and on – eight-twenty-five* – still endlessly saying nothing – *eight-twenty-eight,*

189

twenty-nine, and then – you should have seen Kahr's look of outrage at the interruption – that inexplicable *Phut! Phut!*'

Reinhold paused dramatically, palpably waiting till someone asked him, 'What happened then?'

'Silence, at first – a moment of utter silence! But the watch in Hitler's hand was fully as significant as his pistol. On the very stroke of eight-thirty – at the very moment he first pulled the trigger – the door burst open and in tumbled young Hermann Goering with a machine-gun squad! Steel helmets seemed to appear instantly out of nowhere: at every door, every window, all over the hall itself. And then Pandemonium broke loose! Shrieks and shouts, crashing furniture and smashing beer-jugs . . . punctuated by that short sharp ululation peculiar to women in expensive furs . . .

'Hitler jumped off his table and began pushing to the front, revolver still in hand. Two of Goering's strong-arm boys half-lifted him onto the platform, and Kahr was shoved aside. So there he stood, facing us . . . You know those piercing, psychotic, popping eyes of his? You know that long, comparatively legless body? ('Incidentally you're *another* Alpine, dear boy,' I thought: 'You're certainly no Nordic . . .') But oh the adoring gaze those brawny pin-head gladiators of his kept turning on him from under their tin skull-cups, those ant-soldiers of his (and there seemed to be legions of them, let me tell you, there last night)!

'Now in a moment it was so quiet again you could hear Hitler panting – like a dog circling a bitch! He was profoundly excited. Indeed whenever he faces a crowd it seems to arouse him to a veritable orgasm – he doesn't woo a crowd, he rapes it. Suddenly he began to screech: "On to Berlin! The national revolution has begun – *I* announce it! The Hakenkreuz is marching! The Army is marching! The Police are marching! *Everybody* is marching!"' Dr Reinhold's voice rasped harsher and harsher: ' "This hall is occupied! Munich is occupied! Germany is occupied!

Everywhere is occupied!" ' In his mimicry Dr Reinhold glared round the room with quivering nostrils, as if daring anyone to move in his seat. Then he continued: ' "The Bavarian government is deposed! The Berlin government is deposed! God Almighty is deposed! – hail to the new Holy Trinity Hitler-Ludendorff-Poehner! Hoch!" '

'*Poehner?*' said someone incredulously: 'That . . . long, stuttering policeman?'

'Once – Gaoler of Stadelheim! – Now, Bavaria's new prime minister!' said Reinhold with ceremony: '*Hoch!*'

'And Ludendorff . . . so Ludendorff *is* behind it all,' said someone else.

'Ye-es – in the sense that the tail is "behind" the dog,' said Reinhold: 'Commander-in-chief of a thrice-glorious (non-existent) National Army – *Hoch!* It's Lossow who's to be minister of war. I tell you, when Ludendorff at last came on the scene he was in a smoking rage: it was perfectly obvious Hitler had bounced him – he'd known nothing about the coup till they got him there. He *spoke* honeyed words, but he *looked* like a prima donna who's just been tripped into the wings.'

'And Egon Hitler himself?'

' "*Adolf*," please . . . our modest Austrian Alpine? He asks so little for himself! Only . . .' Reinhold stood exaggeratedly at attention – 'Only to be Supreme Dictator of the Whole German Reich – Hoch! Hoch! HOCH!'

Someone in Reinhold's audience made a more farmyard noise.

'My friend – but you ought to have been there!' said Reinhold, fixing him with his eyes: 'I couldn't understand it . . . frankly, I can't understand it now so perhaps you clever people will explain it to me? Hitler retires to confer in private with Kahr & Co. – at the pistol-point I've little doubt, for Kahr and Lossow were flabbergasted and palpably under arrest – while young Hermann Goering in all his tinkling medals – all gongs and glamour – is left to keep *us* amused! Back comes Hitler: he has shed his trench-coat now and there his godhead stands revealed – our Titan! Our New Prometheus! – in a slop-shop tail-coat nearly reaching to his ankles, *das arme Kellnerlein!* But then Hitler begins to *speak* again : "November criminals" and "Glorious Fatherland" and "Victory or Death" and all that gup. Then Ludendorff speaks: "On to Berlin – there's no turning back now . . ." "That's spiked Kahr's separatist, royalist guns pretty thoroughly," I thought : "and just in the nick of time! Prince Rupprecht is right out of it from now on – he's missed his cue . . ." But no! For then the notoriously anti-royalist Hitler chokes out some intentionally only half-audible laudatory reference to "His Majesty" : whereon Kahr bursts into tears and falls into Hitler's arms, babbling about "Kaiser Rupprecht"! Ludendorff can't have heard what Hitler said or Kahr said either – fortunately, for he'd certainly have burst asunder . . . but as it is, everyone shakes hands all round . . . then State-Commissioner Baron von Kahr speaks, then Commanding-General von Lossow, then Chief-of-Police Colonel von Seisser – all licking the Austrian ex-corporal's boots! All pledging him their support! Not that I'd trust one of them a yard if I were Hitler . . . any more than I'd trust Hitler's new-found reverence for royalty if I were Rupprecht.

'So much for the stage and the professionals : in the audience we're all jumping on our seats and cheering ourselves silly. "Reinhold Steuckel, you level-headed eminent jurist!" I kept telling myself. "This isn't politics, its Opera. Everyone's playing a part – but everyone!"'

'Grand Opera – or Opera-bouffe?' asked someone behind the speaker.

Reinhold turned right round in his chair and looked at his interrogator very seriously : 'Ah, that's the question! And it's early days really to know the answer,' he added slowly. 'But I *think* it's what I hinted earlier : something not quite human. – Wagner you say? You're thinking of that early, immature thing of his, Rienzi? Perhaps. Yes, the score is recognizably at least *school* of Wagner . . . ah, but those ant-soldiers – all those sinister, animated insects and those rabbits and weasels on their hind legs . . . and above all, Hitler . . . Yes, it *was* Wagner, but Wagner staged *by Hieronymous Bosch*!'

He said all this with such compelling earnestness, enunciating those last words in so sibilant a whisper, that a chill hush fell on the whole room. Dr Reinhold had not gained that courtroom reputation of his for nothing.

Chapter 20

Dr Ulrich kept bees, and the little honey-cakes which were being served (with liqueurs) were a speciality of the house: 'Famous!' his guests exclaimed: 'Wonderful – delicacies of the most surpassing excellence!' It quite shocked English Augustine to hear *men* sitting around and all talking so excitedly about food.

'Hitler would adore these cakes of yours, Uli,' said someone.

'But Herr Hitler adores *anything* sweet and sticky,' said someone else: 'These little beauties would be wasted on him.' The speaker smacked his lips.

'That must be why he's got such a pasty complexion,' (it was only Dr Ulrich himself, it seemed, who had hardly heard of Adolf).

'Does anybody know just when Hitler clipped his moustache?' Franz asked his neighbour suddenly. But nobody did . . . 'Because, the first time I ever saw him it was long and straggling.'

'No!'

'He was standing on the kerb, haranguing. And nobody in the street was listening: not one. They walked past him as if he was empty air: I was quite embarrassed . . . I was only a boy, then, really,' Franz added apologetically.

'That must indeed have been most embarrassing for you, Baron,' put in Dr Reinhold sympathetically. 'What did you do? Did you manage to walk by too? Or did you stop and listen?'

'I . . . couldn't do either,' Franz confessed: 'It was all *too* embarrassing. I thought he was someone mad, of course: he looked *quite* mad. In the end, rather than pass him I turned back and went by another street. He'd a torn old mackintosh

194

which looked as if he always slept in it yet he wore a high stiff collar like a government clerk. He'd got floppy hair and staring eyes and he looked half-starved . . .'

'A stiff white collar?' interposed Dr Reinhold: 'Probably he slept in that too. What the title of "Majesty" on the lips of his pawnbroker means to an exiled monarch at Biarritz, or the return of his sword to a vanquished general, or his dinner-jacket to an English remittance-man on the Papuan beaches – *that clerkly collar!* His inalienable birthright as a Hereditary Life-member of the Lower Middle Classes – *Hoch!*'

'It can't have been my lucky day,' Franz pursued, smiling wryly. 'There was another prophet in the next street I turned along, too! And *he* was dressed only in a fishing-net: the chap thought he was St Peter.'

Augustine liked Dr Reinhold: intellectually he was obviously in a different class altogether from Walther and Franz (surely it was symptomatic how much Franz himself seemed to alter in Dr Reinhold's company!). So now Augustine slipped out of the seat he had been planted in, made his way over to Dr Reinhold and began talking to him without more ado about a boy at his prep-school who hadn't just thought he was God – he knew it. The boy (a small and rather backward and inky specimen) knew it beyond any shadow of doubt. But though he was Almighty God in person he had been curiously unwilling to admit it openly when questioned in public – even when taxed with it by someone big and important, with a right to a straight answer even from God (some prefect, say, or the captain of cricket): 'Leighton Minor! For the last time – Are you God or aren't you?' He'd stand on one leg and blush uncomfortably but still not say Yes or No . . .

'Was he ashamed of His Godhead? Considering the state He's let His universe get into . . .'

'I don't think it was that: n-n-no, it was more that if you couldn't spot for yourself something which stood out a mile like that it was hardly for Him to make a song about it – altogether too self-advertising...'

Dr Reinhold was delighted: 'But of course! Incarnate in an English boy how else could God behave? It's how you all do behave, in fact.' Then he enquired of Augustine in the meekest of voices: 'Mr Englishman, tell me please because I should be so interested: are you God?'

Augustine's jaw dropped.

'You see!' cried Dr Reinhold triumphantly. But then he turned to Franz and said in tones of contrition: 'Introduce us, please.' And thus – rather late in the day – Reinhold and Augustine formally 'met'.

The German clicked his heels and murmured his own name, but Augustine just went straight on talking: 'Sometimes we had to twist his arm like anything to make him own up to it.'

'Himmel!' Dr Reinhold regarded his new friend with owlish anxiety: 'Considering ... who He was, wasn't that just a tiny bit unsafe?' Then he clapped his hands: 'Listen, everybody! I want you to meet a young Englishman whose idea of a wet-afternoon's harmless amusement for little boys is twisting the arm of ... of Almighty God!'

'He'd better meet Hitler then,' said a square woman sourly.

'It isn't as if the Kampfbund themselves took Hitler seriously,' said someone. 'He's not one of their *big* men.'

'It's all Putzi's fault,' someone else was saying, 'for bringing him to people's parties: it has given him ideas.'

'He ruins *any* party ...'

'Oh no! When he talks about babies he's really rather sweet...'

'Putzi Hanfstaengl was with him last night looking like Siegfried,' Reinhold murmured: 'Or rather, looking as if he felt like Siegfried,' he corrected himself.

'It isn't only under the Hanfstaengls' wing: nowadays some people actually invite him ...'

'Then they deserve what they get. I remember one dinner-party at the Bruckmanns . . .'

'What – the famous occasion he tried to eat an artichoke whole?'

'Even two years ago in Berlin, at Helene Beckstein's . . .'

'At Putzi's own house – his country cottage at Uffing . . .'

'The formula is much the same everywhere these days,' said a rather squat actor-type, rising and moving down centre: 'First: a portentous message that he'll be a bit late – detained on most important business. Then, about midnight – when he's quite sure that his entrance will be the last – he marches in, bows so low to his hostess that his sock-suspenders show and presents her with a wilting bouquet of red roses. Then he refuses the proffered chair, turns his back on her and stations himself at the buffet. If anybody speaks to him he fills his mouth with cream puffs and grunts. If they dare to speak a second time he only fills his mouth with cream puffs. It isn't just that in the company of his betters he can't converse himself – he *aims* to be a kind of social upas, to kill conversation anywhere within reach of his shadow. Soon the whole room is silent. That's what he's waiting for: he stuffs the last cream puff half-eaten into his pocket and begins to orate. Usually it's against the Jews: sometimes it's the Bolshevik Menace: sometimes it's the November Criminals – no matter, it's always the same kind of speech, quiet and winning and reasonable at first but before long in a voice that makes the spoons dance on the plates. He goes on for half an hour – an hour, maybe: then he breaks off suddenly, smacks his sticky lips on his hostess's hand again, and . . . and out into the night, what's left of it.'

'How intolerable!' exclaimed a youngish woman, angrily. She had an emancipated look rather beyond her years.

'At least there's this about it,' said Dr Reinhold thoughtfully: 'No one who has once met Herrn Hitler at a party is likely to forget it.'

'But they'll remember him with loathing!'

'Dear lady,' he answered sententiously, 'there's one thing

even more important for a rising politician than having friends; and that is – plenty of enemies!'

'That doesn't make sense.'

'It does. For a politician rises on the backs of his friends (that's probably all they're good for), but it's through his enemies he'll have to govern afterwards.'

'Poppycock!' said the sensible young woman – but too sweetly, she calculated, for it to sound rude.

Suddenly Mitzi, forgotten in a corner, gave a startled, poignant cry. But in that buzzing room almost nobody heard it – not even Augustine, for Dr Reinhold had just offered to show him Munich and Augustine was just saying with alacrity 'When shall I come?'

'Tomorrow, if you like,' Dr Reinhold smiled. 'But no – I was forgetting the revolution . . . better give that a day or two . . . say, early next week?'

Thus Augustine was one of the last to notice Mitzi's curious behaviour. The room had dropped almost silent, for after that cry she had stepped forward a pace or two and was now standing with both groping hands held straight out in front of her. The tears of final defeat were running down her face.

'Is that child drunk?' asked the sensible young woman, loudly and inquisitively.

But in almost no time the now stone-blind Mitzi had got control of herself again. Hearing the question she turned and laughed, good humouredly.

Chapter 21

There had surely been something a little brittle and heartless about that party at the Steuckels all through (or so it seemed to Augustine and even Franz too looking back on it afterwards): the talk was all just a trifle noisier than need be, the attitudes more striking: there was an evident bravura and a bravado about all these people. For these were in fact all people somehow, some way, riding the Great Inflation. Thus in their manner they reminded one rather of skaters caught far out too late in a thaw, who know their only but desperate hope lies in speed. The ice is steaming in the sun and there can be no turning back. They hear anguished cries behind them but they lower their heads with muffled ears, they flail with their arms and thrust ever more desperately with their legs in their efforts to skate even faster still on the slushy, cracking, sinking ice.

Anything rather than get 'involved': whereas Lothar and his lot pursued 'involvement' as if that were in itself salvation.

Franz felt he never wanted to see the Steuckels again – he was done with all that sort.

They got back to Lorienburg soon after dusk, just as the new moon was setting.

Naturally it was not till the first shock to them of Mitzi's disaster had begun to wear off and they were alone together late in the evening that Franz told his father and uncle the story of the Beer-hall Putsch.

'What stupidity!' said Walther. 'It almost passes belief.'

'So our "White Crow" has managed to push his nose into the big stuff at last,' said Otto. 'Well, well!'

'You said once he had served under you during the war,' said Franz. 'What on earth was he like as a soldier?'

'As a lance-corporal?' Otto corrected him a trifle pedantically: 'He was a Regimental Messenger, which rates as a one-stripe job . . .' Then he considered the question conscientiously: 'adequate, I suppose – by wartime standards: he hasn't the stuff in him for a peacetime Regular N.C.O. of course.' Otto set his lips grimly.

'Who are you talking about?' asked Walther absently.

'After the war,' Otto continued, 'Roehm's intelligence outfit at District Command found him a job as one of their political stool-pigeons – spying on his old messmates for pay, not to put too fine a point on it. That started him: now, he seems to consider himself something of a politician in his own right – in the beer-hall and street-corner world, he and his fellow-rowdies. But it's Roehm who still pulls the strings, of course.'

'Oh, that chap of Roehm's? – Yes, I've seen his name on the placards,' Walther remarked.

'But in the regiment?' Franz persisted.

'I can't really tell you much,' said Otto a little haughtily. 'He did what he was told. He . . . wasn't a coward, that I'm aware of.' Otto paused, and then continued a little unwillingly: 'I never cottoned to him. Damned unpopular with the men too: such a silent, killjoy sort of cove. No normal interests – he couldn't even join the others in a good grumble! That's why they all called him the "white crow": in anything they all took part in, Lance-corporal Hitler was always the odd man out.'

'I don't much like your Captain Roehm either, what I've heard of him,' said Walther.

'Able fellow,' said Otto: 'A fine organizer! He's invaluable to the Army. – But it's that snort of his, chiefly: though he can't help it – nose smashed in the war. But it makes him seem a bit abrupt, and he's conscious of it. – Don't call him "my" Captain Roehm, though: *he* wasn't in the regiment. – We had his young friend "Gippy" Hess for a time,' Otto suddenly grimaced: 'Frankly, in the List Regiment we were a pretty scratch lot, all told.'

No one commented: they both knew it had been quixotic of Otto to accept that wartime infantry posting.

In the pause which followed Otto's mind must have reverted to his 'white crow'; for '... half-baked little backstreet runt!' he muttered suddenly – and with surprising feeling, for an officer, considering that Hitler had been merely an 'other ranks'. Franz eyed him curiously. Clearly there'd been some clash.

Meanwhile the telephone kept ringing. Munich was still 'no lines' but all that day rumour had succeeded rumour: rumours that the Revolution was marching on Berlin, rumours that the Revolution had failed, and that Ludendorff and Hitler were dead. Dr Reinhold of course had left Munich for Röttningen before dawn that morning: he had known no more than the next man what had happened *after* that Bierkeller scene.

Lothar had been there, in Munich; but Lothar's excitement that momentous night had reached such a pitch that in his own memories afterwards of what had happened there were inexplicable blanks. Scene succeeded scene: but what had happened between them, just how one thing led to another, seemed subject to total non-recall.

Years later Lothar could still vividly remember the mounting elation and the rhythmic, stupefying effect of the Nazi march down the Brienner Strasse, the crowd growing like a snowball ... that absurd tumbling urchin ... the woman smelling of carbolic soap who sprang forward out of the crowd and kissed him ... that other woman who marched beside him and kept thrusting a crucifix under his nose as if he was a condemned criminal bound for the scaffold.

But the whole troop was bound for the Bürgerbräu, surely (where the Revolution was), by way of the Ludwig Bridge? How was it then that the next thing he could remember he was somewhere different altogether and quite alone?

Scene Two.

It was dark. Lothar was in some enclosed place, and the darkness was only relieved by the murky trailing flames of torches held by hurrying hooded monks. It wasn't a gun Lothar was carrying now, it seemed to be a pick. No Fritz, no Willi – none of his friends were here with him; but one of those hooded faceless figures was padding along ahead of him, guiding him and hastening him on. The air was warmer than the chill night air outside but close and dank – a sort of earthy, cellar-warmth. The smoke of his guide's torch made him cough, and his cough echoed – these were vaults . . . there was a damp smell of mould, a smell of bones . . . this was a place of tombs, they were deep underground, these must be catacombs . . . they were treading in a deep, down-soft dust that muffled sound – it must be the dust of bones.

The small Nazi working-party they came to were older men mostly – none of them ones Lothar knew. From a different troop. They worked by the light of the monks' torches in reliefs of sixes, for there was no room for more to wield picks and shovels at one time and anyhow the dust hung so heavy on this dead underground air that one soon tired.

The thickness of the masonry they were digging through seemed endless. Lothar found it hard to believe this was just some bricked-up vault: for who would have bricked up an *entrance* with masonry more than four feet thick? When at last they did break through, however, the whole thing was plain: for this they were entering was no ecclesiastical door. Efficiently sealed off and sound-proofed from the barracks above, moreover: the reason being eight thousand rifles hidden here from the Allied Disarmament Commission – and theirs for the taking!

'*Von Kahr himself signed our orders – the old fox!*' – 'Eh? Surely not!' – '*Yes indeed! Our officer had to show them to the Prior . . .*' – 'But surely he'd have intended this backdoor for royalist uses; and no doubt that's where these simple monks think the rifles are going even now!' – '*But Kahr has joined us with Lossow and Seisser, hasn't he?*' –

202

'Ye-es . . . or so Herr Esser said: but he's such a slippery cove, Dr Kahr . . .' – *The old fox! But he's trapped at last . . .*'

Eight thousand rifles, well-greased, neatly racked – what a sight for weapon-hungry eyes! Re-inforcements of friendly Oberlanders arrived, and a living chain was formed to pass the guns from hand to hand, along the tunnels, up the torch-lit steps, along the corridors and cloisters – all the long way through these dark and silent sacred places out to where Goering's plain vans were waiting in the street . . .

It went on for hours.

Scene Three.

Lothar was dripping wet and had lost his boots. It was early morning. He was agued with cold so that he could hardly speak . . .

Lothar must have swum the river, but he had little idea why he should have had to swim: presumably the bridges were closed – or he had thought they might be . . . or else, perhaps someone had thrown him in.

But he had to reach Captain Goering, had to tell him . . .

In the gardens below the Bürgerbräukeller brownshirts were bivouacked, but it was perishing cold and no one had slept. Dawn was breaking at last, still and grey with an occasional lone flake of snow, as Lothar picked his way among them. In the entrance-corridor of the Keller was huddled a civilian brass band, the kind one hires for occasions: they had just arrived, they were in topcoats still and with shrouded instruments. They were arguing: they looked hungry and obstinate: their noses dripped. They were being shepherded unwillingly into the hall where the meeting had been, now full of brownshirts camped among the wreckage; but the bandsmen were demanding break-fast before they'd play to them – and at that word Lothar's saliva-glands stabbed so violently it hurt like toothache.

Then someone took pity on the shivering Lothar and pushed him into the cloakroom, telling him to help himself.

The place was still littered with many of last night's top-hats, furs, opera-cloaks, uniform-coats, dress-swords . . .

'They were all in too much hurry to bother,' said a sardonic voice: 'All the upper-crust of Bavaria – and when *we* said "Scat!" they were thankful to run like rabbits. Take your choice, comrade.'

The speaker was a portly little brownshirt with a kindly, humorous face. In private life he was an atheist and a tobacconist, without reverence for God or man; and now he was drunker than he looked. It tickled him to wrap Lothar in a fur-lined greatcoat with the insignia of a full general on it. If Lothar had noticed those badges of rank, as a good German the very thought would have burned him to a cinder – like the Shirt of Nessus; but now his new friend was pouring a hot mugful of would-be coffee into him, and he noticed nothing. Lothar *must* see Captain Goering – and at once – about those rifles . . . But no one seemed to know whether Goering was even in the building. However, some of the other high-ups had just got back from a reconnaissance in the city, someone said: they were in a room upstairs . . . Hitler, General Ludendorff . . .

So Lothar, warmed a little at last, wandered off upstairs unhindered. The length of this vast greatcoat almost hid his stockinged feet, but he was just as wet underneath as ever and left wet footprints everywhere on all the carpets. *–He must find Captain Goering . . .*

In the half-darkness of an upstairs corridor Lothar met a hurrying orderly and stopped him imperiously: 'Where are they? I have to report!'

'This way, Excellency,' the man said, saluting (but Lothar was too pre-occupied to notice, for those rifles might have reached God-knows-whose trusting hands by now). Then the orderly led him through a little anteroom where piano and music-stands had been shoved on one side to make room for a chin-high pile of packages, and opened a door:

'. . . be hanging from the lamp-posts in the Ludwigstrasse,' a cracking, nervous voice was exclaiming within.

Chapter 22

On the threshold, Lothar checked himself in dismay. Goering wasn't there; and clearly this wasn't a Council of War at all, for there were only two people in the room and by their dress both seemed civilians. In a thick and fragrant haze of tobacco-smoke a stout old gentleman all puffy dewlaps and no neck sat stolidly sipping red wine and pulling at his cigar alternately: he was staring at Lothar – but only as if his gaze had already been fixed on the door before it opened – with dull, stony, heavily-lidded eyes. Under his scrabble of grey moustache the open, drooping mouth was almost fishlike, and he had dropped cigar-ash all down his old shooting-jacket. Beyond him Lothar glimpsed some nondescript with his back turned, gnawing his fingernails and violently twitching his shoulders as if some joker had slipped something down his neck . . .

A *waiting-room!* But Lothar had no time to waste – he *must* find Captain Goering at once and tell him those monastery rifles were useless, they'd all had the firing-pins removed.

Lothar retreated, leaving the door ajar. But in the anteroom the orderly was already gone, and Lothar paused – at a loss.

'Tonight we'll be hanging from the lamp-posts in the Ludwigstrasse!' The interruption had been so brief that these histrionic words seemed still suspended on the stale air.

'Nevertheless we march,' the seated one replied flatly and with distaste.

In the ante-room Lothar stood rooted – he knew *that* voice (why hadn't he known the face?): it was General Ludendorff. Then of course the other . . . this wasn't at all his platform voice, but it *must* be . . .

Inside the room, Hitler turned: 'But we'll be fired-on if we do, and then it's all up – we can't fight the *Army!* It's The End, I tell you!' Then, as if he had forgotten who he was talking to, he added, ruminating: 'If we appeal to Rupprecht, perhaps he'd intercede?'

For their impromptu Revolution was already running on the rocks. Hoodwinked by the 'earnest of good faith' of those useless rifles, Hitler had let Kahr go; then Kahr, Lossow and Seisser – the all-powerful triumvirate – once safely out of his hands had turned against him. Prince Rupprecht had unequivocally refused to rise to Hitler's fly – not with Ludendorff's big shadow darkening the water; and that had decided Kahr. Lossow had been virtually arrested by his own city commandant till he made clear his obedience to Berlin. Seisser too had dutifully bowed to the will of the police-force he commanded. So now the Kampfbund was to be put down by force unless it surrendered.

Government re-inforcements had been pouring into Munich all night, and the 'Vikings' had already deserted to them. The Nazis held the City Hall – for what that was worth – while Roehm with his Reichskriegsflagge had seized the local War Office and now couldn't get out of it again; but all other public buildings were in the hands of the Triumvirs. *They* held the railways, the telephones, the radio station – indeed no one in the Nazi camp had even thought of securing those vital points, there can seldom have been a would-be coup-d'état so naïvely impromptu and unplanned.

Troops were reported to be massing now in the Odeonsplatz, with field guns . . .

Lothar peeped in again unseen. The general still sat his chair as heavily as a stone statue sits its horse and his eyes were still set in the same stare, though lowered now to the carpet just inside the door.

General Erich Ludendorff was only fifty-eight: not quite the 'old gentleman' Lothar had taken him for, but nevertheless his mind like his muscles was becoming a little set. Nowadays pre-conceived ideas were not easily shaken and if they were tumbled they left a jagged gap: Kahr's double-crossing Ludendorff could take, for the man was a civilian and though a protestant was in the Cardinal's pocket one could only expect of him the moral standards of ... of cardinals: but a world where a Lossow – Commander-in-chief of the Bavarian Army – could break his 'word as a German Officer' was a new world altogether for Ludendorff!

The old order was ended for the old war-lord, and he knew it; but his puffy features were quite without expression, as if their soft surfaces had no organic connection with nerve and muscle and bone and brain within, and he sat staring without visible surprise at those wet foot-marks on the carpet – the marks of two naked feet where lately a German general in full-dress uniform had stood.

'Eh? – We march,' said Ludendorff again. His voice remained firm as a lion's, and this time it was unquestionably a command.

But when Ludendorff had said 'We march' (as he presently explained) he hadn't meant it in the military sense. No soldier would try to capture Munich – or even to relieve Roehm beleagured in the War Office – by doing as Ludendorff now proposed: by marching three thousand men through the narrow streets of the Old City in a kind of schoolgirl crocodile sixteen abreast. But a clever (and desperate) politician might.

A military operation would cross by the Max-Josef Bridge in a flanking movement through the English Garden – some tactic of that kind: but what would be the use? That fellow Hitler (thought Ludendorff) was right: they couldn't *fight* the Army. But suppose that instead, in all seeming confidence and trust like friendly little puppy-dogs, their whole companionage paraded peaceably right onto the points of the Army's bayonets ... would German soldiers ever fire on inoffensive brother-Germans? And once contact was made, once the officers saw their old war-lord Ludendorff in front of their eyes and had to choose, was it conceivable they would prefer to obey the unspeakable Lossow who had turned his coat twice in one night? Barely an hour ago the streets were still placarded with Lossow's name linked with ours ... 'And once the Army obeys my orders again, the road to Berlin lies open!'

Lothar was so bewildered that he stood listening outside dumbfounded and dripping among the bales of bank-notes which half-filled the ante-room, and scarcely noticed Captain Goering as the latter strode suddenly past him and entered the room beyond.

Goering listened to Ludendorff's plan; but then his eye met Hitler's. These two had rather less faith in the magic of the 'old war-lord's' name and presence nowadays than the 'old war-lord' had himself. Ludendorff had been slipping – didn't the old boy realize how much he had slipped these last few years? That flight to Sweden in '18, and all those antics since ...

Goering suggested instead a retreat on Rosenheim – to 'rally our forces' there, he hastened to add. But Ludendorff fixed this bravest-of-the-brave with his stony look: Rosenheim was all too convenient for the Austrian frontier! Hitler also turned his blue stare on Goering: for reasons best kept to himself, escape into his native Austria held no attractions for Hitler.

Goering dropped his eyes and did not press it. But the suggestion all the same tipped the scales in Hitler's mind, for any alternative was preferable to 'Rosenheim'; and he turned to Ludendorff's plan after all. Hitler's own 'magic' at least was new; and if that called out anything comparable with last night's cheering crowds they would march behind such a screen of women and children that no one could fire on them!

A coup-d'état by popular acclamation? Maybe it was a forlorn hope. But at least it meant, for Hitler, sticking to the one technique he was yet versed in – the technique of the public meeting.

Blindly Lothar wandered away, not knowing whether he was mad or sane, awake or dreaming. Goering . . . he had a message for Captain Goering, something about some guns.

Chapter 23

One thing, the arch-plotters agreed, was essential: if this gigantic confidence-trick of Ludendorff's was to work the marching men themselves must have no inkling that Munich was in 'enemy' hands, for they must positively radiate friendliness and trust. No one must know the real state of affairs outside the innermost circle. So, shortly before eleven, a briefing-parade for officers was held in the fencing-school and there the supreme leaders, beaming, put their next subordinates 'in the picture', assuring them that everything in the city was going like clockwork under the capable management of their obedient allies, Kahr, Lossow and Seisser, and all ranks should be so informed. Today the Kampfbund would parade ceremonially through the city, merely to 'show the flag' and to thank the citizens for the warmth of their support: they would then take up a position for the night outside somewhere to the north, and wait there for regular troops to join them . . . and after that – Berlin!

Officers and men alike, that's what they were told.

Lothar never did get to Goering; and the Oberland adjutant he at length reported to about the defective rifles, being fresh from that 'enlightenment' in the fencing-school, took it not at all tragically. He burst out laughing: 'Kahr – the old fox! He just can't change his habits, that's all . . . I admit though I was surprised when he *volunteered* those rifles!' But it didn't really matter, he explained to Lothar, for everything was going swimmingly: they could collect and fit pins this evening at the latest, and meanwhile it was only a parade the arms were wanted for.

Lothar was thoroughly bewildered; and Hope that wiry young woman awoke anew. Could he have been quite wrong about what he thought he had heard upstairs? For this was evidently the latest news, and this was 'official' – straight from the horse's mouth . . . but yet . . .

The adjutant stole a doubtful look at Lothar's dumb-founded face. What ailed the boy? – As for all this about the rifles, the men mustn't *know* they were armed with guns which couldn't be fired: could this lad be trusted to hold his tongue or had he better 'disappear' – be put under arrest for something, perhaps?

But just then Putzi Hanfstaengl's giant frame began to be made manifest – feet first, like a proper deus ex machina; for he was coming downstairs from the council room (something seemed to have wiped the grin off his handsome great jaws for once – till he emerged into public view). So the adjutant whispered to him; whereon Hanfstaengl turned, and his powerful pianist's fingers gripped Lothar by the arm: 'You're coming to the city with me, my lad!' he said.

Lothar hardly reached to his breastpocket, but Putzi lowered his face almost level with the bedraggled, hollow-eyed youth's to add confidentially: 'I must have an escort – to protect me!'

Dr Hanfstaengl was such a famous tease! Lothar blushed; and then, in spite of the turmoil in his head, climbed into the car after his new master as proud as Punch to be in such important company. There he tried hard to sit upright in the back seat with proper military stiffness; but before they had even reached the bridge he was sound asleep. Thus Lothar's friends Fritz and Willi both took part in the famous march but not Lothar, who slept like a log for hours.

When Lothar woke at last he found himself on a floor somewhere. It was the sound of two voices talking urgently which woke him, one of them unmistakably philosopher-editor Rosenberg's. Lothar's head was on a bundle of galley-proofs, and his eyes opened with a start only a few inches from the turn-ups of Rosenberg's bright blue trousers and dirty orange socks with clocks. So he must somehow be

211

in the offices of the Völkischer Beobachter, he guessed.

But as the clouds of sleep began to clear Lothar realized these people too were both talking and acting as if the Revolution had failed. While he talked, Rosenberg was cramming clothing into a broken briefcase on his desk as if for a hurried departure (doubtless preferring brighter and looser neckwear than that usually worn by politicos on lamp-posts). For a second or two the stained tail of a crumpled purple shirt trailed across Lothar's face; but he shut his eyes and listened and lay still, his temples bursting with sweat. For what he heard next was even more incredible still. That whole briefing parade had been one deliberate, colossal lie! Indeed, the men 'had had the wool pulled properly over their eyes', said Rosenberg's companion approvingly. The march was on, and they were all going like lambs to the slaughter! Rosenberg himself was so certain it would end in a massacre that he for one wasn't waiting to see it. Putzi Hanfstaengl too (one gathered) had gone home to pack . . .

Even the leaders who were marching had made their arrangements – or arrangements had been made for them, whether or not they knew it. There would be a car waiting for Hitler (Rosenberg's companion said) in the Max-Josefs-Platz with engine running: he could nip down Perusa Street to it – if he survived that far. Goering too had sent some-one home to fetch him his passport . . .

Now Rosenberg was choosing his own passport – *choosing* it, he seemed to have a whole drawerful of them.

When the two men left at last Lothar was not far behind them. He thought of Fritz and Willi and all his other noble friends going unwittingly to their deaths and his bowels yearned.

But then once again something black descended like a blind over Lothar's power of reason. It was simply not possible (he told himself) that the Movement had been lied to deliberately by its leaders like that. Hitler loved his men, he would never knowingly lie to them this way and lead them into danger; and as for the heroic, gallant Goering . . . let alone General Ludendorff! – No, if these leaders had indeed had evidence of the Triumvirs' treachery they hadn't believed it because they were too noble to believe; and it was just this noble incredulity the beastly triumvirate had banked on, to lure the Army of Light into the depths of the city so that when the jaws of the trap closed the slaughter might be all the more complete.

Devils! Lothar bounded down those office stairs four at a time, as if every bound trod underfoot a triumvir. Somehow he must find Fritz and Willi – somehow he must warn them . . .

And warn Captain Goering . . .

But as he neared the route the city seemed solid with police, and half the streets were closed.

Chapter 24

Five years ago almost to the day Kurt Eisner too had marched into Munich – with flying beard and floppy black hat like a seedy professor of pianoforte, having half the hooligans of Munich at his heels – and so come to power.

But November 7th, 1918 had been unseasonably warm: perfect Putsch weather. Eisner had the advantage of surprise too, for he marched first and announced his revolution afterwards. There was little risk of organized opposition since the troops were still at the front and the whole city numbed by defeat.

On November 9th, 1923 the prospects were chill and grey. It was unseasonably cold – bitterly cold, with a biting wind now and occasional flurries of snow. When the march at last began the buglers with their chapped lips found it difficult to blow. Fritz and Willi shivered in their cotton shirts with no tunics and their chins were raw: the moment they stopped singing their teeth chattered. The 'cheering crowds of spectators' could be counted in twos and threes, and were chilled to the bone.

It had been past twelve when the march moved off from the Bürgerbräu and a few yards down the hill it had halted again. Peering over the heads in front, big Fritz could see there was some sort of scuffle going on down at the Ludwig Bridge. It was apparently the police-cordon there making trouble – the wooden-heads! But then a mixed bag of fifty or more leading Munich Jews padded past the waiting column and on down to the bridge at the double. A wave of laughter followed them; for whatever their past dignities (and many were elderly, prominent citizens), today they were all dressed only in underwear and socks: they'd been locked all night in a back room of the Bürgerbräu like that. Captain Goering himself, with his elfin humour, must be taking the situation in hand. Indeed Goering must have threatened to drop all these hostages in the river to drown if the police didn't show more sense; for almost at once the column began to move forward again, and at last the river was crossed.

Four hundred yards into the Old City however they halted a second time. This time it was their own leaders who halted them, wanting to make quite sure everyone was fully 'in the picture' in case of misunderstandings. Any soldiers or armed police they might meet (they were told) would be patrolling the city 'on behalf of our revolution, understand! In the Odeonsplatz maybe we'll find a detachment of regulars drawn up apparently to face us: with guns to their shoulders, even ... but don't be nervous, that's just to cow any hostile rowdies in the crowd lining our route so sing 'em a rousing chorus, boys, and give them a hearty cheer as we draw level with them . . . Oh, and just in case of accidents in these crowded streets we'd better not march with rifles loaded.'

When the marching column reached the Marienplatz they found the city hall festooned with swastika flags, and in the open square in front they were cheered by a small but milling crowd. That crowd had just been whipped up by Julius Streicher in his juiciest vein. Indeed that was why Hitler had sent Streicher on down there ahead; for here, potentially – if Streicher had really done his stuff – was the human screen Hitler needed.

If only *enough* of these cheering citizens would tag along with the marchers from now on, keeping between the moving columns and the guns ... If *only* it hadn't been so beastly cold today ...

But the wind was indeed too bitter. Struggling to reach the Marienplatz Lothar could make little progress against the solid mass of citizenry hurrying away.

Chapter 25

As the procession moved off from the Marienplatz again Ludendorff took his place in the van, on foot, in front of the standard-bearers even. On that, Hitler and one or two other notables and would-be notables jostled their way to his side: they had convinced themselves by now that there would be no shooting, that the trick would work.

The Odeonsplatz was their objective, for that was where the troops were said to be waiting for them: that was the psychological point d'appui. From the Marienplatz two routes converge on it, like the uprights of a capital 'A' with the short length of Perusastrasse for a cross-stroke, and that bit of pseudo-Florentine nonsense the 'Feldherrnhalle' loggia in its tip. The route they chose was the left-hand one, the Wein-and-Theatinerstrasse; and the leaders were already half way along it before seeing that the far end was indeed blocked solid by a small detachment of soldiery – with guns.

Here at last, then, straight ahead, were those bayonets Ludendorff was to deflect with the magic of his presence! Those triggers no German finger could pull...

We have only to march straight up to them, straight on... (Was conviction weakening?)

How far have we got? *Tramp, tramp* ... just ahead lies the corner of Perusastrasse – the *last* side-turning, before ...

'Look,' said someone excitedly to Lothar in the thinning crowd, 'there's *Ludendorff!*' The fabulous, the Army's idol, walking straight towards those Army guns in his old shooting-jacket ... 'And that beside him's Hitler, his faithful friend; and God-knows-who ...'

Tramp, tramp, and flags waving and a band somewhere tootling and the men singing, *tramp, tramp* ...

And most of the remaining spectators, cold and bored, remembering their lunches and turning away to go home.

Thirty yards more ...

In the throes of their fore-knowledge the leaders now felt their feet going up and down like pistons, as if they were not really advancing at all, *tramp, tramp.* No, it was the muzzles of the guns which were all the time moving nearer.

Twenty yards more ...

Hitler keeps his eyes fixed sternly ahead, yet out of their corners can't but be acutely aware of the delicately-nurtured schoolgirl wheeling her bicycle at his very elbow. 'She's trying in vain to match her stride to *my stride* ...' Quite easily, though, she matches the men's voices in song with her surprisingly deep contralto.

Fifteen yards ... Ten ... and now on the right the opening of Perusastrasse is bearing irresistibly down upon us, an open mouth ...

'My God I'll give up politics! Never again ...'

It came like the sudden inexplicable unwilled lurch of a planchette at a séance, that sudden unanimous swing of the whole group of leaders into a right-wheel turn – away from the guns, straight into the shelter of that side-street! It was so sudden that the girl taken unaware fell over her bicycle and tore her stockings, and that was the last they saw of her.

The whole cheering follow-my-leader crocodile followed, of course – without a thought, without a worry, singing their heads off in the honour of the troops whose guns at point-blank range were still trained on their defenceless flank as they wheeled. *They* still hadn't an inkling of what they were now right on the very edge of.

For the leaders the respite was brief: in a very few yards this short cross-street would reach the open Max-Josefs Platz. To the left, then, would lie the narrow canyon of Residenzstrasse – the other, perhaps less well-guarded route to the Odeonsplatz . . . the route in any case they now *had* to take . . . Ah, but had they? For also from this Max-Josef Square a broad, broad boulevard led back totally unmenaced straight to the river again: the primrose way of retreat.

A primrose-yellow car was parked there, by the monument. As they neared the corner it was young von Scheubner-Richter (Ludendorff's right-hand-man) who recognized it as Hitler's – and he sucked in his cheeks. Straight way he locked his arm very firmly in Hitler's. *He*'d see to it the old general wasn't left in the lurch.

But now somebody had ordered another halt, *another* rifle-inspection: officers were to make quite sure again that every breech was empty.

That primrose-yellow car was trembling slightly – so its engine was running, ready! Max Erwin von Scheubner-Richter at Hitler's side stood still and tightened his comradely grip. Meanwhile, in the ranks behind, Willi was yawning with the cold and his stiff fingers fumbled on the bolt. Was there no end to inspections? He was getting horribly bored. Fritz blew on his fingers, and cursed – he had broken a nail. Were all revolutions as dull as this one? It was a relief to them all when the march started again.

But the tense troop of police waiting among the statues in the Feldherrnhalle had heard that echoing rattle of bolts as hundreds of breeches at one time were flung open for inspection, and drew their own conclusions. So the rebels were loading: they meant with their vastly superior numbers to rush it. And the police were so few . . . but that last hundred yards of the Residenzstrasse was a Thermopylae – fifty men could hold it against five thousand, if they were resolute.

At the corner of the Square Willi had thought he caught a glimpse of young Scheidemann near that purring yellow car. He seemed to be trying to signal to them, and Willi

218

nudged Fritz – but this chap looked so doleful it surely couldn't have been Lothar!

Funny, though, how empty the streets were, suddenly: what had become of all those cheering spectators who had filled the Marienplatz? As the troop in front wheeled left there was not a single civilian who followed it into the Residenzstrasse – only one funny little dog in a winter waistcoat of Scotch plaid, looking important.

When Princess Natascha (for that girl with the bicycle was Mitzi's Russian friend) had picked herself up, the head of the procession was already out of sight and Perusastrasse chock-a-block with them; but she guessed they would turn left again up Residenzstrasse. She had better get to the Odeonsplatz ahead of them if she wanted to see the fun; and indeed she was determined to miss nothing, for the lonely young exile was impervious to cold and quite intoxicated with the singing and the marching and the general community and exaltation of the thing. She mounted her machine and bicycled up the few remaining yards of the Theatinerstrasse as if the troops in front of her just didn't exist (and they were in fact very few).

'Damn her!' muttered the officer in command. 'She's right in my line of fire!' So he let her through, and thus Tascha found herself the only civilian in the whole empty centre of the Odeonsplatz with every window looking at her; but she wasn't embarrassed at all, it wasn't her nature to be. Pedalling hard, she gave a wide berth to the one armoured car stationed there, but it took no notice. Good! The top of Residenzstrasse was open, she'd ride down and meet them: she could hear already the tramp of the approaching marchers, and as she got to the corner she caught the gleam of their bayonets. But just then a troop of armed police appeared out of the Feldherrnhalle and stretched right across the street in front of her, right to the Palace wall. An absurd thin line; but she had to jam her brakes on, and dismounted close behind them. *Tramp, tramp* . . . between the policemen she could see the procession coming now: Nazis with fixed bayonets and Oberlanders without, side by side, sixteen abreast, a veritable horde. This pitifully thin string of policemen could no more halt them than the winning-tape halts a race, they'd be trampled underfoot if they didn't skip jolly quick. *Tramp, tramp* . . . she was dancing in time with it. *What* a juggernaut!

No one was singing now, and she heard a voice among the marching leaders suddenly cry out to the police: 'Don't shoot – it's Ludendorff!' and then a policeman fired.

It had seemed a juggernaut; and yet when that ragged unwilling volley at last rang out it melted clean away.

Chapter 26

At the sound of that first shot Hitler dropped so violently to the ground (accelerated moreover by the stricken weight of Ulrich Graf on top of him) that the arm locked in Scheubner-Richter's was dislocated at the shoulder. This saved his life, however; for a second later young Scheubner-Richter collapsed dead in his stead, his chest wide open. Almost all the leaders, their nerves already keyed to snapping-point, had flung themselves down instantly like Hitler, performing the old soldier's instinctive obeisance to the flying bullet: this briefly exposed the dumbfounded men behind them – till they too collected their wits enough to fall flat as well: thus it was they who chiefly suffered, not the leaders.

The reluctant police were mostly pointing their carbines at the ground; but that saved no lives, for the flattened bullets bouncing off the granite setts only made the uglier wounds. After those few seconds of nervous gunfire there were many wounded. Moreover there were sixteen men stone dead or dying: the street darkening before their eyes, their souls at their lips.

The whole world was flat, the living among the dead, except for Ludendorff. For generals tend to lose the instinct to lie down as well as the agility; and the old war-lord's magic was worth just this much still, that no one did aim at *Ludendorff*. He had stumbled and nearly fallen, but then with his hands in his jacket pockets he continued his stroll without one glance back at the dying and wounded and frightened men behind him, straight through the green line of police (which opened to let him pass). He seemed deep in thought. As he passed Tascha she heard him murmuring, 'One, and nine, and two...' Then he was gone.

No one fired twice – but it was enough. As soon as the

noise ceased all who were able sprang to their feet and vanished. They were headed by the little dog in the plaid waistcoat at full speed, but Hitler – unhit, though stumbling from the pain and awkwardness of his shoulder – lay a good second in the race.

The sound of the firing had carried right to the rear of the column, and the rest of the parade too instantly dismissed. The police stood aghast. At that moment a dozen men could have rushed them; but there weren't a dozen.

Stretcher-bearers appeared.

In front of Tascha lay Ludendorff's young von Scheubner-Richter: his lungs had burst from his chest. Poor Max-Erwin! She'd met him at parties: he'd had so much charm ... and beside him lay someone else whose brains spattered the roadway for ten yards round. Weber, the Oberland leader, had staggered to his feet and stood leaning against the palace wall, in tears. Young Hermann Goering with two bullet-gashes in the groin was trying to drag himself behind one of the stone lions in front of the Residenz palace.

The street was bright with blood. As soon as the fumes of the carbines cleared you could even smell it; and at that something mad seized Tascha. She jerked into the saddle and bicycled wildly down the street, wobbling her course between the dead and dying. Tascha's one object was to get plenty of splashes of blood on her bicycle-wheels (Hitler's if possible: surely she had seen him fall?). But in point of fact even before Tascha had mounted, Hitler, legging it, had reached the Max-Josefs-Platz and been hustled into that waiting yellow car and was gone. Lothar caught a glimpse of him climbing into the car – he held his arm queerly extended, as if carrying something. So Tascha had to be content with quite anonymous blood: it was mostly Willi's, as it happened.

Ludendorff continued his way unhindered across the empty square. As soon as he had added together the digits of this fatal year 1-9-2-3 and registered that their sum was 15 his mind went suddenly blank. He continued to march straight forward like a mechanical toy – quite without object, merely without impediment, *plod, plod* . . .

He had already turned into the Brienner Strasse like that, *plod, plod*, when all at once he halted, thunderstruck – his brain suddenly springing into action again. But of course! *Fifteen was the same total 1-9-1-4 added up to!* – Fifteen! *Ten* and *Five:* applied to the alphabet these digits gave the letters 'J' and 'E' – the first two letters in JEhovah . . . yes, and in JEsus too! Thus *both* years were auspicious years for *both* Germany's joint enemies – the JEws and the JEsuits!

1914 . . . the 'JEhovah-JEsus' year when the noose of International Jewry-cum-Papistry had first closed so tight that Germany had been forced to strike back – in vain. Now, *1923* . . . No wonder we've failed!

But at that moment a policeman dared at last to address him, politely requesting His Excellency's attendance at the station. At the station however they were not quite so polite. A one-eyed wooden-faced sergeant looked up from his ledger and asked this distinguished client his name and address and made him spell it. The constable looked at his superior in surprise: why, surely Sergeant knew that face – and knew how to spell *Ludendorff*? Hadn't Sergeant lost his eye (he always told them) in the ill-fated 'Ludendorff offensive' of 1918?

Chapter 27

The little dog in the waistcoat at last found his master again – an elderly, frock-coated, elegant citizen with so neat a spade beard it deserved a prize (he slept with it in a net); and they both rejoiced. Willi meanwhile sat on the pavement outside the Post Office in the Max-Josefs-Platz, applying a tourniquet to his own copiously-bleeding leg, his head in a whirl. Tascha had the misfortune to have her bicycle stolen while she was being sick in a ladies' lavatory, and hurried home on foot to write her letter (in two-inch script) to Mitzi.

The public health department cleaned up the messy Residenzstrasse with wonderful speed and thoroughness: it was the sort of job they excelled at. The police put on ferocious airs as if one and all they habitually ate Kampfbund kids for breakfast, and made numerous difficult and dangerous arrests (such as Willi, who was too giddy to stand up). Then one by one the shops and restaurants on the route of the march re-opened (the others elsewhere had never closed) and all was as before. Lothar slipped quietly home for a quick change and was back at his desk at the Bayrischer-Hof, shaved and in a neat grey suit, without anyone quite seeing him arrive (at the Bayrischer-Hof few were even aware any disturbance had taken place).

Meanwhile the police had already raided that gymnasium. There they found Augustine's ten-shilling note in the till, and showed it to the Press. Once again that note turned out a windfall; for wasn't it proof positive the Nazis were in foreign pay?

Ludendorff was (rather unflatteringly) released on bail, and carried his dudgeon home with him to Ludwigshöhe.

Goering's brownshirt friends found Goering in a rather bad way, behind a stone lion outside the palace, groaning: they took him to a Jewish doctor, who patched him up with infinite kindness (a kindness Goering never forgot) and hid him in his own house: so Goering did get in the end to Rosenheim and thence into Austria as he had all the time intended. There he found Putzi Hanfstaengl and others who had arrived before him: not Rosenberg, though, who after all was hiding in Munich. Nor Hitler, of course: Hitler in a depressed state was driving about Bavaria at top speed without the least idea where to go. Finally he fetched up at Uffing of all places – at the Hanfstaengl country cottage, which was bound to be searched sooner or later – and was hidden in the attic where they kept their emergency barrel of flour.

Most of these things had happened before the Steuckels' party had even begun; but true news travels slowly, and the party had dispersed before the upshot of the Putsch was known. When a full and authentic account of it all did at last reach Lorienburg with the next morning's papers it caused little stir there for the only politically important fact in it was already surmised – that Kahr's planned restoration of Rupprecht had after all not come off.

Moreover a miss-fire like this might mean that it had to be put off for quite a while. That led to some desultory abuse of Ludendorff, whose clumsy, amateurish interference had upset all von Kahr's delicate timing. Ludendorff would now be totally discredited for keeps: there was at least that much to be thankful for. And that silly little Hitler too: like the frog in the fable he had tried to play a role too big for him and burst. After this we'll hear no more of Hitler – and that too's a good riddance! I expect when they catch him he'll just be pushed back over the Austrian frontier as an undesirable alien.

As a proved incompetent, *Exit the White Crow!*

Thus it was all soon forgotten. For the Kessen family had now something on their plates even more important than politics, for once: a family problem – what to do with Mitzi now she was stone-blind.

BOOK THREE

The Fox in the Attic

Chapter 1

In the darkness of the unvisited attics the bats flitted endlessly or huddled in bunches against the cold, and under the heavy pile of furs in the corner the sleeping figure stirred and moaned.

The very young face with its closed, wide-set eyes was contorted. He was having one of his 'red' dreams, when everywhere there was always blood. Tonight he was dreaming that his legs were paralysed and he was dragging himself on his elbows across a heap of bodies, and from their open bellies the living entrails writhed towards him. When they wound themselves round him they were barbed, like barbed wire; and the fetid, dully-crimson air was full of twittering though there was nothing winged here . . .

This winning, open-faced boy having his nightmare in the attics was the missing Wolff, Lothar's warrior-brother: Franz's best schoolfriend, and still his guiding star.

Wolff woke, half-swallowing a scream. His lips were dry and his mouth tasted of blood from a bleeding gum (he had pulled his own tooth himself, the day before). His body was wet and for a moment he thought that was blood too, but it was only his sweat, under too many furs. Hauling himself out of his dream by main force he deliberately recalled to the surface of his mind that day four years ago when his troop was storming the signal-box on the Riga railway and he stumbled in the hidden wire and fell into Heinrich's body that was burst and steaming and the wire had held him there, in that motherly warmth, while round him the bullets splashed in the waterlogged meadow like rain.

Wolff flashed his torch. The beam lit a chin-high stack of ancient account-books covered with bat-droppings, for this hiding-place of his was a kind of muniment-room – the only room right up here close under the castle clock and the great water-tank ever finished since the castle was first built. In the shadows two red eyes were watching him, and the air smelt strongly of fox.

The torch-beam shifted, and shone on what looked like a gigantic snail. This was a coil of climber's rope he kept there, covered in cobwebs. Even after the Baltic collapse those dedicated young men Wolff and his like-minded fellow killers had kept on killing 'for Germany' – though killing *in* Germany and killing secretly now. But ever since Rathenau's death the police-net had never relaxed: Wolff was deeply involved, and for the past eight months had never once set foot on the ground outside.

In the wavering beam the watching red eyes blinked, and Wolff snapped out the light. But he dared not drift off to sleep again, and to keep awake in the dark and to soothe his jangled nerves he made an effort to think about his 'Lady'. For Wolff had fallen deeply in romantic love, last summer, with that fair-haired girl in the garden below who was unconscious of his existence even.

But tonight she eluded him, for tonight he was wholly in the grip of images of a sort yet more compulsive still than hers: that cat, for instance, in the drawing-room of the little deserted manor in the Livonian woods . . . a fat, white cat . . . willy-nilly he began to recall it all, now, nervously smiling the while.

It had been one day they were looking for a missing re-connaissance-party of their own men that they came on this modest house, hidden among the birches and pines. There were fresh pink English hollyhocks round the door; but although it was nearly noon the green shutters were all closed as though the house were sleeping. Whoever had been there last had gone, and had clearly left it empty. But those shutters fitted so close that coming in from the sun you couldn't at first see: only stand there listening to the drawing-room clock that was still ticking, and wait for the dazzlement to wear off. This happened to be Wolff's sixteenth birthday, and at the sound of that clock the boy had felt desperately homesick.

Moreover, he could hear a purring . . .

But soon the pupils of his eyes dilated enough to see that the room was heaped with bodies – their missing friends. The bodies were mutilated in the usual Lettish way; and these men hadn't died fighting, this had been done to them alive.

The purring cat had been sleeping luxuriously on the sofa in this very room when the searchers arrived. But now she took refuge on the top of that ornate mantelpiece clock, arched and spitting, her drawn claws slipping as she scrabbled to keep her balance on the smooth marble. Underneath her the clock whirred, then started to strike with tuneful silvery chimes.

In his rage he had torn the cat to pieces with his bare hands, then slipped in the mess on the floor and twisted his ankle. Meanwhile the others had rushed outside to search the buildings; but they found nothing living out there either except one cow. Her they killed too: they'd have killed even the tomtits if they could have caught them.

Now Wolff himself, as he remembered it all, lay there purring . . .

Conscience had first sent Wolff east, to those freelance wars in the lost provinces where his birthplace was; and a conscience blindly indulged like his tends to acquire a stranglehold. 'Conscience' had now become the one call he could no longer ever resist. The fighting had long been over; but those Baltic years of the beastliest heroism had been the years while Wolff grew his last inch of height and his spirit set in its mould; and nowadays the dictates of his conscience had become quite invarious: always the simple command to kill.

Hidden here, and now no longer able to go out and

murder, Wolff was in every sense an exile from 'life': even from its warm trickles in the house he hid in. No human sound reached here: only from close overhead all night the huge clock's slow, loud, heavy ticking.

Chapter 2

In the roof the castle clock thumped the hour and on the last stroke Mitzi woke.

It was pitchy black, and a smell of outdoor furs. There was not even a glimmer from where the window lay opposite her bed; yet Mitzi was broad awake, and agitated moreover by a sense of urgency. She reached for the box of matches by her candle and struck one . . . and nothing happened. She heard the usual sputter, but it made no light.

It was only then that she remembered. But . . . but however could a person have forgotten she had gone blind?

No no no! Surely this sudden blindness was only a bad dream Mitzi had just woken from – in the dark!

But that smell of furs . . . suddenly yesterday's sleigh-ride came back to her. Moreover this wasn't really at all the normal blackness of night: rather it was the negation of seeing, the absence of any visual sensation whatever. It was merely Memory which had translated it into the visual terms of darkness, as being the nearest equivalent Memory knew. She tried by an effort of will to see it as 'darkness' again, but almost at once a chaos of meaningless sight-sensation began to wake in the deprived optic nerve – like the sensation Uncle Otto said he felt sometimes in the leg which wasn't there.

In fact, there was not any proof even that this still was night-time! It might just as well be broad day – and hence the feeling of urgency Mitzi had woken with.

Certain, now, she had overslept and was going to be late for breakfast Mitzi sprang out of her bed to find her clothes. Normally she folded them on the chair by the window, where in the morning the dazzling entering daylight would direct her to them again; but in the misery of last night,

233

had she remembered to do this? Anyway, where was that window? She had taken a few steps from her bed without thinking, and could no longer be sure which way she was facing.

Moreover those phantasms of colour and shape chasing each other across her mind's-eye had now become violently vivid – like solid objects flung at her, so that involuntarily she winced to dodge them. Panicking, she began blundering about with her hands stretched out to find some bit of furniture whose touch she could recognize; and in that big room of hers she was soon completely lost. It was difficult to keep one's balance on this ancient undulating floor without eyes (even purblind ones) to help one: her toe tripped on a tilted board and she reached out to stop herself falling . . . her hand touched something, and grabbed it – but only to feel an agonizing pang of pain, for it was the nearly red-hot iron flue of the stove she had seized for support.

The pain brought Mitzi back to her senses. She knew now just where she was, for she could feel the warmth coming from the stove several feet away – as she ought to have felt it before if she had kept her head instead of blundering right against it. As she stood there with her burnt fingers in her mouth it occurred to her she must henceforth learn to use such areas of local heat and cold for finding her way about: she must learn to steer by the radiant heat of the many stoves, the cold air near windows and the draughts through open doors – no longer by the direction of the light (by day from windows and by night from lamps) which formerly had fitfully pierced her private fog like lighthouse beams.

Then Mitzi remembered too the yapping of the fox the night before, and the changes in resonance when first he was in the big open hall, then on the enclosed stairs, and then in the attics above. So perhaps she could use resonance too to help tell where she was – out in the middle of a room, for example, or close to a wall?

Mitzi began moving about again, feeling for her clothes.

This time she quickly found the window-chair – but they weren't on it. So as she zig-zagged to and fro across the room she began uttering little staccato fox-like cries and tried consciously to interpret their reverberation for she was desperate – she *must* find her clothes! By now, the level morning sunlight would be shining straight in – though she couldn't see it. She knew she was late, and Papa hated one being late.

A heartfelt urgency crept into her feral yapping.

Franz woke, that yapping tingling in his tuned ears.

For a moment he thought it really was their little fox as before; but he soon realized this was no natural fox. Indeed it was a most queer, uncanny sound: moreover it was coming from the room next to his: from Mitzi's room. Something was in there with Mitzi.

A were-fox? – He shivered, and his skin prickled with goose-flesh. But an instant later he recognized the voice for Mitzi herself and fright turned to anger. The little fool! What was she up to, rousing the whole house – had she gone out of her mind? He felt so cross with her his hand trembled as he lit his candle, and he barged in on her filled with an elder brother's righteous wrath. Four in the morning! Was she out of her senses? What a time for a girl to stand in her nightgown in the pitchdark in the middle of her bedroom, *yapping!*

Mitzi could hardly believe him when he told her the real time, and she burst into tears as he drove her back into bed.

But then suddenly Mitzi heard a ringing slap – and Franz's scolding voice ceased abruptly. It was replaced in her ears by another voice: a cracked old voice that was chanting a familiar little childhood jingle:

> *'Der Mops kam in die Küche*
> *Und stahl dem Koch ein Ei:*
> *Da nahm der Koch den Löffel*
> *Und schlug den Mops entzwei . . .'*

'*Dear* old Schmidtchen . . .' How often, long ago, that ditty had served to lull a feverish or a fractious little Mitzi off to sleep!

Mitzi gave a deep sigh. But still the saga continued:

> '*Da kamen alle Möpse*
> *Und gruben ihm ein Grab . . .*'

Candle in hand, the old nurse – her dwarfish figure swathed in three dressing-gowns, the few grey locks on her nearly bald head standing out like sea-urchin's spines – bent over her afflicted young baroness and gave her a troubled, searching look while she continued to intone:

> '*Und setzen ihm ein Denkmal*
> *Darauf geschrieben stand:*
> "*Der Mops kam in die Küche*
> *Und stahl . . .*" '

– and so on, round and round: for the song is endless.

But already Schmidtchen's little Baroness was sound asleep; and as for the young Baron, he had long ago slunk back to his room – his tail between his legs and his boxed ear still stinging.

Chapter 3

When that sluggard Saturday's dawn came at last it found fifteen-year-old Lies already kneeling on the cold castle stairs; for the snow of Friday's boots still lay there unmelted, each morning it had to be swept up with dustpan and brush.

Augustine was not awake yet: by the time he woke, Lies was already in his room. On his wash-stand steamed the jug of hot water for his shaving wrapped in a towel and the girl was down on her knees in front of his stove, coaxing it with fir-cones and the breath of her powerful young lungs. Lies wore her skirts kilted for work, and rolled her stockings; and on the backs of her broad bare white knees the rolls of puppy-fat still lingered. Augustine's sleepy eyes opened on them as she knelt there – surprised to find legs could look quite so soft (and indeed almost babyish) on any young woman quite so stalwart as Lies.

Contemplating them, suddenly the thought struck him: 'Suppose you couldn't see?' – and once again a pang of pity for Mitzi racked him like an angina.

True, one could learn to thread the obstacle-race of this three-dimensional world without eyesight: that Augustine discounted. But to the *joy* of seeing Augustine was perhaps exceptionally addicted, as if his whole consciousness were concentrated close behind his eyes and almost craning out of them, like someone who can't tear himself from the window. Among the five senses sight was incomparable. Indeed, sometimes he thought he would as lief be deaf as not in this world where everyone always talked so much too much: he was not humanly musical, and the only sound he would really miss aesthetically (he thought) was bird-song.

Smells too were mostly *un*pleasant – since petrol, and since even respectable women had now taken to powder and scent. Taste . . . Touch . . . even Movement! He would rather break his back and live out his life in a wheeled chair than be blind, for there was an almost infinite and incessant pleasure to be got from just 'looking': even (but now he averted his eyes) at a young peasant-girl's fat knees.

How much Augustine preferred watching people to hearing them talk! When he was a boy of eleven a kindly astronomer had helped him build a telescope. It was meant for nebulae and the rings round Saturn and moon-mountains and so on; but soon he was spending hours with it by daylight too, turning it onto people. Being of the astronomical type it stood them on their heads, but one got used to that. And it was powerful: framed in a circle like specimens in a microscope slide, *his* soundless specimens could be observed unawares as closely as if they were with him in the room. How different people's faces do look when they think no one sees them and so they stop gesticulating at you with their features! It gave the boy quite a Godlike feeling, thus to 'know their downsitting and their uprising, to understand their thought afar off.' For he was seeing natural human nature, which the human eye so rarely sees (even if he did see everything upside down).

For a time this human bird-watching had been almost an obsession; but at last it was brought to its own abrupt and wholly shaming end. For the view from Augustine's bedroom window at home had included another garden, and there had been three little girls who used to play there. They weren't quite gentry children, so he never came into normal naked-eye contact with them – he never even knew their names. Indeed he was then at an age to shun little girls like the plague in real life; but this was different, and soon these three were much his favourite object of nature-study. He came to know intimately almost every hair of those three heads; for the telescope brought them seemingly within touching-distance. I suppose he fell half in love with them,

238

impartially with all three: a little private, abstract seraglio – so very close to him always, and yet ethereal visionary creatures without even voices. And so the idyll had continued, till that day when the one he happened to be watching wandered off from the others and, as he followed her with his eye curiously, suddenly bobbed down between two bushes.

When it was over the young peeper was appalled: he had seen what no boy's eye ever ought to have seen, he had broken the strongest taboo he knew. It was weeks before he used his telescope again and then it was only at night, to study the moon: the uninhabited, infertile, utterly geological safe moon.

That moon is covered with mysterious ring-mountains; some with a solitary peak rising at the very centre, like a little tongue – surely utterly unlike anything to be seen anywhere on this earth? Soon he became so enthralled he planned to map the whole moon's surface, and tried to draw pictures of those rings.

As for picturing more mundane things, it was galling for someone so eye-conscious to have no aptitude for painting, however hard he tried. But Augustine's natural skill at shooting was some consolation, for here it was the exact visually-imagined pattern in space and time of the bird's flight intersecting with the brief trajectory of his pellets that was the attraction: that, and the utter loveliness of the plumage of the fallen bird.

Only one thing equalled this last – the utter loveliness of Mitzi's hair; and at the thought of that, this morning, in his warm body under the warm bedclothes his heart glowed warmer still.

Yet Augustine this morning – though he would not admit it – was really in two minds about Mitzi. His heart might be warmed by the generous fires of love but the pit of his stomach had its sinking moments, its moments of chill. He loved Mitzi and Mitzi only and would love Mitzi for ever –

and even more so for her blindness! Yet, to be coupled till death did them part with a blind girl was a bit like ... entering a three-legged race with a partner who has only one leg.

As a budding lover Augustine had developed some at least of the instincts of a grown man but he was still an egoist also, with still the instincts of any normally self-centred child: too much of an egoist, perhaps, to tolerate yet the full 'we-ness' of true marriage. So he clutched unconsciously perhaps at Mitzi's blindness as something by which his separateness seemed permanently guaranteed. But the human personality like the plant has its 'growing-point' with a foresight and wisdom all its own: a foresight insistent (in this case) that so infantile an egoism could not last for ever, that to seek to perpetuate it by a lame marriage must prove a disastrous thing. Hence, then, perhaps, these queer flutters of panic. He never for a moment consciously contemplated *not* marrying Mitzi yet something within him prompted a curious lack of impatience about going to her and actually Saying the Word – although he longed to say it.

With luck there would be an empty place next to Mitzi at breakfast. Thereafter (Augustine told himself) he would refuse to be parted from Mitzi all day: he would devote himself openly and unequivocally to her, claim the privilege of guiding her from room to room, of fetching and carrying for her ...

But when Augustine got to the breakfast-table he found no Mitzi. Cousin Adèle was preparing a tray: Mitzi would be breakfasting in her own room, and so after all the moment of final commitment was postponed! Augustine was desolated; and full of jokes.

Chapter 4

Permission to breakfast in one's own bedroom was rare in the annals of Lorienburg: one always had to appear even if one ate nothing. So Mitzi was indeed grateful not to have to appear today, when such waves of black despair were rolling over her it would be impossible to keep her feelings from appearing in her face.

For blindness was not an affliction which would pass – like a pain, or like an illness which either gets better or kills you. She was blind now she was young: she would be blind middle-aged: she would still be blind when she was old – she would die blind. She was going to be blind all her earthly life: only beyond the grave would she again have eyes to see.

The length of life – oh, its interminable length! Almost she formulated the wish to be struck dead that minute; but something smote her inward lips as with an actual blow of the hand, preventing them from quite uttering any wish so wicked.

Why had God done this to her? What had she done to deserve it? When she felt it coming on, had she not prayed with every breath of the lungs of her soul? Why hadn't God answered her prayer, then? If He'd let her off this she'd have adored Him all her days and laid her whole life as a thank-offering on His altar, gone out to nurse lepers ...

Why had God done this to her? Because she had sinned? But everyone sins. Granted she was more sinful than average, one of the most repellent of all His creatures; but on the other hand no sin can't be forgiven and she'd gone to confession regularly, received absolution. Had the priest's absolution then been somehow always unavailing? It must have been! For a just God would have had to count up against her *un*forgiven every sin mortal and venial she had sinned since babyhood to judge her worthy of *this*.

'*Most merciful Father . . .*' But the gates of His mercy were shut against Mitzi, it seemed. 'Holy Mary, never was anyone who sought thy intercession left unaided . . .' But Our Blessed Lady had withheld her intercession from Mitzi.

From Mitzi – the pariah of Heaven.

The meaningless chaos of sensation in the optic nerve still revolved without intermission.

Would she had never been born! Would that the day she was to be born could have been left out of the calendar, the darkness of the night preceeding it joined mercifully without any intervening day to the darkness of the night that followed, rather than that Mitzi had ever come into being as the living human soul in whom *this* unending frenzied darkness should come into being! Why had life been given her, to be so miserable in, so bitter?

What had God put her into the world for at all, if having put her there He *couldn't* forgive her?

But forgiveness, she knew, is only for the truly penitent: without the sinner's contrition absolution is a mere form of words snatched from the priest's lips by the Powers of the Air, blown back like smoke.

Had Mitzi never truly repented, then, in her heart, of the sins her lips had confessed? Since He had not forgiven her, Reason answered 'that must be so'. – Then again and again she had taken the Holy Sacrament impenitent, thus eating her own damnation!

At this sudden thought of damnation Mitzi sweated with the absolute of terror; for in that case this blindness was a mere earthly foretaste of the horror to come. In that case even the grave could be no 'bed of hope' for a Mitzi; for its bottom would open under the weight of her sins to discharge her incontinently into the bottomless everlasting fires of Hell...

Oh how *short* is that brief postponement of punishment we call earthly life, and how awful the everlasting wrath of God!

Mitzi's mind was young and single, her faith unquestioning and her imaginative powers vivid. Her agony of mind was now passing beyond what tender human nerves can bear: like the point at which some poor soul trapped in the top of a blazing building at last makes the necessary leap from the sixth-floor window into the smoke.

Chapter 5

When breakfast in the dining-room was over Augustine found himself at a loose end, for Walther shepherded Adèle and Otto and Franz into the drawing-room and shut the door. Evidently some sort of family council was going into session (under the fatherly eye of Good King Ludwig III). Nervous, and with time to kill till Mitzi appeared, Augustine's first thought was to spend it making friends with the younger children at last. But that might not be easy: to begin with there was the difficulty of his 'good' German, and moreover morning and evening they were all made to file round the table ceremoniously to kiss his hand which put one on altogether the wrong footing. Better wait till later, perhaps (he had never before funked children, but he'd never before struck quite such a formidable quartette). Moreover he had just remembered that this was Saturday: Augustine had spent three whole nights in Germany without sending Mary so much as a picture-postcard yet.

Augustine had already had one letter from Mary, here. 'Polly has a cough . . .' (Mary had said nothing about Nellie and the dead child's father coming to the lonely neo-Gothic 'Hermitage' to live: she thought that wound better given a little time to heal.)

But when Augustine went to his room and began writing he found it difficult to keep bent on his travelogue a mind that kept turning to Mitzi. However, he didn't want to tell Mary about Mitzi quite yet: not till he had spoken to the waiting Mitzi and even her father and it was all settled. It never occurred to him Mary could think thirty-six hours from first meeting rather *soon* to have made up their minds: he was sincerely afraid if he couldn't tell her something definite she would think them hopeless ditherers to have havered so long.

Thus Augustine's letter-writing limped, and presently he laid down his pen and mooned round the room examining the pictures all over again. There was a distant group of figures in one of them, on the banks of a river, which had intrigued him before; for they were so minute he couldn't make out what they were at. Were they bathing – or ducking a witch?

If only he'd been standing on yon tufted abbey tower with that telescope he'd had as a boy turned on them! Vividly Augustine recalled the pleasure he used to get from studying just such distant groups, himself unseen. But then a new thought struck him: now – and without any telescope at all – he could study a blind Mitzi just like that! He could gaze right in her face at six inches range without giving her offence, just as long ago he used to study those . . . those distant little girls in the garden! At the queer thought of it his heart jumped like a fish in his breast.

The recollection of his telescope made him turn automatically to the window, and look down from it into the great courtyard underneath. And there, to his astonishment, went Mitzi herself – quite alone, and blundering through the snow.

Mitzi (he saw) was purposefully feeling her way along the façade of the house: she had followed it right into the corner of the court where the snow had drifted: she was floundering almost waist-deep in snow. But then she turned at right-angles along the side-wall (evidently she hadn't dared risk a bee-line in the open): found the door she wanted: unlocked it, and vanished inside.

Chapter 6

For at the moment when Mitzi had felt herself to be at the implacable very bottom of despair, beating her head against the bars of her imperfectly-remembered religious instruction like a bird in a trap, a voice as real as the hand which had smitten her inward lips had said: 'Think, Mitzi – THINK!' and suddenly the answer had come to her. There was indeed one damnable sin she had never repented nor even confessed for she had never noticed till now she was sinning it: all her life she had allowed herself to feel afflicted because she could not see as other children saw: she had never once *thanked* God for what little sight she had.

Now she had lost it she realized what a treasure even that purblind sight had been. Finding her way about used to seem difficult – yet how easy it had then been in comparison with now! Moreover, how singular had been the beauty of that peculiar world once hers! Those soft-edged, looming shapes things had: the irised patterns of colour changing from moment to moment as when a kaleidoscope is shaken, the flickering fringes of bright violet round where windows were and the gorgeous coronas that meant lighted lamps: the veined and marbled skies, the moving dappled pillars that were her friends and the standing ones that were the trees . . .

She, who had always hovered halfway to blindness – surely this should have been a perpetual reminder to her that sight is not intrinsic to humanity: that sight is a gift – which God gives, or God withholds. Yet all this she had enjoyed and never once thanked God for it.

It was at this instant of perfect contrition for her ingratitude to God, the realization of the worthlessness of all her petty repentances of sins that were so minuscule in comparison with this one, that her intolerable nervous tension snapped and Mitzi at last made her necessary 'leap' into the stretched blanket.

Thereafter all fear of Hell – all *thought* of punishment even – was suddenly gone as completely as a finished thunder-storm is gone. What remained was a feeling of floating: of floating on God's love. It soaked her through like sunshine. She felt God incomparably nearer than ever before: God held her whole being nestling in the hollow of His infinite hand . . . or no, God wasn't even that much outside her – He was running in her veins. *He* was the tongue speaking in her mind's ear and He was the mental ear which listened, He was the very mind in her which did her thinking. There was now no obstacle at all between herself and God: her will and His were one. Once, Mitzi had made her sight into a barrier between herself and God: so God had touched her eyes with His healing finger and now that barrier was gone . . . and how she loved and adored Him for it!

Mitzi believed herself already quite lost in God. But was she, wholly? Surely there was still one tiny part of this neophyte which even now watched the transaction as it were from outside; and, curiously, that outsider was the 'I' at the transaction's very heart. That 'I' in her which couldn't help feeling just a little bit cocky that *she* had been chosen for an act of such exceptional grace; for after all, it isn't everybody God thinks worth striking blind to bring her to Him.

But it is difficult to express this cavil at all without exaggerating it. For the moment at least the voice of this outside watcher inside Mitzi was in comparison as faint as the piping of a gnat dancing in the spray of a roaring waterfall: the Mitzi-of-the-Adoration was scarcely aware of it, and let it pass; and presently her desire for prayer and praise – to thank God for her new blindness as the source of this ecstasy she now enjoyed, of this foretaste within Time of the

Eternal Life – had become so insistent her ordinary weekday room could no longer contain it, and she felt her way to the door.

No one saw Mitzi cross the hall; for that family council (which had met to decide what was to be done with Mitzi) was still in session: a conference at which the chairman – the late King Ludwig – watched, but said never a word. Thus no one saw, no one heard Mitzi creeping down the stairs. Even Mitzi herself never noticed when she tripped and nearly went headlong, so intent was her whole thought on reaching her goal.

It was not till she was right out in the courtyard, fumbling her way through the snow to find the door which led through the vestry into the castle chapel, that Augustine alone at last caught sight of Mitzi from his window – and darted down after her with thumping heart.

Chapter 7

Augustine was an adept wildfowler and his shoes had thick crêpe-rubber soles. The door Mitzi had entered still stood open and he slipped inside, careful to make no sound.

He found himself in a room lined from floor to ceiling with noble old cupboards and presses in painted pine – like the changing-room of an eighteenth-century football club, he thought (if the eighteenth Century had had football clubs), but this changing-room had a faint ecclesiastical smell and he observed a holy oleograph of exceptional crudity (a rather disgusting surgical item, a bleeding heart) on the only bare patch of wall. However there was no Mitzi here; so he continued equally stealthily through a further open door and found himself in what he at once knew must be the chapel: and there he stood aghast.

For the little family chapel at Lorienburg was a baroque confection of exceptional splendour. Augustine had been reared in an Anglo-Gothic reverential gloom; but this was all light and colour and swelling curves. There was extravagantly moulded plaster and painted trompe-l'œil, peeping angels, babies submerged in silver soap-suds and gilded glittering rays . . . Augustine had *heard* of Baroque – as the very last word in decadence and bad taste; but anything so outrageous as this was incredible in a secular . . . and this was a *sacred* place! Even the professing atheist could not but be shocked.

Yet Augustine soon realized he ought rather to be reassured. Hitherto he had shirked wondering whether Mitzi was really a believing Christian; but even if she thought she was, a religion which expressed itself in a place like this couldn't possibly be more than skin-deep – something easily sloughed, under his teaching. Yet could any teaching of his be needed? Surely the utter callousness of what had just happened to Mitzi must already have taught her more forcibly than any words could that the Universe has *no* heart. Mitzi *must* know now there was no one else in heaven or earth to love her – only him.

But in that case why had she come here? And where was Mitzi? For he hadn't found her, still.

Seeking her, Augustine peeped gingerly into the dark confessional; then he tiptoed to the sanctuary rails. But his eyes soon began to wander, for though the general effect of this awful place was so utterly wrong all the same there were details which plucked at his eyes so that he could not help but look. Even the billowing chaos of colour and glitter above the altar once he examined it began to assume shape and meaning: patently it was intended for an enormous storm-cloud with the rays of God on top – and then suddenly Augustine noticed that from every cranny and interstice of that vasty tornado towering under the God-light from above there were miniature heads of child-angels peeping! In their rather sweet way these were quite lovely – and palpably all portraits: every child in the village that long-ago year must have been singly portrayed here: this was a whole child-generation of Dorf Lorienburg. One Sunday centuries ago all these fresh young faces up there must have been mirrored by the First-Communion young faces bowed over the altar-rail below, each carved face with its own living counterpart. But whereas in time those faces at the rail had grown old and disillusioned and coarse – and had all died, generations ago – these through the centuries had remained forever singing: immortal, and forever child.

All portraits, and all singing: as the eye travelled up the cloud from parted lips to parted lips it seemed inconceivable one couldn't *hear* that singing: the eye filled the laggard ear with visionary sweet sound . . .

'Gloria in excelsis Deo . . .'

250

– in thin, angelic treble unison the ancient and holy chant was floating on the air; and with a sudden shiver up the spine Augustine realized he *could* hear the singing.

Augustine's scalp pricked; but a moment later he realized this must be only Mitzi – just Mitzi somewhere, and the echoes that she woke. Momentarily he felt furious with her, as Franz too had been furious when her yapping duped him in the night. What did the little fool think she was up to, *singing* – here, alone in this empty frightful chocolate God-box?

Where had she got to? He turned where he stood, and glared all down the nave.

Augustine found Mitzi in the end crouched before something in the far corner: something of which he had been half-conscious all the time, for though it was part-hidden by a gorgeous catafalque it still showed up incongruously in all this welter of colour, being carved in dark unpainted wood: an object palpably much older than anything else here, as well as nobly different in style. It was a great thirteenth-century Deposition, more than lifesize; and half-hidden at its foot knelt Mitzi.

The thin but almost faultless voice had finished the ecstatic Latin chant, and fallen silent. Mitzi was silently praying. She was still, and hardly seemed to breathe; and the big black bow was coming off her fair plait of hair.

He longed to retie it for her . . . oh how he loved her – and what poles apart they were!

Mitzi was praying for a miracle, no doubt – to that bit of wood! Or, was she merely the hurt child who clings leech-like but hopeless to her teddy bear? Was it, then . . . was it possibly *better* at least for the time being to leave her with her religious illusions, if these were a comfort to her?

Perish the thought! It can never be better to believe a lie; and surely 'God' was the biggest lie ever uttered by the human race!

How thankful Augustine now was he had yielded to his returning instinct for watching unseen – with the sense it conferred of almost supernatural guardianship over the loved one, on this mysterious solitary sortie of hers!

But Mitzi's hair . . . Augustine's fingers of themselves were craving for the touch of it just as the parched tongue itself craves for water; and at once he could think of nothing else. Dropping on hands and knees he inched forward across the floor-matting without sound – himself now scarcely daring to breathe. Delicately he lifted his hand and at last as lightly as touching a butterfly's wing just touched the tip of her hair.

But instantly he withdrew his fingers for even that contact had so quickened his breathing that now she surely could not help but hear!

Chapter 8

Indeed Augustine's heart was beating so wildly that only her rapt religious state could possibly have kept him undiscovered long. For although he realized it would be fatal to be discovered now he had presently begun acting as uninhibitedly as if he wore a cap of darkness indeed – fluttering noiselessly about Mitzi, as she moved from one devotional spot to another, in a kind of one-man unwitnessed ballet. And when at last Mitzi left the chapel, as she locked the vestry door Augustine glided to her side 'as if' to take her arm and guide her – so close their two bodies were almost touching. They moved off like that, too – he hovering over her mothlike. His right arm even started its own passionate makebelieve, raised 'as if' round her.

Augustine was trying to *will* Mitzi into the right path through the snow; and they must have looked unequivocally a pair of lovers as the two of them plunged together into snowdrifts and out again as if neither of them had eyes at all for the outside world; for what else could prompt so wildly erratic a course but the mutual blindness of love? But so intoxicated was Augustine now with his role of Zvengali-cum-Invisible-Man, he had quite forgotten that the only eyes to which he was really invisible were Mitzi's. Thus it was now Augustine's turn to be watched unwitting – from the dormer so mysteriously unboarded – by the truly Invisible Man (that existence in the attics nobody knew about except Franz).

Nor was that watching eye benevolent – or harmless.

Augustine had meant to speak to Mitzi as soon as they reached the hall – as if meeting her there. But when they got there the two little girls were framed in the dining-room

253

doorway; so he hesitated, and Mitzi made a bee-line for her room.

He'd lost her! But no doubt she'd be out again soon, so he'd wait; and in the meanwhile Augustine was in such a gay, exalted and rather fantastical mood, so bubbling over with makebelieve, that children to work it off on seemed a godsend – if only he could get these ones to accept him at last!

Augustine advanced on the children all smiles, and mooing like a cow (so tiresome, this language difficulty!): then, changing his note, stood still and bleated like a lamb. The effect was not quite any one might have expected. There was the first shock of bewilderment of course (and embarrassment, for at eight and nearly ten the two little girls were surely too old for quite such nursery tactics); but what was odd was that then they ran towards him apparently in an access of extreme friendliness. They began chattering away to him nineteen-to-the-dozen; and so far as he could make out, they were saying there was something lovely they wanted to show him – to show *him* especially, their dear Uncle: something quite wonderful . . . downstairs.

Taken aback, Augustine studied their faces: for this just wasn't true! They were laying on all the charm of two elderly experts; but behind all the smiles and cajoling there was fright in those four eyes like little grey stones.

Through the dining-room door, too, came the unmistakable clink of metal on metal. Augustine had to use sheer muscular strength to shake off their pulling and plucking, but then he peeped through. The air in the dining-room was thick with feathers. There was white down everywhere, swirling in the currents of hot air the stove set up. Feathers covered the floor; and in the midst of it all, of course, were the Twins. Heavily armoured (indeed they could hardly move) in real shirts of chain-mail reaching their ankles and even trailing along the floor, and with real swords, they were acting out some legend of their race. It was evidently a fight in a snowstorm; for they had slashed open a big down cushion and had hung it from the great central chandelier –

and here an occasional whack from a sword sent still more down and feathers eddying on the air. Already their well-greased armour was sicklied o'er with feathers.

But at that very moment Augustine heard the distant drawing-room door open and voices down the hall. The Council was at last adjourning: from the far end of the hall Walther was advancing, and behind him Adèle, Franz and Otto.

With an urgent whispered 'Achtung!' Augustine turned to face them. What was to be done? The two failed sentinels still stood at their post but their crestfallen faces had gone as expressionless as Christmas annuals: they were beyond even trying any more. So it was Augustine himself who babbling of forestry or something somehow contrived to head Walther and the rest of them off, and lead them harmlessly elsewhere.

Thereafter Augustine returned to his own waiting-post in the hall: he lingered there till it was time to eat, but even then Mitzi still didn't reappear.

Luncheon was always rather a movable feast at Lorienburg, but that Saturday it was quite exceptionally late. In the meantime some skilled sympathizer (Augustine suspected Lies) had been in the dining-room and made a wonderful attempt at clearing up the mess there; but when the meal was at last served there were still feathers here and there, as Walther – evidently wholly bewildered how they had got there – rather pettishly kept pointing out.

The children ate their food without seeming to hear him, but Adèle was profuse in her apologies to her guest: 'It's that little fox,' she explained – 'he must have got in here and disembowelled a cushion and played at chicken-coops with it . . .

'But alas!' said Adèle. 'As Walther says, you can't punish *foxes* – they don't understand!'

With her serious watery-blue eyes she fixed Augustine's – and winked.

Chapter 9

So Lorienburg went about its normal business that Satur-day. Mitzi kept to her room while Augustine roamed rest-lessly looking for her the whole afternoon: no one men-tioned yesterday's revolution and Hitler seemed already quite forgotten.

But in the meanwhile the discomforted Hitler – a proved failure now, a fugitive hurt and hopeless and with the Green Police on his trail – had finally gone to earth in Uffing. Uffing is a village on the edge of the Staffelsee, that lake of many islands at the foot of the towering Bavarian Alps where the broad Ammer valley leads up towards Garmisch. Hitler went there not because he saw there any hope of safety but because the hopeless hunted animal tends always to bury its head in some *familiar* hole to await the coup de grace. Some years past Putzi's American mother had acquired a farm near Uffing, and last summer Putzi and Helene themselves had bought a little house there too: Putzi and Helene, that young couple who alone perhaps in all Germany seemed to Hitler to be fond of him for his own sweet self.

'Putzi' – or Dr Ernst Hanfstaengl, to give him his proper title – as a half-American had taken no part in the war. Before it broke out he had been a student at Harvard and later he had married a German-American girl in New York. Here in peacetime Germany, naturally this gifted and musi-cal German-American couple moved in circles more intelli-gent and civilized than any their park-bench protégé had previously known: yet they didn't seem to see Hitler at all like the nasty caricature Dr Reinhold and his cronies elected to see. True, when they tried to introduce into those circles of the wealthier Munich intelligentzia this tiresome but vital,

this incredibly naïf yet incredibly gifted and indeed sometimes entrancing performing pet of theirs, then things tended
to happen which embarrassed and galled Hitler, so that
Hitler was never really at ease there and retaliated with an
assumed contempt. But on musical weekends here at Uffing
with Putzi and Helene themselves (alone or with only the
clammy gloomy young Rosenberg for a foil) he could always
entirely uncurl. He could be then all soul and wit: and how
they responded! Baby Egon in particular adored his 'Funny
Uncle Dolf': for Hitler could always be marvellous with
children (which seems to be a common corollary of an
addiction to chastity, even so secret and compulsive and
perverse a chastity as his).

The mother's pretty farm was ten minutes out in the
country, beyond the sawmill and the river. But the young
couple's was a neat and homely little house close to the
maypole and the church: it was plumb in the middle of
the village, though backing onto fields: squarish, and unlike its neighbours built of stone. Moreover with some vague
premonition of trouble Putzi had surrounded his pocket-
size property with a five-foot stone wall as if to turn it into
a dwarves' castle; and Hitler had only the happiest memories
of this friendly little fort.

Helene had been alone at this 'villa' except for her two-
year-old child and the maids when Hitler had himself
secretly dumped there, arriving on foot, through the fields,
after dark, late that Black Friday evening, muddy and hat-
less and his shoulder queerly drooping and with a man each
side of him holding him on his feet. 'Al*so*, doch!' she greeted
him; for Helene herself had been in Munich that very morning yet had heard nothing there of that disastrous march,
and only after her return had heard (and till now, dis-
believed) the village rumours.

Helene learned little factual now, except what was to
be gleaned from incoherent ramblings about the Residenzstrasse and the bullets and the blood. ' – But Putzi ...?'

she asked him. Putzi was all right, Hitler assured her with unconvincing conviction. Ludendorff was dead, though: the credulous old fool who had trusted the 'honourable' von Lossow! You should never trust generals: with his own eyes (he said) he had seen Ludendorff killed . . .

But Herr Hitler must be mad (thought Helene) to have come here! This house was bound to be searched (yes, and the nearby farm as well) even if only for Putzi! Once the police came meaning business Putzi's pitiful stone wall would hardly keep them out – it was only an added advertisement of mystery. Perhaps the Bechsteins would help? Ah, but it would be crazy to use the phone . . . All the same, Herr Hitler had to be got away again somehow and smuggled into Austria (yes, why on earth hadn't he already crossed into Austria long ago?).

Now, though, the man looked half fainting: for the moment the one thing he needed above all else was a bed. So she told his two friends to take him away upstairs.

Hitler went up with them docilely, in a miserable daze, and they took him to the big attic he knew so well of old – all full of Putzi's books. But not to bed! For once they had got him alone up there they stretched him out on the floor and knelt on him. One was a doctor, and they wrestled again and again with that dislocated shoulder to get it back into joint. They had no anaesthetics and for a long time even downstairs and with the doors shut Helene could hear him: while the frightened baby woke and wailed.

But it was all too inflamed by now to discover that as well as the dislocation the collarbone was broken; and so, for all the doctor's skill, they failed – and finally they gave it up and left him.

Hitler was left, all among Putzi's books: but he was much too distraught to read. He was panting, and for a moment he leaned against an incongruous open flour-barrel which these queer Hanfstaengls kept too in this attic-bed-room study; but then he saw the bed, and the bed had Putzi's English travelling-rug folded on it. So Hitler rolled himself in the rug as tight as a cocoon to ease the pain, and lay there in the corner with his face to the wall.

Hitler had been already half-delirious with pain and frustration when he arrived: now he was growing more feverish still. The torn and twisted sinews were shrinking, the broken bone grated, and pain was piled on pain. If only Putzi had been there to play Wagner to him, as David's harp soothed Saul! It was faithless of Putzi to absent himself now just when he was needed; and mentally Hitler chalked a bad mark against him.

Hitler was alone, in the dark, and could not hope to sleep. His mind was wandering. From below came the interminable rise and fall of voices like the sound of rain (for the doctor in his excitement was sitting up to tell Helene his whole life-story). It sounded like rain ... or like a river ... like the Danube flooding its banks in the spring rising, gurgling into cellars, murmuring, menacing, still rising. The sounds from downstairs woke in Hitler his obsessional fear of water, but he could not escape for the barrage of perpetual pain whined low overhead like the English shells and pinned him down.

So, after an immeasurable time without sleep, daylight had at last come again: the same Saturday daylight that at Lorienburg had found Lies kneeling on the cold stairs. For Hitler it began a Saturday of conferences and alarms and futile planning. Even at this stage of history Hitler had already developed his famous technique of that kind of 'leadership' which divines uncannily what most of the conference wants and propounds that as the Leader's own inexorable will: thus today he presently heard himself propounding that the Bechsteins must instantly send their closed car to drive him into Austria (he could never go to Austria, of course, or he'd have fled there in the first place like those others. But time enough to cope with that when the car did come: meanwhile, conferences and air-castle planning at least helped to hold captive his ballooning fevered mind).

Noon: at Lorienburg the knightly duel among the

feathers, and at Uffing the unquiet doctor starting for Munich to fetch a confrère. Hitler himself had already dispatched the other man to contact the Bechsteins: so this left Hitler alone with Helene (and the maids of course, and the child). Hitler wanted to keep her always with him, talking: but she dared not leave for long the equally excited child: twice she had just caught little Egon outside trying to climb the wall, for he wanted to shout to the whole world the good news that Uncle Dolf had arrived.

Dusk again. Why had the Bechstein car not come yet? Hitler had forgotten by now it could do no good if it did come: he had sent for it and so it MUST come.

Dusk again, and the baby at last safe in bed. Presently a car did come but still this wasn't from the Bechsteins: it was only the two medicos from Munich (so once more two angels wrestled with their wretched Jacob, and once more in vain). Finally the doctor swathed Hitler as he was in bandages like swaddling-bands, and the car took them both off again (for good, this time).

Thus began Hitler's second night at Uffing. He was again alone. Outside in the darkness and out of due time a village cock crowed. Then came the knocking . . . or was it only a dream that there was a strange man trying to get in, saying he had a message from Ludendorff 'for your visitor here'? But Ludendorff was dead . . . a messenger from the shades, then – or a Judas? Helene 'had no visitor', and sent the man away.

Midnight, and still no Bechstein car had come; but so far, neither had the police.

Suddenly Hitler started out of a half-doze, for a calm Sibylline 'voice' was ringing in his ears. It had only spoken six words and those as if the whole thing was ancient history, over and done with. But what it had said was, 'In the end he shot himself.'

It was only a dream, of course.

Chapter 10

With Sunday's daylight the man who had knocked was back again. Hitler found he knew him by sight so this time he was let in; but he had suspiciously little to say (except that Ludendorff was certainly alive), and soon went off again no one knew whither. Why worry, though, where the man went or what he told? For after questioning him Hitler was overwhelmed with such a nausea of fatigue he went back to his bed behind the barrel: he must, *must* get some sleep.

Ever since the 'March' Hitler had never quite slept: yet he was never quite awake, and this second day at Uffing found it difficult to speak coherently or even think. He must rest: and yet it was even worse alone, more difficult to keep hold. Now, as he lay there on his side sleepless and poring over the past, even his own legs would no longer obey him: they kept trying to run of their own volition like a dreaming dog's. Indeed his whole nervous system seemed to be dissevering itself from central control; that superb instrument he had been used to playing on at will now twanged suddenly and discordantly like a concert-piano when a cat jumps on the keys. He couldn't stay long in one position. He couldn't keep his eyes either open or shut, and whenever his eyes opened they saw books leaning over him in their cases. Hey presto before his very eyes those books had started exchanging titles like jugglers throwing balls to each other! They were doing this to distract his attention: once they managed that they were planning to fall on him, leaning cases and all.

It was at this moment that suddenly the bells started ringing: the Sunday bells of Uffing, beating on his ears with their frightful jarring tintinnabulation. Whereon somebody must have started pulling a clapper in Hitler's own head too, for his own head started chiming with the bells of Uffing. His head was rocking with the weight of its own terrible tolling.

Flinging back the blanket Hitler gazed desperately round. His trusty whip stood just out of reach, but how he longed to hear again instead of those clanging bells the whirr of its clean singing thong of rhinoceros-hide – the whirring, and the *crack*! If he had given those traitors a taste of it instead of letting them through his fingers he'd have been in Berlin by now – yes, in BERLIN!

'Woe to the bloody city! It is all full of lies and robbery ... the noise of a whip ...' (To think that this very hour he should have been riding triumphant through Berlin!) *'... the noise of a whip, and the noise of the rattling of the wheels, and of the prancing horses, and of the jumping chariots ...'* (In Berlin, scourging the money-lenders from the temple! A city in flames!) *'There is a multitude of the slain, and a great number of carcases; there is none end of their corpses, they stumble upon their corpses ...'*

Scourging the hollow barons ... scourging the puking communists ... scourging the Lesbians and the nancy-boys with that rhinoceros-thong!

But that barrel – it was changing shape: now tall now short, now fat now lean ... erect, and swelling ... and out of the swelling barrel a remembered figure was rising – smooth, and gross, and swaying and nodding like a tree. It was a man's figure from his own penurious teen-age in Vienna: it was that smooth-faced beast at the Hotel Kummer, bribing the bright-eyed hard-up boy with cream puffs, promising him all the pastries he could eat and daring to make passes at *him*, at Adolfus Hitler!

Then under the hammering of the bells the figure collapsed – suddenly as it had risen.

Scourging the whores, the Jews ... scourging the little flash jew-girls till they screamed ...

Now the dark corners of the room were filling with soft naked legs: those young Viennese harlots sitting half-naked in the lighted windows all along the Spittelberggasse (between the dark windows where 'it' was already being done). For once upon a time the young Hitler used to go there, to the Spittelberggasse: to ... just to look at them. To harden his will; for except by such tests as these how can a lad with the hair new on him be assured that his will is strong? The boy would stare, and walk on a few yards; then come back as 'strong' as ever – back to the most attractive and most nearly naked and stare her out again, pop-eyed.

He called it 'the Flame of Life', that holy flame of sex in the centre of a man; and he knew that all his whole life *his* 'Flame' had to be kept burning without fuel for at the first real touch of human, female fuel it must turn smoky, fill his whole Vessel with soot. This was Destiny's revealed dictate: if ever Hitler did 'it' the unique Power would go out of him, like Samson and his hair. No, at most if the adult male flesh itched intolerably it might be deviously relieved.

After all, how could that monistic 'I' of Hitler's ever without forfeit succumb to the entire act of sex, the whole essence of which is recognition of one 'Other'? Without damage I mean to his fixed conviction that he was the universe's unique sentient centre, the sole authentic incarnate Will it contained or had ever contained? Because this of course was the rationale of his supernal inner 'Power': *Hitler existed alone. 'I* am, none else beside me.' The universe contained no other persons than him, only things; and thus for him the whole gamut of the 'personal' pronouns lacked wholly its normal emotional content. This left Hitler's designing and creating motions enormous and without curb: it was only natural for this architect to turn also politician for he saw no real distinction in the new things to be handled: these 'men' were merely him-mimicking 'things', in the same category as other tools and stones. All tools have handles – this sort was fitted with ears.

And it is nonsensical to love or hate or pity (or tell the truth to) stones.

Hitler's then was that rare diseased state of the personality, an ego virtually without penumbra: rare and diseased, that is, when abnormally such an ego survives in an otherwise mature adult intelligence clinically sane (for in the new-born doubtless it is a beginning normal enough and even surviving into the young child). Hitler's *adult* 'I' had developed thus – into a larger but still undifferentiated structure, as a malignant growth does.

In Mitzi – as could perhaps happen to you or me – with the shock of her crisis the central 'I' had become dislodged: it had dwindled to a cloudlet no bigger than a man's hand beneath the whole zenith of God. But in this suffering man always and unalterably his 'I' must blacken the whole vault from pole to pole.

The tortured, demented creature tossed on his bed . . .

'Rienzi-night', that night on the Freinberg over Linz after the opera: that surely had been the climactic night of his boyhood for it was then he had first confirmed that lonely omnipotence within him. Impelled to go up there in the darkness into that high place had he not been shown there all earthly kingdoms in a moment of time? And facing there the ancient gospel question had not his whole being been one assenting Yea? Had he not *struck* the everlasting bargain there on the high mountain under the witnessing November stars? Yet now . . . now, when he had seemed to be riding Rienzi-like the crest of the wave, the irresistible wave which with mounting force should have carried him to Berlin, that crest had begun to curl: it had curled and broken and toppled on him, thrusting him down, down in the green thundering water, deep.

Tossing desperately on his bed, he gasped – he was drowning (what of all things always Hitler most feared). *Drowning?* Then . . . then that suicidal boyhood moment's teetering long ago on the Danube bridge at Linz . . . after all the melancholic boy *had* leaped that long-ago day, and everything since was dream! Then this noise now was the mighty Danube singing in his dreaming drowning ears.

In the green watery light surrounding him a dead face was floating towards him upturned: a dead face with his own slightly-bulging eyes in it unclosed: his dead Mother's face as he had last seen it with unclosed eyes white on the white pillow. Dead, and white, and vacant even of its love for him.

But now that face was multiplied – it was all around him in the water. So his Mother *was* this water, these waters drowning him!

At that he ceased to struggle. He drew up his knees to his chin in the primal attitude and lay there, letting himself drown.

So Hitler slept at last.

Chapter 11

The sergeant had hayseed down his sweaty neck and had taken off his cap for a good scratch. What lovely clear cold weather this was! The invisible frost fell on his baldness out of the bright sky like minute pinpricks, and he stood for a moment relishing it before putting his cap on again. The snowy mountains above Garmisch glittered in the evening sun: it was early for really good snow, but how he wished he was off up there now for a Sunday's skiing! The Ettaler-Mandl above Oberammergau was caught in a particular gleam.

'No rest for the wicked,' they say, but it's the wicked rather who allow policemen no rest. They had spent half this lovely Sunday afternoon searching the American lady's farm: they had probed haystacks, turned over the fodder in the mangers, crawled through apple-lofts, climbed in and out of cornbins, tunnelled under woodpiles (which fell in on them), crept under the beds of maidservants (who boxed their ears), ransacked cupboards and tapped walls: and now those damned dogs of theirs had broken into the beehouse and the whole lot were howling. Lord, what a din! All the same, through the open door he could still hear the Lieutenant bawling the old girl out for trying to telephone – the silly old trout.

When her mother-in-law's voice was suddenly cut off like that Helene put back the receiver slowly. So this was the end! They had left it too late now.

Today she couldn't make Herr Hitler out. At lunch he had seemed better after his rest: he had joked with little Egon, who was much impressed with the figure Funny-Uncle cut in the vast old blue bathrobe of Daddy's he was wrapped in. Then when the baby had gone to rest Hitler had begun to wax furious about the Bechstein car not coming: yet, when she offered to have him whisked over the pass to Austria with the plumber's motor-bike concealed in the sidecar (transport far less likely to be searched at the frontier than the big Bechstein Limousine), he would have none of it. So she had thought up all sorts of plans for hiding him in the forest, in some woodman's hut the police would never think of; but he would still have none of it. It was the Bechstein car in style, or nothing.

So now it was – nothing.

Hitler was sitting upstairs in a daze again dreaming of suicide when his Mother walked into the room. She told him the world was ended, and then took out of his hand something . . . it was something he didn't really want.

That woman who had come into the room was Helene, of course. And when she told Hitler the police were at last on their way here he had gone apparently demented: still wound in the big blue bathrobe he began turning like a top in his efforts to draw his revolver with his one good arm: 'Those swine! Never shall they take me alive!'

She grabbed at the gun in his hand, but with only one arm to use and all wound up in the bathrobe for a moment Hitler still seemed to struggle demoniacally. And yet it was no real struggle, for when she let go of him and told him not to be so silly he gave up, and let her take it. Disarmed, too, the frenzy suddenly left Hitler and he realized who this really was. Yet he hardly seemed to realize what had just been going on here though he himself was still panting from it: he looked at her wonderingly, surprised to see the beautiful Helene of all people just a wee bit dishevelled. Then he sank into a chair and hid his head in his hands and groaned.

To give him something to think about she urged Hitler to compose his political testament while there was yet time; and leaving him scribbling she quietly dropped the revolver into that open barrel of flour, harmless. It sank in the soft flour without a trace.

Dark had just fallen when there was a sudden roar of powerful engines: then a screech of brakes, and the ominous whining of big dogs. Hitler sprang to the window: he saw there was a truck down there – two trucks, with greenfly swarming on them.

Helene slipped quietly downstairs and told the girls to keep Egon in the kitchen with them. As soon as the door of the lighted kitchen was closed she felt her way in the pitch-dark to a shuttered window giving towards the street.

Meanwhile the police had surrounded the house, each man with a dog at his side. Except for one light upstairs the place seemed to be in darkness and downstairs all the shutters were closed. The sergeant vaulted the wall and crept close to a window, hoping to peep in where he thought he saw a chink, and flashing his torch found himself staring straight in a woman's eyes. Startled, he jerked the leash in his hand; and startled in its turn his dog barked. That set them all off and soon the quiet village sounded like a kennels at feeding-time.

As soon as they were quiet again the Lieutenant knocked. It was Frau Hanfstaengl herself who answered, and taking the sergeant and one man with him he followed her up the stairs. She opened a door – and bless me, there the blighter stood, dressed up like one of the Christmas Magi! So he must have been here in the village all the time – not hidden at all!

When the officer rather apologetically told him he would be arrested for 'Treason' then Hitler really did let fly. For at the sight of those three rosy faces goggling at him his brain had cleared. He felt his 'Power' returning: it was a fire in his bones, it was mounting in his throat till it overflowed, it was new wine in a barrel without a vent. Moreover, speech might be the last shot in his locker – but surely this his last bullet was a silver one! For you just had to press the right button as so often before, pull the right lever . . .

these three should be his first new converts, he'd march back to Munich at their head!

'Wiry little chap, yon,' thought the sergeant: 'but he don't look as though he meant to put up a fight . . . though *Mutter-Gottes* what a noise he's making! Voice like a jay . . .' For a flash the sergeant was walking with his Gretl in the June woods and the jays were screaming.

Not for one moment did it occur to the sergeant that he might hear what the prisoner *said*, any more than the jays: for policemen have invisible scramblers in their ears whenever 'the Prisoner' speaks. In the context of his arrest every man is a thing only, so any sounds he makes are mere meaningless noise such as all things tend to make – doors slamming, rivers roaring, jays . . .

June, and Gretl in her dirndl with him in the woods . . . the sergeant's mind's arm gave his mind's Gretl a hearty, a corset-bursting squeeze. But just at that moment the spate of sound ceased abruptly, and the prisoner stood there looking like . . . *Pfui*, for all the world he resembled in spite of his queer get-up (and rather as some comical mimicking insect might) any popular platform-speaker waiting for the applause! One hand was still held aloft, as if ready to pluck fresh arguments out of the lamplit air. Whereon the sergeant stepped forward and clapped him briskly on that drooping shoulder.

The night was bitter and the trucks open ones so they took Hitler downstairs still wrapped in the bathrobe (though he refused a beret), and trailing Putzi's prized English rug by one corner like a child who has been playing Indians (but his whip was forgotten). Then the men closed in and hustled him expertly into the foremost truck, jumped up after him and drove him off to Weilheim gaol.

Egon had run out, and the last the sleepy baby saw of dear Uncle Dolf once his pale face had vanished among them was that empty whip-hand, helplessly thrumming the air. Indeed that was all there was to be seen of him; for now they were all 'things' together those were bigger things than he was.

The trucks left Uffing with Hitler jammed among his captors' bodies too tight to move; and for a minute he felt curiously at peace. But as the fact sank in of this his incredible constraint by *things* and so of his utter impotence always over deaf adders who chose to stop their ears his belly griped suddenly as in a colic-cramp. He felt in his rage as if he was being assaulted by climbing snakes; though these were only the cramps running up and down him from head to foot, his own rebellious muscles each writhing of their own volition all up and down his skeletal frame.

But that too soon passed, overwhelmed by the nausea of weariness once more. Damn the woman for taking his gun! Even in that he had failed.

Did Hitler attempt to speak again, in the back of that truck? Who cared? Who possibly knows? For one of them had brought his accordion and they all began to sing. The sergeant had a lovely baritone, and the song was sickly-sweet.

Chapter 12

That Sunday of Hitler's arrest was November the Eleventh: everywhere throughout England they had been celebrating Armistice Day. The fifth anniversary of the day *all* war had ended . . . but how had that lovely belief arisen, and why did it linger? Perhaps for no better reason than that nothing less seemed counterweight to the load of death all their boys had died.

In the morning, everywhere the solemn two-minute silence. It fell like an enchantment: indoors and out no one spoke, nothing moved: the cars and buses and drays in the streets halted, the carts in the lanes, the cowman in the stall stood still. Then, as the buglers in the churches everywhere sounded the last note of the resurrectional Last Post, came the moment of release – like the prince's kiss. Men in their civvies ramrod-stiff at attention relaxed and smoked. Women spoke, children ran, cars started, hooves trotted.

But now it was tea-time. Mellton church was empty – only their guerdon of Flanders poppies and the carved names remained there, while at the vicarage the Vicar of Mellton munched fruit-cake and put the last touches to his evening Armistice sermon.

At the lonely Hermitage on the downs Nellie had just set the wash-tub in the new sink.

In Gwilym's sanatorium the nurses all wore poppies, and there were poppies pinned to the King's portrait on the wall. Gwilym was already putting his things in order – tearing up letters, and so on – ready tomorrow to go home; for he had been quite right of course, he was now so much better they *had* to let him go home. Gwilym had few possessions, but there was a pencil-sharpener he could give his friend in the next bed to remember him by. As an afterthought he gave him a red pencil too, and they both wept.

The Sister had told Gwilym well in advance that he was going, in the hope of distracting his mind from the death of his little girl. But it had been difficult for even the doctor to make him understand it must be months 'before he could work again'. They put this down to his throat, for his throat is a preacher's most precious organ: in particular Gwilym *must* rest his throat!

As a matter of fact Gwilym's throat had been cauterized too drastically and the vocal cords had been completely destroyed. It was impossible he should ever speak again except in a whisper, but that they hadn't told him.

'How long must I rest it?'

'Oh . . . six months, at the very least.'

(Gwilym, they thought, could hardly last six months.)

Six months! For someone expecting to die, so short a reprieve; but to Gwilym, expecting to live, an interminable time to have to wait for his health back. And yet it's a queer thing, this Spes Phthisica: though confident he would soon be a giant refreshed and raring for the pulpit at the same time Gwilym knew perfectly well he would never get better and was going to die. His mind just kept both bits of knowledge apart so they need not contradict.

At the times when he contemplated death his heart welled over with pity for poor Nellie. So soon would *he* find Little Rachel waiting on Jordan's further shore to greet him; he would enter his Maker's presence with that dear hand warm in his. But Nellie might have many dreary years to wait before seeing her lost child again. *Two* children dead, and now her husband dying: poor emptied heart of Nellie's! Gwilym prayed with all his soul that little Sylvanus might grow to fill it again. Indeed Gwilym's mind dwelt much on this baby he had not yet even seen. As soon as he was fit again he and Nellie must visit Rachel's grave on the bare hill above Penrys Cross; and they would take Sylvanus with them, for he must be taught from the first to love and revere the sister he had never known – that little angel God had lent them for awhile, who now from heaven was loving him and watching him grow. They must teach Sylvanus to try to live always worthy of that angelic love: never to do anything or even think anything it would pain those innocent eyes to see. Bit by bit the boy must be brought to realize that always from heaven *his Sister was watching him.*

For, apart from religion, the happiest thing Gwilym had to dream about now was the joy of bringing up his son. He made endless plans for it (particularly in the evenings, after his temperature had risen): all the things he and the boy would do together, as the boy grew.

'The boy and he *together*'? – Ah, there lay the sharpest of all death's stings.

The Sunday paper discarded on Gwilym's bed carried little news of the Putsch in Munich – and spelled 'Hitler' wrong. It was all of no interest to Gwilym, naturally. But in Mary's paper 'Munich' caught her eye, though only because her brother must have been there about then. She jumped to the conclusion he'd have seen the whole thing and his first letter would be full of it: she'd better know what it was all about. But Gilbert would hardly look at the paragraph: Bavarian antics were of no conceivable importance to England, and a politician must always keep his eye on the ball. For these were crucial times! Baldwin had forestalled Lloyd George in calling for 'Protection' and this had driven L. G. back on to uncompromising Free Trade, of course. Baldwin's change of heart moreover was a complete ratting on his party's election pledges only last spring, so it meant yet another General Election almost at once; and that closed the Liberal ranks willy-nilly – for the next week or two.

'What chance have we got of turning out the Tories?' – Today's cake had seeds in it, and absently Gilbert picked his teeth with the wire stem of his poppy while he pondered.

Chapter 13

At the lonely Hermitage on the downs Nellie had just set the wash-tub in the new sink. Beside her, in a warm corner near the fire, baby Sylvanus (now three weeks old) was sleeping in his basket. Cold water from the bucket, hot from the steaming kettle on the hob . . . Nellie tested the temperature with her bare elbow to get it just right, and then – discarding her poppy for fear the wire might scratch the infant – lifted the tiny object out of its warm snuggle and laid it on her knees to undress it.

Waking abruptly it wailed, and began to quiver. She had laid it face-down, and in its anger the scalp blushed reddish through the sparse black hair. The simple seminal ego within it was awash with rage. In the transports of its rage the transparent skin on its tiny naked back suddenly marbled with quick-flushing veins, while the helpless waving fists were drained of their blood and turned a bluish-grey. Then she rolled the object over face-up again. Now apparently it was too angry to cry out at all – it hadn't the breath; but the chin quivered like the reed of a musical instrument and the whole face crinkled.

Competently and gently, like dusting fragile porcelain – but a bit absently, as if the porcelain was unloved – Nellie wiped the eyes with a swab of cotton-wool. Then she made little spills of the cotton-wool, dipped then in oil and twiddled them in those defenceless ears and nostrils. The infant's head was too heavy for it to be able to move it but every other inch of its body jerked and shook in paroxysms of rage and sneezing, and at every such movement all its tender contours crumpled and collapsed like a half-deflated balloon.

It was only now Nellie remembered to swathe it in the towel which hung warming before the fire.

Indoors the light was already failing, and Nellie stopped for a moment to light the lamp. But from outside through the open door still came the sound of sawing; for Sunday or not the carpenter had to get that shed finished in time, and it was quite an elaborate piece of work.

Sighing (from mild indigestion) Nellie soaped the wobbling heavy head, then held it out over the sink to rinse it. Next, her large hands began soaping the convulsive, prehominid little body and limbs. But now the carpenter's dog Charlie – a young spaniel with a talent for comedy – had grown disgusted with the smell of sawdust outside with his master and wandered into Nellie's kitchen. After one quick apologetic smirk at his hostess he began nosing around eagerly; but each time he found some new smell that amused him he glanced again momentarily at Nellie, and smirked his thanks politely. With her eyes on this engaging dog and hardly aware what she was doing Nellie submerged the baby's body and rinsed that too. At the benevolent touch of the warm water rage instantly subsided; but his moment of comfort was brief, for she lifted him out to dry him – and instantly rage returned.

Then Nellie opened her own box of powder that she had set ready on the Windsor chair at her side. It was a cheap brand, and the scent drove the dog completely dippy. Doing the familiar job by rote Nellie watched him – and broke into a smile for the first time for ages. For Charlie would fawn towards the powder-box and then halt, humbly, at least two feet from it. There he bowed deeply, right to the ground, and took one distant sniff. Then he danced round the room like a ballerina till his ecstasy was expended: then he fawned back again, praying to the gracious box for yet one more replenishing sniff. When Nellie actually began powdering the baby, for a dog's nose no doubt that scent billowed on the air and so his state of religious ecstasy was rendered continuous. He ran round the tiny room at incredible speed; though how he avoided colliding with the crowded furniture was pretty miraculous, for he ran with his eyes rolled up to heaven till the whites showed – and Nellie laughed aloud.

Engrossed as she was in watching Charlie, none the less she powdered the baby's body expertly all over in every crease: with scarcely a glance she folded clean napkins and put them on him and pinned them, and wrapped him again in the flannelette nightgown that did up at the back with tapes. But there was one item of common practice Nellie left out. I don't mean just that she had forgotten to oil his bottom before putting the napkins on (she remembered that afterwards, when it was all finished and he was back in his Moses-basket – but what the hell, just for once!): no, I mean that she hadn't kissed him. That was something as yet Nellie had never ever done.

Before he was born Nellie had hated him. But now she was completely indifferent to him, for Rachel's death had numbed her. That indifference wouldn't last much longer, however; for if Nellie couldn't escape like Mitzi out of disaster into God, neither could she long remain like Hitler – cooped up with his disaster in the prison that was the ring-fence of *himself*. For Nellie's central 'I' was minimal. Hers was a 'self' consciousness only really vivid ever towards its periphery – at its sensitive points of contact with other people: whatever happened at the centre to Nellie always surfaced out there sooner or later, transmuted into enigmatic compulsions of love or hate. Before long, Nellie's numbness *must* melt in a very cataract of feeling: but of love . . . Sylvanus her only son and she a widow? Or of hate . . . had Sylvanus never been conceived Little Rachel need never have died? Or both?

Tonight, as Nellie carried the bathwater to empty it outside, she caught sight of Little Rachel smiling down at her from her fretwork frame on the kitchen wall and burst into tears.

Charlie nuzzled her knee with his soft nozzle. How passionately she wished that Charlie was hers! But now the carpenter was whistling for Charlie: Gwilym's shed was almost ready – and just in time – but the daylight was quite gone now and he had to stop.

Packing his tools, the carpenter hoped kind Mrs Tuckett had saved him a good tea. "Night, Missus: marnin' to finish un'!'

Somehow Nellie managed to answer 'Good night.' The man and the dog were gone; and only the faint evening churchbells of distant Mellton floated to Nellie on the still air, sounding infinitely remote.

Chapter 14

Past midnight now; and the only light still showing in all snowy Lorienburg shone from the window of Otto's office, for Sunday or no Otto would go on working just so long as he could keep awake: Otto dreaded his bed. Everyone else seemed to be sleeping. All their sealed windows were dark. Heavy curtains occluded even the nightlight burning in the twins' room: within, its gleam just revealed them as two mere molehills in the middle of the blankets evidently not needing to breathe. And likewise (through the door he always left open on to the stairs) the faint glow from his overheated stove just showed Augustine: he was smiling in his sleep, and stroking the pillow. But elsewhere the darkness of the silent house was everywhere profound. Mitzi, in her own private darkness within it, dreamed she was weightless and climbing a ladder; but each rung beneath her vanished as she took her foot off it, and the ladder was topless.

Only in the billowing darkness of the attics above two eyes were open, and staring. Endlessly cooped-up there, knowing he could never again leave these attics alive, something long under intolerable strain in Wolff was beginning to break at last.

November the Eleventh: in Wolff's eyes and many others 'blackest day in the calendar, day that the traitors sold Germany down the river . . .'

Germany had not been defeated: whatever the world pretended, she had not been defeated! For in childhood the axiom that Germany *could not be* defeated had been embedded in Wolff deep in his core of intuited knowledge, far below all corrective reach of perception or reason.

This, then, was the early but abiding disaster of Wolff and his kind: transcendental truth had set them at loggerheads with all reality, a deadlock Wolff could not break. However, in the course of his self-immolation on the altar of 'Germany' Wolff's over-altruist self had by now so atrophied it could no longer contain this his Disaster: yet of its nature that disaster allowed no normal outlet – neither into God nor man. Final escape could be only into the absolute unreality of death; but in the meantime Wolff had turned, as to Death's twin and surrogate-on-earth, to Romantic Love: sole comparable realm, with Death's, of the Unreal.

Thus, in the same knightly way as Palamon in his Athenian tower, this Wolff had also fallen deeply into romantic love last summer with the unknown girl seen 'romen to and fro' beneath him in the garden. For Mitzi's yellow hair too was

> *'broyded in a tresse*
> *Bihinde hir bak, a yerde long I gesse,'*

and like Palamon, the moment he saw it Wolff too had

> *'bleynte, and cryde "A!"*
> *As if he stongen were unto the herte.'*

Wolff still knew nothing about Mitzi; for she was too sacred to speak of even to Franz. They could never meet: this girl called 'his' must never know he existed . . . But that was all as it should be, for this kind of loving alone could have suited Wolff, and his love was all the more deep and poignant for being unreal.

Now Reality had broken into even this charmed circle too, so that tonight Wolff knew his jangled nerves might no longer turn for solace to what had lately become its habitual source for him – to inward dramas of killing himself in Mitzi's presence, to the exquisite pleasure of dying with his face bathed in Mitzi's scalding tears. Yet even tonight his homing thoughts unwatched kept creeping back willy-nilly towards this their usual performance, and each such time his reverie was shattered anew by the recurring shock of those two lovers seen stumbling together through the snow!

Each such blow left something defenceless in Wolff weaker, till finally the intolerable tension snapped at last. *A German girl who accepted an Englishman's advances, and this her guilty lover* . . . THEY MUST BE KILLED. It was a very voice from outside: the most compulsive call of Conscience even this addict had ever heard.

Why had Wolff not plunged on them from his window that first moment he saw them together – like a plummet, like an avenging Lucifer destroying himself and them together all three?

Perhaps he might have – had they come near enough. Yet for him that would surely have been altogether too soon! For this was murder; and surely the essence of murder lies always less in the final perfunctory act than in the malice prepense: in the turning it over and over and over beforehand in one's mind. No, this must be carefully planned. Wolff was ignorant even, as yet, who slept where in those storeys downstairs he had never entered. No precipitate act, this; but rather, a passionless duty he had to perform, a punishment he had to inflict: his last and supreme sacrifice to offer on Germany's altar, this was an act to be done in the coldest of cold blood . . . yet at the very thought of coming on Mitzi asleep and killing her an excruciating flame lit in the pit of his stomach, constricting his breathing!

The supernatural voice had hit Wolff at first with the suddenness and violence of an electric shock, striking him rigid; but now the rigor had passed, leaving all over him a heavenly glow. Vividly now Wolff saw himself creeping through the dark and silent house like the angel of death:

he saw himself silently opening a door, within which lay Mitzi still and white on her bed with her eyelids closed and her hair all dispread: he stretched himself on her like Elisha on the Shunammite child ... and saw his two hands close to his own eyes as they smothered her with the pillow ...

Wolff was huddled the while face-down on his attic floor, and the heart in his breast thumped wilder and wilder for beneath his taut overlaying weight on the lumpish furs he could feel Mitzi's heart beating under him. He could feel it flutter, and stop. At that a thunder as of falling towers was all about him, setting his ear-drums ringing: he felt giddy to bursting, almost as if about to vomit.

Or, ought Mitzi perhaps to die by the knife rather? Yes: for 'I ABHOR THINGS STRANGLED' came from the darkness the cold divine command.

Repeating his scene da capo Wolff now dwelt on his teasing point pricking through the thin nightgown to the naked skin so that she half-woke: then the sudden thrust into the throbbing heart itself, the knife pumping in the wound, the withdrawal and the hot blood welling to his elbow. And this time, how peaceful that moment of vision! Wolff's giddiness was gone: in spite of his heart's thumping his troubled spirit was nearer tranquillity now than for many months past.

'A passionless duty ...?' Wolff was contrite. But nothing could still the new life which coursed in his veins tonight as he slipped quickly out of his wraps, in the dark, and crept down the stairs in his socks.

Chapter 15

At nightfall the day's drowsing doubts, like roosting owls, tend to take wing and hoot. Alone in his office tonight Otto could nohow get Mitzi out of his mind. It was their decision at Saturday's conclave that gave him no peace: Had it been right, that decision? For what, after all, had been their real motive in reaching it?

One thing Otto couldn't forget was the tone of Walther's voice exclaiming that there'd never been a blind Kessen ever before: he had sounded almost accusing, as if being born physically faulty meant she *deserved* to be banished from everyone's sight. No one had seemed to consider if she'd be happy 'there': how to make up to Mitzi for her affliction.

Surely there was doubt she'd be even accepted! Normally they'd never take someone so handicapped: at the least it meant special permissions.

Otto sighed. He knew very well, really, that Influence could cope with all that. There'd be benefactions. They'd never refuse ... not a hope. And if they did refuse, what was the alternative? (Otto was holding his list of timber prices close to his eyes but they still wouldn't focus: annoyed, he turned his oil lamp even higher; but it only smoked.) He had to admit Adèle had been unanswerable: marriage was out of the question, for what sort of a Schweinhund would ever marry a blind girl? Some insensitive climbing clerk, for her dowry and connections? Surely even this was better than that!

What other solution was there?

Mitzi wasn't to be told yet ... yes, and how would she take it when they did tell her? But Otto was aware this was something no one would ever quite know. Mitzi had too much courage – too much self-control. When they told her, she'd just obey orders, poker-faced: make the best of it.

Looked-at like that the whole thing was near-blasphemy! But reason told him there must be plenty of similar cases.

Otto was still turning this treadmill when the clock struck two. – Bed! He was doing no good here. So at last he lit his carrying-candle and put out the lamp. But this dimmer light only made vivider his mental image of the niece he was soon so totally to lose. Mitzi had never been his favourite among Walther's children (surely one always likes boy-children better than girls?) but he was deeply concerned for her; and now as he passed her door on his way to his own room this concern turned to an impulse so strong it surprised him: he *must* see how she was! Quietly he opened the door, and listened candle in hand to the darkness inside.

Not a sound. She seemed to be sleeping, but he'd better make sure. So Otto pushed the door wider, and went in to look.

Chapter 16

As Wolff had reached habitation-level, the first door he came to stood open on to the stairs. Since it was right on his line of retreat (this room normally not used), he slipped inside to investigate; and by stovelight recognized his English rival.

'THIS ONE SHALL DIE BY FIRE . . .' The Voice was so loud Wolff wondered it didn't wake the sleeper; but Augustine never stirred.

Fire . . . Wolff knew at once what to do, when the time came (for he had done the same thing once before, to a police-spy at Aachen): he must drag this young man out of bed pinioned in the sheet and too suddenly for any struggle and kill him by holding his head against the red-hot stove. Already (remembering Aachen) Wolff heard the sizzle, smelt cooking bone and hair. It ought to be quite easy – *when* the time came: but that was not yet, might not even be tonight. For this kind of killing was not like a quiet stabbing: even if he gagged his victim too with the bedsheet he could hardly count on no noise at all; there was Mitzi, and he must not risk rousing the house till there was only himself left to kill.

He knew now where the Englishman slept. But Mitzi came first: it might be more difficult to discover which room was Mitzi's, nevertheless that was the next thing Wolff had to find out.

Augustine stirred, and half-woke just as a reddish shadow vanished through his door.

Quiet as any shadow Wolff prowled on down into the pitch-dark hall. Here there were many doors. But here again Fate was smoothing his path tonight; for one door stood ajar, with a light inside. Through the chink Wolff could just

284

see the head of the bed; and at what he saw there his skin flushed hot from head to foot – for it was all coming true. That hair spread over the pillow in the candlelight was Mitzi's!

The candle which lit the room was hidden from outside, where Wolff stood. But just then the shadow shifted, and warned him just in time that someone else was in there before him! He checked himself on the threshold.

Standing at the foot of the bed, Otto had just raised his candle to look at her.

Asleep (Otto thought), with her hair all loose undone, Mitzi looked not even a young girl yet – only a child. Asleep, he saw with relief, she shut her eyes exactly as everyone else does: asleep, no one could tell.

Walther and Adèle – even Franz – had they no imagination? Surely they loved her more even than he did: then had they no notion what the life they were sending her to must be like for her? For someone so immature still, so human, so . . . earthly? Almost one heard those great gates creak as they slowly crushed shut on her!

Otto pitied his niece so deeply that almost (he thought) it were better the poor girl had died.

Outside in the hall a loose tile clinked as Wolff retreated. He was back in his attics long before Otto had left Mitzi and gone to his room.

Wolff knew now where they *both* slept: he could do it whenever he liked! Fate whose servant he was wasn't fickle (said Wolff to himself as he ousted the fox from its nest in those warm abandoned furs): Fate was helping him; and Fate wasn't fickle! When the time did come for a killing she always gave him the signal: till then, he must wait.

Chapter 17

Morning again! Monday's wintry sun up, and those twin molehills in the blankets erupting into two little boys pulling on leather knickerbockers much blackened and polished at the knees and seats: buckling on belts which each carried a decorative sheath-knife, its handle a roe-deer's foot.

After breakfast Augustine praised those knives loudly; for he saw they were cherished cult-objects and he hoped to give pleasure. But this marked praise seemed only to cause consternation; and it mystified him still further when, in a solid glum lump, all four children followed him to his room.

For a moment the lump blocked his doorway in silence. Then, 'Have you told yet?' ten-year-old Trudl asked him in a deep, harsh voice.

Trudl was speaking 'good' German carefully, for Augustine's benefit; but what did she mean by 'told', he wondered? – Ah, about that fight-in-a-snowstorm of course! But after himself saving the situation for them why on earth should she think he'd 'tell'?

'No,' said Augustine, smiling.

Trudl nodded (after all, if he had told Papa they'd have heard of it!). Then she signed to the two little boys, and with yard-long faces they began unbuckling their belts. Trudl snatched both the knives and held them out to Augustine: 'Here you are, then,' she said, and watched him intently.

'It's a waste!' said the younger girl, Irma. She addressed the ceiling cynically: 'If he takes them he can still "tell" just the same.'

'No! D-d-don't give them yet!' stammered Rudi. 'Make him swear first!'

' "Make him *swear*" !' jeered Irma. 'When he's English, you little nit-wit? What good's that?'

'B-b-but . . .' Augustine was so flabbergasted he even caught Rudi's stammer: 'I-I-I . . . don't want your knives!'

'We all thought that was what you meant,' explained Trudl, nonplussed. 'You as good as said so!'

For answer, Augustine thrust back the two knives violently – and they fell to the ground.

'He wants something else, then,' said Irma, flatly. Heinz fumbled out a rather sticky pre-war fifty-pfennig piece, looked at it disparagingly and returned it to his pocket. There was a pause.

Then, 'What will you take, to promise?' asked Trudl anxiously. 'If it isn't the knives you want?'

'I expect all he wants is to tell – when he's ready,' Irma suggested. 'He likes keeping us waiting: it's fun for him.'

But at this Trudl flung herself furiously on Augustine, grabbing his jacket as if she was trying to shake him. 'You must say what you want!' she cried: 'You must you must you must!'

'Yes, now's your chance, Greedy!' said Irma, addressing Augustine directly for the first time. Then she exchanged glances with the twins: 'Else we'll tell Papa ourselves and take our whacking – and that way you'll get nothing!' she added spitefully.

'Yes – serve him right!' said Rudi, refixing his knife to his belt. After all, even a caning might be better than blackmail: 'Who minds a sore b-b-bum?' he added, lordly.

'*I* do . . . he *must* promise,' Trudl miserably muttered. Astonished, the others stared at her hostile and uncomprehending: 'I'm too old to be beaten, now . . . it gives me the "funny feeling". I'm older than any of you!'

The situation was so bizarre Augustine hardly knew if he was on his head or his heels. In vain he tried to convince them he'd hate for them to be beaten: that he'd no intention of telling tales – but all gratis, he wanted nothing: but no, his silence had to be bought! Their attitude was that otherwise no Englishman's word could be trusted. This astounded Augustine, for surely 'an Englishman's word is

287

his bond' is known the world over? (It astounded this anti-patriot, too, to discover how angry this ignorant attitude made him!)

In the end, Augustine gave in. 'Very well,' he said, 'I'll tell you.' There was an anxious silence, while resources were inwardly totted. 'I want the biggest snowman there's ever been; and you've jolly well got to build it for me.'

They stared at him in paralytic astonishment. A grown-up want a snowman? Mad . . . utterly mad! Eight eyes fixed on him fearfully, the whole body retreated backwards.

'Before lunch!' Augustine called after them cheerfully: 'It's a bargain – don't forget!'

Whew! he thought: and these were her brothers and sisters – the same flesh and blood as his Mitzi!

What a fool he'd been, Saturday, not to take his chance in the chapel and speak to Mitzi! He'd had no other chance since; and indeed so long as she kept to her room how could he – short of going to Walther and demanding to see her?

No doubt Cousins Walther and Adèle were wondering what he was waiting for; but what did the old idiots expect? Augustine was quite prepared to ask Walther's leave for the marriage *after* speaking to Mitzi, but it was just too Victorian if Walther expected to be asked for permission *before!* 'Leave to address my attentions . . .' yes, it looked very much as if that was what Walther did expect, hiding Mitzi away like this!

As for Mitzi herself, what must she be thinking? She'd be feeling deserted, she'd be asking herself what sluggard sort of lover was this: she might think he'd had second thoughts . . . she might even suppose that sacred moment of one-ness in the courtyard had meant nothing to him!

All eyes were upon him – so Augustine supposed: everyone was waiting for Augustine to speak! It never occurred to him no one – not even Mitzi herself – had *noticed* him falling in love.

288

Chapter 18

Mitzi was indeed feeling deserted that morning; but deserted by God, not Augustine.

Waking (for Mitzi that morning) had been like waking in an unexpected empty bed: *God wasn't there* – it was as simple as that! Yesterday God talked in her ear, breathed over her very shoulder: wherever she turned there wasn't the tiniest interstice but God was there: yet today, when she called to Him she could hear the words of her prayer travelling outwards for ever into infinite empty distances. Nothing even echoed them back to her – for *nothing* was there.

So today Mitzi was indeed alone in her darkness, and indeed in despair.

Mitzi had taken for granted that first day's first ecstasy was going to be her condition from now on for ever. It had never occurred to her once God had found and possessed her she could ever lose Him again. Had her eyes of the spirit also been smitten with blindness? Was that possible? For God *must* be there!

Mitzi thought of that game where the seeker is blindfold but the onlookers help him by saying 'You're cold!' or, 'You're hotter now . . .' Surely she was not truly alone, with the glorious saints (she was told) all around her? Crowds of them, clouds of them – *onlookers,* all of them seeing where God was? Would none of them say 'hot' or 'cold' to her? For God MUST be there!

Or had Mitzi but eyes, to read with! The Learned Fathers (she knew) had all been here before her, in this 'dark night of the spirit': at least they'd be company for her – give her hope.

St Teresa of Avila . . . Teresa had written of 'seasons of dryness', times when even that greatest of the mystics found prayer was impossible; but surely Teresa had something too, somewhere, about the 'three waters' which solace that dryness? Mitzi alas had paid little attention in school when the nun read that bit aloud to them: now she hadn't the haziest notion what those 'three waters' were (and for that very reason felt certain that here lay the key to her problem). The 'first water' was . . . what was it? Oh had she but *eyes*, to read that book over once more!

But again, *why* had God done this? Why (and now her soul trembled in mutiny), why show her the depths of His love if He meant to withdraw it? Oh cruel the love that so used her! Truly Mitzi had welcomed her blindness, if nothing but blindness could open her heart to His sweetness: but would she had never known bliss rather than know it and lose it – on top of her blindness.

Yet Teresa . . . Oh could she but READ . . . and that was the state of her mind when she heard a knock at the door, and her uncle walked in.

It had struck the uneasy Otto that morning how lonely the girl must be feeling: so far as he knew, no one much visited her except old Schmidtchen – and it couldn't be good for her, moping alone in her room all day with nothing to do. Leg or no leg he must get her to come for a walk with him. Of course, he himself couldn't walk far; so perhaps it would be better after all if Franz took her? Or what about that young Englishman: surely he'd spare an hour to give the poor girl an outing?

He must find out if she'd like that; and so he had come to her room. But one glance was enough: Mitzi was huddled in a chair beside her untasted breakfast, and her face wore a look of such strain she was certainly fit for no stranger's company. She answered incoherently, too: she seemed unfit to converse, even with him.

But Otto was determined not to leave her like this, now he had come. Perhaps she would like him to read to her? At that suggestion she trembled, but nodded. 'Well: what shall I read, then?'

But alas, to listen to 'Teresa' with him watching! It must strip Mitzi's soul bare, and today her horrible soul wasn't fit to be seen – not by anyone's eyes. Just because she so longed for Teresa, then, Mitzi chose at a venture Thomas-à-Kempis. Thomas seemed safer – more congruous too (she told herself) with her uncle's disciplined mind. And who knows? He *might* even prove helpful.

But Otto's calm unspeculative voice made Thomas's dry medieval apothegms sound even drier still: Otto gave the words a sharp intonation like musketry instructions and Mitzi's attention soon wandered. *She had been green, and now she was cut down – dried and withered like grass . . .*

'*Shut your door, and call to you Jesus your beloved: Stay with Him in your cell . . .*'

– came Otto's confident voice. – Yes, all very well! But suppose you call and He won't come?

Mitzi was getting sulky with Thomas. *God had taken her up like a toy . . .*

The thing finally and supremely necessary for the Christian (read Otto presently) was

'*That, having forsaken everything else, he leave also himself: go wholly out of himself, and retain nothing of self-love . . .*'

Then for a moment the reader glanced over his shoulder; for silently Franz had looked in, made a face, and withdrawn. Perhaps it was that momentary tiny change in Otto's voice; or perhaps it was only the image of her own unique ill-treated 'self' so vivid that very moment in her mind that made the bald words hit Mitzi like a thunderclap. She shuddered violently: for what did that mean? Was Thomas saying that if she was to return to God, then even to *herself* her 'self' must become indistinguishable – no singer may single the sound of her own hosanna in the chorus of the heavenly host?

Must she forego even her own 'I am' – the one thing she had thought nothing could take from her – not Death, even? But how could she, by sheer act of the will, do just that? How could she forget she was 'she'? The task was both unexpected and plainly impossible: *if God existed, so must she.*

For Science can prove most things – or disprove them, sooner or later; but there is one thing Science can't prove or disprove and nobody asks it to because everyone knows it already: each knows his own '*I*-ness'. Other people's unproven '*I*-nesses' he is willing to surmise, by analogy; but he can't be directly conscious of them from within as he is of his own. Indeed there seems to be no other concept in quite the same category – I mean, something without intervention of the senses or logic a direct object of consciousness – except for people like Mitzi *conscious of God:* that is, of the '*I*'-ness of God. For it would be an understatement to say that Mitzi 'believed' in God; she was conscious of His great 'I AM' in the same way – in the very same breath of partaking – as she was of her own little 'I am' that reflected the image of His. Say, rather, that she 'believed' the existence of the people around her – her Mother, Franz, Otto, Natascha! But God's existing Mitzi 'knew' – from within it, just like her own.

In the squeeze of the dilemma Thomas had posed her, for the first time it occurred to Mitzi that being 'with God' is never a static condition: it is rather a journey – and endless.

The discovery was visual. Far below her – like the lights of an inn left behind in the valley when a sudden turn in the mounting road shows them again but now directly beneath you – she saw, in the likeness of a pinpoint of light far down underneath her, that first day's simple, sweet happiness: and now she could never go back to it. Nor did she want to, she found! For she who seeks God must press *forward* (thought Mitzi): lost sight of, God lies always in front.

Something of that moment of vision must have shone in her face; for, watching and part-comprehending his niece's emotion, Otto felt – yet hardly dared feel – a sudden elation. Could it be after all . . . against all odds . . . that their decision was the utterly right one?

If so, then some Saint had taken a hand since everyone's motives in reaching it had been so utterly wrong.

Chapter 19

Franz had looked in on his sister because he too was growing uneasy about that decision as time wore on. Franz too couldn't get Mitzi out of his mind.

Yet surely Franz at least knew *his* motives had been of the noblest? For his iron duty it was to keep his hands free, his back unburdened for whatever burden Germany might lay on it (so Wolff had taught him). Each son and daughter of Germany these desperate days must be devoted wholly to Germany; and what could a blind girl hope to do for a Germany in travail except one thing – avoid hampering the activists, take herself out of their way? Like Agamemnon at Aulis, Franz had been called to bind his nearest and dearest on his country's altar . . . and very noble he was to do it, no doubt.

Yes . . . but would Mitzi herself see it that way unless he explained to her? Franz must at least have a talk with his sister and so he had gone to her room – but found his uncle in there before him.

Uncle Otto was reading to Mitzi, and reading moreover some of that anaemic soul-rotting drivel no good German might believe any more . . . Ah, but Mitzi of course from now on . . . it cut Franz to the quick, how far apart already he and his dearest sister had drifted.

Disgruntled, Franz crept away without interrupting them – up to the attics. For the root of Franz's new feelings of guilt about Mitzi was undoubtedly this: she was to be sacrificed to the 'Cause', but that Cause (if he would but admit it) was in fact in a state of utter stagnation. Ever since Rathenau (more than a year ago) nothing had been *done*. Their mystic goal of Chaos seemed now remoter than ever:

even Friday's enigmatic upheaval in Munich had only left Weimar stronger. Meanwhile, the legions of the Activists were ... were inactive. Kern their old leader was dead, and Fischer: even the noble young Salomon was in prison: weaklings had joined the Nazis: that really only left Wolff to lead them, and Wolff all these long months ...

'*Wolff!*' Franz halted, trying to adjust his eyes to the dusk. 'Wolff, where are you? I want to talk.'

Huddled in his furs, the recluse was crouched in the open dormer staring out at the bright interminable sky. Wolff was the same age as Franz but appeared even younger, for the idealist's generic tendency to moral insanity had left the generic innocent charm quite unaffected – or had even enhanced that youthful magnetism of altruism and singleness of purpose.

At long last Wolff's climbing rope was uncoiled again: he was running it like a rosary through his fingers. From far below in the courtyard the Englishman's voice floated up to him (in his British impudence hectoring German children! But his time would be short ...).

Reluctantly, and with a rapt visionary look in his blue wide-set eyes, Wolff turned away from the light. For the last hour or so Wolff had been absorbed in his dreams of killing Mitzi and naturally was loth to return to earth. But he must: for ... heavens, *what* was this good fellow saying? (It was indeed something new to be criticized by worthy little Franz.)

'Wolff, I do wish you'd listen! What I mean is, oughtn't you to ... well, in fact isn't it high time now we ... look, why don't you come out of here and put yourself at our head?' Wolff stared at him in silence. 'Then at least we could all die gloriously like Kern and Fischer,' Franz added a little lamely. 'But ever since Rathenau ...'

The great Rathenau – the king-pin (they had thought) without which the whole hated edifice must collapse – Weimar's only genius! Walther Rathenau was a Jew, and had just signed a treaty with the Bolsheviks; but that wasn't the reason they had killed him: that had meant nothing to Kern and Wolff and all their likeminded fellow killers, for these were no bourgeois predictable Nazis. No: with the complete open-mindedness only true fanatics can afford they had read all his books with deepening admiration, hung on his lips till they reached at last the mystic conviction that here at last was the one wholly worthy sacrifice for Germany's redemption which Fate must accept. It was not till they at last knew they almost *loved* Rathenau that they had heard that final categorical imperative to kill him.

With an effort Wolff forced himself to answer: 'Franz! Don't you trust me any more?'

'Yes of course, Wolff, but . . .'

'Do you suggest I am shirking my duty?'

'No of course not! But . . .'

'Then can't you trust *me* to judge when the time is ripe?'

Yet Wolff's words rang hollow even in his own ears; for what nonsense they both were talking! He would never come out, he knew that. Wolff couldn't say so to his only disciple, but there was nothing left now to put himself at the head of! All that was *kaput* – since Rathenau. Now that Kern and Fischer (the protagonists in that sacrificial killing) had died fighting in a deserted tower of Saaleck Castle the whole Noble Army of Martyrs was on the run. 'The king-pin, without which the whole hated edifice must collapse?' But it had not collapsed: instead, the nationwide horror and revulsion of feeling had infected even their own ranks and now Wolff had no friend or follower left in all Germany but silly Franz.

'Wolff, you must break out – not stick here rotting! A hundred heroes call you!'

But Wolff only smiled a rather superior smile. He had nobler things to think about now, did Franz but know it. Anyway, how could he wish to leave here even if he was able? In a whole year spent here he had grown into a unity with the very timbers of these attics (to express that unity he now knotted his rope to one). Look! Like the bones in

Ezekiel already these beams were covering themselves with flesh, with skin – and it was *his* flesh and skin they were growing (delicately Wolff stroked the wood with one affectionate finger, tracing beetle-paths in the thick dust). He would breathe into these dry beams soon, and then these attics would live . . .

Though perhaps the whole range of them was too large to vivify: enough his one particular corner, his own bundle of furs . . . Indeed, better still when he had something quite closed-in – say a box – to lie in. He must ask Franz for one . . .

'*Wolff ! ! !* – For the LAST TIME!'

Franz looked so funny in his ignorant, puny vexation that Wolff started to laugh. Little this booby knew what final exploit for Germany Wolff was planning: that made it funnier still! So funny, Wolff laughed and laughed . . . he'd a good mind to tell Franz all about it just to see how he took it.

Franz left finally almost in tears. But even before he was gone Wolff had forgotten him, back in his dreams of destroying those two.

After all, he would not do it while they slept: no, he'd kill them together – and so that they knew. One day they'd go for a walk in the forest; and he would follow them. He would stalk them, flitting from tree-bole to tree-bole. By the end, deep in the forest and far from all help, they'd suspect something was there and yet never see him. He would circle them round – like this noose he was knotting. Fear would seize them: they'd cling to each other, and – hidden – he'd mock them. Then at last he'd come out to them, slowly, and kill them, and bury them deep in the snow where no one would find them till spring.

Mitzi's hair . . . blood, running in its fine gold, running down till it crimsoned the snow.

Mitzi's blood, spouting – floods of it – lakes of it, warm and exquisite! – *Seas* of it . . .

Look! The sun himself dangled a rope of glutinous blood from his globe – emulous, wanting to join those seas like a waterspout.

On a fountain of blood like a bobbing ball on a waterjet Wolff's soaring soul was mounting to heaven – high into the interminable blue . . . but then something bit it! Bat-winged and black, something sunk teeth in it, tore it.

The abominable attack was so sudden – no time to recall Wolff's soul to his body, it was caught out there bare: spirit to spirit in hideous unholy communion. *Despair!* Down he was rocketing falling twisting . . . oh agony agony! Black-ness, everywhere black: noise . . . pain, everywhere pain – *unbelievable* pain!

'I ABHOR THINGS STRANGLED . . .'

From his temples the sweat spurted, and his teeth met through his tongue.

Chapter 20

Below in the sunny courtyard the children were wildly laughing.

Augustine had driven them hard: he had kept them working on that colossal snowman a whole hour without respite. But when it was done he had remodelled its nose with his fingers a minute or two, added his own hat and pipe and scarf – and lo, it was *him!* Then Augustine had been the first to knock the hat off with a snowball, and now they were all pelting it madly (not entirely without rancour, however, and the laughter was rather high-pitched).

Otto was in his hot little office again, where almost nothing was audible from outside; where the only sound was the slow, stuttering thump of his typewriter as he sat at it, sweating.

Under Otto's window Franz was alone – skiing, hurtling down the almost precipitous castle mound between the close-planted trees and missing them by hairs'-breadths. It was madly dangerous, but his spirit with its newly-broken navel-string was now in that kind of turmoil only deliberate danger can ease. Walther had been away since early, in a distant part of the forest where there was work to be planned. Adèle was down in the village.

Thus the whole house was empty except for Mitzi, still in her room.

There, everything was quiet. Even the voices of the children she couldn't hear; for Mitzi's window was on the far side of the house, over the river. But then, in the stillness, her acute ears caught an extraordinary sound: a human and yet inhuman sound, a sound she could only describe to herself as *worse* than groaning and it came from overhead – no doubt of that, it came from somewhere in those empty

299

floors above her. There was someone up there: someone who needed help.

Mitzi went to her door and called Franz: no one answered of course. Then she called to her father; but the house was utterly still and now she had that certainty one feels sometimes in an empty house that it *is* empty. There was nothing else for it: she would have to go up there herself.

Crossing the hall at a venture she luckily struck the door to the stairs first shot, and with her hand on the wall to guide her began to feel her way up them. Slowly passing Augustine's door (which stood open as usual) she spoke his name into it, quietly – though certain he wouldn't be there. Then she went on as fast as she dared, to the heavy door at the top.

Hinges and latch had been recently oiled: the door swung open without the creak she expected. This second floor, she remembered, consisted of 'rooms', like the first floor: finished, and even furnished – only not used since the war so that everything here was lifeless, and shrouded moreover in dirt and dust: her sensitive fingers abhorred it.

She stood still here a moment, and listened; but there wasn't a sound. The groaning had ceased. Something told her, though, it had come from much higher than this – that terrible groaning.

As best she could Mitzi felt her way to the next flight of stairs (which she dimly remembered were brick ones) and started to mount them. These stairs were uneven and narrow: she hadn't been up here for years and no longer could picture properly what lay in front of her.

So she reached the next storey, and it was from this point she reckoned that nearly the whole building lay open right up to the roof: a timber skeleton only – rooms never partitioned, floors that had mostly never been planked. But in that case, surely she ought to . . . wouldn't she hear the roof-clock clearly, not muffled like this?

She should have, of course! And this muffled sound convinced her she'd made a mistake. So long was it since she'd been up here she'd counted them wrong: there must be another flight yet before one got to the attics. This was a whole storey of rooms she'd somehow forgotten . . . and just then she tripped over a jug.

Again Mitzi started to mount; but confused now, for having once made a mistake she could no longer imagine at all what her eyes should be seeing. Progress was nightmarishly slow although the need for haste was so desperate for she had to trust wholly to feel, and feeling explored no more than one arm's-length ahead every time.

Then her ears told her she had got there at last! The slow, clear tick of the clock . . . a feeling of space all around her, the breath of a draught . . . and again Mitzi stood still and listened. Though clear and sharp it was still far above her, the *tick* . . . *tock* . . . of that clock. From far above, too, came the sizzle of water that trickled into the tank in the roof through a half-frozen ball-cock. And the squeaking of bats.

From here on, the stairs were a makeshift: little more than a ladder. She needed her hands to climb with. Then she came to what must be some sort of platform, for her shuffling foot felt an edge – with nothing below; and her fingers confirmed it.

The sound of the clock and the sizzling water were nearer now. But now there was something else too – a faint sound of movement . . . quite close to her . . . yes, the sound of . . . Someone *was* there!

Mitzi opened her lips, and licked them, and called: 'Who is it?'

No answer; and yet the faint sounds continued.

'Don't be afraid!' she called clearly: 'I'm coming to help you! Where are you?'

No answer; yet still that rustle, of somebody moving. A creak – very close to her now.

The fox had been here: Mitzi smelt him. She dropped to

301

a squatting position calling his name, and he thrust his wet nozzle into her hand with a stifled half-howl. The creature was in a queer state: she could feel it, and caught the infection. Suddenly she too was thoroughly frightened.

That faint sound *was* movement – within feet of her surely! Nearer than ticking clock or dribbling water, although so much fainter. Mitzi wanted to call out again 'Who is it?' but now her voice wouldn't come. *The stairs!* Could she find her way back to the stairs if . . . if she had to? But she mustn't think about stairs yet: she had come here to bring *help*.

'*Sub pennis ejus sperabis,*' Mitzi breathed: '*Non timebis a timore nocturno. A sagitta volante per diem, a negotio perambulante in tenebris, a ruina et dœmonio meridiano . . .*' As that gabbled childhood spell again the dark had always done long ago, now too the sacred words began to work in her instantly. 'Under His feathers thou shalt find hope,' she repeated (in German this time). 'Thou shalt not be afraid for any terror by night, nor for the arrow that flieth by day . . .' and now fear totally left her: and left of 'her', seemingly, nothing but a love that spread outwards like pulsing chimes from a bell.

But then in a puff of sound the distant happy voices of the children floated up to her followed by Franz's scandalized voice that admonished them. That recalled 'Mitzi': for the sound must come through a window, and this meant that now she knew where she was – somewhere close to the dormer! This platform must be the narrow planked catwalk that led to it.

On her hands and knees she crept there. The dormer was open! Something smelling of ammonia was close to her . . . She craned out and called to him:

'*Franz!* – Quick, *Franz!*'

'COMING!' he shouted.

The children – this was what had scandalized Franz –

302

were chasing Augustine out through the Great Gate pelting him with snow: so neither they nor Augustine heard Mitzi. But Franz heard, and flight after flight he bounded upstairs, burst into the attic, then up the ladder . . . and saw them – there, by the perilous window! His sister was crouched at the low sill. Close behind her was Wolff, looming over her. Close to Mitzi – as in life he had never been close.

For this was Wolff's body, hanged from the beam. The feet were clear of the gangway – out over nothing. The body was swinging a little still, and slowly turned from the tension it put on the creaking rope.

Franz's first thoughts were none for his hideous friend but all for his sister: how could he get her away unaware of what was hanging right over her? Any moment she'd stand up and bump into it.

Franz grabbed her, but Mitzi strongly resisted: 'No!' she cried. '*Idiot.* There's someone up here, I heard him! I called you . . .'

She only gave in when he told her, sharply, that Wolff was beyond help.

Chapter 21

Buckets ringing like bells on the cobbles: the early-morning carolling of boys with December voices still hoarse from the pillow, with unwashed eyes still sticky from sleep and new-donned breeches still cold to their bums! Jinglings from the saddle-room, whinnyings from the stalls: a smell of leather, metal-polish, saddle-soap, of linseed bubbling on the stove, of warm new dung being shaken, of sizzling urine . . . bobbing lanterns haloed in mist, rime on the great yard pump ghostly in the gloaming – and a huge forkful of hay travelling high like a giant's head on a pike . . .

Two weeks to Christmas – and the stable clock striking Six! For life began mighty early in Mellton stables under Mary's regime even if this wasn't a hunting morning (hunting had stopped even in this scrambling Mellton country because of the iron frost).

Polly in her nightgown hung out of the nightnursery window, listening to it all and trying to watch. Alas that it was all too far off to be smelt also; for in Polly's nose nothing after Gusting's smell equalled the smell of stables, not even a rabbit-hutch full of her own particular rabbits. As she leaned from the window the December air was raw and her teeth started to chatter, but Polly paid no attention: it was better to be cold than bored. Polly's purgatory was that every single day she woke soon after five; and unless Augustine was in the house, at five no one seemed to welcome a visit. But except Christmas and birthdays Polly wasn't allowed to dress till years later – not till Minta came at the dreary hour of seven. If only they'd let Polly take her rabbits to bed with her or even a kitten she'd have stopped on in bed, perhaps; but not just with teddies, for teddies smelt only of shop, she'd no use for teddies . . . Oh lucky stable-boys (thought Polly) allowed to get up at half-past five every day of their lives!

Polly had told Willie-Winkie once how lucky he was; but he only made noises for answer, and the noises were rude. All the same, Wee-Willie-Winkie was her favourite (fourteen, yet almost Polly's own size). Willie smelt of gin and tobacco as well as of horses and 'boy': he was aimed for a jockey, he told her. Willie was clever too: she had seen him bridle a hunter of seventeen hands; he tempted its head down with an apple laid on the ground, and then when the horse's head went up again wee Willie went up with it.

Now the stable clock struck half-past, and Polly could stand it no longer. She would creep downstairs to see what the housemaids were up-to, enjoying their brief hour of sovereignty now while the house was exclusively theirs. As she opened the door Jimmy scuttled past down the passage, his arms full of boots and his mouth full of jokes. Then she found Gertie brushing the stairs: Polly stepped over her carefully, but Gertie tickled her legs with the long-haired banister-brush as she passed.

When Polly got to the drawing-room, Rosamond was dusting the Cupiddy ceiling with a bunch of cock's-feathers on the end of a twelve-foot cane. Polly hoped to be chased with it; but Rozzie was 'busy' ... The dining-room, then? But Violet was sweeping the dining-room and Violet was always a cross-patch, so Polly tiptoed away unseen. However, in the morning-room she found Mabel, lighting the fire and singing. Mabel had polished the grate till it shone, and Polly by now was shivering (she'd forgotten her slippers and dressing-gown) so sat herself down on the fender to admire it, watching the flames as they grew and warming her toes. She and Mabel were friends: Mabel let her stay on (but, 'Now then, Polly Flinders!' said Mabel, and stopped her playing with coal).

When Mabel departed at last she forgot her black-lead, and Polly – deeply admiring the shine on the grate – thought

suddenly how very much nicer the rocking-horse up in the
nursery would look . . . so annexed the saucer of wet black-
lead and the brushes and (remembering Gertie to pass)
secreted them under her nightgown. But they were awkward
to carry that way, and she dropped them twice before she
successfully got to her room. Just as she got there moreover
the clock chimed the three-quarters: Minta might come
any minute, so prudently Polly hid her spoils in her bed and
climbed in on top of them. Thus at Seven, when Minta did
come at last, against all precedent Polly was fast asleep.

At Eight, kitchen-breakfast was over and Lily – you remember young Lily – was out in the scullery washing it up.
For Lily this was a fine coign of vantage for saucing the
postman (a light-weight boxer of note); for at Eight the post
was delivered. The mail for the Chase arrived grandly, in
their own private leather dispatch-box with the Wadamy
crest: Mr Wantage it was who unlocked it and gave out the
post, and as usual he made this a solemn occasion. The
Master's and Mistress's letters he would sort and set out
with his own hands by their places at breakfast, with the
'halfpennies' underneath the real letters (today the Mistress
had one with a foreign stamp: he would put this on top).
Any letters for Kitchens he gave to Cook to distribute.
Today there was one for Mrs Winter: that went to the
Room. There was a letter today too for Nanny Halloran;
and this he entrusted to Minta.

Minta took Nanny's letter up with the Nursery breakfast,
and as soon as Nanny had drawn an elegant 'P' in golden
syrup on Polly's plateful of Force she opened it. The letter
came from Minta's forerunner, Brenda (an orphan, Brenda
was devoted to Mrs Halloran and still looked to her for
advice when she needed it).

Brenda had gone temporary now to Lady Sylvia to help
'Mumselle' with little Lady Jane; and the letter was dated
from a village near Torquay, for in spite of the season Her
Ladyship had packed Janey off into lodgings – as far from

Eaton Square as she could. Now, Brenda wanted advice about giving her notice. 'Tchk, Tchk,' said Nanny, pursing her lips as she read it and absently cooling her tea in the saucer: for Janey (it said) the very first day there had locked Mumselle in her bedroom and gone off ferreting with some village boys. She enjoyed this so much that next day she and the boy at the lodgings decided to go on their own; but, not having a ferret, took the cat with them instead. However, it seems that when the boy pushed his cat down a rabbit-hole the cat had objected. It tried to get out, and so Janey sat on the hole. Thus began a battle of wills; for the half-suffocated cat was desperate and yet under the boy's eyes Janey just *couldn't* give in. It bit and it scratched, but she sat and she sat. In the end, she 'come home with her knicks all blood and fair tore to rovings' – and also minus the cat.

'Tchk, Tchk,' said Nanny, passing the letter to Minta. Then she added: 'Of such is the Kingdom of Heaven!' and sighed at the prospect. 'When that one was old enough,' Nanny went on, '*I*'d send her into the Navy – if she wasn't a girl.'

'If she was a boy, you mean,' put in Polly.

'That's what I said: "*if* she wasn't a girl".'

'But she might be a dog,' said Polly, her eyes shining with logic: 'Not everyone's boys or girls.'

'Eat up your Force, dear,' said Nanny.

Mrs Winter's letter was propped beside Mrs Winter's breakfast egg in its green crochet-work cosy, and the post-mark was 'Flemton' ('Proper mad-house!' Mrs Winter muttered: 'Ought to be certified the whole lot of them.'). The letter of course came from Nellie's mother-in-law; and it was certainly short. The old lady was well but wanted a catapult and hoped dear Maggie would send one.

Chapter 22

When Gwilym's mother first had that seizure at the mortuary she was taken to the Penrys Cross infirmary, but when she was better they had wanted to send her home. Where should they send her however? She was a bit 'funny' after her illness: she certainly mustn't live alone any more. Could she come to her son at the 'Hermitage'?

She'd have to sleep in the kitchen of course, and if she was bedridden . . . but still, if they had too . . . Nellie herself was prepared. All this ought to have worried Gwilym, no doubt; but nowadays Gwilym seemed to have lost the power of worrying just as he had lost the power of using his legs. It certainly worried Nellie! But what could be done? Maggie was adamant the old lady mustn't come to the 'Hermitage'; but Nellie couldn't even get away to go down there and see to things (nor could she have borne to go there). So, in the end, Maggie it was who went.

This had been Mrs Winter's second visit to Penrys Cross: she had gone to the funeral (sole family mourner thereat), and after had called on the coroner to learn all she could. So now she went straight to the one person she knew at the Cross. Luckily this was one of Dr Brinley's 'good' days: when she showed him how hopeless it was to think of Gwilym and Nellie he promised to fix it. 'A bit funny, you say? Then it means finding suitable lodgings.' He would find the old lady somewhere in Flemton (a place where no one thought anyone *inside* the community odd).

On the orders of Dr Brinley, therefore, Alderman Teller, who combined a moribund sweets-and-drapery business with marketing prawns, agreed to let her a room; and there Mrs Winter installed her. After that, Mrs Winter had to go home.

The room was lofty, and panelled, and musty, with an elegant marble mantelpiece (gone a trifle rhomboidal); and for company, plenty of mice. The mice had shocked Mrs Winter; but the old lady took to them and started a war at once to protect them from cats. For at Alderman Teller's (all former High Stewards had this courtesy-title of 'Alderman') the cats of the town roamed in and out as they liked. They seemed to find Teller mice extra-desirable – because (she supposed) of some special bouquet these acquired from their diet of prawns; and soon it was war to the knife between her and the cats. Thus the mice were in clover at Alderman Teller's: what with unlimited prawns, and with snippets of velvet to upholster their holes, and now the old lady's protection; and she too was in clover – what with the mice, and the Tellers couldn't be kinder, and even in bed she could hear the roar of the sea which she loved and the far-off occasional *ping* of the cash-till as sixpence went in.

True, she couldn't see out much unless the window was open; for the glass was frosted with salt and scratched and pitted by a century's driving sand. Some days it had to be tight shut, for at times she felt she was floating and might float out of it. But the days she felt stable enough to risk it she kept the window wide open – to harass the cats, whose favourite way into the house was a broken pane in the window directly below hers. At first she was able to check them by waving her arms out of the window and cursing; but in time they got used to that, and ignored her and still went in and out as they chose. However, someone had left a salmon-rod in her wardrobe. So she plugged up the hole in the glass downstairs, and went back to her room. There she waited till a queue of frustrated cats had formed on the sill underneath her, then leaned right out and swept them all off with the rod (two tabbies, three tortoiseshells, one semi-demi-Persian, and the old red tom with one ear).

After that, as the cats grew warier she too grew warier: she developed her sport to an art. As for Flemton, Dr Brinley was right: at the spectacle of an old lady fishing for cats all day with a salmon-rod from a second-floor window not even the children looked twice.

To get back to the railhead at Penrys Cross Mrs Winter had travelled by carrier's-cart on top of the Alderman's prawns; and His Worship the driver was Tom, the present High Steward himself. From a lifetime of lifting weights, Tom's bull-neck and shoulders were prodigious: he was solider far than his horse. His manner was always laconic: he drank like a fish: his schooling had been kept to a minimum: but Tom was no fool. Tom's brother George owned the 'Wreckers', Hugh fattened store cattle on the Marsh and together these three were the power in Flemton, with the 'Worshipful Court' and all that in their pockets (there was a fourth brother too but he didn't count. Aneurin was a coasting-smack skipper whose ships always sank and who now had set up as a dentist – or so his brass plate described him, but no one had ventured inside).

Jogging along the lanes Tom had given Mrs Winter some news which surprised her: Newton was going to be sold! Oh yes, Tom was sure of it: the young squire had decided to sell (Tom glanced at her sideways) and any day now the bills would be out for the auction ... though some said the place had been sold already – a war-profiteer it was who had bought it, one who Lloyd George had turned into a Lord. After all, why wouldn't he sell? Nice welcome he'd get if he ever came back here (Tom glanced at her sideways again). 'But some say it's entailed and mustn't be sold.'

When Tom wanted to find something out he never asked questions: he formed working hypotheses, announced them like this and observed the effect. But although Mrs Winter hadn't known this and was taken by surprise, Tom's 'method' had at last met its match in her habitual discretion: she listened politely but gave him no shadow of lead. Tom lashed at his willowy dawdling horse and lapsed into silence. The point was that just now Tom was thinking

310

of buying a bus and this made it vital to know whether Newton was going to be sold, for when an estate like Newton comes under the hammer there are pickings which mustn't be missed. If Newton was up for sale, then the brothers would need all the cash they could raise and the bus would be better postponed.

'After all,' he resumed, 'now Young Squire has turned Roman Catholic and settled in Rome . . . bought a very fine house there they tell me, next door to the Pope . . .'

'P.S.,' wrote old Mrs Hopkins, 'and better send pellets.'
'Proper mad-house indeed!' thought Mrs Winter again as she buttered her toast.

Chapter 23

At Nine, Mellton's day really began: for at Nine the Master came down.

Gilbert's post was a large one, but today he gobbled his breakfast and left his letters to read in the train. He had to get up to Town in a hurry. The election was over last Thursday, but no one knew yet who had won: the cards had been dealt but the hands had still to be played.

Baldwin had gone to the country on 'Protection': Liberals and Labour alike had stuck to Free Trade. Clearly the country rejected Protection since less than five and a half millions had voted for it while more than eight and a half voted against; but there all clarity ended, for the 'defeated' Protectionists were still the largest party in a House where no single party had a majority (and where Labour had now somehow got thirty-three more seats than the Liberals had). Suppose, then, that when Parliament met in January the Tories were forced to resign, who ought to succeed them? The party second in strength, the Socialists? But if eight and a half million votes had rejected Protection, *nine* and a half must be reckoned as anti-Socialist votes! Only the Liberals opposed *both* policies the country rejected: thus in a true sense only the Liberals represented the popular will. The Liberals themselves then? No doubt some Tories would have supported them to keep the Socialists out: all the same, since the popular will had made them the smallest group in the House . . .

(Mary's post was more moderate in size than Gilbert's, but the German stamp was on top and she wanted to read Augustine's letter at leisure: she would wait till Gilbert was gone.)

. . . The practical answer of course was simple in principle. Since a Liberal administration was really out of the question and the very word 'Coalition' these days was something which stank, either the Protectionists must stay in office but at the price of forswearing Protection, or the Socialists must forswear Socialism and step into their shoes. In either case Centrist policies would have to be carried out – by n'importe qui, provided it wasn't the Centrists. So the Liberals though the smallest were today the most powerful group in the House, having absolute power to decide who should govern (provided that wasn't themselves), and how they should govern, and for how long ...

(Without opening the envelope Mary pinched it with her fingers: it was certainly bulky.)

... Well then, which should it be? Should the two elder parties combine to 'save the country from Socialism', or shall we let Labour in on Liberal leading-strings? 'In such a dilemma,' said Gilbert, 'Ethics must guide us not Interest. I abhor Socialism – at the very thought of a Socialist government my being revolts. But I see this as just a plain question of right and wrong, Mary: whatever the pretext it would be morally indefensible to cheat Labour of the prize their electoral victories have earned them.'

For a moment Mary looked puzzled. After all, whichever party was forced into office on such miserable conditions must cut a pretty poor figure there: at the next election *they*'d be bound to be out for the count ... In other words, which did the Liberals hate most? ' "Electoral victories"?' she queried: 'Oh, I see what you mean: put them in because *they*'re the ones who've been pinching rightful Liberal votes!'

But Gilbert was gone. Now his mind was made up he was off to London post-haste.

... For several days the police were in and out all the time [Augustine had written], comic little chaps in green looking more like gamekeepers – no helmets even! Something about a body being found somewhere Irma told me (she is one of the children). Irma said he hanged himself in the attic but she must have made that up the little ghoul for how could a stranger have got in and got up there?

(Mary wondered if Mr Asquith would listen to Gilbert: he'd better, this was jolly ingenious!)

. . . But if it had just been a tramp died of cold in a barn or something why the police buzzing around all that much? Then a very decent-looking old boy turned up who Trudi said was the father [Trudi is the eldest *he had written in afterwards*] and this is interesting, he had a young chap with him I more or less knew, he changed some money for me at that hotel I spent my first night in Munich at! It must have been the funeral they came for but it was all kept mighty quiet . . .

(Jeremy had once defined 'political instinct' as 'letting one's transparent nobility of character compel one to some highly profitable course of action'.)

. . . and Walther and Franz both said nothing to me with such emphasis it obviously wouldn't have done to ask questions.

(Jeremy's an absolute pig!)

The kids are a lot of fun now though they were a bit sticky at first, I suppose my being foreign and I don't think any-how they are used to a grown-up spending most of his time with them, in *their* world, in fact treating them as fellow-humans with equal rights . . .

With the tail of her eye, through the window Mary caught sight of a groom walking her horse up and down (Heavens, she was supposed to be riding up to the Hermitage this morning!). She had better stop now and get changed. She would take the letter upstairs and read some more while she dressed. But she mustn't be long or the horse would get cold (and Nellie might want to go out).

The other day, Trudl and Irma . . .

Chapter 24

Nellie had been at the Hermitage for more than a month by now, and somehow – with Mrs Wadamy's help, and Maggie's – a whole new rhythm of living for Nellie had bit by bit grown up.

Milk had seemed an insuperable difficulty at first, since there were no farms in the chase. But Mrs Wadamy had evolved an ingenious plan whereby a farm-lad on his way home from work every evening left it in a hollow oak only half a mile from the house: from there Nellie lantern in hand fetched it as early as she could fit in the time (though sometimes this wasn't till near midnight, after the baby's last feed). As for the water, each bucket took seven minutes to draw (it was lucky that Nellie for all her book-learning was strong as a horse). There was one advantage in well-water, though: there were no pipes to freeze, now that even in England it had turned really cold (especially up here in the chase).

In short, things weren't easy for Nellie. Some people find even a baby a whole-time job, while Nellie had the constant care of an invalid as well and on top of all that the shopping. In the past, Nellie's housekeeping had been of the town kind which includes constant poppings round the corner for little things forgotten, the matching of rival shop-windows for bargains – a penny off this or that at So-and-so's this week. But Mellton village had only one shop-of-all-sorts, and here the prices were uniformly higher than town prices: all the pennies were on, not off.

Mrs Wadamy rode her horse over three times a week to see all was well and generally she brought something in her saddle-bags, but these little presents were 'extras' – calves'-foot jelly and the like: the shopping still had to be done.

Maggie had lent her sister her bicycle, and this was an enormous help; but even then Mellton, nearly five miles away, was a major expedition to be made as seldom as possible and loads were heavy in consequence. Wheeling the old machine all hung round with stores (and with its tattered dress-guard of lacing that kept catching in the spokes till Nellie took it right off) it was a long pull up the hill to the chase gates; and Nellie was always in a hurry to get home, for she was acutely anxious every minute she had to leave Gwilym in his bed alone. Already the disease had begun to attack his spine and he had bad bouts of pain.

Whenever Nellie went out, Gwilym insisted on having the baby's Moses-basket put in his shed with him where he could look after the little fellow and talk to him. Gwilym couldn't get out of bed unaided so there was nothing he could do about it if the baby did cry: this distressed Gwilym, so Nellie made plentiful use of a soothing-syrup if ever she had to go out. Thus, mostly they enjoyed undisturbed their long conversations together, the father and his sleeping poppied son: conversations adapted to whatever age the son was supposed to have reached that morning.

'That's it, Syl: hold on to my finger . . .' (for today he was teaching Syl to walk). Another day he would be sitting by a four-year-old's cot at bedtime, telling him Bible-stories – the infant Jesus, and Joseph with his many-coloured coat. 'Well, what did they teach you today, Syl?' – for now a bright-cheeked boy had just run in from school. His father heard him his three-times, and (a few years later) helped with his prep . . . while the baby lay all the while in his basket and bubbled.

'Syl! What's that one called, Syl?' For sometimes they went for long walks in the woods together, that father and his growing son, and Gwilym taught him the names of the birds and Syl showed him the nests he had found. Then they talked about God, who created all those beautiful birds and painted their eggs; and the baby still bubbled.

When Sylvanus entered his teens his Dad insisted on

serious practical talks about all possible sorts of jobs, though knowing full well the one thing Sylvanus wanted was to be a preacher like Dad (but every call to the ministry has to be tested like this). Whereon the baby woke up and crowed, and opened a mouth toothless as a tortoise's in a wide smile, dribbling and showing his gums.

But always, whatever the boy's age at that moment, Gwilym talked to him endlessly about that little angel who sat at a window in Heaven and watched him whatever he did, the guardian-sister whose love he must learn to deserve: 'Syl, if ever you're tempted to think about girls with . . . in a way you know to be wrong, just say to yourself five words: "My angel-sister was one".'

All this made Gwilym blissfully happy, and he often thought how lucky he was. Nowadays it never struck him as in any way sad that the boy's whole upbringing had to be condensed like this into a few months at most.

On fine afternoons – at least on the days when Gwilym's back was a little less bad – Nellie used to take both of them out for their 'walk' together. She half-lifted Gwilym from his bed into an old wicker Bath chair Mary had lent them, and tucked him up well with blankets topped with an old horse-rug from the Mellton stables. Then she set the baby on Gwilym's knee, and trundled them a few hundred yards over the frozen turf to the edge of the escarpment where the whole deep river-valley lay spread beneath them, and there they rested awhile. It was a perilous journey, for the topheavy Bath chair was not intended for such rough going; but the view at the end was well worth it at least so far as Gwilym himself was concerned. Far beneath them the river curled: in the distance the downs rolled and rolled: on clear days you could even see Salisbury spire. For now he was ill Gwilym found an infinite pleasure in this beautiful terrestrial world: no longer was it the arid 'vale of woe' he had once decried from the pulpit, and he took to writing poems.

An idyllic life while it lasted: till Gwilym's accident, that later was to leave such a load of guilt on the wife and child, occurred.

Chapter 25

The horse Mary was riding was an old cob steady as a billiard table (and much the same shape), for Mary was now two months gone with child and her doctor did not really approve of her riding at all. But surely sitting on Cherry hardly counted as 'riding'! Cherry was more stable than the hills; for according to the psalmist the hills can skip -- but certainly Cherry couldn't. The doctor moreover had prescribed a daily walk, so for part of the way Mary got off and led him. This gave her an opportunity too for another mouthful or so of Augustine's letter:

... I must say, they have got plenty of guts...

(Who? Oh, those everlasting Kessen children of course!)

... especially the twins. You remember that horse-sleigh I told you we went out in that day? Yesterday the horse bolted with it (empty) and little Heinz fell down right in its light. He just lay still, though, and one of the runners went right over him and I thought he would be cut in half but he was sunk right into the snow and the empty sleigh was so light it went right over him without the runner even touching him. What saved him of course was because he had had the nerve to lie still. But the others just hooted with laughter and he was laughing too when he got up, while the horse charged on down the hill like a dog with a tin can on its tail – you ought to have seen it! The sleigh swinging from side to side and banging on the trees till it smashed to matchwood. End of sleigh! Trudi (she's the eldest) laughed and laughed till it gave her a pain.

Tomorrow though I'm off to Munich. Frankly, I have been here exactly three weeks now . . .

Mary turned back to look at the date: yes, this *had* been a long time in the post . . .

exactly three weeks now and it is high time I saw something of the real, new Germany for a change. Lucky I don't just judge present-day Germany by this place or I'd come home knowing no more than I set out. Actually of course all this is right out of the picture, the whole set-up here is just a left-over from the past. They are even R.C.'s still, here! Judging just by here you would hardly guess the new Germany with its broad-minded peace-loving spirit and its advanced ideas and its Art existed even, but I met an awfully nice chap that day we went for the sleigh-ride and he has invited me . . .

Even that wasn't nearly the end, but Mary pushed the sheets back in her pocket and remounted. An odd sort of letter from someone of twenty-three and intelligent! That last paragraph – *really*! Indeed the whole tone of the letter was childish. Like a kind of regression. What an unexpected effect for travel to have on Augustine! It worried her rather. She knew he had taken his guns, but no mention of shooting . . . in fact, Augustine seemed to like messing around with small children better than being with his natural companion Franz – let alone with Walther or Otto. Trust Augustine to be adored by the children wherever he went – but not, *not* to waste his whole time with them this way: he didn't do that even with Polly, and she was his niece . . .

Trudi the 'eldest', he had said? Trudi hadn't been born . . . Funny none of his letters had mentioned once that eldest girl Mary remembered. Little Mitzi'd be now . . . what, seventeen? 'I suppose,' thought Mary, 'she must be away at school.'

In the far distance a few small patches of snow on the hilltops seemed to float in the haze, each with its own dollop of white mist like wool clinging close to it. Otherwise the day was a grey sort of day: dead still, with a faint haze the sun just showed through like a small, watery-yellow pea. The light was indefinite: a dim, ominous, over-all glare that was shadowless.

Slowly Cherry plodded his uphill way on a long rein, gently rocking under Mary like a ship. Fleetingly for no reason she found herself recalling her father who had died when she was a child . . . tweeds like nutmeg-graters for bare skin to sit on, and his long moustache that smelt of tobacco and tickled . . . But suddenly Cherry blew a deep organ-note through his nostrils – tremolo, so that with its vasty vibration Mary's legs quivered like jellies and the whole landscape shook.

When it settled again, lo – there were the chase gates in sight now, and Nellie running towards her half tripping over the ruts in the turf that the workmen's cart had made weeks ago. Nellie was panting and her eyes starting out of her head: would Mrs Wadamy *please* go at once for the doctor? Something about Gwilym being worse, and a frightful accident yesterday: it was all Nellie's own fault, she would never forgive herself . . .

In later years Gwilym's 'accident' came to loom so large we had better be quite clear what did happen, that frosty day on the downs.

Yesterday the baby had had a stomach-upset and so couldn't go out. But the weather yesterday had been wonderful, so rather than do Gwilym out of his walk Nellie had wheeled him to his usual viewpoint and left him there by himself while she dashed back to see to the baby. She meant just to give Sylvanus his peppermint-water and come straight back to Gwilym again; but the little wretch wouldn't stop crying, so she stopped with him.

Gwilym must have dozed off, for the heavy horse-blanket

321

slipped from his knees and he woke feeling cold. In trying to retrieve it he overbalanced the chair and was spilled out on the ground. There he lay, too weak to get up by himself. Nor could he even shout: his cauterized throat could only *whisper* 'Help!' He was blue with cold and nearly unconscious when at last the terrified Nellie got back to him. Strong as Nellie was she had a terrible struggle to get him back up into his chair off the ground.

That evening Gwilym's temperature had soared to new heights, but Nellie dared not leave him to go for the doctor. How could she? She *had* to wait for the morning and hope that Mary would come.

When Mary did bring the doctor at last he looked grave: a touch of pneumonia, he said. The patient might live through the attack but it would certainly leave him weaker.

In Nellie's mind as the years passed it became more and more that accident which had tipped the scales: without it the sick man might have – *must* have recovered. Little Sylvanus was a murderer before he was born, twice a murderer ere he was weaned.

Chapter 26

Far more lay behind Augustine's disgruntlement with
Lorienburg and his exeat to Munich than he chose to tell
Mary. At the time of writing he had been in love for a whole
three weeks yet his progress was nil. True, Mitzi appeared
at meals now, but she seemed more distraite than ever
and vanished as soon as she could. The only person she
seemed to respond to ever was Otto. In short, Augustine
could sometimes feast his eyes on her now (and he certainly
made the most of it); but he never again got a chance like
the one he had missed in the chapel of talking to her, he
never once saw her alone.

Somehow it never entered Augustine's head to offer to
take Mitzi for a walk. But once, greatly daring, he did
summon up courage to offer to read to her: 'Schiller or
something.' Mitzi thanked him warmly, which made his
heart hop like a bird: but instead of taking him to the empty
library she led the way to the drawing-room, and thus the
reading took place with her mother there and her two
younger sisters as well (for the children shadowed Augustine
now like dogs everywhere, and they wanted to make him
come out and play in the snow). The two little girls were
palpably bored by Schiller and longing to carry him off for
themselves: Adèle jumped like the toothache at every mis-
pronounced word: Mitzi showed no reaction whatever till
he paused, when she thanked him again and slipped away
to her room. The reading was *not* a success, and was never
repeated. How he cursed the German language! For in
English he knew he read rather well.

To forget his woes he did indeed make use of the children:
he spent whole days with them, for entering into their minds
at least took him out of his own. But this 'regression' of

Augustine's was not always wholly successful either: far too often he would lead the twins into some shocking piece of mischief and then at the crucial moment his mind would revert to Mitzi, so that by sheer inattention to business he landed them all in a mess. Walther couldn't understand Augustine's behaviour at all: he seemed 'totally lacking in seriousness: quite irresponsible!' As for Franz, over-buoyant now with the weight of the world off his shoulders at last, he was longing to be off to the mountains skiing: with his guest for excuse he might have wangled it if only Augustine had shown the least interest ... Franz found him rather a bore.

The sensible part of Augustine knew well that the sensible course was to go away, at least for a while. His hosts would have welcomed it: indeed at the time of Wolff's funeral (it had been touch-and-go, that police inquisition: it had called for endless pulling of strings) they had almost openly wished he would take himself elsewhere at least till that business was over. Yet it wasn't till a fortnight after the funeral that Augustine remembered Dr Reinhold's offer to show him Munich: a proposal which his hosts, when he finally broached it, effusively approved. So at last he wrote to Dr Reinhold, and at last his going was fixed.

Dr Reinhold had a large flat on the Odeonsplatz close to the Theatinerkirche (he would have had a wonderful view of the end of the Putsch if he hadn't left Munich so soon). A bachelor and a bit of a sybarite, with a married couple for butler and cook, his place was impeccably run; yet he seemed to be hardly ever in it himself, so Augustine found. Dr Reinhold went to his office at nine, and thereafter his guest was left to his own devices: 'showing him Munich', it seemed, consisted chiefly in planning sight-seeing tours which the guest carried out on his own.

Moreover, departure to Munich did nothing (Augustine discovered) to empty his mind of Mitzi. Indeed she kept cropping up in the unlikeliest contexts: in the Dom, for instance, while they were showing him the Devil's Footmark he spun round on his heel for he felt her right at his shoulder. Certainly 'selling Newton' was an idea which never entered his head: he was far too busy just now envisaging Mitzi as its mistress and major adornment for that: Mitzi under his guidance learning to find her way all over the house: Mitzi learning the feel of the furniture with his fingers covering hers: Mitzi learning the changing seasonal smells of an English garden, the songs of the birds, the voices of all his friends . . . he would get that old harp in the small south drawing-room restrung for her (blind harpists are always the best).

Augustine was sent, of course, round the corner to the Königsplatz where the galleries were. There were wonderful things in them: acres of pictures, famous pieces of Greek and Egyptian sculpture already familiar in photographs; but the galleries themselves were vast, altogether dwarfing their contents. Thirty or forty minutes of looking at masterpieces Augustine intensely enjoyed; but, because of this very intensity, he couldn't stand longer. At the end of that time he felt a pain in the back of his head: he suddenly felt what a waste of time *everything* was without Mitzi: he suddenly felt a passionate longing for beer.

Hurrying out of the Glyptothek thus, with his eyes unfocused to give them a rest, he barked his nose on the door.

Chapter 27

The churches here Augustine was sent to admire, however, really shocked him; for they all, excepting the Dom (late Gothic) were baroque or even rococo. This confirmed what he had already felt at Lorienburg: people who found such things beautiful must be essentially unserious people: their religion (and so, Mitzi's) *must* be only skin-deep: their culture, a froth and a sham. Was it conceivable that the sensitively cultured Dr Reinhold with real Art in his blood sincerely admired these sugared monstrosities, or had he his tongue in his cheek? The 'Asam-Kirche', for instance: where here was the classic austerity (hall-mark of all true art), the truth to nature? The bareness of line, the restraint?

'Baroque isn't even non-Art, it's anti-Art,' he tried to argue with Reinhold, but failed. 'This must just be a blind spot in old Reinhold,' he was forced to decide (to Reinhold of course the blindness was all in Augustine).

This argument happened one Sunday morning. Outside in the Square where a few weeks back the police had fired on the Nazis a band had struck up with selections from Strauss, and the two men moved to the window to look. In the sharp winter air the notes of the band swirled up to the sky while coveys of pigeons swirled down to the ground, and Reinhold pointed out the kerchiefed little old women assembled to feed them: the famous 'Taubernmutterl', the 'little dove-mothers' of Munich. The small dog with the plaid waistcoat was back there again – brisk, intent, and important: his elderly dandyfied master followed behind on a lead. The whole scene touched a chord in Augustine and he sighed, windily, wishing that Mitzi was here . . .

But Sunday was Reinhold's holiday, so presently he suggested a visit to Schwabing together: ' "The Quartier-Latin of Munich" they call it,' he explained (with an almost invisible moue). 'Anyway, it's the home of all the Munich poets and painters who count.' Augustine pricked up his ears: this surely was what he had come for even more than the galleries. 'Genius!' Reinhold continued, observing his mood: 'Genius in studios, genius in garrets, genius in basements – back-bedrooms – mezzanines: Nordic and Latin, Gentile and Jew: genius spilling out on the pavements . . .' He sighed. 'So we'd better take plenty of money to pay for their beer.'

' "Schwabing" you call it? Is it far?'

'Right here on our doorstep,' said Reinhold. 'In fact, here we are now,' he presently added as they passed by the Siegestor. 'We're arrived at our "Chelsea".'

'Odd,' thought Augustine. 'I've walked round here dozens of times without guessing: it's more like the Cromwell Road.'

For a while they moved in a great half-circle sampling bars and cafés ('For sheer joie de vivre', thought Augustine, 'they're much like South Kensington private hotels.') on the look-out for celebrities. But in all those places they found only one such, and this was that selfsame emancipated young woman from the party at Röttningen. At the sight of her Augustine flushed blackly and stopped in his tracks on the threshhold; but Dr Reinhold bowed with empressement, whereon she waved a long cigarette-holder and smiled invitingly. Augustine tugged at Reinhold's sleeve and said 'No!'

'No? Too small game for you?' Augustine left it at that and they beat a retreat. 'Come, these places are no good: I'll take you to Katty's.' So they turned down the Türkenstrasse, and halted outside a little boîte where the sign was a red bulldog baring his teeth. ' "Simplicissimus",' said Reinhold. 'With luck we'll find old T. T. Heine here, and Gulbransson.'

'Who are they?' asked Augustine.

'Look!' said Reinhold, nettled: 'What living artists *have* you heard of?' He paused on the doorstep.

'John,' said Augustine. He hesitated for more names, then added: 'Sargent's no good of course; but there's Eric Kennington, I've bought one of his.'

'But apart from Englishmen?'

'*Foreign* artists? Mind you, I genuinely liked some of the settings for the Russian Ballet,' he admitted.

'Derain and Picasso you mean? "The Three-Cornered Hat"? But have you seen any of their real work –or Matisse? Van Gogh? Cézanne?'

'N-n-no . . . but do I really want to? Isn't that lot all a bit . . .?'

Reinhold groaned. Then he tilted his chin, and called – apparently into the sky: 'Come down, Jacinto, and have a drink with us horrible Philistines! Help us to wash out our sins.'

Augustine looked up. At the top of a tall lamp-post, squatting cross-legged on the very lamp itself and in spite of the weather dressed only in vest and running-shorts, was a dark young man who looked like a prentice yogi. But the yogi up there only shook his head slightly, finger to lips. From the first-floor window beside him came the rhythmic sound of a burgher's Sunday siesta.

'Jacinto's a young Brazilian sculptor of distinct promise,' said Reinhold. 'He's also a first-class professional runner: he lives for his art but runs for his living.' He regarded the silent, immovable figure up there with interest: 'Moreover he would now appear to be cultivating a connoisseurship in snoring.'

'In *snoring*?'

'Precisely. Doubtless he sprints from superlative snorer to snorer all over the city – I bet he's just finished his rounds. – Come down!' he shouted again. 'You'll catch cold!' The solo ended abruptly and the agile young man slid to the ground and joined them. 'Tell me,' asked Reinhold anxiously. 'Is it possible to translate the essential rhythms of a snore like that into marble?'

For answer Jacinto made a rapid and complex series of movements in the air with his hands, then dropped them to his sides helplessly.

'I was afraid not,' said Reinhold sadly, and the trio moved inside.

Chapter 28

Reinhold ushered them into a tiny room too dark to see anything at first, and where the only sounds were the unmistakable sounds of drinking. When their eyes got used to it the two famous cartoonists (Gulbransson and Heine) turned out to be absent, but there were other celebrities here: 'That,' said Reinhold behind his hand, 'is no less than Ringelnatz! – Servus, Joachim!' he called. 'Join us, my treasure!' The sailor-poet was drunk already and joined them with difficulty. 'And that,' said Reinhold indicating the Jew in the corner, 'is Tucholsky himself.'

'Don't catch his eye!' hissed Jacinto through chattering teeth. 'I dislike him.'

'So? All the same, Kurt's a brilliant writer and our young English friend here . . .'

'If Tucholsky joins you I go!' said Jacinto with such finality that Reinhold gave in, ordering beer for only the four of them. ' "Our young English friend here!" ' quoted Jacinto and examined Augustine owlishly. 'Can you run?' he asked with a note of anxiety.

'Yes . . . no, I mean not like you can.'

'What a relief! Then I needn't challenge you when I'd far rather get drunk.'

Meanwhile Ringelnatz was clumsily trying to cover his mug with a large slab of cheese: '. . . keep out the goblins,' he muttered. But the cheese fell into the beer and then when he tried to drink got in the way of his nose, so he burst into tears.

'If you don't run what *do* you do?' Jacinto pursued. 'I mean, for a living?'

'He snores,' said Reinhold wickedly. 'London theatrical

managers employ him to snore off-stage when it's needed in plays.'

But Jacinto was not to be deceived: 'Impossible! He hasn't the nose.'

'Nose?' broke in Ringelnatz angrily. 'Who's talking of noses?' *His* nose was a large one and he never liked noses discussed; but especially now when his own was dripping with beer.

Presently Ringelnatz wandered out to the back, and when he returned he had borrowed Katty Kobus's own dressing-gown to wrap round the shivering Jacinto. But Jacinto was oblivious of the kindness, for the talk had got onto Aesthetic and Jacinto had gone like a person possessed. Reinhold was delighting in the scrimmage he had managed to stir up between Augustine and Jacinto: he kept himself in the background but from a safe distance was egging on both and sniping at both.

In any such argument with an Augustine Jacinto was at several advantages. To begin with, the Brazilian could talk with his hands (which the subject required): his hands served Jacinto as slides serve a lecturer, he drew so fast in the air the whole line seemed simultaneously there. Second came something always essential for absolute clarity of thought: he had read almost everything which agreed with his theories and nothing whatever which didn't, whereas Augustine's notions were merely an unorganized ten-year deposit from many conflicting sources. And third, most important of all, was his passion: hearing and seeing him talk you realized that verily 'Significant Form' was for Jacinto almost what the Cross of Christ Crucified was for St Paul.

Augustine admitted at once that *of course* there was more in Art than mere imitation: there was something . . . 'like the wipe-round with garlic essential to a good bowl of salad?' Reinhold suggested . . . but it staggered Augustine when Jacinto allowed in Art no role for imitation at all. 'But you can't make a salad out of *only* that wipe-round

331

with garlic,' Augustine argued. Jacinto however took all Augustine's representational notions and tore them to shreds. He lashed into Augustine as Paul lashed into the Galatians (those two-timing Gentile Christians who hankered after obedience to Mosaic injunctions 'as well'). Once you discover Significant Form (said Jacinto) and know this alone is what matters you must 'stand fast in that liberty' (as Paul told the Galatians), and never be entangled again with the representational yoke. 'Significant Form . . .'

' "The contemplation of beautiful objects",' Reinhold quoted: 'The first of the only two valid rules of conduct, according to your own Moore's "Principia Ethica" – the bible of Bloomsbury, Augustine! Have you read it?'

'. . . is the sole meaning of things,' Jacinto pursued, 'without which the universe were a kind of visual gibberish . . .' And so on, and so on. Jacinto had a fourth advantage in argument: Augustine listened, and so was pervious to conviction however unwilling, but Jacinto listened to no one.

By now, moreover, Jacinto had also a fifth advantage: the powerful nature of Munich beer. Ringelnatz of course had a start, but now Augustine was becoming inarticulate too.

Ringelnatz had long been beyond interfering – beyond listening even. Just now when Augustine had emptied his pockets to pay for a round he had inadvertently left on the table his last-year's rover-ticket for Lords, and this circle of cardboard so beautifully printed in gold had fascinated Ringelnatz: indeed he admired it so much that presently he spread it with mustard: later he had added a slice of salami and topped it with beer-washed cheese and now he was munching it, his thoughts far away on Parnassus.

Though Augustine liked drinking he hated getting too drunk (something associated with mindless hearties at Oxford). But tonight, being too deeply absorbed in the argument to notice how much he was drinking, it caught him unawares. The first he knew of it was a roaring in his ears that had nothing to do with Jacinto and the coldness of sweat on his forehead: then the slapping beer in his stomach seemed almost to top his oesophagus ... Augustine had drunk a little too much that first night at Lorienburg but this was something more dire; for the room was losing its equilibrium and even its shape, it resolved into separate revolving planes if he didn't prevent it and only by Herculean efforts could he hold it together and upright.

Augustine had no ears now for Jacinto: every effort had to be concentrated on keeping control or the ceiling lost its balance and swooped, while the menacing floor hung over his head by a thread ...

'Significant F-form ...' That's the thing: hold on to Significant Fff ... Fff ...

So he held on, as long as he could: then slid to the floor.

Chapter 29

Never in his life before had Augustine been so drunk. Even two days later when (on his way back to Lorienburg) he pondered this ignominious ending of his visit to Munich he could still recall nothing, from the moment of losing his desperate struggle to keep Space loyal to Euclid, till he woke in his bed at the flat and found it was Monday and midday. He was wearing pyjamas, so *someone* had undresed him and put him to bed . . . it was utterly shaming to think that this must have been Reinhold.

Lord, too, what a head he had had! When he first sat up his skull had come apart like a badly-cracked cup in the hands of a housemaid. At that awful moment of waking he had thanked heaven that Reinhold by now would be out for the day; for how could he ever face Reinhold again, he had wondered (yet when Reinhold did come home in the evening he had been wonderfully decent about it). What a way to repay Reinhold's kindness . . . what must his host think of him . . . what a FOOL he had been!

After drinking a quart from the water-jug and splashing his face with the rest Augustine had felt better, and dressed. Then he went for a walk, crossing the square into the Hofgarten, under the arcade. It was there, in the frosty air of the Gardens, that he first realized the momentous thing which had happened to him under the shock of the alcohol: that in spite of his headache his mind was unprecedently clear – *and clear because it was empty!*

Even now in the train next day Augustine was still enjoying the pristine freshness of that empty-headedness; for all those old outworn ideas which had cluttered his mind for so long had been swept away in a kind of spring-cleaning – he had been brain-washed in beer ('Good Gracious!' he thought. 'Perhaps then one *ought* to get drunk every two or three years to get rid of the rubbish!').

The result of the riddance was that two things alone stood out clear in his mind, now; and one was the image of Mitzi, washed free of any last trace of hesitation or doubt. 'Heavens!' he had thought in the Gardens. 'What on earth am I doing in Munich when I ought to be back at her side? How can I bear to stay away from her one minute longer? Indeed, why on earth did I ever come away to Munich at all?' He must go back to Lorienburg at once and claim her at once.

But inside Mitzi's image stood now one other idea, and that was 'Significant Form'. In this respect, how describe what had happened to him? In spite of himself that Gospel phrase 'being born again in the Spirit' occurred to him; for though Heaven forbid all this should be concerned with religion, still that done-away-with clutter had indeed been replaced by one single overwhelming idea: the concept of 'Significant Form' as an immanence in the perceived which the painter's eye can uncover. A *physical* immanence mind you; for though this transcended the merely physicist's-real it was still a wholly physical kind of super-reality. 'I mean,' thought Augustine, 'it isn't the philosophers or the scientists any more than the saints who have discovered the meaning of the universe, it's the painters! That "meaning" is something that can't be intellectually expressed, it's something essentially visual.'

'The eye is the light of the body ...' How Augustine longed now to look fresh with his under-used eyes at familiar pictures – yes, and also to turn this new 'light of the body' on to the new art Jacinto had talked of so reverently – Matisse, Cézanne and the rest! If only the next stop was Paris ...

But it wasn't, of course: the next stop was Kammstadt, and by the time Augustine had changed trains and was chug-chugging up the valley again from village to village more and more was it Mitzi who filled all his thoughts, filled his very fingers and toes: less and less (for the moment) Significant Form. For he meant to go straight to Mitzi the moment he got back. He began rehearsing what he would say to her – even filling in her answers. His life's supreme moment was come. When they were married he must teach Mitzi about . . . but . . . but how on earth do you teach a blind person about Significant Form? Yet he felt even that wasn't impossible to the strength of his love.

When the train at last reached Lorienburg and Augustine jumped down on the line he found that the children had all come whooping to meet him. All four of them fought for his bag (too heavy for even all four of them), then dropped it and fought for his arms and his hands. They all talked at once and no one listened to the answers he gave without listening either. When they got to the village however they stopped for Augustine to buy them sweets and the atmosphere grew calmer: calm enough, at least, for him at last to ask after Mitzi.

'You'll just be in time to say good-bye to her: she's off to a convent.'

'For long? Are they teaching her Braille there or something?'

'What do you mean, "long"?'

'Mitzi's going to be a Religious.'

'She's taking her vows.'

'A Carmelite Sister: she's wanted to, for ages.'

'They've accepted her now; and Papa says she can.'

'Don't you understand? Mitzi's going to be a nun . . .'

'Is something the matter?'

'Come on, Stupid, what are you waiting for? You've got your change now so *come on* . . .'

Chapter 30

How the rest of that day passed Augustine never knew: he was a walking zombie, with no mind for things to make any impression on.

When he woke next morning and remembered, his heart went at once so leaden in his breast that it pressed on his stomach and made him feel quite sick. When he opened his sticky eyes it was almost as if he had gone blind himself; the colour had gone out of the world, and all solidity. His surroundings were so wraithlike they were more like memories of things seen long ago than fresh sense-impressions. Even solid Lies kneeling at his stove was faded and immaterial as a ghost.

Augustine's legs carried him to breakfast: he drank some coffee, but ate nothing.

Today Walther and Adèle (contrite perhaps at their own inhospitable feelings of a week or so ago) were full of plans for his amusement. The sleigh 'smashed to matchwood' had nevertheless been repaired, and was at his disposal: 'Would you like to see some churches?' asked Adèle, explaining that one of the finest baroque masterpieces of the Asam Brothers was only five miles away: or, in the opposite direction there was that little shrine with its quaint votive pictures of every kind of rustic disaster and disease ...

'Nonsense!' said Walther. 'He'll have seen enough churches in Munich – haven't you, my boy?' It transpired that what Walther wanted was to send him off with the foreman to a distant part of the forest, there to decide whether the frost was yet hard enough for a bottomless bog to bear heavy cart-loads from the castle cesspool to where their nutrients were needed most. 'It takes longer for that bog to freeze properly than the Danube itself!' Walther explained:

warmth, engendered by the decaying vegetation in it no doubt: Augustine would find it all most interesting, and (he added as a tactful afterthought) he would value Augustine's advice. Franz too was agog to teach him skiing: it was a lovely day, and the snow was just right at last. As for the children – their parents' presence constrained them to silence, but they were miming to him imploringly through the open door.

Of the whole sort of them, only Adèle noticed at all Augustine's curious condition. She wondered what on earth could have happened to the young man in Munich: bad news, perhaps, from home? But Adèle had an unshakable belief in the powers of sightworthy objects to distract the mind and assuage the troubled heart, and only pressed her sight-seeing proposals all the more.

What Augustine wanted, of course, was simply to be alone; so he let the torrent of conflicting plans roll over him, made the best excuses he could to the adults, dodged the children and set off by himself for a long tramp in the snow.

The meaningless sky was without a cloud, and set in it was a sun that gave him neither light nor warmth.

At first his legs felt nerveless. He had hardly got outside when they wanted him to stop, and for a while he leaned over the broken palings of the old skittle-alley opposite the great Crucifix, contemplating with downcast eyes three dots sunk blackly just below the surface of the snow under the overhanging linden. Three tiny shrunken bats they were, that had frozen to death hanging in the twigs above and dropped there.

. . . That ever Mitzi should shrivel to a nun! In a mind's-eye flash he saw Mitzi lying white in the unending darkness of her night with tell-tale toothmarks on her throat . . . Augustine wouldn't look up at it but turning with eyes still lowered shuddered at the very shadow on the snow of that (to him) grisly vampire-figure clamped too insecurely to its rood above him; and hurried off long-legged like someone at nightfall with twenty miles to go.

Augustine was already crossing the wide field beyond the road with the same idiot haste and now knee-deep in snow when the children from the castle spotted him far-off and making for the forest without them. How had he forgotten them? They ran out after him; but the snow was soon too deep for them, and to their astonishment he paid no attention when they yelled to him to wait. Yet they wouldn't give up till a waist-deep drift in the middle of the field almost engulfed them. Here even Trudi was forced to a halt, and the twins showed little but their heads above the snow.

He *must* have heard them, on so still a morning! Yet with lowered eyes Augustine hurried on, never even looking behind him when they called. At this incredible betrayal the twins did what they never did – burst into a wail, puncturing the surrounding snow with tear-holes while Augustine vanished out of sight.

There had been no new fall lately, and in the thinner snow on the fringes of the forest the surface had recorded for Augustine's earthbound eyes all the criss-cross passages of animals and birds for the past few nights and days. Idly he scanned them: the neat-punched slots two-and-two of roedeer: the marks of a fox's pads, set after each other in one straight line like the track a cog-wheel would make: the arrowed tracks of all kinds and sizes of birds, with the delicate imprints of their trailing tails and wings like fossil ferns. It was as if all these creatures had been here at the same time together, summoned to a compulsory dance of all creation without pattern or purpose.

The only living creature in sight now was a single blackbird about to alight. The dazzling snow made her misjudge her height as she came down, so that she tail-slipped the last two feet to a false landing with claws outspread in front of her and tail-feathers sticking into the snow. As Augustine turned into the forest the bird called after him: 'You're well out of it – you don't know when you're lucky!'

Augustine turned round in surprise; but he was wrong, it was only a bird.

In the airless gloom of the forest Augustine threaded his way between the tree-trunks – smooth tubular boles showing a cold blue-grey against the dull green foliage lining the heavy, high-overhead canopy of snow. These endless rows of immensely tall evergreens without branch or twig for fifty or sixty feet were all exactly alike and closely and evenly spaced. There was no undergrowth. Because of their precise spacing and the lack of any lower branches or foliage their echoing was voluminous and sinister whenever the silence was broken. One yapping farm-dog in the far distance sounded like a whole pack of hounds in full tongue – or like a distant riot.

But presently Augustine debouched from the thick trees quite by chance on to a broad drive, and for a time followed along it. This was the selfsame drive that had taken them a month ago on their way to Röttningen; but that at first he failed to notice. Then something familiar must have struck him; for suddenly he remembered the sound of their sleigh-bells, and that frost-pink face peeping from her furs . . . how happy he had been even next-but-one to Mitzi on the box-seat, that day a month ago!

At first Augustine had been wholly numbed by despair; but now that he had begun seeing his surroundings again a little he also began again, just a little, to think. Was it after all even now too late? It was not as if Mitzi had gone to the convent already and the gates had shut on her: then, doubtless, they'd never let her go. But as long as she was at home they surely couldn't compel her. Had he perhaps given in too easily – stunned by the first obstacle just *because* he had taken for granted the prize was there for the plucking whenever he chose? If he went back now and declared himself, surely this whole crazy nunnery-project must vanish like smoke! Surely (and at this idea his heart kicked like a backfiring engine) Mitzi was only doing this because she despaired of him: for how could any healthy, normal girl like Mitzi want to become a nun?

'Fool!' he replied to himself: 'You don't understand her. You haven't a hope.'

For that was the point: if in a human way Mitzi had turned him down for another chap . . . but there wasn't one! Only that ever-living ever-dying figure on the Cross which Augustine used to think nothing of, but now made him shudder so.

What sort of a mediaeval, then, must Mitzi be – inside of her – that she could even consider going into a convent? It beggared comprehension! How could such a person nowadays even exist? And how could her parents allow it instead of sending for a psychiatrist? He couldn't understand them either, not at all. But then, did he understand *anyone* here? Perhaps not even dear Reinhold. They were all . . . cock-eyed, somehow, when you got under the surface (why, look at Franz!). You thought you could see how the wheels went round but really you couldn't at all. They weren't the same kind of beings that you were, these Germans.

These Germans . . . all this passion for politics, as if any human 'collective' was something that really existed! *These trees* . . . all these millions of sinister similar mangrown evergreen trees . . .

'*Christ I want to get out!*' he shouted out loud; and quick as a bullet's ricochet the tree-boles snapped back at him '*Get out!*'

Chapter 31

After trudging aimlessly in the forest for several hours Augustine suddenly found himself coming out in the open. Here the country before him was strange to him. Under the trees he had lost sight of the sun, and had no idea even of the general direction he had taken: he might have walked in a circle so that 'home' was just round the corner, or it might be ten miles away. There was nothing in sight he could recognize.

Augustine felt dog-tired. Normally he could walk thirty miles without tiring at all, but today the state of his nerves had set up in his muscles numberless minute internal tensions and now these had fought each other to a standstill: he ached.

Augustine had come out of comparative darkness to the edge of this dazzling snowfield, so he had to shade his eyes with his hand from below as he scanned the landscape for someone to tell him the way. As luck would have it, there was a farm not very far off, and briskly walking towards it a middle-aged man – thick-set, and dressed as a well-to-do peasant. Augustine forced himself to a jog-trot to intercept him; and when the man saw him, he waited.

When the farmer saw this obvious foreigner and obvious gentleman, who was also so obviously lost, trotting towards him over the snow, three emotions combined to make him ask in the stranger: curiosity, compassion, and pride in his home. Augustine was too nerveless to resist, and anyway, longed for a chair to sit down on. He followed his host in without looking round him – for once, he was himself in no mood to be curious. All that really interested him was something to sit on awhile.

He was taken into a parlour where the walls were covered with horns, and regaled there on layer-cake sodden in rum; but in his present state the cake seemed to him tasteless and he could hardly swallow it down. But then they gave him a generous tot of home-distilled plum brandy and that made him feel better at once.

Augustine began to look round him at last. Those hundreds of antlers and horns . . . were they trophies of the chase, decoration, or simply to hang your hat on (or rather, your hundreds of hats)? Instead of a dog on the hearth-rug – incidentally, there wasn't a hearth for it either – the fur rug had itself once been a dog! What a compendious arrangement . . . he bent down and tickled its ear (they offered to fill up his glass, but he firmly refused – Gosh their plum stuff was strong!).

Almost wherever the horns left room on the walls there was a carved crucifix or a carved cuckoo-clock – one or the other: there were also two terrible portraits in oils, and it gave one a jolt to see how like was his mother's picture as a bride to this elderly farmer himself, in spite of his whiskers. Augustine turned, and smiled at his host benignly – the nice old three-hundred weight!

Again they tried to fill up his glass, and again he refused.

Meanwhile the questioning went on. It was all so courteous and terribly tactful that everything had to be carefully answered. They seemed thrilled to learn he was English, and wanted to know all he could tell them about King George.

Before Augustine quite knew what was happening they were showing him round. Never had he seen anywhere quite so crammed with possessions. Bedroom after bedroom had three or four beds in it: each bed had three or four mattresses and then was piled high with all kinds of other things so that no one could possibly sleep on it. Every wardrobe was bursting with clothes and had cardboard boxes on top of it: everything had to be taken down, unfolded and shown. All these things had accumulated in dowry after dowry over

343

three generations, he gathered. None of them seemed to be used – they were wealth, like the gold in a bank. Yet the tiptoe possessors seemed radiant . . . *these* were people who knew beyond doubt what they wanted – and had it! Sorrow suddenly rose in his throat, but he swallowed it down.

They told Augustine he was not far from the Danube and also the railway, but further on down the line than Lorienburg was. The station was two miles off, and it was getting time for the train but still they insisted he just saw the cows – nothing else – before he departed.

A door opposite the parlour-door opened off the front hall straight into the stable (so he had just to look at the horses). Beyond lay the piggery (he also looked at the pigs), and furthest of all were the cows – rows and rows of them, all red-and-white ('What kind of cows has King George got at Sandringham?' How on earth should he know!). But the Sandringham cows couldn't be finer than these were: indeed at the sight of all his own wonderful cows the farmer seemed ready to float; and in spite of himself Augustine was intrigued by them. A boy had just brought in the calves to be suckled: Augustine couldn't help watching how the milky little nit-wits tried all the other mothers as well as their own, and how mildly those other ones kicked them aside.

Just as they were leaving the cows, one of them lifted her nose from her calf and called after Augustine: 'You just don't know when you're lucky!'

Augustine looked round in surprise; but he was wrong, it was only a cow.

The visit had done Augustine good, but as he hurried off along the lane once more his melancholy kept hitting him in waves as sea-sickness does. When that happened the colour in everything faded, and the legs under him almost refused.

Even at the best of times Augustine's surroundings in Germany never seemed to him quite 'real': they had a

344

picture-book foreignness, down to the smallest detail. The very snow he was walking in differed from English snow. Those distant forests were coloured a 'Victorian' green – the colour of art-serge curtains rather than trees: the edges of the forest were all sharp-etched (outside of them no loose trees stood around on their own) and yet these plantations were formless, for their arbitrary boundaries seemed to bear no relation to Nature or the lie of the land. Thus the landscape (in his eyes) had none of the beauty almost any English landscape (in his eyes) had got.

Augustine kept passing wayside shrines, and even the farms had each its own little doll's-chapel outside with a miniature belfry and an apse as big as a cupboard. Taken all together and on top of the churches they added up to a pretty frightening picture ... Often these chapels were almost the only outbuildings the farms had got, apart from a crow's-nest up an apple-tree for potting at foxes.

Indeed these hardly looked like 'farms' (which are, surely, essentially a huddle of big byres and barns with a tiny house tucked away in the middle?). These (because the animals lived indoors on the ground-floor) looked all 'house'.

Since landscape changes like this from country to country it must owe very little to Nature: Nature is no more than the canvas, and landscape the self-portrait the people who live there paint on it. But no, hold hard! Surely, rather the people who *have* lived there; for landscape is always at least one generation behind in its portrayal (like those other portraits that hung on the parlour wall). This was Augustine's 'new' Germany, but the landscape here was unchanged since Kaiserdom or even before: whereas the people ...

But at that point Augustine stopped dead in his tracks, for something had struck him – something so obvious why on earth hadn't it struck him before? *The people were also pre-war.* History has to use second-hand timber when she builds a new edifice – like those awkward post-war chicken-houses people build out of bits of army huts and old ammo-

boxes, with 'W.D.' stamped all over them and costly enig-
matical fittings too much trouble to unscrew. Likewise the
people the new Germany was built of were the self-same
people the old had consisted of before the structure was
smashed and they were ripped out of their places in the
ruins and . . . but could you call the new Germany 'built'?
No! Just at present these were more like rooks sent wheeling
about in the sky when their rookery-tree is felled. One day
they would settle . . .

When Augustine at last reached the plain of the river-bed,
he was surprised to find there no snow at all. There was ice
there instead : on the road it had been swept into untidy
heaps like a dump for shattered window-panes : on the fields
it just lay around on the ground like more window-panes
shattered. Round each of the trunks of the roadside tree
three feet from the ground there was a kind of ring-table of
ice you could picnic on . . .

They explained it all to Augustine when he called at the
village Gasthof for a drink (after all, he had made good
time). A week ago (they told him) the Danube had frozen.
Dammed with the barrier its own ice-floes had piled up, the
river had flooded out over the plain and begun to freeze
again, like a lake. But then with the weight of the water behind it the dam had broken and the floods had subsided –
deserting their new ice, which was left in the air unsup-
ported, and broke. Now, in sheets and fragments and splin-
ters for miles it lay in the sun and glittered : only those
'tables' of ice round the trees remained as witness to the
depth of the floods.

In the middle of the village, the market-place had a kind
of Xanadu-wonder because of the trees. For their branches
and twigs were feathered with white ice that glittered in
the sun : they were like cherry-trees every inch in bloom,
and whenever the faint breeze breathed on them they tinkled
like tiny bells.

The road to the station took Augustine close to the river

346

itself. Even now the river was not everywhere frozen: here and there where the current was strongest there were still patches of dark grey water that steamed in the sun, so that the solitary swan indefatigably swimming there was half-hidden in vapour. But elsewhere the Danube seemed to be frozen solid in heaps. It was wild, yet utterly still. Huge blocks of ice had jostled each other and climbed on top of each other like elephants rutting and then got frozen in towering lumps: or had swirled over and over before coagulating till they were curled like a Chinese sea. None of them had remained in the place where first it had frozen: each block was complete in itself but now out of place – like a jig-saw puzzle glued in a heap helter-skelter so that now it could never be solved.

It was all such a muddle! Although it was utterly still it expressed such terrific force it was frightening: the force that had made it – thrusting floes weighing hundreds of tons high into the air, and the force it would release when it thawed. When that ice melted at last it would go thundering down the river grinding to bits everything in its path. No bridge could possibly stand up to it. The longer you looked at its stillness, the greater your feeling of panic . . . Augustine *hated* Germany: all he wanted now was to get away as quick as he could.

The moment he got back he would go straight to Walther, tell him in ten words that he *had* to marry Mitzi; and then go straight to Mitzi and . . . and not take 'no' for an answer. For he couldn't possibly leave Mitzi behind in all this: no longer just for his own sake but for *hers* he must rescue her – take her to England (and make a reasonable Englishwoman out of her like everyone else).

Augustine jumped from the train the moment it stopped. He galloped up the hill. Still out of breath he asked for Walther at once. But the Baron (they told him) was out. Augustine stamped his foot in fury: every minute's delay was intolerable! When would he be back? – The Baron and

Baronin wouldn't be back till tomorrow . . . surely the Gentleman knew that *today* they were taking the Young Baroness to her convent? They had started at noon. – No, *she* wasn't coming back with them of course: the Baron and Baronin would return alone in the morning. But the Young Baron would be here for dinner tonight, and the Colonel-Baron: three gentlemen dining alone, Good Appetite to them!

So this was the end! From his protestant upbringing Augustine knew that what once a convent has swallowed it never gives up . . .

Flinging his things into the old Gladstone bag that had once been his father's he could hardly see what he was doing: he was more like a boxer practising on a punch-bag than a young man packing his clothes.

Where was he going to next? Anywhere anywhere anywhere! Over the frontier to whatever other country was nearest! But then, as he turned again to the wardrobe his bag called after him: 'You don't know when you're lucky!'

Augustine turned round in surprise; but he was wrong, it was only a bag.

Acknowledgment

The knowledgeable reader will have recognized for himself
how deeply this volume is indebted to Bullock, Wheeler-
Bennett, Hanfstaengl, Kubizek, Salomon and other published authorities, as well as to private sources.

A long list of these latter would defeat by tedium the
purposes of gratitude but I cannot leave unnamed Baroness
Pia von Aretin: she gave me access to her father's memoirs
and in every way she and her family have helped me im-
measurably. I must also thank particularly the only living
person in a position to describe to me first-hand the whole
forty-eight hour period when Hitler was in hiding at Uffing.
(Neither of these however, is blameworthy for my opinions.)

At certain points my narrative of the 'Putsch' differs
materially from others previously compiled. But I have imported almost nothing fictitious except the little dog in the
plaid waistcoat, and the historian may be interested to know
that much of this narrative – including the whole episode in
the crypt, the crucial briefing in the fencing-school with all
that implied, and the correct route of the march – is based
on a vivid contemporary account by an actual Nazi partici-
pant, a Major Goetz. This account was contained in a letter
to a friend dated November 26th, 1923, which some weeks
later found its way into the German press. Its very mistakes
authenticate it, but it does not seem to be well known.

I am also more deeply indebted than I can express to
the skilful and patient private critics of my manuscript.

R. H.

349

OTHER TITLES BY RICHARD HUGHES IN TRIAD/
PANTHER BOOKS

IN HAZARD

A sea story in the finest tradition, *In Hazard* tells of a
modern cargo-steamer caught in a hurricane in the Caribbean,
and of the men who fought the sea to save her.

'*Here is the old simplicity, surprise, outrageous humour. But
the most outrageous quality of* In Hazard *is not its humour
but its daring to take the same subject as Conrad in* Typhoon
*... it would be foolhardy if it were not triumphantly
justified*' – GRAHAM GREENE

'*A tremendous piece of dramatic, narrative description
... magnificent*' – DESMOND MacCARTHY

'*I enjoyed it so much I kept exclaiming with pleasure as I
read it*' – DAVID GARNETT

60p

A HIGH WIND IN JAMAICA

A High Wind in Jamaica is the classic novel of childhood in which Richard Hughes describes with perfect insight not only the adventures of a family of children caught up in the company of pirates but also, with magical clarity, the tropical landscape the children leave behind them and the endless ocean which they must cross.

'*It has genius because it sees something that a million people have seen before, but sees it uniquely*' – HUGH WALPOLE

'*Vivid, exciting, delicate and swift. The strangeness is never exaggerated, the descriptions are exact as well as beautiful*' – CYRIL CONNOLLY

'*Mr Hughes has the divine gift of imagination. His phrases have often the fatality of poetry and often the unexpectedness of wit*' – THE OBSERVER

'*The style is brilliant, the ingenuity of the narrative is brilliant, the characterization is brilliant, and the total effect of the story completely satisfactory*' – ARNOLD BENNETT

85p

| A HIGH WIND IN JAMAICA | 85p ☐ |
| IN HAZARD | 60p ☐ |

All these books are available at your local bookshop or newsagent, or can be ordered direct from the publisher. Just tick the titles you want and fill in the form below.

Name ....

Address ....

....

Write to Panther Cash Sales, PO Box 11, Falmouth, Cornwall TR10 9EN.

Please enclose remittance to the value of the cover price plus:

UK: 25p for the first book plus 10p per copy for each additional book ordered to a maximum charge of £1.05.

BFPO and EIRE: 25p for the first book plus 10p per copy for the next 8 books, thereafter 5p per book.

OVERSEAS: 40p for the first book and 12p for each additional book. *Granada Publishing reserve the right to show new retail prices on covers, which may differ from those previously advertised in the text or elsewhere.*